# The
# Silver Moon Elm
## A JENNIFER SCALES NOVEL

*MaryJanice Davidson*
*and*
*Anthony Alongi*

ACE BOOKS, NEW YORK

THE BERKLEY PUBLISHING GROUP
Published by the Penguin Group
Penguin Group (USA) Inc.
375 Hudson Street, New York, New York 10014, USA
Penguin Group (Canada), 90 Eglinton Avenue East, Suite 700, Toronto, Ontario M4P 2Y3, Canada
(a division of Pearson Penguin Canada Inc.)
Penguin Books Ltd., 80 Strand, London WC2R 0RL, England
Penguin Group Ireland, 25 St. Stephen's Green, Dublin 2, Ireland (a division of Penguin Books Ltd.)
Penguin Group (Australia), 250 Camberwell Road, Camberwell, Victoria 3124, Australia
(a division of Pearson Australia Group Pty. Ltd.)
Penguin Books India Pvt. Ltd., 11 Community Centre, Panchsheel Park, New Delhi—110 017, India
Penguin Group (NZ), 67 Apollo Drive, Rosedale, North Shore 0632, New Zealand
(a division of Pearson New Zealand Ltd.)
Penguin Books (South Africa) (Pty.) Ltd., 24 Sturdee Avenue, Rosebank, Johannesburg 2196,
South Africa

Penguin Books Ltd., Registered Offices: 80 Strand, London WC2R 0RL, England

This is a work of fiction. Names, characters, places, and incidents either are the product of the authors'
imaginations or are used fictitiously, and any resemblance to actual persons, living or dead, business
establishments, events, or locales is entirely coincidental. The publisher does not have any control over
and does not assume any responsibility for author or third-party websites or their content.

THE SILVER MOON ELM: A JENNIFER SCALES NOVEL

An Ace Book / published by arrangement with the authors

PRINTING HISTORY
Berkley JAM trade paperback edition / June 2007
Ace mass-market edition / June 2008

Copyright © 2007 by MaryJanice Davidson Alongi and Anthony Alongi.
Cover art by Keith Birdsong.
Cover design by Lesley Worrell.
Text composition by ReadSmart® from Language Technologies, Inc.

ISBN: 978-0-441-01601-3

ACE
Ace Books are published by The Berkley Publishing Group,
a division of Penguin Group (USA) Inc.,
375 Hudson Street, New York, New York 10014.
ACE and the "A" design are trademarks belonging to Penguin Group (USA) Inc.

PRINTED IN THE UNITED STATES OF AMERICA

10   9   8   7   6   5   4   3   2   1

*For Annie and Jessica,*
*who make our universe*
*that much more pleasant to be in*

*Have love for your friend up to a limit, for it is possible he may turn into your enemy some day; and hate your enemy up to a limit, for it is possible he may turn into your friend some day.*

—ALI IBN ABI TALIB

*It is easier to forgive an enemy than to forgive a friend.*

—WILLIAM BLAKE

# PROLOGUE

## *Thursday*

*Lying on her belly and sobbing, Jennifer Scales wanted to die.*

*The crescent moon slid peacefully through the twilit sky, shedding enough light on her surroundings for Jennifer to lose all hope.*

*There was no refuge in this forest. The foreign sounds of unknown things filled the air, murmuring a restless siege. She sat up at the gathering noise and tried to collect herself. They were closing in. Maybe a minute left before the end.*

*Friends? None left. She thought of them all—Susan, Eddie, Catherine, Skip—and a new wave of despair crashed over her with the memory of each one.*

*Family? Jennifer began to cry again at the thought.*

*And there was no place else to go.*

*Her tear-filled gaze went up to the crescent moon. She cursed it under her breath. So much pain had come into her life since she had discovered its power.*

*She released herself from dragon form, for what she knew would be the last time. Back in the shape of a fifteen-year-old girl, she felt around with her hands for a sharp fragment of stone. Lifting a small, jagged rock in her hand, she thought wistfully of her beautiful daggers. She had lost them. She had lost everything.*

*Holding the stone firmly in her right hand, she held out her left wrist. She flexed her fingers and watched the blue veins shudder under her starlit skin.*

I miss you so much, Mom. You, too, Dad.

*The noises in the forest were closer. She could make out movement in a few of the taller trees. They would be upon her in seconds.*

*She pressed the sharpest edge of the stone against the skin, saw some blood seep out . . . and then abruptly stopped. Gritting her teeth, she removed the rock from her wrist and stood up.* Not like that, *she promised herself.* I won't do it for them.

*"Come on!" she screamed out to her predators in the dark. The stone felt fierce in her hand. "Come on!"*

*She did not see the attack come from behind.*

# CHAPTER 1

## The Previous Saturday

*This is almost as good as flying,* Jennifer Scales thought to herself ecstatically with gray eyes closed.

The November wind whipped through her shoulder-length platinum blonde hair, good music washed over her numb ears, and the sunlight shone on her reddening cheekbones. It was chilly, to be sure—but she had a sweater, jacket, and scarf to keep most of her warm.

She snuggled farther down in the Ford Mustang convertible's leather passenger seat and turned to the driver.

"So how often does your grandmother let you use this car?"

The dark olive features of Catherine Brandfire lifted from the attention of the road long enough to flash perfect teeth at her friend. "All the time, when I'm not grounded."

"Like you are today?"

Catherine laughed. "You know this weekend was an exception. Besides, if I know her at all, Grammie Winona will be more annoyed at *you* than me!"

Jennifer bit her lip. This much was true. At fifteen years old, she was already a legendary figure among her people, a unifying presence who blended all three dragon races and more. Most weredragons forgave a lot about her—not least the fact she was half beaststalker because of her mother. While beaststalkers were among the sworn enemies of weredragons, Jennifer Scales was an ambassador between the two peoples.

But that didn't mean everyone in Crescent Valley was going to be happy with what she was doing.

Turning to the backseat and the three friends shivering with goofy grins under several coats and blankets, she lingered over the face of Eddie Blacktooth, her childhood friend and a young beaststalker. Eddie's sharp nose and soft brown eyes stared back at her, sparrowlike. He smiled at her and she smiled back, thinking of the strange turn of events that had wounded his mother, Wendy, alienated his father, Hank, and led him into the guest room at her own house.

This weekend's trip to Crescent Valley would be a landmark of sorts—the first time in her people's memory that a beaststalker had come to the most hidden and sacred of dragon refuges. Winona Brandfire would welcome Eddie, Jennifer knew. After all, it was the eldest dragon who had suggested such contact.

Susan Elmsmith—Jennifer's best friend, shivering next to Eddie—would probably also get a gracious reception. At least Jennifer hoped so. Susan was neither dragon nor stalker—she was 100 percent American girl, with no additives or preservatives, as the two of them occasionally joked. In any case, Jennifer wouldn't keep Crescent Valley from her friend—after more than a year of hiding uncomfortable truths, she had resolved there would be no more secrets between them.

"What?"

Jennifer broke from her reverie, realizing her friend was looking back at her. *Oh!* "Uh . . ."

Susan blindly wiped her nose on her own sleeve, which sent her brown curls bouncing around panicked blue irises. "Have I got something on my face?!"

"Yeah, my fingers." The passenger on Susan's other side reached over and lightly pinched her nose, causing her to snort and giggle. Jennifer turned all the way around in her seat to flash him an affectionate grin.

It was, she considered, the warmest reception he'd be likely to get for some time. The eldest of all dragons had given no permission for the *third* visitor her granddaughter and Jennifer were bringing with them. Skip Wilson was a werachnid—another one of the sworn enemies of weredragons, whose oversized spider and scorpion shapes emerged under the same crescent moon as Jennifer and Catherine's people. Jennifer knew she was taking a chance in bringing Skip to Crescent Valley. She knew some dragons—maybe even Winona Brandfire—would be furious with her.

But she didn't care. She was sick of secrets, and sick of hiding parts of herself from her friends. Crescent Valley was part of who she was. Skip was her friend—and might have been more, she remembered ruefully, had she been more forthcoming with him in the past.

*Full disclosure—the way to go.* Weren't their high school English literature classes full of long, boring examples of characters who would have fared much better had they pursued a policy of honesty? Didn't modern singers generate hit ballad after hit ballad where a love was lost due to deception? Didn't movie stars play one forgetful (and eventually regretful) liar after another? As the lyrics or plot always revealed, cover-ups never worked. Secrets were the butt-biting boomerangs of modern pop culture.

Anyway, Skip had promised to be on his best behavior. They were off to a good start. In this trip to her grandfather Crawford's cabin—*Scratch that,* she reminded herself ruefully, *it's not Grandpa's anymore, it's Mom and Dad's*—so far, Skip Wilson had been a perfect gentleman, complimenting the girls on their fashionable autumn coats, thanking Catherine for giving them all a ride, and even making nice with Eddie. That last part was no small feat, since the two of them had started their sophomore year at Winoka High at each other's throats.

The year had gotten off to an awful start, she had to admit. In a mere two months, her world had churned violently. Not only had Eddie made an ill-advised (and ultimately failed) attempt at "coming of age" as a beaststalker by attacking Jennifer, but a promising relationship with Skip had been cut short, Susan had gotten hurt, Catherine had nearly been trampled to death, Skip had beaten Eddie into unconsciousness, her mother had been hospitalized . . . and worst of all, her grandfather Crawford had been murdered.

Not just murdered by anyone. By his own granddaughter Evangelina—a half-sister Jennifer hadn't even known she had until just recently. The young woman had been beyond insane. Evangelina was an abandoned, disturbed, and deeply vengeful dragon-spider hybrid. Only just before she died, when confronted with new emotions such as love and mercy, did she show a glimpse of humanity.

*Too late for her now,* Jennifer mused. *And too late for Grandpa.* Consumed in thought, she barely heard Susan's voice in the backseat, a soft complaint about the cold—then a muffled giggling as Eddie and Skip both tickled their friend warm. *But not too late for us.*

Susan's giggles burst into a whoop of alarm as Skip's hand strayed too high from her ribs. "Hey! Those aren't ticklish!"

"Accident!" he protested, raising his palms and smiling nervously as Jennifer's head whipped around. She tried to give him a hard stare, but Susan's continued chuckling forced her to face front again. *You can't get mad at him for flirting with other girls,* she chastised herself. *Not if he's not your boyfriend anymore.* She swallowed hard and lifted the collar of her coat up against her ears.

Catherine noticed the movement. "You want me to pull over and raise the top?"

"It *is* November." A sudden bad mood made for a harsh tone.

"But it's a convertible!" Susan objected as Catherine pulled the Mustang gently into the breakdown lane. "You can't put the roof up on a convertible! It's sacrilege!"

"It's sixteen degrees!" Jennifer snapped, pointing at the digital display on the polished maple dashboard. "You just said yourself it's chilly!"

"Yeah, but I'm getting warmer." Her best friend snuggled up against Eddie, and did not protest when Skip brought his right hand back down over her slight shoulders and long black curls. The car came to a full stop, and silence descended upon them all.

It took exactly twenty-three seconds for the convertible top of the Mustang to extend itself and settle into position. Jennifer knew this because she counted each one off by grinding her tongue between her teeth while she stared at the scene in the backseat. Meanwhile, Catherine whistled a jaunty tune at the steering wheel; Eddie focused on the nearby speed limit sign with an embarrassed shade on his cheeks; Susan had the decency to look down with fluttering lashes; and Skip stared right back at Jennifer with calm blue-green eyes as he teased Susan's opposite earlobe between thumb and forefinger.

*Jerk.* She briefly considered reaching back and tearing out his jugular. *He just can't resist a good confrontation. Or a bad one.*

Finally, Susan gently brushed away his hand. "Skip, stop it."

Jennifer's squint shifted to the right. *Nice of you to notice it bothered me.*

Eddie's cough was obviously fake. "Wow, Catherine, it really warms up fast with that roof up. Thanks."

The non sequitur irritated Jennifer. "Oh, shut up, Eddie."

Catherine put a soft hand on her shoulder, and her lean Egyptian features closed in for a whisper. "Easy does it. You can't have global harmony if you bust up your friends on the car ride there."

The older girl's voice soothed Jennifer. She relaxed, curled up a corner of her mouth, and tossed a casual glance back at Skip. "If you get a hand back under her shirt, don't be surprised if it doesn't find much."

Skip and Catherine burst out laughing as Susan gasped. "That's not fair!"

"Oh, it's fair," Catherine countered as she accelerated the car back onto the highway. "If you flirt with a girlfriend's ex, she gets to make rude and superficial remarks about you. It's part of the code."

Susan appealed to the boys, eyebrows high in desperation. "No, really, it's not fair! Jennifer's got perfect *everythings*, and have you seen her mom? Of course she's going to have bigger—"

"So *anyway*, how much longer until we're at . . . wherever we're going?" Eddie asked, even redder than he had been before.

"We're almost at her family's farm," Skip answered before Jennifer or Catherine could say anything.

"The family farm? You've been to Jenny's grandpa's place?"

No one answered; there was no point in denying it. Skip had been to the farm weeks ago, when Jonathan Scales invited him there to talk about Evangelina. After all, she was his half-sister as well—the daughter of Jonathan Scales and Dianna Wilson.

Eddie turned to Jennifer with a hurt expression. "You always told me no one besides family was allowed at your grandpa's place."

"Um, that's not true. Catherine's been there lots of times." *How is that an answer?* she asked herself before plunging forward. "It's sort of a dragon hideout. Anyway, er, Skip, er, didn't stay long."

"Is that where Crescent Valley is?" Susan interrupted helpfully. "At the farm?"

"Sort of. It's . . . close by." *Why am I being evasive? We're all going there soon enough.* "It's kinda hard to explain. You'll see."

The car swerved. Alarmed, Jennifer looked over at Catherine, who was clutching her right shoulder. "You okay?"

"It's getting kinda hard to keep this shape," her friend replied through gritted teeth. "Normally I'd've changed by now . . ."

Since it was almost noon, she could not easily see the moon in the sky. But it occurred to Jennifer that her father had left their house in Winoka earlier this morning—like most weredragons, he was compelled by the crescent moon to change shape. Only she among her kind, and Skip among his, were able to decide when and where they morphed.

"Oh, that's . . ."

"You do not," Susan commented, "look well."

Jennifer resisted the urge to grab the wheel. "Pull over!"

Catherine did not argue. She whipped open the door and tumbled out of the car even before it had completely stopped. Jennifer followed her friend into the ditch and picked up the shoes, jacket, yellow pullover, and faded jeans as they were shed and tossed to the ground.

"Wow," she heard Skip mutter back in the car.

"Grow up!" she shot back, trying to interpose herself between the gawking boys and her friend, who was slowly easing into her new shape.

Except for her father, Jennifer had never watched someone else change into a dragon. It was fascinating, though brief after the first (quite painful) time. Tramplers like Catherine were one of three distinct dragon breeds. They were powerfully built, with only rudimentary wings but terrific musculature and impressive nose horns. A scarlet fire burned behind their eyes, and many had what Jennifer privately thought of as "peacock scales" . . . green under most lights, but with hints of yellow and blue when the sun or moon were right.

When Catherine was finished, she showed two rows of sharp teeth. "Looks like you get to drive us the rest of the way there, Jennifer."

"Oh! Um, sure—"

"No, wait, I can drive! I have my learner's permit and

Jennifer doesn't." Susan shrugged out of the backseat while calling out the window.

Catherine wrinkled her nose. "Um, no offense, Susan, but—"

"But she just met you this morning and trusts me more than your little piece of paper. Return to your station in the backseat, trollop."

Susan grinned back at Jennifer and settled down. "Fine. Eddie, our friend Jennifer is colder than the weather. Care to warm me up?"

That was enough for Eddie, who quickly opened his door, scrambled away from Susan, raced around the back of the idling Mustang, and slipped into the passenger seat.

"Hmmph! Fine. Skip, you'll do . . ."

"I'll do what?" With a traitorous grin, he pushed Susan over into the spot Eddie had occupied. "Keep your distance, before you get us both into more trouble."

The grimace of hurt and anger was gone so quickly, Jennifer wondered if she'd imagined it on Susan's face. She forced her mind back on track and settled into the driver's seat. "Fine advice," she said with faux enthusiasm. She turned the key in the ignition. The resulting sound was terrifying.

"Um, Jennifer, the engine's already started."

"Also fine advice. Thank you, Eddie. Let's go. Catherine, flap those wings hard and try to keep up!"

She gunned the engine, and the Mustang spun gravel into the air as it thrust back onto the highway.

"Geez, won't people see her? I mean, it's broad daylight!" Susan gaped out the rear window at the winged shape that glided behind them. Every few hundred yards, a giant hind leg would smash into the ground, propelling its owner farther.

Jennifer shook her head. She had learned that most people did not see dragons—not because dragons were invisible or had any special mental powers, but because it was just too darn difficult for the average person to admit that things like dragons, and giant spiders, and soldiers who devoted their lives to slaying such things, could exist. *Wow, great special effects, what movie are they shooting?* Or, *Huh, I must not have shaken the flu like I thought.* Or, *Whoa, is the Air Force testing new funny colored jets around here or what?*

After that initial burst, she kept her speed down so that Catherine could keep up—the trampler had a hard time moving much faster than forty-five miles per hour. Fully adult tramplers could gallop much faster, Jennifer knew—she and her father had been on hunts where tramplers had moved in coordinated, predatory herds that topped sixty or more miles per hour. But she stayed patient with Catherine. After all, there was no hurry. This was her first time behind the wheel of a car, and despite the automatic transmission, she was anxious.

"What if the state patrol stops us?" asked Eddie, voicing Jennifer's primary concern. "I mean, we're breaking the law here."

"Correction: *Jennifer's* breaking the law," Skip said. "*We* are innocent bystanders. Hostages, really, to her ferocious temper."

"It's just to the cabin," Jennifer answered. "Maybe five more miles, tops." Her nerves did not stop jangling, however.

"So how will we get home?" Susan's tone was more concerned than accusatory. "It'll still be a crescent moon for a few days. We're not staying that long, are we?"

There was no easy answer to this question. Nobody offered to take Jennifer's place, not even Susan. Driving the rural route the last few miles to their destination was one thing; braving state highways for the long trip back to Winoka was something else again.

"Let's worry about that when we go back." Jennifer decelerated to take a right turn onto an unpaved county road. The ground shifted uneasily beneath the tires, as if the earth itself were aware of her moving violation. This was dumb; why didn't they let Susan drive? Sure, that would have been technically illegal, too, but at least her friend had had lessons. And a police officer would probably look more kindly on a learner's permit than a blank stare.

The Mustang rolled agreeably enough along the dirt highway, shifting abruptly an inch or two left or right just often enough to keep Jennifer's knuckles white on the steering wheel. Catherine's winged form sailed across the potato field to their left, anticipating the farm, which would be just past that line of trees up ahead, and then around the bend where the wildflowers and grasses grew . . .

When the first of her grandfather's enormous beehives emerged from the grassy knolls to their left, Jennifer let out a breath she hadn't realized she was holding. The neat hives lined the south lawn like buzzing sentry towers, and behind them were the fields of strange wildflowers and the herds of sheep, still faithfully maintained. Beyond them, the sparkling lake shimmered through the copses of maples, pines, and oaks to the north. Not far from its shore was the farmhouse: sprawling, white, green-shuttered, with a wraparound porch and more rocking chairs in sight than she could count. She knew the large porch and grill were in back, along with a larger barbeque pit for guests . . . and off to one side, the grave marker her mother and she had set up for Crawford Scales. Just a few steps from the marker, it was possible to fall into the lake, cool and with a taste of liquid diamonds.

The car stopped with a small, quick squeal of brakes at the end of the driveway, and as one the gang unsnapped their seat belts. "C'mon," Jennifer said. "I'll show you round the back. Stay behind me, because—"

Skip almost shoved her aside in his rush to get around the corner of the "cabin" (as the Scales family still affectionately called it). "Whatever. What's the big freaking—*whoa!*" His feet stuck to the bed of pine needles that lined the gravel driveway. Eddie and Susan pulled up short behind him, and Jennifer heard Susan let out a small whimper.

A few feet from the back porch, a pit that would have swallowed the Mustang was filled with fire and the delicious smell of roasting sheep. Around the smoke-filled edges, in murmured conversation punctuated with raucous laughter, were a dozen dragons. As one, their necks craned and they took in the visitors with reptilian coolness.

"Hey, Joseph," Jennifer called out after an uncomfortable silence.

Joseph, an eighteen-year-old lavender creeper who looked after the farm for the Scales, snorted. "Hey, Jennifer. You brought friends."

"Yeah." She momentarily reconsidered the wisdom of bringing them all here. After a brief surge of anxiety, she straightened her shoulders. "Did Catherine already show?"

His dark, scaled claw pointed to the porch doors. "Inside."

"Great. Save a bit o' mutton for me, guys." With that, she led the others inside.

"Um, Jennifer." Susan's voice was very small as they hustled themselves into the library. "There are twelve dragons in your backyard."

"Twelve *big* dragons," Skip chimed in. He was still grinning, but there was a certain awe in his voice. "And I'm not sure they're all thrilled we're here."

Susan tried on a smile for her best friend. "Good thing we're with you!"

Skip sniggered. "I don't think all of them are that crazy about Jennifer, either."

"She's not in dragon shape," Eddie observed quietly. It was the first time he had spoken since they had arrived, and he stared at the gathering by the fire pit. "They don't like the reminder of her beaststalker side."

Jennifer ignored the uncomfortable turn the conversation had taken. "Hey, Catherine. You around?"

"In here!" Catherine's voice came from the kitchen. "Car still intact?"

"Give or take a wheel. Bring out the ketchup, will you?" Jennifer turned to the other three. "There's plenty of snacks in the refrigerator, if you don't want sheep. I remember the first one I had—it was a bit weird."

As Eddie and Susan headed into the kitchen, Skip turned to her. "You and Catherine going outside to eat?"

"Yeah, I have to—it's been a rough few—Eddie's right. I should try to make nice with them. There are dragons around who still wonder about me and my mom."

"So we eat in here. You eat out there."

"Yeah."

"Interesting." His expression wasn't quite readable.

"What? It's not like you're in any danger or anything. I just thought you'd be more comfortable in here."

"I'll eat out there. With you."

"What, so you're going to make Susan and Eddie eat in here alone?"

His hands spread out. "They can come outside if they want."

Catherine ambled out on all fours, one wing claw clutching a squeezable ketchup bottle. "Who can come outside?"

Jennifer turned to Skip. "I'm not going to get into an argument with you, Skip. You want to come outside? Come outside. Be an hors d'oeuvre. The rest of us will remember you fondly as we continue to Crescent Valley."

A few minutes later, she was grumbling to herself as all five of them sat around the pit with the dragons, eating barbeque and swapping stories. Susan was full of nervous laughter as she told these strangers about her childhood memories with Jennifer; Skip and Catherine chatted together about life without parents; and Eddie gave short, one-word answers to the occasional question from a dasher or trampler.

"That's right," Susan was saying cheerfully to a bright violet creeper sitting to her left. "Jennifer can breathe fire, twirl a knife around her wrist, and do all sorts of amazing things. And I sculpt things out of rocks and wet dirt."

"Beautiful things," Jennifer spoke up loyally, thinking of the small dragon Susan had made for her earlier that year. Susan gave her a grateful look.

She noticed that this group of dragons was younger than average—all in their very late teens or early twenties, like Joseph. A few had lived in Eveningstar like Jennifer, before it burned down; but they had no memories of Pinegrove, so there was caution but little bitterness in evidence toward beast-stalkers.

Finally, Joseph turned to Skip. "So what's your story, buddy? You a beaststalker like Eddie here, or a pure human like Susan?"

Jennifer's insides clenched. Skip flipped back his chocolate hair and looked up at the treetops. "Neither."

A dasher with deep blue-green undertones and quills bristling from the nape of her neck winked. "But that's impossible. You're not pure human, and you're not beaststalker. Jennifer here is the only dragon who can hold human shape under this moon."

Joseph's gray eyes narrowed. "So what *are* you?"

Skip lowered his gaze with a cold smile. "I'm like Jennifer. Except a bit different."

The dasher spit out a gobbet of sheep and licked her full array of teeth. "*How* different?"

With a low growl, a trampler at the far end of the pit joined the conversation. "*Eveningstar* different?"

Skip remained calm. "That's one way of putting it."

Joseph gave Skip a hard stare, and then turned to Jennifer. "Do the Elders know about this? Does your father know?"

She returned a defiant look. "Come on, guys. I'm full. Let's go back inside. We've got to get ready for Crescent Valley."

"You're taking *all* of them to Crescent Valley?" The dasher was up on her hind legs now, pointing at Skip with a trembling wing claw. "Including *him*?"

"Including him."

"Inside, inside," Catherine stressed, pushing the others in front of her.

"This was a bad idea," Eddie groaned as he stepped through the porch doors.

"Grow a pair, Blacktooth." Skip was the last to enter the house, letting Catherine herd the others inside while he kept eye contact with Joseph. For a moment, Jennifer thought he would close the door behind them and rejoin the dragons at the pit, at whatever cost. But he did finally come inside.

"That was scary," Susan whispered.

"Please," Skip retorted as he watched the barbeque through the glass doors. "They're not that scary!"

"Are you looking at the same dragons I'm looking at? You almost got roasted!"

"Susan, they're just talking tough. But all they have are teeth and—"

"Fire-breathing! They *breathe fire*, Skip. Can spiders do that? I mean, I'm sure the webs you can weave are pretty and all, but—"

"It doesn't matter," Jennifer cut in. "We're going."

"So are they," Catherine groaned. She was watching the dragons outside as they doused the fire and extended their wings, making for the lake. "The crescent moon is up over the treetops. They're going to make it to Crescent Valley first and tell the others what we're doing!"

"Let them tell," snapped Jennifer. "We're not doing anything wrong."

"We should go now—they'll be expecting us!"

This was exasperating. Jennifer stepped up and flicked her friend's nose horn. "Excuse me, but I'm in no rush. My plan was to spend a fun weekend with my friends. And I don't know if

you noticed, but we are now five teenagers with the place to ourselves, with no adults telling us what we can and cannot do."

"Now you're talking my language." Skip chuckled.

"Stow it," she replied kindly. "After we kick back and relax
with our own fire, there are enough bedrooms here for us to each
get our *own*. To *sleep* in. No nighttime visitors!"

Skip poked Susan's ribs. "That goes double for you, Elmsmith."

"Grammie will be so ticked off when she hears about all this,"
Catherine murmured as she watched the lake's surface. "And then
the whole Blaze will be waiting for us! You sure we shouldn't
go now?"

"They'll be calmer tomorrow," Jennifer pointed out. She
yawned. "And I'm getting too tired to fly more, and then face
everyone. Plenty of time."

"She only told you to bring back beaststalkers, Jennifer. Maybe Skip should stay here? And maybe Susan, too?"

Before Skip or Susan could react to that, Jennifer held up her
hand, five fingers extended. "All five of us, Catherine. All together. All the time. Got it?"

Catherine gulped. "Okay."

Skip's voice floated in from the kitchen. "Hey, toaster waffles!"

# CHAPTER 2

## Sunday

"Cripes, Skip, could you just change back? You're creeping me out."

"Lighten up, Susan."

"Lighten up?! You have a poison stinger, Wilson. Ugh, I cannot believe I let you feel me up in the car."

"If Jennifer and Catherine can be who they are in this place, so can I."

"Skip, it is a bit much to take—"

"No one asked *your* opinion, Blacktooth. Don't you have a sword to bust into pieces somewhere?"

"Skip!"

"Aw, Jennifer, I'm just messing with him . . ."

"Can we get *on* with it?" Catherine asked miserably, tapping a toe claw, which gouged divots of dirt the size of dessert plates. "You guys have been drying off for the last hour. We got off to a late enough start this morning—we should get moving."

"Jennifer was right yesterday. What's the big deal? She wanted me to come, and I'm here. If the Blazers can't handle that—"

"Blaze," Jennifer corrected him uncomfortably. It was a bit much to have this conversation with a six-foot-long fat-tailed scorpion. The yellow and gray segmented body dried more quickly, she supposed, than Skip's normal clothing would. But still . . .

"Blaze, whatever. Anyway, I'm going to have to change when we get going again. Catherine and Jennifer can't carry all three of us at once."

She tuned out the conversation and took in the scenery. They were on the shore of the other side of the lake, huddled around a quick fire Catherine had spat up. Everyone had come through the water just fine, with only a bit of shock at the thought that there was a whole other world through the bottom of her grandfather's lake.

With only twilight to see by, her dragon sight could still make out the gorgeous expanse of moon elms that got thicker and taller to the north and west. Far above the treetops was the eternal crescent moon, which rolled through the sky without ever changing shape.

She had been thrilled to see the moon welcome them with its traditional signal of fire. Her grandpa Crawford was up there now. *Would he be proud of me?* she wondered. He had always had a tense relationship with her beaststalker mother—but then, he had gone ahead and left the farm to her as well, to look after.

He would agree with Jennifer bringing Skip along, wouldn't he?

As if in answer, a distant chord of howls wafted through the trees. Catherine's head immediately perked up.

"Newolves!"

"New*what*?" Eddie's nose wrinkled.

"Newolves. They're like wolves, except they help us hunt, and—"

"Catherine's barely ever seen one." Jennifer giggled, her mind returning to her friends' conversation. "But she still managed to write a whole thesis on them."

"You want to be banned from the Mustang for life?"

"By which I mean to say, Catherine is a genius on the esteemed topic of newolves."

"Yeah, well, whatever they are," Skip guessed, "I'm sure they won't be thrilled about me either."

"You could try *not* being a scorpion," Eddie offered.

"And *you* could try getting bent."

As the two of them hurled insults at each other, Susan bent over and whispered in Jennifer's ear, "Which one do you think will pee harder?"

"Do scorpions even pee?"

Susan giggled, which made Jennifer feel better. She knew

this world was impossibly strange for her friend—the cellolike crickets in the distance, the luminescent morning orange lichen hanging from a few of the moon elm branches, and, of course, the way three of her friends turned into exotic beasts.

"Let's go turf-whomping," she suggested to Catherine. "Skip, if you're going to keep up with us, you're going to have to shift into something that can jump."

"I can arrange that." A few moments later, he was something furry and black, with white stripes and three rows of dark brown eyes. "This type runs in my dad's side of the family an awful lot."

"Swell. Catherine, why don't you carry Susan—she's lighter. Eddie, climb on."

Skip snickered at Eddie, who gave Skip a rude gesture before he straddled Jennifer's back.

Off they went, leaping through the forest, Jennifer and Catherine gouging great tufts of turf with their claws, Skip leaping alongside them, eight legs pumping effortlessly to push him thirty feet in the air without breaking a sweat. Assuming spiders could sweat.

Eddie's legs clenched around Jennifer's kidneys, and she felt his heartbeat race against her scaled spine. "Slow down!" he finally called out after they had nearly hit a large moon elm branch.

"I thought you went riding all the time on your family trips to Wales," she replied, amused. She rotated just enough to squeeze between two half-fallen elm trunks that were thicker than their own bodies.

"Horses! I like riding *horses*! You are not a horse! There's no saddle! No reins! No spurs!"

"Damn right there're no spurs," she snickered. "Just don't barf on me."

"No promises."

"Also, watch out for fire hornets."

"Fire *what*?!"


"*So how the hell* do you brush your teeth in the morning?" Susan asked Skip. Her open disgust had largely passed, and she seemed genuinely curious.

"Mandibles," he corrected her, merrily clicking them. "And we don't brush them. We wash them in human blood."

"Ugh, Skip, that's—"

"Kidding." He sighed. "Geez, Susan. If Jennifer had said something like that, you wouldn't have taken it seriously."

"Jennifer doesn't have eight legs."

"She—"

"Jennifer doesn't have mandibles."

"But—"

*"Jennifer doesn't look like the eternal predators that scuttle across the shower wall and freak me out even when they're only one-inch long."*

"You're prejudiced."

"I can't help my natural instincts. I see lots of legs, I squash."

"Skip, you probably *should* change back to human form," Jennifer piped up as she did so herself.

"Why?" Skip asked with all the enthusiasm of an angry cobra.

"Skip."

"This is the real me!"

"Skip."

"I'm being myself. Isn't that what Crescent Valley is about?"

"Skip!" She held out her human hands, presenting herself. The message was obvious: *If I can do this, so can you.*

"Fine." He shrugged four of his limbs and shifted back to a human wiseass. "Happy?"

"A minor improvement at best," Eddie chirped. He had his land legs back and appeared ready for whatever came next. "How far are we from the Blaze?"

"The amphitheater is right over this hill. Come on, we'll walk there together."

"Oh, man," Catherine said with a sigh as they started. "Grammie is going to be *so angry.*"


"*Now the Blaze* might be a bit edgy—"

"You think?" Skip grinned. He took in the vast amphitheater of grass and stone, with an aged dragon perched on each rock. Very few of them were smiling at any of them.

"It's possible they're a bit anxious," Eddie observed. "Jennifer, where's your dad?"

"Right here," came a voice behind them.

Jonathan Scales, one of the youngest Elders, was a creeper dragon with shining indigo scales and three horns on his crest. Despite his modest age he still commanded high respect among the members of the Blaze. Jennifer supposed being the father of the Ancient Furnace had its perks. However, his expression suggested the current costs were likely outweighing the benefits.

"Jennifer," he greeted her with sharp, gritted teeth. "You brought quite the crowd with you."

She stared defiantly at him without a word. He was either going to accept her and her friends or he wasn't.

To his credit, he got the message. He let a sigh replace the lecture that must have been forming in his head, and turned to Skip. "Skip. It's good to see you again. A couple days ago when you disappeared from our house, I was afraid you were dead."

"Mr. Scales." Skip nodded slightly. Jennifer guessed he was trying to figure out the Elder's tone, just like she was. Skip's disappearance from the house had coincided with Evangelina's attack on Elizabeth Georges-Scales—and while Jonathan's wife was now fine, forgiveness may or may not have been in this dragon's silver eyes.

His glance moved to the others. "Eddie. Welcome to Crescent Valley. It makes sense that Jennifer would invite you. I'm glad she did. Thanks for coming."

Eddie's sharp features reddened a bit, not entirely a reflection of the fires that surrounded them. "You don't have to thank me, Mr. Scales. I should be thanking you. I don't know if you heard yet, but your wife—Dr. Georges-Scales—well, I asked her if I could stay at your house for a while. My dad and I are still working a few things out."

Even though Jennifer knew this was the first he was hearing of this, Jonathan Scales did not hesitate. "You stay with us— at our house, or in this world—as long as you like, Eddie. Take your time. Do what you need to do with your parents."

Eddie nodded a bit. Jennifer almost hugged her father. *Aw, hell.* She stepped up and hugged him. "Thanks, Dad."

"You're welcome. I know it will mean a lot to your mom, too. Speaking of your mom, why isn't she here? Is it because of Wendy?"

Jennifer nodded. "She's going to go see Eddie's mom at the

hospital later today. I'm bringing her back with me after this. We figured you'd understand her—you know, her not coming right away."

"I understand."

"Great. Um, do I have to shift into dragon shape now? I would have before, but I figured with Eddie and Susan—"

"Keep your shape, ace. I get it—you want to make your friends more comfortable. It's a good idea."

"Wow. You're in super-Dad mode." An idea seized her. "Um, can I have a Ford Mustang convertible? Catherine has one and it drives real—"

"No."

"Worth a shot."

"No problem, ace." He turned to Susan and embraced her. "Susan. I can't tell you how pleased I am that Jennifer decided to bring you. How's your dad?" Everyone heard the unspoken question: *What did you tell him about the last few days?*

"Hey, Mr. Scales." She patted the bony crest at the back of his head, then winced and wrung her hands. "Dad's good. Jennifer's mom called him and straightened everything out. I'm not in trouble for smashing the car; he's just glad I'm okay."

"It's probably good he doesn't know you smashed it into my half-sister," Skip joked.

Everyone stared at him.

He shrugged one shoulder. "Not ready to joke about her yet?"

A ripple of discontented colors washed over Jonathan's scales. "Not yet."

"Where's Xavier?" Jennifer blurted out.

Her father turned to her with a wry look. "Xavier Longtail is patrolling the ocean shores of this world, with a few of his relatives. I imagine he timed his absence to coincide with your arrival."

"Good." Jennifer had no need of Xavier Longtail right now—the Elder dasher had made her miserable when the Blaze discovered her beaststalker half, and while he went along with the Blaze's plan to make Jennifer an ambassador, he had made his skepticism known.

"No kidding," Catherine added. "The last thing we need is for that geezer to—"

"Catherine." The voice of the Eldest was unmistakable—

Winona Brandfire, Catherine's grandmother and an elderly trampler, stooped but still powerful. "We are in Blaze."

"*In* Blaze? I thought they *were* Blaze," Susan whispered.

"You can use it both ways," Catherine whispered back quickly. "As long as it's not too confusing."

"Granddaughter!"

"Sorry, Grammie." Catherine waved a sullen wing claw at Jennifer. "I guess I should go sit with the others now."

"Stay here with me!" Jennifer was surprised how much the plea came out sounding like a command. The others seemed surprised, too. But Catherine didn't seem insulted. "Please?" she added, just in case.

"We should start," Winona announced, licking her teeth. Susan and Eddie took a step back at that gesture. It may have been absentminded on Winona's part, but Jennifer didn't think anything this woman did was unintentional.

"Eldest." Jonathan put a wing claw on Jennifer's shoulder. "My daughter, Jennifer, Ancient Furnace to her father's people and ambassador to her mother's, has arrived with guests."

"So she has," the Eldest replied. Her inscrutable olive features took in Jennifer, then Susan, then Eddie, and then (with slits of red eyes) Skip. "I've heard enough about each of these individuals to have little doubt about who they are. This is quite . . . something."

"M-maybe we should go," Susan stammered. Her forehead glistened. "I mean, I'm not a dragon, and I'm not a—"

"Susan." Jennifer reached out with her right arm and took her friend by the waist. "It's okay."

Susan gave her a nervous grin. "Who says?"

"*I* say." She looked at Winona, who could plainly hear them both. "I know no one here has a problem with this."

"No one present, perhaps." The Eldest stretched her wings and looked up at the deepening sky, gazing to the north and east. "But you are aware this Blaze is not unanimous in their trust of your judgment, Ms. Scales. Perhaps you could have started with a crowd more . . . true to your original mission?"

"I brought a beaststalker," Jennifer pointed out. "Two, if you count me. And my mother's coming next time." Resentment welled up inside of her. "And why am I explaining myself? These are my friends."

Her father took a half-step toward her. She didn't look at him, but she did exhale. *Right, Dad. Got it. Calm down.*

Winona's half-smile didn't budge the scales on her severe reptilian face. "I have friends, too, Ambassador. Regardless of what you may think of me, I do not spend all my time on this mountainside. In my considerable years, I've managed to make quite a collection of friends, colleagues, and acquaintances. Not all of them are dragons. But I know the rules. The dragons can come through to this world. The ones who aren't, stay on the other side. They never even hear of Crescent Valley. That's why it's still here."

"I really should go." Susan gave a pleading look. "I'm causing trouble. I don't want to." She called over Jennifer's shoulder. "Ma'am, I don't want trouble. I'll just—"

"You're not the problem, Susan." Skip bit his lower lip as he looked around the towering amphitheater with defiance. "I am."

Winona did not say anything. *She doesn't need to,* Jennifer thought. Should she have left Skip behind? She just wasn't ready to admit that yet. Having him drive up with them just felt so right—even if he did feel up Susan in the backseat.

"I don't belong here," he called out to the other dragons as much as to Susan or Jennifer. "It's okay, I'm used to it. It's not the first time I've run into people who've made up their minds about me before they really know me. I mean, I thought you all might be a bit more like Jennifer here, but I guess—"

"A lecture," Jonathan firmly interrupted, "may not be the best course of action here, Skip."

"That's funny coming from you, Dad."

"Irony noted, ace. Skip, perhaps you could let Jennifer introduce Eddie. Then the Blaze could engage an actual, honest-to-goodness *beaststalker,* as it expected to do today. After that, we can schedule a discussion of whatever cultural or philosophical shortcomings you believe dragons have. Think you can step off the soapbox long enough for that?"

Skip turned to face Jonathan in full—face, shoulders, and body. His high cheekbones darkened, and his fingers twitched. *What's he doing,* Jennifer wondered, *some spider version of* High Noon?

One glance at her father was enough for her to know she needed to intervene, now. He was not amused by the challenge, and his posture was becoming predatory . . .

"Skip, please!" She interposed herself between them. Skip hesitated, and she used the time to talk him down. "Dad's being an ass, but he's right: This shouldn't be about you. Let them talk with Eddie."

"Eddie." He practically spat the name, but he relaxed and sat cross-legged on the amphitheater stones. "Yeah, sure, go ahead, Eddie. Be a hero, if you can."

Nose down and chin stuck to his chest, Eddie stumbled forward a couple of steps. Jennifer was pretty sure Susan had pushed him.

Winona seemed glad of the change in focus. "Edward Blacktooth. What can you tell us of the mood among your people in Winoka? Do you think there is an honest chance for reconciliation?"

Eddie stared at the ancient presence before him and bobbed his lips a few times. Sensing his need for moral support, Jennifer sidled up next to him and held his hand. The move helped a little in that he stopped gaping at Winona; but now he started gaping at Jennifer.

She stared hard at him, willing him to talk. *Say something, Eddie!*

He finally snapped out of it. "Er, sorry, Ms. Bran—I mean, Ms. Drag—I mean, Eldest. My people? It's hard to say. Nowadays, with Jennifer and her family making waves, it—er—um . . ." With an apologetic look at Jennifer and Jonathan, he trailed off miserably.

"Go on," Jennifer urged.

Shrugging his shoulders, he continued. "It's just that Winoka seems kinda split right now. I know some folks who think Jennifer and her parents are great. I know others who want to hurt them."

"Who want to *try*," Susan mumbled behind them.

"Ms. Scales is our ambassador to you," Winona told Eddie. "She is tasked with finding more beaststalkers like you. Warriors who would talk with us. Are you willing to help her? Can you convince other beaststalkers who might speak up in Winoka for peace?"

His eyes went wide. "Geez, I want to help Jennifer. But I don't . . . I'm not . . . I couldn't even finish my rite of passage—"

"To be fair," Jonathan said grimly, "you would not be standing here if you had."

"I don't know that I had much say in it all." Eddie's completely blunt response made Jennifer smirk. She *had* kicked his ass. "And failing that test is probably the worst thing I could do to gain the respect of other beaststalkers—especially since I'm already friends with you and Jennifer, no offense."

"What about the guys you started hanging out with earlier this year?" Susan's suggestion made Jennifer recall the clique Eddie had begun to hang out with when the two of them were unfriendly. "Bob Jarkmand may be a bit of a dunce, but he's got lots of friends. And he'd be a big friend to have—literally."

"It's not a bad idea, Susan. Bob's a big guy, and he'll probably be a heck of a beaststalker someday. But I think Jenny kinda blew that deal when she brushed him off at the hospital . . ."

Jennifer winced as Susan gaped at her. "Bob Jarkmand asked you out? And you shot him down?"

"Yeah." She felt hundreds of stares upon her as she related the latest quirk of her crazy love life. "I know that he comes from a beaststalker family, but I couldn't . . . I'm not . . . he's just . . ."

"Undateable?" Catherine guessed.

"Right on. Hey, listen, folks, if I've gotta date every beaststalker boy in Winona just to give peace a chance . . . I just don't have the energy."

"Or the contraceptives!" Susan teased, ignoring Jonathan's glare.

"If we could get back to conventional diplomatic methods," Winona almost begged. "Mr. Blacktooth, we need your leadership. Can you talk to other beaststalkers and get them to join you?"

Eddie, who for the last few moments had appeared to want to sneak out of the amphitheater, flinched at the return of this topic. His shoulders were slumped and his hair hung limply over his sparrowlike features. "You don't understand, ma'am. Bob Jarkmand, he won't—I mean, I don't think anybody would pay much attention if I—"

"But will you *try*?" The trampler leaned in, her voice burning with ferocity.

Jennifer took Eddie's hand again and squeezed. He looked at her, but all she could see in his brown eyes was fear. Fear of

Bob Jarkmand, and the other kids at school. Fear of his parents, and what they would say. Probably even a little fear of Jennifer herself. *Come on, Eddie. Stand up. Take the lead. I'll help you.* She wanted to say these things, but she knew Eddie had to answer for himself.

He finally turned away from Jennifer and mumbled at the ground in front of the Blaze's Eldest. "I could talk to one or two friends, I guess. But I don't think they'll listen. I mean, I can't even hold a sword right . . ."

Winona ground her teeth in obvious frustration. Jennifer let go of his hand. *Oh, Eddie.* She didn't know what made her feel worse—the boy's complete lack of confidence, or how his spinelessness had cost them all a chance to come together.

"Perhaps when my wife arrives, Eldest," Jonathan suggested, "we might have better luck devising a diplomatic strategy." He didn't seem too optimistic.

Winona rubbed the ridge of her skull with a wing claw. "Perhaps so. In the meantime, Mr. Blacktooth, as Elder Scales has already told you, you are welcome to stay among us. All I ask is that you remain under the escort of the Ancient Furnace, or her father."

"What about us?" Susan piped up nervously. "Can we stay with Jennifer, too?"

The trampler ignored Skip's cynical snort from his cross-legged position on the ground. "Ms. Elmsmith, I believe the Blaze can make an exception this once for you. But that is only once, and only for you. Mr. Wilson—"

"—is already on his way outta here," Skip interrupted, getting up to leave. "Thanks for the tea and biscuits, motherfu—"

*"Skip!"* Jennifer slapped a hand over his mouth. He didn't try to resist, but he did lick her hand a few times. Grossed out, she kept it there anyway.

"You can't just kick him out, Grammie!" Catherine's outrage was a pleasant surprise to Jennifer—she had just met the boy. "He has no way of getting home!"

"I'm sure Elder Scales will not mind if his daughter's friend stays at their farmhouse for a couple of days, on the proper side of the lake."

Jonathan shook his head, but it was not in deference to the Eldest. "He'd have my permission, but frankly, I don't think that's wise, Winona. There are young weredragons around the farm right now, and—"

He trailed off, but everybody including Jennifer knew what he meant: It wouldn't take long for Skip to get into a scuffle with someone.

"I'll drive him home," Susan spoke up with pride. "I mean, I only have my permit, but it's not like my driving is so bad I'll crash a car . . . um, *again*, that is . . ."

She took Skip's hand and led him out of the amphitheater. Jennifer and Catherine watched them go with alarm.

"Grammie, you can't be serious! She's only fifteen!"

"There are no adult drivers available," Jonathan pointed out. "Jennifer's the only dragon who can change shape at will."

"But the convertible . . . !"

"I would rather risk the convertible," Winona replied coldly, "than this refuge. Jennifer, see to it that they both get through the portal again safely, and that they are driving in the right direction. Then come back so that your friend Edward here—"

"We all came together, and we'll all leave together," Jennifer snapped. "Come on, Eddie. Let's go. Catherine?"

Catherine teetered in the space between her grandmother and Jennifer. Her reptilian features creased with worry, and Jennifer belatedly realized she had put her friend in a horrible spot.

"Catherine, it's okay. If you want to stay here—"

"No, I'm coming." The resolve was sudden and filled Jennifer with an unexpected warmth. "Just let me say good-bye to my grandmother, and I'll catch up."

"Sure." Jennifer turned to her father. "Will you need to see us off? Make sure we're driving in the right direction and not doubling back against orders?"

"Hey, ace. Easy. It's me." He curled a wing around her shoulders and walked her away from the Blaze with a downtrodden Eddie in tow. "You wanna go, go. Just do me a favor and fly home. It's safer than driving, at your age. Deal?"

She relaxed under his wing. "Deal. Sorry I lost my temper, Dad. It's just that this place . . ." Looking around, she couldn't place the emotion. "It means so much to me. When you first brought me here, I finally felt like an adult. Hunting here with you and Grandpa was special. Bringing Catherine here made our friendship stronger, even though it ended up being dangerous for her. And then when the Blaze talked about banishing me when they found out I was a beaststalker—I just couldn't bear the thought. And Grandpa's buried here, and now he's up above with the only sister I've ever known, and—"

She found herself crying as she walked out of the amphitheater. "This place makes me so happy, and it ticks me off so much, and it's dangerous and sad and beautiful all at once! I wanted to share it with my friends, because I thought they—"

"You thought they might feel it, too," he finished for her. "Look, Jennifer, you're right to want to share this place with your friends. And it's going to happen for you, I'm sure of it. But you can't expect everyone to grow up for you, all in a day. Not Winona, not Xavier, not Skip, not even me, or yourself. Be patient."

Nodding, she gently shrugged his wing off and looked around at the mountainside. "It wouldn't be so bad to have werachnids visiting here in Crescent Valley. Maybe even living here someday. Right, Dad?"

He shuddered and chuckled. "I guess, ace. Your vision is a bit more progressive than mine. But time is on your side. Use it."

*"So go ahead,* Jennifer. Let me have it." They were relaxing in the living room of the cabin on the other side, drinking lemonade and watching out of the window as winged shapes soared and dived. They were all in guest bathrobes (except for Jennifer and Catherine, who kept their dragon form), while their clothes enjoyed a dryer cycle.

"Oh, Skip. I'm not going to let you have it." She watched a dasher nip into the cold lake just briefly enough to pull a large walleye out. "I don't blame you for anything you said."

Truth be told, she was more annoyed at Eddie. His pathetic "commitment" to talk to one or two of the less scary kids at school was hardly the heroic start she had hoped for in dragon-beaststalker relations. She tried hard not to look at him, choosing instead to turn back to Skip. "I just feel badly that I can't bring you back. I mean, I suppose I *can,* but I really shouldn't . . ."

He wiped his hands on the hem of his robe. "Don't worry about it. I don't want you sticking your neck out for me with those old farts."

"Those old farts?" Catherine raised her scaled chin up from

the carpet. *"Those old farts* are my grandmother and her friends. She raised me after my parents died. You're cool and all, Skip; and I'll support Jennifer because I think she's right. But don't bad-mouth my family."

Skip rolled his eyes but didn't argue the point.

"When will the clothes get out of the dryer?" asked Susan, shivering in her robe.

"Give it another half-hour," Jennifer guessed. "You sure you're okay to drive, Susan? I mean, with all of us here, maybe the weredragons won't give Skip or you any trouble—"

"I want to leave," Skip said. "If I need to call my aunt Tavia and have her come pick me up, fine. But I'm not staying here."

Jennifer's face crumbled in despair. This was her fault—she never should have brought him. She thought she was helping all of her friends get closer together, but this trip had just caused trouble for everyone. Skip had nearly started a fight, Susan would have to drive illegally, Catherine was arguing with her grandmother, and Eddie . . . *Who cares?* she thought bitterly.

"You don't need to call your aunt, Skip." She sighed. "We'll get you home."

"Home," he repeated. He plainly didn't like the word. "I don't know why I care so much. Like I told Catherine's grandmother—I don't belong there, or here, or Winoka, or anywhere else. None of those places has ever felt much like home."

"So where *is* home?" Catherine asked him.

He wrapped his hand in the robe's belt and didn't look at any of them. "Far away," he finally said.

"What, like, Iowa?"

He gave Susan a short push, but didn't return her smile. "Not Iowa. It doesn't matter. It's not like I can take all of you there now, like Jennifer tried to do for us. Jennifer, I'm sorry this didn't work out. I know it meant a lot to you."

"Thanks, Skip." She looked at him, then at Eddie again. *See?* she almost screamed at the young beaststalker. *He can stand up tall, talk straight, look me in the eye. Why can't you?*

As if hearing her thoughts, Eddie chose that moment to get up and leave the room.

"Unbelievable," Catherine muttered as soon as he was out of earshot. She rolled onto her back and stared up at the ceiling fan. "My grandmother makes one request—talk to some beaststalkers—and he punks out. Jennifer, I thought you said he was your friend?"

"He is." Jennifer felt her neck get warm, since she had just been thinking the same thing. "He's just going through a tough time. Give him a break."

"We all go through tough times, Jennifer." Susan didn't seem happy about arguing the point, but she went on. "I understand Eddie's mom is in the hospital and his dad's a jerk. But there are people I know who get knocked down and then stand back up." *Like you*, her look told Jennifer.

"He'll come through." She tried to sound more certain than she felt. "Eddie just needs something to believe in again. His family let him down. I let him down."

"Skip kicked his head in," Susan added.

"Doesn't matter," Catherine insisted. "Eddie let everyone down. Did you see the look on Grammie's face? I thought she was going to pinch his head off and toast it, she was so upset by his answer."

"He'll come through," Jennifer repeated.

"Whatever you say," Catherine said and sniffed. She got up and ambled into the kitchen on four legs. "I'd like a bite before we go. Skip, you didn't eat all the toaster waffles last night, did you?"

# CHAPTER 3

## Sunday Afternoon

During the drive home, Catherine and Jennifer stayed in formation close to the ground so they could talk and whomp.

"Your dad seemed to stay pretty cool," Catherine commented as her large hindclaws crushed the brown weeds alongside the highway with leap after leap.

"Yeah, he's all right," Jennifer allowed, whomping the grasses right next to her friend. "We still get along okay."

It was a while before Catherine said anything. Then, "I told Grammie before we left that she should listen to you more. And your dad. But she's too—too *Grammie*. Know what I mean?"

"Yeah." *No clue.*

"I mean, she raised me from since I can remember. She's always been right, about everything. Or so I thought. But the more I see of Crescent Valley and other dragons, the more I wonder. I mean, who cares if someone like Susan or Skip visits Crescent Valley? They're friends."

"My thoughts exactly."

"I think the pressure of being Eldest is kinda getting to her. Whenever I try to talk to her about stuff, she gets really freaked out. Especially if it's about beaststalkers."

"Why's that?"

"Beaststalkers have *not* been kind to our family. She's told me some pretty nasty things, about killings, and hobblings, and skewered newolves . . ."

Jennifer was just about to ask what hobblings were, but then the image of a skewered newolf made her stomach churn. "Ugh. How would newolves and beaststalkers ever meet?"

"I'm not sure. Grammie's talked a bit about some newolves coming over to this side, as guards or escorts."

This much was true. Jennifer recalled the previous spring, when her father and grandfather had arranged for newolves to patrol the forests near the farm. She wondered how they crossed over. Did they swim? Did they need to have the wearer of the Ring of Seraphina with them?

And did beaststalkers really have to *skewer* them?

They went on, staying within sight of the Mustang, which only swerved once in a while when it drifted too far to the right and hit the rumble strip.

"Jeez," Jennifer remarked the fourth time this happened in the past half-hour. "Do you think Susan's just tired, or what?"

"More likely fending off Skip's advances" came the sly response.

"Okay, was that supposed to be funny?"

"I'm just saying—"

"Because I know funny. I'm a funny gal."

"She doesn't exactly *stop* him when he grabs her under—"

"And that? Not so funny."

Jennifer punctuated the last remark by launching herself intentionally into Catherine's side. She knocked both of them into a cornfield, which fortunately had been harvested weeks ago and only contained snowy mud and stalk residue. They somersaulted several times before they were able to stop, and they were both giggling as they got up.

"I'm glad *you're* not driving that car anymore," Catherine said. "Steering like that, you'd have hit the ditch miles ago."

"Yeah, but I would have taken down the sassy bitch in the next car with me."

"We'd better catch up. I want to keep an eye on them."

"Me, too."

"Not for that! I mean, we should make sure they get home safely. You know, Skip seemed kinda down. And, er, Eddie, too."

It took a few jumps before Jennifer realized something. She sailed at her friend again, this time merely bumping her a bit off course. "*You* like Skip!"

"Hey! Well, *like* is a strong word. I think he's . . . kinda interesting."

"He called your grandmother an old fart."

"She *is* an old fart."

"Catherine!"

"It doesn't mean I don't love her." They were even with the Mustang again. "It just means Skip said something insexy—er, incisive."

"Oh, sweet, merciful . . ."

"Before you broke up with him, did you consider how firm his butt is?"

"That's it. I'm ripping the roof off of your Mustang, right now."

"Don't be surprised if you find them making out in there."

"At fifty miles an hour?"

"You're right. Too slow for making out. They're probably just feeling each other up."

"You are *so* not my friend anymore. Go back to your old fart of a grandmother."

"See, it's not as sexy when *you* say it."

WINOKA
POP. **19,502**
*SAFE HOMES, STRONG FAMILIES*

"You sure you won't come into town?"

"Naw." Catherine shifted her weight nervously as she leaned against the Winoka city limits sign. One wing claw reached back to scratch her spine. "I figure Susan can avoid crashing the car from here. I'll go back to Crescent Valley and let Grammie and your dad know everyone's back home. You still coming back tomorrow with your mom?"

"That's the plan." The thought of bringing her mother to Crescent Valley made Jennifer immediately feel better. That was a trip that would go more smoothly.

"We'll see you later, Catherine!" Susan was almost back in the car before her sentence ended. The engine revved back up. Skip and Eddie waved from the inside; Skip's face was full of rash confidence. Jennifer squinted—was that lipstick on his cheek? It was hard to tell in the dim light of a dismal November afternoon. Maybe that was a hickey on his throat . . . or maybe it was mascara . . .

*What would her eyelashes be doing on his neck? Cripes, Jennifer. Get a hold of yourself.*

"Hey, listen." Catherine woke Jennifer from her reverie. "I'm not supposed to talk to you about this, but I can't resist. Don't be surprised if something cool happens later this week!"

"What do you mean?"

But Catherine only flashed her perfect teeth and leapt off the ground, bouncing several yards away as she began to turf-whomp her way back to Crescent Valley.

"Hey, that's mean!" Jennifer called out. Catherine was already too far away to hear.

"Can you believe she—" But Jennifer was already talking to a cloud of gravel and dust. She began to hack as the Mustang ripped back onto the road and through the outskirts of Winona. She pointed across the highway. "Guys, wait up! Don't you want to get ice cream at the mall or something?"

Because she could fly normally now, she cruised a few yards behind the Mustang, shifting the scales on her skin to make herself less apparent to bystanders and trying hard to peer through the rear window and see if any silhouettes were getting too close to each other.

It was not far to Skip's house, a two-story Cape Cod with brown shingles and a bright red door, which complemented the pale yellow trim. Skip lived with his aunt Tavia Saltin, sister to the late werachnid sorcerer Otto Saltin, who had tried to imprison and abuse Jennifer when she first became a weredragon.

But there wasn't anything sinister in view as they pulled up into the short driveway. Out of deference to Skip's aunt, Jennifer shifted out of dragon form as she opened the passenger side door.

"All right, lover boy. Out."

"In a second." He didn't even turn to look at her, Jennifer noticed as his body leaned closer to Susan and his voice sank to a whisper. She heard Susan giggle, and her grip tightened on the top of the open door.

*If I slam it hard enough, maybe it will blast off its hinges, fly across the seat, and crush them against the fine, leather-trim interior.*

He finally got out, a wide grin on his easy features. Jennifer left the car door open for Eddie, who had quietly gotten out of the back so he could slide into the passenger seat, and followed Skip up the walk to his front door.

"Well," he drawled with his hand on the doorknob. "Thanks for a fantastic overnight."

She returned the ironic lip curl. "Same here. You sure do know how to show a girl a good time. Multiple girls, in fact."

"Oh, hey." His grin lost some of its edge. "Nothing happened with Susan and me. I was just . . ."

"Making an ass of yourself? Studying for biology class? Handing me a murder motive?"

". . . trying to get a rise out of you," he finally admitted. His hand came off the doorknob and rubbed the back of his neck.

She bit the edge of her tongue, considering. Then, though she didn't know why she said it, she told him, "Catherine thinks you're kind of cute."

"Does she?" His face twisted with surprise, as though he had never really considered the possibility. *Why would he,* she told herself. *He just met her and insulted her grandmother.*

"Yeah. You know, just if. You know. If you wanted to know that."

"Huh." He kept rubbing the back of his neck. "Yeah, though. You know. Doesn't live around here. Northwater, right?"

"Yeah."

He whistled. "Ways away. I mean, I don't see. You know, she's your. And, a ways away."

"Yeah. Though the car."

"Right. The car. She has that for when."

Her tongue was getting sore from the chewing. "Yeah. Anyway. If you want to ask her and." *Don't or I'll stab you both to death.* "You know."

"I guess I could think about. You know. If I see her again when. Whenever."

"Well." They both jumped at the smooth voice coming from the direction of the door, which was now wide open. Edmund Slider sat in his wheelchair, watching them from just inside the foyer. Mr. Slider was a mathematics teacher who had just moved to Winoka that year, and had begun dating Tavia Saltin. The forced smile on the man's face betrayed a resigned sort of dismay.

A long, delicate finger came up and pulled a blond lock of

hair out of his face. "As an educator, I am once again humbled by the remarkable display of conversational flair today's teenagers have stitched together for my benefit. If only you two could keep this up for another few minutes, I might be witness to an actual coherent and complete English sentence."

Jennifer coughed and took a step away from the door. Skip's ears turned maroon with embarrassment.

"Where's my aunt?"

"Out gathering supplies for her musical therapy group. She should be back any moment."

"Have any of her patients seen any results from that?" Jennifer knew Tavia Saltin was an ophthalmologist who was pioneering music-based therapy for those who were blind or losing their sight. Whether this therapy used science or sorcery was uncertain. The late Otto Saltin had been one of the rare werachnids who could weave sorceries, and Jennifer assumed his sister, Tavia, could do the same.

Mr. Slider shrugged. "I'm not an expert on music, or on eyesight. So Skip, am I to understand that your overnight trip to the Twin Cities with Jennifer's mother was a smashing educational success?"

"It was awesome," Skip answered. "I'd never seen surgery done before, and Dr. Georges-Scales is amazing. I gotta say, I thought Career Day was kind of a stupid idea when Mr. Pool suggested it, but I'm actually thinking medicine might be kind of a cool career for me."

Jennifer was quick enough to nod at the same time as Skip. "Mr. Pool's a good guidance counselor. He told me I should do another Career Day with someone different, since I've seen surgery with my mom before." She turned to Skip. "You think your aunt might be willing to let me watch her work for a day or two?"

Skip's look was pure gratitude to her for going along with the cover story.

"Wow." Mr. Slider gave a gracious laugh. "You two are *really* good under pressure. I can't believe I made fun of your conversational skills. All right, let's cut to the truth: I am not as naïve as your aunt, Skip. We all know you two were off on an unapproved overnight teenage outing. May I at least assume that you were intelligent enough to avoid truly irresponsible behavior, in the absence of adult supervision?"

Jennifer turned to Skip. "Okay. You're on your own, Skip. Nice knowing you."

She turned and walked back to the car, careful not to look back as Skip gave an exclamation of protest and Mr. Slider began to laugh.

*By the time* they got to Jennifer's house, they had agreed that Susan should leave the car there. The Elmsmiths lived just a few houses down Pine Street from the Scales.

Jennifer insisted on walking Susan home. After unlocking the front door at home for a very quiet Eddie—Elizabeth's shift at the hospital had not yet ended, so there was no one to let him in—and letting her collie-shepherd mix, Phoebe, out, the two girls started off down the road together. Jennifer let the dog trail them at a respectful distance; Phoebe was fairly obedient to voice commands.

They were both quiet for a while until Susan finally said, "Jennifer, I'm sorry about Skip. I didn't—"

"Forget it." She tried to sound stern, but in truth Jennifer was delighted her friend had broken the ice. "I know you two were just messing with each other. And me."

Her friend exhaled. "Thanks. And thanks for taking me to Crescent Valley. Jennifer, it's so beautiful! And I know it's an important place to you."

They could see Susan's house now, an older brick house ("Built in 1890," she would often say with a sigh, "long before things were cool.") with faded shutters and a curiously long, deep garage where horses were once kept. It was set into part of the hill that dominated this end of Pine Street. With no wind on the chilly air, their footsteps on the asphalt were the only sounds that broke through the early twilight.

"I wish I could take you back there."

"Don't worry." Susan squeezed her hand. "I'll go there again someday. I know we'll find a way."

They approached Susan's driveway. Jennifer let out a heavy sigh. "I'm not looking forward to going back home right now."

"Yeah, I don't expect Eddie will be great company tonight. Where's he gonna sleep while he's staying with you?"

"Mom was going to make up the guest room for him, before

she headed off to work. Honestly, Susan, I'm glad we can help him out, but I'll be super-happy if he just goes into his room and closes the door for the next three weeks. I was thinking of bringing him back with my mom and me tomorrow. But there's no way I'm doing that now. Every time I look at him, I just want to strangle him."

"He'll enjoy having the run of your house while you're away," Susan offered. "How long do you think you'll be gone this time?"

"We'll leave after school tomorrow, probably stay overnight. I don't expect we'll be back in time for school Tuesday. You wanna get together Tuesday night?"

"I can't do weeknights this week. I've got an advanced sculpting class at the community college. Dad says I may have potential."

"That's great! Good for you. Um, okay. Friday?"

"Friday."

"Mall?"

"Mall."

*Jennifer started to tiptoe* into her house, then jumped as Phoebe bolted in behind her and realized how foolish it seemed. She clomped into the kitchen and found Eddie eating a banana and peanut butter sandwich (*blurgh!*) and flipping through *Popular Mechanics*.

"Hey."

"Hey."

She thought about saying more, but couldn't. She spun away from him and went upstairs, telling herself it was because of the sandwich.

# CHAPTER 4

## *Monday*

Winoka High School was a large public school, built on the east edge of town near some of the last farmland within city limits. The school had been rebuilt about a decade ago, after beaststalkers demolished one of the last few public buildings they had left standing after invading Pinegrove and renaming it fifty years prior.

The faculty and staff of Winoka High worked hard at their jobs and were highly productive, torturing over 1,500 teenaged souls on a daily basis. A few veteran teachers were unsurpassed in their ability to bore even the most enthusiastic students; others were at various stages of disillusionment with their chosen career path.

Pockets of resistance persisted: Jennifer had several favorite teachers who had not yet let go of their dreams, and who could engage her and other students in lively discussion. Mr. Slider, despite his dry and occasionally chilly manner, inspired Jennifer with his challenging classes and calm wit.

However, she wasn't looking forward to geometry class this morning: What with all the doings over the weekend, she hadn't finished any homework. Slider was likely to be merciless and cutting, which she supposed she deserved.

So she and Susan were scrambling next to Jennifer's locker to copy each other's notes—a strategy that seemed likely to fail, since Susan hadn't had time to get homework done either—when a voice interrupted them.

"Jenny!"

Jennifer recognized the voice immediately and nearly fell into her open locker. Putting on as fearless a smile as she could manage, she turned to behold the most popular sophomore girl in Winoka High a mere two feet away, beaming at her.

Well, not *her*. Amanda Sera's baby blue gaze was riveted to the small silver compact she held as she touched up her lip gloss. Meanwhile, her three most famous satellites—Amy Collins, Anne Hutchinson, and Abigail Whittier—clustered behind her back. This foursome was known as the A-List. Every boy at Winoka High wanted any one of them. Every girl scrambled to get out of their way, lest their combined fury destroy an innocent reputation. Until this day, they had not had a word for Jennifer Scales. Ever.

"What's up, Jenny? Hey, Sarah."

"Susan." To her friend's credit, the tone held no impatience.

"Hey, guys." *What on earth could you possibly want?*

"My parents are out of town Friday night." Amanda smacked her lips and kept her bright eyes on her mirror image. With her spare hand, she twisted three perfect curls so they fell over the left side of her face. "Sooo, party at my place. You wanna come, Jenny?"

"You bet," Jennifer blurted without thinking. *Wait. She didn't ask Susan, even though she's right here. That was rude. And why do I want to go to this girl's—*

"Cool. Bring a mack."

*Ugh.* "Um, yeah. Sure." *Who the heck am I going to bring?*

"You *got* a mack, Scales?" Amy Collins sneered under carefully coiffed brunette bangs as she put a hand on Amanda's shoulder. "'Cause I hear you and Skip Wilson are history."

"Too bad," observed Abigail Whittier, her thin cocoa features betraying boredom as she stared at random students walking by. "Skip's a stud."

"Yeah, why'd you dump him, anyway?" Anne Hutchinson was the only one of the four who appeared remotely interested in Jennifer. Her reddish-blonde curls danced around curiously freckled cheeks.

"He, ah, you know. Changed."

"Yeah, I getcha." Amanda snapped her compact shut and checked her jeweled watch. "Word's out that Bob Jarkmand's kinda sweet on ya. Bet he'd go."

"Yeah, maybe," said Jennifer doubtfully. Hadn't the A-List heard about her stiffing Bob already? Heck, Eddie and Susan had known. Of course, she had told them—but she always as-

sumed the A-List knew stuff like this instinctually. Like how a
little seagull chick knew to peck at its mother's throat to get re-
gurgitated food, so must high school girls know—

"Omigod, here he comes! See ya, Jenny, bye, Stacy!" Amy
pushed Amanda away, which appeared to form a sort of gravity
well of popularity down the corridor. Abigail and Anne fell into
it, giggling, and the four of them were gone in an instant.

And just like that, Bob Jarkmand was right in front of Jennifer and Susan, his massive, jacketed torso sporting the school's
colors and a prominent "W" for his promising young career as an
offensive lineman at Winoka High.

"Hey." His massive-shouldered posture was nonthreatening,
his acne-pocked face seemed bland. Possibly vacuous. He turned
to Susan. "Steph, can you give me 'n' Jenny a sec?"

Susan's face narrowed. "I promise to leave, just as soon as
someone in this school gets my name right."

"Susan, please?" Jennifer's heart fell. She already felt bad about
how the A-List had blown her off, worse that she had accepted their
party invitation anyway, and worst of all that Susan now had to
leave to give this dimwit a moment of Jennifer's time.

Without taking her glare off of Bob, Susan backed down the
hall exactly four steps, and then waited. Her intransigence seemed
to confuse the hulking boy.

"Uh. 'Kay. Um, Jenny, there's a party at Amanda's this Friday."

"Yes, there is." Jennifer's head began to ache, and his voice
sounded far away.

"I was thinking maybe you and me could—"

"Go together? Yeah, that would be great."

*WHAT?*

*Don't worry,* the other half of her brain desperately tried to
assure the first half. *I've got a plan. I must have a plan.*

"Wow!" Bob's simian face brightened. "Really?"

*And your plan is?*

*Um. It's a secret?*

*Idiot.*

"See you Friday night," she said quickly, and turned to shuffle
past Susan, who was gaping.

She was halfway to geometry class before her friend's voice
caught up with her.

"What was *that*?"

"That was a date," Jennifer replied simply.

"A date? With Bob Jarkmand? For a *macking* party?"

"Geez, Susan, what do you want me to do? Go to this thing without anyone?"

"No, but what about going with an actual member of the human race?"

"Hey, Bob asked me. Amanda and the others find him acceptable. I'm taking what I can get."

"What a terrific way to pursue true love. Will you let him down your pants if Amanda and the others say it's okay?"

"That's cute, Susan. Could you be a little more insulting?"

"Sure, how about this: Since when did the Almighty Dragon Princess start blowing off her friends to go to parties with those *bitches*?"

Jennifer stopped short and faced Susan. "Is that what this is about? Them?"

Her friend stared at her as if she had polka dots on her nose. *"Duh! Yes!"*

"I'm sorry I said yes to Amanda, okay? And I'm sorry I said yes to Bob. But I don't have lots of choices, Susan. Bob's a beast-stalker, or a beaststalker-in-training, anyway. And haven't you ever noticed? His family hangs out with Amanda's family, and I'll bet Amanda's one, too. Heck, the whole freaking A-List could be beaststalkers. Someone's got to reach out to them. Eddie's not stepping up. That leaves me."

"So because Eddie punked out, you'll ditch me and become an A-List whore?"

Jennifer let a hiss escape through her her teeth. "Will you stop overreacting? It's one stupid night. I'm not blowing you off—"

"We were going to go to the mall together Friday night. Remember?"

The words hit Jennifer across the face like a dasher's spiked tail. She couldn't think of anything to say.

"I guess not. Like I said: Blowing Me Off!" Susan raced off to geometry class.

Jennifer stood there—still in shock—for a good few seconds before she caught movement in her peripheral vision.

"So how'd it go, Jenny?"

It was Amanda. She was focused on using a tiny lint roller to remove invisible specks from her perfect wool skirt and cashmere sweater. The other three girls were in tight formation behind her.

"It went fine. I gotta go to geometry."

"Bob's coming to the party with you?"

Aggravated, Jennifer pursed her lips and put her hands on her hips. "Of course he is. What, you think he's saying no to *this*?"

That got Amanda to look up and grin. Abigail let out a whoop of laughter, and the others tittered nervously.

"He'll have his hands full," Amanda said, scanning the length of Jennifer's body as if recognizing her for the first time. "Make sure you don't tell anyone else about this party. I don't want to wreck the place or my parents will kill me. Sally's cool with not going?"

It was barely a question. Jennifer cast her gaze down the hall. Her friend had already disappeared among the crowds of roving teenagers. "*Susan* will be fine." But she wasn't sure of that at all.

"Where do you get your 'do done?" Anne took a cautious step forward and reached out to touch Jennifer's platinum hair. "That color is insane. I want it!"

Feeling brave and still a bit angry, Jennifer reached up and held Anne's freckled nose between thumb and forefinger. She shook the girl's head back and forth with gentle mischief. "Oh no, cutie! You don't want to go through what I had to go through to get this hair. Believe me."

Anne gasped and took a step backward, breaking contact. The other three girls stared at the two of them, stunned by Jennifer's audacious move. *I dared touch one of them!* The giddy thought raced through her mind with a mixture of surprise at her own transgression, relief that Amanda would probably disinvite her from the stupid mack party, and horror at what rumor they might generate to torture her for the next two and a half years.

Then all four of them started giggling uncontrollably, and Jennifer knew all was truly lost. *They have accepted me. I have become one of them. Kill me now.*

"Oh, Jenny, you are a *riot*!" Amanda reached out with her lint roller and rubbed it over Jennifer's own sweater, as if leaving her own scent all over the new girl. "There. Much better. Hey, you wanna go to the mall tonight?"

Another twinge of regret rankled Jennifer at the mention of the mall. She would have to make it up to Susan when they got back from Crescent Valley. Heck, maybe she could convince her parents to keep the visit brief enough to come back early in the morning, or even tonight . . .

"I've got plans," she finally said without paying much attention to Amanda's look of astonishment. Apparently, not too many girls at Winoka High turned down the A+ of the A-List. "Thanks, though."

"Huh. Yeah, well, see you around."

The A-List turned as one, flared wool skirts all flipping in unison, and walked away.

A boy's whistle behind her made her turn. "Oh, it's you."

"Wow." Skip couldn't take his eyes off the retreating foursome. "You *know* those girls? How come you never introduced—"

"Forget it."

"Yeah, I don't suppose any of them want a guy with a brain above the belt, anyway. Speaking of which, are you honestly going to a party with Bob Jarkmand this Friday? I mean, that's a joke, right?"

Her jaw dropped. "You heard already?"

His expression froze somewhere between amusement and amazement. His thumb jerked. "I ran into Susan back there. She filled me in. I *thought* she was just screwing with my head." Adjusting the backpack on his shoulder, he looked at Jennifer with more confusion—and perhaps less respect. "Bob Jarkmand, eh?"

"Skip, I really don't have time for—"

"Where's your necklace?" He was suddenly alarmed that the wooden necklace he had given her last spring, with the carved image of the Moon of the Falling Leaves, was not hanging around her neck as it usually was.

She looked down at the sterling silver chain and prism pendant she had decided upon that morning, and then shrugged. "I just figured I would wear something different today. What, doesn't this look good?"

"It looks great. You look great. But I kinda hoped you'd keep—"

"What? Wearing your necklace? It's not like we're going out anymore," she interrupted hotly. "I mean, I should probably give it back to—"

"No!"

She took a step back, startled. "Geez, Skip. Fine. I'll keep it. But do you mind if I accessorize myself in the morning?"

"You should wear it," he replied with thin lips. Then he shook his head. "More often, I mean."

As patronizing as this was, she couldn't hold back a laugh. "Skip, this morning was the first time I took it off since June! What, you want me to stuff it down my bra?"

Her joke relaxed him a little, but his grin was still nervous. "Yeah, I guess you're right. Sorry for freaking out. See you around. Say, you still going back to Crescent Valley tonight?"

"Oh, um." She hesitated. Of course he had known she'd planned to return with her mother—but he looked quite vulnerable right now, and she didn't want to start another fight. So she steeled herself and lied. "Naw. It's not that important. I'm still angry at them for booting you and Susan. I told my mom I'd take her another time."

The news did seem to brighten his mood. "I appreciate that. Thanks. But geez, you don't have to— Anyway, if you go, you should wear the necklace." He soothed her with a soft touch under her chin. "All I mean is, it looks beautiful on you when the crescent moon's out."

With a long bat of her lashes, she pushed his hand away. "Sweet talker."

*As it turned out,* she forgot to put Skip's necklace back on that afternoon before she and her mother left in the minivan for Crescent Valley. To be fair, she had a lot on her mind.

First, her backpack was full of geometry homework—an unreasonable amount, even for the enthusiastic Mr. Slider. During class, he had handed out binders full of proofs and problems, chirping over student protests that a busy geometry student was a happy geometry student.

Second, word of her upcoming Friday night date with Bob Jarkmand had washed through the school like floodwaters, penetrating every nook and cranny of the classrooms and hallways until she was drowning in schoolmates' furtive looks and giggles.

Eddie, however, hadn't been giggling as they walked home together.

"Are you kidding me?"

"It's no big deal, Eddie." She wondered why she cared what he thought. "You hung out with him yourself earlier this year. Remember the Halloween Dance?"

"Yeah, but we didn't . . . *go together*," he sputtered. "It wasn't like he and I would ever plan to make out at a party!"

"Gosh, I don't know, Eddie. You two would make an adorable couple."

"He's a bully."

"He's my date."

"You can do better!"

"Yes, well, right now better boys aren't exactly popping out of school lockers."

"They're out there."

There, she had lost her temper and snarled at him. "If they are, they've lost their nerve."

That had shut him up.

Third, Elizabeth Georges-Scales was in a huge rush to leave—the tall, lithe doctor had barely let Jennifer slide the backpack off in the mudroom before claiming she was going out to warm up the minivan and they were leaving in five minutes, or one of them would be left to fly to the farm.

*Oh yeah?* Jennifer had grumbled to herself up in her bedroom, in a flurry of packing and tidying. *What would you do with yourself once you got there, old woman?*

But she was down in the minivan in time, waving with limp enthusiasm to Eddie as he watched them go from the front door.

"It hardly seems right to leave him alone tonight," Elizabeth observed with concerned emerald eyes as she slowly backed out onto the street. "Are you sure he doesn't want to come with us?"

"Definitely sure."

"Maybe I should drop him off to see his mother . . ."

"Mom. You left him with two hundred dollars for the night. If he wants, he can get a taxi to the hospital, order a catered meal from the nearest gourmet restaurant for both himself *and* Mrs. Blacktooth, and then take a limo back here."

"I just feel strange leaving him alone at our place overnight, after what he's been through."

"He's fifteen. He's a big boy. You'd rather stay home and baby-sit him?"

Elizabeth smirked, tucked a blonde strand behind her right ear, and put the minivan into drive. "Okay, honey. You've made your point. I guess it's all for the best. This way, we can spend some quality time with your father."

"In Crescent Valley."

Her mother's green eyes glowed, but the rest of her face stayed composed. "In Crescent Valley."

"Where you've never been before."

"Where I've never been before." Long fingers tapped anxiously on the steering wheel. They were off Pine Street and heading for the town limits.

"And where you've been dying to go ever since you met Dad."

*"Yes!"* To Jennifer's delight, she had finally cracked her mother's composure. Elizabeth bounced up and down in her seat. *"Where I've been dying to go ever since I met your father!* Jennifer, you can tell me now. What's it like? Where is it? Is it in the forest? It's in the forest, isn't it? On the other side of the lake. I tried to check it out back there once in the car, but there aren't any roads after a while and the trees got really thick and there were some enormous wolves running around and *that's where it is, isn't it?* I can tell from your face!"

Jennifer couldn't help laughing—her mother was positively ebullient. "Mom, relax! You've gone years without knowing. Can't you wait another couple of hours?"

"Jennifer Caroline Scales, you tell your mother this instant where Crescent Valley is or I'll gut you with my sword."

"Did you bring it?"

"Hell no. I'm not showing up in front of your father's Giant Angry Lizard Club with a weapon."

"We're closer biologically to birds than lizards, Mom. Remember?"

From the older woman's expression, it was obvious her mother was thinking back to Jennifer's first night as a dragon. "Yeah, I remember. That was quite a night. You called us clueless."

"Well, you were."

"But we were right about a lot of things, weren't we? You have to admit: Parents know more than teenagers want to admit."

Jennifer traced a wavy line down the frosty passenger window with her fingernail. "Mom, just wait until you see all the stuff you don't know!"

# CHAPTER 5

## Monday Night

Back on the farm, Joseph greeted both Scales family members with more enthusiasm than he had shown Skip and the others. Mother and daughter looked over the grounds briefly and gave Joseph some help on a few maintenance issues around the stables. Then Jennifer thoughtfully packed a waterproof overnight bag for her mother, secured it to her hindclaw, and invited her mother for a ride.

"Is this really necessary?" Elizabeth asked, climbing on. "And why do you have one of your grandfather's old duffel bags strapped to your— Hey!"

Jennifer was off like a rocket over the lake, and was not too far from the shore when—

"Hang on tight!"

—she plunged into the moonlit surface.

They came out the other side moments later. As they gently treaded water, they witnessed the venerables' belt of fire course around the crescent moon and listened to the strumming of the surrounding insect life. Elizabeth had calmed down enough by now to slap her daughter gently across her spiked head.

"You could have warned me."

"What? You're the one who thought we were going across the lake, not through it. Anyway, it's not like you had to hold your breath. The ring was protecting you."

"Thanks for explaining it all so clearly. Are you going to fly us anywhere now, or do we just soak here for a while?"

Jennifer imitated her mother's voice. "Watch your tone, young lady, or you'll be *swimming* to shore."

"Hmmph."

They were on shore shortly, and under the gently swaying moon elms Elizabeth changed into dry jeans, a sweater, and a suede jacket.

"I guess it's a pretty casual outfit for a diplomatic mission," Jennifer apologized as her mother rummaged for a scarf and gloves.

"It'll work fine, honey. Where's your dad?"

"I imagine he's been watching the moon for the signal from the venerables. He should be here soon."

He was indeed, and watching him put his wings around her mom as she stared at the wonderful world around her was a sight Jennifer knew she'd never forget.

"Hey, Liz."

"So this is the place."

"This is the place."

Jennifer felt awkward standing there. She took a short walk to give them some privacy, and by the time she came back, Elizabeth was wiping her face with the back of a glove. But they seemed ready to go.

"You need a ride?" she offered her mother again.

"Is it far? I'd rather walk." Elizabeth turned up the collar of her suede jacket and walked over to a moon elm touched with traces of lichen. The cerulean glow lit up her glove as she softly touched the flakes and looked up at the vast network of slender branches. When she turned to her husband, her inscrutable expression was back in place.

"Have you ever seen the silver one here?"

He stepped up to his wife and held her hand. "No. I've never seen the silver one in this world."

Jennifer cocked her head at the exchange. *Silver?*

"These are beautiful anyway," Elizabeth said. "Come on, let's walk."

It was a little awkward for Jonathan—creeper dragons were not made for long walks. But they both agreed it was important for Elizabeth to feel as comfortable as possible—and she certainly felt more comfortable with both feet on the ground.

"I've ridden your father exactly three times," she pointed out to Jennifer. "Always more his idea than mine."

"Uh—"

"I enjoyed myself every time, but it was a relief when he let me get off."

Jennifer shook her head as if warding off a bad odor. "Please don't say things like that. It stings my eyes."

The buzzing of fire hornets grew fainter as they went farther west.

"It's just so—so—" Her mother groped for the right word. "Stunning. The sky and the grass and the air is so clear, it's like wine you can breathe. I wonder if our earth used to smell like this? Before people screwed it up."

"I'm glad you—"

"And the ground! It's like walking on a mattress that goes on forever. And you know the very best, most wonderful thing?"

Jennifer cocked her head in amazement. Her mother, at this moment, the stern Dr. Georges-Scales, was glowing like a teen on prom night. "What, Mom?"

"That you and your father have finally shared it with me." Impulsively, she hugged Jennifer and her husband.

Jonathan looked at Jennifer with the simple gratitude you showed for a person who pleased the love of your life. *Of course,* Jennifer realized, *Mom would never have been allowed here, if it hadn't been for me.*

They rounded the edge of a grove and Jennifer said, "We should be there in a few more minutes. Now, Mom, there's something you should know about some of these dragons. There's this old dasher who—"

Suddenly she stopped.

"Oh," Jonathan said. Then he coughed. Jennifer couldn't even manage a cough.

There were two adult dashers there, drinking at a slow-moving stream. One, Jennifer had never seen before. Her scales were nearly black, with peach accents under the wings. Her tail had two prongs, like Jennifer's, but it also had spikes running down both branches. The strange dasher's gold-orange eyes were full of shock at the sight of the three intruders.

The other dasher, Jennifer knew.

Xavier Longtail's triple-pronged tail twitched at the sight of them, but he did not budge. The other dasher finally moved first, advancing on Elizabeth with a fervor just short of a charge.

"Get out of here!" The woman's voice was clear and

powerful—an operatic alto tinged with the same arrogant tone Xavier could use. "You're not wanted here!"

Elizabeth stepped back in alarm. Jonathan and Jennifer slid in front of her protectively. "This is my mother," Jennifer announced as anxious blood rushed to her head. "She's here as my guest."

"I know who she is, *Ambassador.*" The last word came out bleeding with contempt. "She's Elizabeth Georges, the beast-stalker who murdered my father!"

"Ambassador." Xavier's tone was slightly more respectful. "I don't believe you've met my niece, Ember Longtail."

The revelation surprised Jennifer, but she recovered quickly. "I'm charmed," she snapped. "Now back off."

"Longtail . . ."

Jennifer turned when she heard how faint her mother sounded, and she immediately saw the whitening of the woman's face. Her memory quickly went to the week before, when the Blaze had considered granting her mother sanctuary here in Crescent Valley. Despite the threat of Evangelina, the dragons were hesitant to do so—not least because of Xavier's claim that his brother had died at Elizabeth's hand.

"Yes, *Longtail,*" Ember spat out. "The dragon you performed your sick, depraved rite of passage upon."

Jennifer's thoughts flickered briefly to Eddie, and his half-hearted attempt to murder her. Of course, Elizabeth Georges would have been successful, in her own youth. *When Mom tries something, she succeeds. I'll bet it was brutal.* Her stomach churned at the thought of her mother as a killer.

"She swore off that violence!" Jonathan pushed his wife farther behind him. "For years, she's devoted her life to healing. She's saved other dragons' lives!"

"She killed twice after that!"

"Th-that's not—sh-she . . . it was only in self-defense!" Jonathan sputtered—but Jennifer heard the desperation in his voice. *He knew this would come back to haunt us,* she guessed. "Two dragons ambushed her!"

"Ambushed *us,*" Elizabeth interrupted softly but firmly. "Jonathan, why—"

Jonathan ignored the interruptions. "They set upon her and she had to fight to survive."

Elizabeth whirled upon her husband with a look Jenni-

fer couldn't understand. The two of them stared at each other
for a moment, and then her mother turned to the dashers and
cleared her throat. Jennifer knew her mother had a great deal of
pride—perhaps too much to apologize. But she also knew her
mother despised killing.

"Ms. Longtail. I don't know what to say. If I could take
back—"

The gust of flame that swept out of Ember Longtail's mouth
would have consumed Elizabeth if Jonathan had not wrapped his
wings around her.

"Ember!" Even Xavier seemed alarmed at the attack.

Jennifer did not wait for the Elder's help. She steeled herself
and drove her head into Ember's neck, snapping the latter's jaws
shut and sending them both tumbling to the ground. The sound of
a tail whistling behind her head warned her in time to flinch, and
the dasher's tail spikes missed her narrowly.

"Why you . . ." She slapped her opponent's tail down with
her own. It was hard to tell in dragon shape how old this woman
was—a little slow for a teenager, but not quite slow or powerful enough to be an Elder. Jennifer had never fought an adult
dragon before, in any shape. She wasn't sure if she was in over
her head.

After several moments of rolling and wrestling (and making
a pretty good showing, she thought), she felt her father's wing
claws on her shoulders and reluctantly scrambled to her hind
legs. Xavier pulled up his niece at the same time, whispering
harshly in her ear. But Ember broke free of her uncle's grip and
lunged at them both.

This time, it was her mother who intercepted the assault.
Armed with nothing but her jeans, suede jacket, and leather
gloves, Elizabeth slid between them all with hands held high.

"Okay, stop! You want me? Here I am! Just don't—just please
don't fight each other anymore!"

"Mom!"

"Liz, get the hell back!"

Ember looked at them all in disgust. "You're all pathetic," she
hissed with forked tongue. "The murderous beaststalker, the trai-
tor who married her, and the atrocity they spawned together!"

Wind whistled in and out of Jennifer's clenched teeth, and
her hind legs kicked at the thick turf beneath, but her parents

held her back. Somewhere in the distance, they could all hear the low, cellolike strumming of fire hornets. Xavier laid a dispassionate wing claw on his niece's shoulder. "Ember. We should go."

"No, *they* should go!" The younger dasher slapped her tail on the ground, sending moss and dirt flying. "They should go back to their own world, slink into the Pinegrove home they wrongly took for themselves, gorge themselves on sweets while sharing stories of the dragons they've hobbled or murdered, and then sleep in their stolen beds. That's the beaststalker way."

"I'll be happy to show you the beaststalker way," Jennifer spat between hisses. She was strongly tempted to shift back to two legs and stab the scaled cow in the jaw. "You want to go again?"

Ember ignored her and stepped closer to Elizabeth, seeped in the fumes of her own hatred. Still hissing breath through her teeth, Jennifer began to raise a protective wing, but her mother stood her ground.

"I hope you die," Ember growled over the mounting sound of insects gathering, and then her voice rose to a scream. "I hope you *all die for what you've done!*"

Jennifer felt a strange surge ripple down her spine and tail— it was as if her muscles were racing each other. The noise of the fire hornets was louder than ever, and suddenly she saw a sight that almost made her scream.

A massive, shambling shape came crashing through the near-by brush. Twice as tall as any of them, it was the shape of a dragon—in fact, it suggested a nose horn and double-pronged tail similar to Jennifer's—but it was certainly not a single creature. Rather, it was at least ten thousand fire hornets, each the size of a golf ball. That is, if golf balls were angry, furry, and black with distinctive violet markings.

The swarm moved together with purpose, careening toward the confrontation and spreading its shape to flaunt two furiously buzzing wings—

—and then it stepped right between the Scales and the Long-tails, turned to face Ember, and roared at her in a chorus of fierce strums.

The dasher screamed and scrambled back into the wings of her uncle. Xavier's golden eyes turned to Jennifer in panic.

"You've made your point, Ambassador! Call them off!"

Her jaw dropped. "Call them off? I didn't call them *on*!"

"Actually, ace," Jonathan murmured, "I think you did."

*"What?"*

The droning cloud wheeled around and flexed its limbs, humming contentedly at its effect on the Longtails. Both dashers were backing away with a total lack of grace, unbecoming of such lithe shapes.

"As the Ancient Furnace, you probably have the powers of many Elders and ancestors," her father explained as the swarm held position. "This would be one of them—power over certain insects, such as this land's fire hornets."

"How did I call them? Scratch that, I don't care. How do I get rid of them?" She could make out the soft, hairy shapes of individual hornets. Each bug had an oozing nail dangling behind its abdomen. *Those can't possibly be stingers,* she promised herself unconvincingly.

"Ummm . . ."

"You don't know?"

"I'm not completely sure," her father admitted. "It's an Elder trampler skill, and not one I've seen performed too often."

"Cripes, Dad!" In her fear, she could not hide her exasperation. "I can't *get* you to stop lecturing when you've got some useless piece of dragon trivia to share—and now you don't know? *Now?!*"

"Honey, maybe if you use your beaststalker—"

"No, Liz!" Jonathan interrupted harshly. "No one knows what will happen if she lets go of her dragon shape! Those things could swarm her in an instant. Jennifer, try blowing a bit of smoke their way first. They don't like smoke."

The black and violet blobs hovered ever larger in Jennifer's face. "They don't like smoke? Then why on earth would I use some to piss them off?!"

"Honestly, Jonathan," Elizabeth snapped. "Talk about *blowing smoke* . . ."

"You're not helping, Liz!"

"Neither are you . . ."

"Okay, fine. Jennifer, the swarm's not moving. Just hang tight. I'll go get Ned Brownfoot."

Several tense minutes later, during which Jennifer, Elizabeth, Xavier, and Ember all managed to stare at each other and the swarm simultaneously without saying a word, Jonathan returned with an aged trampler in tow.

Ned Brownfoot was the trampler dragon who had taught Jennifer how to summon reptiles by stomping her foot. She smiled desperately at her gentle mentor as he took in the situation. His soft, crooked grin put her at ease.

"Sometimes, knowin' a little is worse'n knowin' nothin' at all, amiright?" he drawled in a warm, southern Missouri accent.

"If you could just help us out, Ned . . ."

"Sure, Jon. But it's gotta be Jenny here that does it. Her bugs, after all."

"What do I do?"

"Call the queen to your nose horn."

A growl of exasperation escaped. "Which one is the queen, and how the hell do I get her over on my nose horn? *And why would I want a bug the size of a nectarine on my face, anyway?!*"

Ned did not sound any less amused. "The swarm obeys the queen. The queen obeys you. She responded to your first call . . . she'll respond to the same signal."

"But I didn't *give* a signal!"

"You whistled in 'n' out a few times, when your life was in danger. Didn'tcha?"

"I–I–I have no idea!"

"Well, whistle through your teeth three or four more times, 'n' see what happens."

Bracing her forked tongue against her sharp teeth, Jennifer tried to re-create the hissing sound she thought she may have unconsciously made a while ago. It took a few tries, but eventually one of the swarm—easily the largest of the fire hornets—disengaged from the group and landed on her horn. Jennifer crossed her eyes and marveled at its size and the triple violet-stripe pattern lining its body. *Cripes, I can see the tongue.*

She spoke through the corner of her mouth, trying not to move her nose. "Erkay. Nerwhat?"

"Now you talk to her, just like any'un else. Ya give yer orders."

"Huh." Jennifer tentatively worked her mouth open, but the queen showed no sign of aggression. "Um. Hi there. Thanks for coming. You've, er. Done well. I like what you did there, with the dragon shape. Nice . . . er, wings and all."

The queen hopped up and down a bit, humming enthusiastically.

"Yeah. Um, well, you can go now. We've got everything under control. Really, though. Couldn't've done it without you."

Immediately, the queen leapt off her horn and rushed back to the others. Three seconds later, the massive dragon shape had dissipated, and the strumming of the fire hornets was fading back into the forest.

Jonathan exhaled. "Good job, Jennifer. Thanks, Ned."

"Anytime, Elder Scales. Just give me a call, 'n'—"

Elizabeth stepped between the two of them and glared at her husband. "We're going home. *Now.*"

*They went back* through the lake, waited for Elizabeth to dry off in the farmhouse, packed the minivan, and took off for Winoka in complete silence. Between her mother fuming in the driver's seat and her father steaming alongside the minivan, Jennifer certainly didn't want to be the first one to talk.

But she couldn't help herself—one question burned in her mind. She opened the passenger window, letting a blast of cold air in.

"Dad," she called out. "What did Ember mean by *hobbling* dragons?"

"Now is not the time," Elizabeth growled.

"She wasn't asking you, Liz," Jonathan snapped with a quick turn of his reptilian head. He looked at Jennifer as he kept up his cruising speed. "Hobbling is a vicious practice among beaststalkers. Instead of killing the weredragon, they cripple the person's spine. Done properly, it prevents the body from changing."

Jennifer digested that in silent horror for a moment. "So they can't change when the crescent moon comes?"

"No. But their bodies don't realize it, and try to change every time. The pain, I hear, is unbearable."

"Very few beaststalkers do that anymore," Elizabeth interrupted.

"Have you ever done it, Mom?"

Elizabeth glared at her. "That's a disgusting question."

"Which you didn't answer."

"Jennifer." Her father tried to get her attention back, but she was resolute.

"Would asking about the three dragons you murdered be disgusting, too?"

The minivan screeched to a halt, swerving into the breakdown lane with a stomach-turning twist. "Young lady, do you want to get out and *walk* home?"

"I can fly," Jennifer pointed out. "And don't act like we shouldn't talk about this. You're always hush-hush about the past when it suits you. But I deserve answers."

"She's right, Liz." Jonathan had come to a more gentle stop next to them, and he poked his head through the passenger window. "We ought to share—"

*"Shut up!"* Elizabeth reached out with lightning speed and slapped his scaly cheek, right in front of Jennifer. "Don't you dare talk about sharing! I've done my penance for what I did. And for years, you and your . . . your friends have kept that one act dangling over my head. Even though you know it was a horrible mistake." A thumb jerked at Jennifer. "And even now, with her old enough to understand, you have the balls to whisk her away to your secret hideouts and say awful things about us, and *lie* about us, as if every beaststalker is alike, and I can never visit, and even when I do I practically get *immolated*—"

She burst into tears. It was worse, so much worse, than her anger. Jennifer could count on one hand—mostly occurrences in the past few months—how many times she'd seen her mother cry. It was frightening and pitiful at the same time.

"Liz, don't—"

The minivan lurched forward as Elizabeth jammed down the accelerator. Jennifer heard an exclamation of pain as Jonathan yanked his head out of the window a half-second too late.

"Mom!" She tried to look back in the ditch behind them. "I think you really hurt him."

"Good!" The woman was sobbing, and the minivan uneasily straddled the breakdown lane and the righthand lane of the highway. "I hope he forms an embolism."

Jennifer reached out and patted her mother's coat. She wasn't quite sure what to say. Then she caught an image in the sideview mirror. "Huh. He's up." In the faint cherry glow of their taillights, she could make out the sleek, winged shadow of her father as he bolted toward them. "Wow, he looks kinda angry. Maybe you should—"

"How fast can you go when you fly?"

"What? Um, I've never really—"

"I'll bet he can't do ninety."

Like a spaceship launching, the minivan jerked forward with sudden purpose. Jennifer felt herself thrown back against the seat. All she could do was bend her head a bit and watch her father shrink rapidly in the sideview mirror.

"Mom, this is a bit fast."

Her mother didn't answer, and as the minivan's whine raised in pitch to a terrifying scream, Jennifer whitened her knuckles upon her armrests.

"Um, Mom, think of your daughter's safety. Every year at school, they gather us into the auditorium and show us all another video of some car that's been crumpled into a small, decorative box as a result of reckless driving . . ."

The engine's scream raised to a roar. The painted dashes on the highway flew past like deathly pale bullets.

"Um, also, as any child psychology book will tell you, I depend on you and Dad to model a mature, loving, adult relationship so I can form—"

"Oh, shove it! You're on my list, too."

Thoughts of the minivan's unsafe speed flew out of Jennifer's head. "*What?* What did *I* do?"

"Don't use that whiny, put-upon teenager voice with me. I know how much you love taking off with your father and leaving me in the dust. Being a dragon—how exciting for you! You get to fly around together and laugh away, feeling superior to all the poor people down below who can't disembowel sheep with their own teeth."

"That's not—"

"And when someone who disagrees with your point of view comes along, why, you can just incinerate her, or explain her away by calling her a murderer." Now her voice dripped with venom. "After all, no *dragon* would ever kill *anybody*! No indeed. Not unless, you know, they *deserved* it! What a comfortable lifestyle you get to lead."

Jennifer had not the faintest idea what to say, and no opportunity to say it anyway. Something large landed on top of the van at the same time a scaled triangle descended over the top of the windshield—*Dad's wing,* she realized in a mixture of panic and admiration. *Cripes, he can go ninety!*

Elizabeth swore. The van swerved with the added weight and lost aerodynamics. Jennifer's heart stopped as she felt the vehicle veer dangerously toward its right side, and she began to change shape instinctively—a dragon shape would better protect her and her mother from a crash . . .

But the van righted itself in time, and came to an abrupt stop with its hind third still sticking a bit into the highway. She heard her father yell as his momentum threw him off the roof and onto the pavement. As he rolled around in pain, the headlights washed out most of his vivid indigo and blue colors.

"Dad!"

"Don't worry about him." Elizabeth's tone had not changed. She looked over at Jennifer, and for the briefest of moments there was something there—revulsion?—that had never been there before.

Looking down, Jennifer realized she had only morphed half-way. Her flesh was bulging, her hands were covered in a mixture of blue scales and pink skin, and who knew what her face looked like?

"Sorry," she said, at once feeling resentful that she had to apologize to her own mother.

Elizabeth didn't say anything else. Instead, she threw off her seat belt, launched the door open, and ran out in front of the van where her husband lay. Then, to Jennifer's dismay, she began kicking him with a furry Land's End boot.

"What is the *matter* with you?" she was screaming, punctuating each important word with another kick to his midsection. "A *car* with your *wife* and *daughter* is going upwards of *ninety* miles an hour, and *you* decide to *land* on it? We could have been *killed*! *You* could have been killed!"

"Give it a moment," he gasped from the frost-covered, blood-soaked gravel.

She kicked him again with clenched teeth. "Oh, stop the theatrics. You're *fine* and you know it. Superior bone structure and all. It takes a lot more than a roll on the side of the road to kill one of you."

His silver eyes lost their humor and narrowed. "Well, dear, you would know."

*"Don't you say that!"* She threw herself at him and began to throttle him—or at least did the best she could, with her small hands up against a huge, scaled throat. *"Don't you dare say that! I'm not a killer! I'm a doctor! I've saved hundreds of them! DON'T YOU DARE CALL ME A KILLER AFTER WHAT YOU'VE DONE!"*

She stopped trying to choke him and started slapping him, uselessly, around the muzzle and crest. His face softened a bit as he weathered the blows.

"Is that why you tried to throw your life away back in Crescent Valley?" he asked her. "Because you think you're a killer?"

Sobbing, Elizabeth stopped hitting him and covered her face. Jennifer stared at them both as an eighteen-wheeler rumbled by, angrily blowing its horn at the poorly parked minivan. Elizabeth Georges-Scales, a professional doctor, calm and collected, even sometimes cold as stone, was melting down. Jennifer had never seen it this bad. She devoutly hoped she would never see it again.

Jonathan Scales reached up and wrapped his wings around his wife.

"No!" Elizabeth was startled into anger again. She launched herself up and stomped back to the minivan. "You don't get to comfort me! You're a killer, too, Jonathan! Don't forget those two thugs! *Don't forget them!*"

While Jennifer expected him to protest, Jonathan did not move. He just watched his wife get into the minivan, without argument.

*A killer? Him?* Somehow, it was even harder to see him in that role than her mother. And what thugs?

The sound of the minivan starting up refocused her on what was happening. "Mom, no! Wait."

"We're going now."

"No, we're not!"

Her mother turned to her with a poisonous expression. "Don't you talk back to me . . ."

"You can't just leave Dad here!" He was slowly getting up, but his wings were streaked with blood.

"Jennifer, your father's fine. And this discussion is over. We're leaving."

"No, we're *not*." Jennifer flung open her door, ducked out of her seat belt, and was out of the van before her mother could react. "He's hurt."

Elizabeth growled in exasperation and slammed the steering wheel. "Jennifer, get in the car!"

"Mom, look at yourself! Who the hell are you? What are you doing?"

"I'm your mother and I'm telling you to move your ass!"

She tried to stand tall and silent against her mother's withering glare. Finally, she broke and said, "Not until you work this out with Dad."

A delicate balance of a snarl and a sigh escaped. "You don't know what you're talking about! It's been years between your father and me! Years of trust and sacrifice and compromise! I don't need your relationship advice. You have no idea what goes into a relationship, Jennifer. You have no clue!"

"Mom, get out of the car."

"Jennifer, get in the car."

"Get out!"

*"GET IN!"*

Jennifer stepped back and shut the car door. "I'm not leaving him."

"Ask him about the tramplers," Elizabeth growled. "You may change your mind."

With that, she gunned the engine and the minivan's tires squealed with the effort to reenter the highway.

*"Mom!"*

But all that was left was a cloud of gravel, and a pair of vanishing taillights in the dark.

"I can't—she just—did you see—she *left* us!"

"That she did," Jonathan agreed.

"Where the hell are you? I can barely see."

"Over here. You should change—you'll see better, and we're obviously flying home."

"But you can't fly in the shape you're in!" She shifted shape—she was warmer this way, if nothing else. Her father was sitting on his haunches, rubbing the base of his righthand horn.

"Just give me a sec. Your mother was right—I'll be fine."

Jennifer sat down next to him. "What was that she was saying about the tramplers, and about you being a killer?"

He sighed. "I don't suppose there's any way you would accept the truth at a later date . . ."

"No." She felt herself getting angry—not just because she imagined it must be a horrible thing in order to get her mother so upset, but also because it was yet another secret from the past that they had kept from her.

She glued her gaze to the highway while she waited for her father to begin. As a dragon, she could plainly make out the shape of a silver and black Mitsubishi Eclipse as it flitted past them in the far lane. "I'm waiting."

"You're familiar with the beaststalker rite of passage."

"Yeah, from Eddie. I gather it's pretty important to do better than he did."

"Your mother's rite involved Xavier Longtail's brother. Ember's father. She did better than Eddie—in fact, she succeeded brilliantly."

"Right, I got that part. So Mom killed a weredragon, and she's spent a lifetime saving them and other people to make up for it. Where do *you* come in?"

"Let me start a bit before then—to when we first met. It's important you hear this."

Jennifer nodded. She had never really heard this story in detail—just that they met in graduate school, and had worked out the fact that she was a beaststalker and he was a weredragon. She assumed a lot of hot, steamy, parental love figured into the picture somewhere, so she had never pressed for details.

"I met your mother years after her own rite of passage," he explained. "I was a graduate student in architecture at the same university where she was a medical student. She was still wracked with guilt, though of course her beaststalker friends considered her a hero. It did not take long to learn what she was—just a few dates. But by then it was too late. I was already in love."

His voice caught for a moment, and Jennifer waited patiently. The woman he still loved was probably ten miles away by now, and accelerating.

"Of course, I knew it wouldn't work. After all, my disastrous relationship with Dianna Wilson was still fresh in my mind. Weredragons couldn't date their enemies, I was sure. It would break my heart, but I had no choice. I was about to call it off with her, when the most extraordinary thing happened.

"We were on what I thought would be our last date—just an evening stroll by the river not far from St. Paul, with a full moon above us and no one else around. I can still remember your mother eating double-chocolate-chunk ice cream out of a waffle cone she had bought back in town. I think she knew I was going to dump her—she seemed depressed, and she was eating that ice cream awfully fast. Just as I was about to come up with some lame line about wanting to be good friends, she spilled a whole scoop of it on her dress. That started a bit of a fuss, and we were examining whether or not it had made a stain on the hem . . . when we both caught sight of it."

"What?"

"A moon elm leaf," he answered.

"Moon elms? But they don't grow here in this world! They only grow—"

"In Crescent Valley, yes. Yet there it was, a moon elm leaf. And when we looked up, we suddenly found we were standing under an entire tree. It was a glorious, huge, shimmering thing. Unlike any moon elm I had ever seen, and certainly unlike anything your mother had experienced.

"Normally, moon elms have pale leaves that simply reflect the color of the lichen in the forest around them. If you take a leaf out of Crescent Valley and look at it under normal daylight (as I did shortly afterward), it's a sort of unappetizing, milky white. But this leaf—and all the leaves on the tree—were silver.

"I picked up the leaf, and then I immediately realized I shouldn't. I began to change, Jennifer. Change—here, in this world, under a full moon!—the moment I touched that leaf. I dropped it and tried to make my condition look like a headache, convulsions—anything but the truth! I was in a panic; I didn't want it to end like this.

"But I couldn't help it. The change had started, and I was doomed. Moments later, your mother looked upon me for the first time as a dragon. I quickly considered shifting my skin to make myself invisible—then I could just skulk away. But your mother's reaction kept me there."

"What did she do?"

"She broke down," he answered with glistening eyes. "It was not unlike what you just saw here tonight—without the kicking. Oh, how she cried."

"Why?"

"Well, she cried because I hadn't told her the truth right away. She cried because she knew I intended to break things off. And of course, she cried because she was still carrying inside what she had done years ago.

"And while she was crying, the attack came."

Jennifer stiffened. Here was the heart of the matter, she was sure.

"There were two tramplers, a young man and a young woman. They, too, must have touched the moon elm or its leaves, because they were in dragon form under the same full moon I was. Like lightning, they were upon her.

"She didn't carry a sword with her—the rusty one you've practiced with was shiny and new back then, but she kept it under her bed in her dorm room, with never an intention of using it again. Of course, she was still a formidable fighter—but against two dragons and without a weapon, I could see she would lose before long."

"So you helped her."

He nodded. "I helped her."

"You killed those two tramplers, because they were trying to kill Mom."

"Yes. Because they *were* trying to kill her—that much was certain. They even used the name of the dasher she killed—*This is for Longtail,* they said. The Blaze, I learned later, had assigned them to learn the identity of the beaststalker and assassinate her. It took them years to trace her steps—she didn't brag or boast about her deed, like most beaststalkers did—and when they found her, it was her dumb luck that I was there to protect her. Yes, Jennifer, I killed them. Ripped out their throats and tore their heads off, like we do when we hunt oreams at Crescent Valley. Two of our own. I killed them and I would do it again, in a heartbeat."

His voice was hard now, and he unconsciously bared his sharp teeth. Jennifer could almost see the dead, wingless trampler shapes in the cold ditch before them.

"I realized at that moment that I would not leave her. And she realized she would not leave me. We swore our love to each other, under that silver moon elm. And we've been together ever since. The strange thing is, we've gone back to that place quite a few times over the years . . . but the moon elm was never there again.

It was as if it just grew there, for us, that one night."

Jennifer stared at a patch of grass in the ditch for a while, waiting for more. It didn't come right away. "Yes. Well, Dad. I see. You saving Mom's life and then professing your love under an itinerant tree—that completely explains why she's so pissed at you right now . . ."

"I'm getting there!" His wing claws flexed nervously, and he shifted a bit in the gravel. Two sport-utility vehicles cruised by, the second one swerving a bit at the inexplicable shapes it must have witnessed on the side of the road.

"Of course, we had to hide the dead bodies," he said. "So we did, burying them in some caves not far from the river. And then we had to find out what the other dragons knew—would more of them come after her? Would they come after me, too?

"With the help of my father, who sat on the Blaze, I learned the two tramplers had not taken time to report back any information before attacking. They had, everyone guessed, gone straight from discovering who your mother was to launching their attack. Without the crucial information these two dragons took to their graves, the Blaze was nowhere near connecting the beaststalker they still sought, and the woman I was dating.

"As a result, when the tramplers went missing, the trail went cold. The Blaze knew a beaststalker had killed Xavier's brother, and they now assumed that same beaststalker had done away with the pursuit."

Jennifer stiffened. "You never corrected them. You let them think Mom had done it. That's why they blame her not just for the rite of passage, but those two other dragons!"

"That's right. Years later, they traced the killing of Charles Longtail to a beaststalker who fit your mother's physical description. But by then, Dr. Elizabeth Georges-Scales was a doctor who had saved countless dragons' lives. It made no sense to the Blaze that she would be a beaststalker. Of course, your grandfather had figured it out; but he helped me hide the truth."

"I bet Grandpa Crawford was mad at you for making him lie like that," Jennifer snapped. She recalled the difficult relationship her mother and her father-in-law had, even up to his death less than a month ago. Realizing how he had protected all of them just made her miss him more.

"It wasn't until you revealed your beaststalker half in Crescent Valley," Jonathan reminded her, "that Xavier Longtail and the others still searching for his brother's killer put it all together. They made the natural assumption at that point that she had killed not only Charles Longtail, but also the two tramplers. I thought the Blaze would go after your mother immediately, but Winona Brandfire showed incredible restraint that night. The fact that you saved Catherine—that might have saved us all. Winona got everyone to calm down and focus elsewhere. Because of that, we were able to discuss sanctuary for your mother later on."

"Okay, I know the story from that point. So they assumed Mom did it all. And Mom was okay with you pinning it all on her?"

He coughed. "Your mother didn't know, until tonight. For years, she has thought I had owned up to killing those tramplers right away, told the full truth to the Blaze, and received forgiveness."

"I wonder where she got *that* idea," Jennifer fumed.

"Jennifer, please understand. I was young, and—"

"Are you still too young to tell the truth? Were you still too young when I was hauled up in front of the Blaze a few months ago to account for who Mom was?"

He didn't answer.

"Cripes, Dad! What would you do if *I* lied the way you did to the Blaze and to Mom? Would I get a free pass because I'm fifteen years old?"

His reptilian head hung low. "You don't need to try to make me feel worse, Jennifer. I know what I did."

"So when are you going to make it right?"

"My thought was to do it during your mother's visit. Ever since the Blaze granted her sanctuary during our search for Evangelina, I figured the time was coming to set the record straight. The Blaze would not have granted sanctuary to someone they wanted to kill. Everyone has to learn the full truth. We'll never be able to accomplish what we need to accomplish as long as people misunderstand what happened. I will admit to the killings when I return to Crescent Valley. Tomorrow, I suppose."

"Why did you wait so long?" Jennifer asked, exasperated. "It makes no sense! Winona Brandfire defended us against Xavier when I made a mistake. Why wouldn't she forgive you, too?"

Jonathan sighed and scribbled a strange pattern in the gravel with a wing claw. Jennifer recognized the broad swirls and shapes—it was the sort of writing dragons carved into molten rock, when burying their dead.

"Because," he slowly explained, "she will have to forgive me, a friend she has deeply trusted for years, for murdering her daughter and son-in-law."

A complete numbness fell over Jennifer. She was certain she had not heard what she had just heard.

"I know you have never asked Catherine about her parents," he continued. "And I also know she's never offered it. After all, she probably doesn't even know what they were doing when they went missing, less than a year after she was born. But I would imagine someday very soon, you will need to share what you have learned with her."

The words kept coming, and Jennifer kept trying to fend them off—but they were too true, and too hard.

She stared at him and felt the fire come.

He winced. "This may complicate your friendship a bit—"

"You!" She got up and—finding she couldn't help herself— kicked him. Several times. Had her mother kicked him hard enough? *Definitely not.* "You! *You!* You are . . . *you!* You are . . . *ruining my life! Ruining my LIFE!*"

He took the kicks with resignation, moving only a little to avoid getting hit in the same painful locations more than once. "Jennifer, don't be melodramatic . . ."

"*Melodramatic?!* I'm a *freak* because of you! I had a murderous *sister* because of you! And now I'm going to lose one of my best *friends* . . . because of *you!*" She turned to rant at the empty cornfield behind them. "*Why* did I get out of the minivan?!" she asked the dirt expanse. "*Why* didn't I listen to my mother? My own mother! She tried to tell me! She told me, 'Jennifer, get in the van!' That's what she said! And I ignored her!"

"Ace, your mother was driving over—"

"*Why* did I ignore her?" she asked, whirling upon him again with a bonus kick. "She always wants what's best for me! She's told me so! She saved me when Skip's dad used you as bait— we could have left you down there in that sewer system, that's what we *should* have done—and she taught me that neat little thing with the daggers—you know, where I throw them and they hit nasty things like your other daughter—and after all that I ignored her! *Why?*"

"Maybe we should—"

"Maybe you should shove it, Dad." She turned away from him and spread her wings. "Shove it deep, shove it hard. I don't want you in my life. All you ever do is fuck it up."

She took off before he could answer her.

*The flight home was cold* and dark. Jennifer didn't need to look behind her to know that her father followed her the entire way, from a respectful distance. To his credit, she supposed, he didn't try to stop her or slow her down. The effort to keep up an escort in his condition must have been considerable.

So she sped up.

She morphed within a step of landing in front of their house on Pine Street and barged through the front door. Phoebe scrambled to all fours with a startled bark, and then raced forward to lick Jennifer's hand. Eddie was lounging in the living room, with the stereo on a bit louder than necessary, reading a magazine laced with photos of bikini-clad models. *Ugh. Boys.*

"Jennifer!" He jumped up, threw the magazine under a couch cushion, and turned the volume down. "You're back! I wasn't expecting—"

"Did my mom come home?"

He flipped his brown hair back in confusion. "What? No, she left with you. Isn't she still with you?"

"Great." So her mother had taken off for parts unknown. *At ninety miles an hour, she could be anywhere,* Jennifer thought grimly. *Including the hospital.*

She had called the hospital to verify Dr. Georges-Scales wasn't there—either on shift or as a patient—by the time her father skulked through the door, wings folded close to his body and tail down.

Without waiting for him to say anything, she pushed past him and went upstairs. The footsteps behind her were human—Eddie, she guessed, was following her. *Trying to help. As if he could.*

"Jennifer, wait up!" She was right. The boy's voice was concerned. "What's going on? Why are you back so soon? Is your—"

"Eddie, I don't have the time."

"But you're really upset! It must be important. Let me help you."

"Help me?" She put a hand on the doorway to her room and faced him, shaking the platinum strands away from her look of disgust. "*You?* Get real, Eddie. You didn't help me when I needed you last spring. You didn't help me when I needed you at the mall with Evangelina. And you didn't even help me yesterday, when it would have been easy. You're not a help. You're deadweight."

Her words crushed him—she saw that immediately—but she did not take them back. She was too angry at him, and her father, and her mother to care.

"Nobody around here," she continued with all the dramatic flair her teenaged heart could muster, "can help me."

She stepped back and slammed the bedroom door. It would have been more satisfying if Eddie's head had been trapped in the doorjamb. *Maybe next time.*

A sound from within her dark bedroom startled her momentarily. She flipped the light on and saw her gecko, Geddy, scrambling off a terrarium branch and into his log cave. She stepped over to the bucket of crickets, pulled the extraction tube out, and tapped a couple of new victims into his tank. He looked at them, then up at her, then back at the crickets, and then her again. Then he licked his eyeball.

"You said it, chum," she said, and flopped facedown on the bed.


"*Guess you went back* to Crescent Valley after all."

Instantly she rolled over and glared at Skip, who was lounging on her windowsill, only partly blocking a chilly breeze. Skip was one of only a few friends who dared climb the trellis on the back of the house.

"Knock much?"

"What happened?"

"It doesn't matter." She sat up and wiped her eyes, as well as the corner of her mouth. She heard Phoebe whining outside her closed bedroom door, but she ignored it. The dog whined at everything. "It was bad."

"Anything ice cream might fix?" He reached into his coat pocket and pulled out a couple of slips of paper. "I've got coupons for Super Sauce Sundaes at the mall."

Jennifer couldn't help a chuckle. It felt better than lying in her bed, drenched in self-pity. "Whadda big spender."

"What do you care what it costs me? For you, it's still free."

She looked at the clock: It was 9:10 pm. "They'll close soon."

"We'll make it if you fly me there."

Shrugging her shoulders, she reached under the bed. "Let me just . . ." She found her daggers and strapped them on under her modest skirt and sweater set.

He watched the ritual with a friendly leer. "Never leave home without 'em, huh?"

"You got that right." She moved to the window.

"Whoa. Don't forget your necklace!" He grinned easily at her inquisitive look. "Remember how I told you how good it looks on you?"

"Francis Skip Wilson, are you hitting on me less than a week after our breakup?"

He scratched the back of his neck, letting his chocolate hair sway back and forth. "Yeah, maybe. So you gonna cooperate or what?"

"For ice cream, sure." She snagged the emblem of the Moon of the Falling Leaves from her dresser, and put it around her neck hastily. "You know, it's not like you'll be able to see it after I morph anyway."

"I'll know it's there." He climbed onto her back as she sprouted wings, and then he slapped her scaled hindquarters. "Giddyup!"

"Skip."

"Sorry."

She waved to the terrarium with a wing claw. "Bye, Geddy."

As she launched into the dark November sky, she thought she heard the gecko make a noise. But she corrected herself quickly—there were still plenty of woodland animals out here scrambling for food, and the shrill warning shriek she heard made a lot more sense coming from one of them.

*Skip was, as usual,* a charming date. He bought her a second sundae, even though he was out of coupons. Then he let her borrow his jacket as they walked out to a park near the edge of town, because she had forgotten her coat in her rush to leave. Then he offered his gloves as they sat on a park bench and she got drowsy trying to warm her hands.

As she drifted off to sleep, she felt his soothing touch upon her throat. His fingers warmed the necklace charm she wore, and a soft melodious voice—his?—told her it was all right to sleep here, and not to worry about getting home.

*She'll be home soon,* she heard the voice say.

And then the dream started. It began with a simple moon elm branch, thick enough to sprout into two. She got closer and saw tiny shapes leaping from one branch to the other, and then back again. It was amazing how far they could jump—the distance they bridged was hundreds of times wider than any of them. There were four of these small acrobats—spiders, she realized. As each jumped, it left a web strand in its wake, so that each jump built another line connecting the two elm branches.

A Blaze of small dragons, barely bigger than the spiders, came toward the massive moon elm. Maneuvering between the two branches, they got stuck in the web being cast. Like flies, they buzzed and struggled. The spiders did not mind them; they kept jumping and trailing threads, faster and faster. More dragons came. More were caught.

Soon the four spiders were barely visible, they were moving so fast. The web was less like a willowy construct than a barrier now. Pulled together tighter and tighter, the moon elm branches began to groan. Each new dragon that hit the web caused the whole trap to shiver with tension.

Before Jennifer could think to reach out with a blade and cut the webs, one of the spiders spotted her, screamed, and woke her up.

# CHAPTER 6

## Tuesday

Jennifer leapt up from her dream with relief, frozen cheeks, and a sore back. The sun had just barely risen, and she was still on the park bench. A latticework of frosty dew clung to her gloves—Skip's gloves—and she chastised herself for falling asleep in the open during late autumn. *You could have at least woken up long enough to shift to dragon form! Ever heard of exposure, idiot?*

Route 55 was not too far away. Cars were already commuting to work. None of them slowed to look at a transient girl in the roadside park.

Skip was nowhere in sight.

*Still a dream?*

She looked around. There was something not right about the trees. What was it? Beyond the park, the houses seemed normal enough— No, there was one that looked strange. A house where there hadn't been a house before. It was darker than the others and had intricate spires on each of the corners. With limbs on the outside supporting a large abdomen, it almost looked like a—

*So yes, still a dream.*

She identified what was wrong with the trees: They were laced with webs, caught in the branches of nearby oaks and maples like Spanish moss. And she spotted more houses, in places where once there had been parks and open fields.

Not far away, there was a sign by the edge of the highway. It faced away from Jennifer, but she recognized it as the census sign that welcomed visitors to Winoka.

Rubbing her shoulders, she got up and walked over to the sign. Across the road, she could make out the familiar retail stores that anchored Winoka Mall. There was Herberger's, and Applebee's, and the ice-cream store where she had gone with Skip.

*And where is he, anyway? Why isn't he in this dream?*

She reached the sign and looked at the other side. A bright, reflective green, it read in bold white letters:

**PINEGROVE**
**POP. 34,323**
*VISITAR TUTOS, IMPERAR TUTOS*

Why Pinegrove? Why nearly twice the population of Winoka? And what was with that weird town slogan? Her command of Romance languages was shaky, but "imperar" sounded pretty pushy.

A plane soared overhead, miles in the air. She slowly brushed off her—Skip's—coat. Planes, coats, mall, road signs. So this wasn't completely surreal. Usually her dreams meant something, at least since her first dragon change last year. Where was the meaning here? What were the webs supposed to mean? What did this dream want to tell—

"It's not a dream," a familiar voice said behind her, and she turned to see Skip. He had on a new coat, and the gentle wind blew his bangs into his serious face.

She shook her head. "Of course it's a dream. I'm glad you're in it; I was wondering where you were. What do you suppose comes next?"

"What comes next." He repeated the words tonelessly and came closer. "You realize it's not a dream. I'm sorry, Jennifer. I just learned it was happening last night, right before I visited you. I didn't have enough time to prepare you. I barely had enough time to save you."

Jennifer's good mood dwindled. She looked down at herself— she was wearing the same wool sweater and skirt combo under this coat, and her shoes were the same, and so was her jewelry, including the necklace—

*Change.* She ordered it of herself because dreams sometimes cut off options, denied you the chance to think of a way out. In a flash she was in her electric blue skin, stretching her wings and preparing a gust of flame over the ditch, just to prove to herself she could . . .

"No! Change back!" The vehemence behind his words surprised Jennifer, and she obeyed. "Jennifer, you can't do that here. Ever. Jennifer, please let me explain. A group of powerful werachnids has cast a sorcery, and—"

The lowing of cows interrupted him. Jennifer turned to the west, beyond the edge of town. A quarter of a mile away, the farmlands of the surrounding townships stood cold and stark against the advancing development of Winoka—

*Pinegrove?*—and in one of those farms, about a dozen cows were standing and chewing, just like always.

Suddenly, a brown spider the size of a pony leapt from a nearby tree and landed on top of one of the animals, driving its mandibles through the cow's throat and bringing it down amid a strangled, bloody *moo.*

"Cripes!" She felt his arm on her shoulder and let him pull her back a bit. "Skip, do you see that! Werachnids in true shape, this close to Winoka? The beaststalkers will wipe them out! Mayor Seabright won't stand for it!"

"Jennifer. Look at me. This is not Winoka. Winoka never happened."

Distracted, she turned away from the cows. "But we're right across from—"

"This is Pinegrove. What Winoka would still be, if the beaststalkers had never invaded. And if dragons never lived here. Which they never did, anymore."

As quickly as Jennifer had gone from bemused dream to startled surrealism, she now shifted to frightened irritation. "Skip, you're not making any sense. We're right here, in Winoka. We fell asleep last night. You must have woken up before me and gotten a breakfast sandwich from the McDonald's down the road. I'm going to get really mad at you if you don't pull one out of your pocket and share it with me, because that's really selfish you know and what you're saying *just doesn't make sense!*"

"Like I said, some werachnids cast a sorcery. A huge one. It changed a few things in this area. This town, and some others."

"Skip, the mall is right over there. Nothing's changed!"

"Look at that house." He pointed behind him, at the very house Jennifer had noticed before. Its spires tweaked the cool air. Jennifer heard another cow gurgle a ways behind them, but refused to look.

"The house is new," she admitted. "But I'm not a freaking contractor or zoning official. New houses get built in this town all the time! Heck, my dad was probably the architect."

"Jennifer, your dad's gone."

She shoved him back. "Skip, that's not funny. I'm going home. I'll see you in school later. Meantime, try to grow up."

"Jennifer, please come home with me."

"Piss off." She was in dragon form and soaring over the highway in an instant.

*"Jennifer!"* He sounded terrified. Looking back, she saw him shift into the same jumping spider shape he had used in Crescent Valley. In no time he was bounding after her. "You can't do that! People will see you!"

While she didn't want to give him the satisfaction of changing back—what he was saying was ridiculous!—she did find his earnestness unnerving. She flexed her scales and settled into a nice, soft sky pattern. No one below was likely to see her: She had snuck around Winoka a hundred times like this.

He kept after her. "That's not good enough! We can see better than beaststalkers!"

"Calm down, will you! We're almost there."

They approached Pine Street, and Jennifer scanned the treetops for the familiar sight of her house's roof. It would be right . . . right over . . .

Several cold facts hit Jennifer at once. First, her house was not there. In its place was a new structure—another home, she assumed from the size, but like the first strange house she saw, it was bloated and dominated by spires. The whole thing was painted a sickly pale lime, and neither the minivan nor Catherine's Mustang was in the driveway.

Second, if her house was not here, her family was not here.

Third, if her family was not here, Skip was not lying.

Fourth, if Skip was not lying, she was in colossal danger.

She dove to the ground under a line of stark oaks and fluffy pines. These were trees from her backyard, she realized. Yet this was not her backyard anymore.

*I need help.* Attempting a basic trampler skill, she breathed smoke onto the ground and stomped her hind leg.

Nothing happened.

Skip landed and shifted back to human form behind her. "Jen-

nifer, knock it off! That's not going to work. Do you honestly
think there are any reptiles left dumb enough to come to the aid
of a dragon alone in this town?"

She turned and grabbed him by the shoulders.

*"What did you do?!"*

"Jennifer, *I* didn't do anything! I told you, it's a group of—"

"It was your aunt, then!"

"I don't think—"

"How is this even possible!" She screamed it at the trees. "You
can't just go around shifting the universe! Moving people around,
making some disappear, making others reappear!" Another icicle
stabbed at the pit of her stomach. "Who else is gone?"

"I don't know. To make a universe where there are more werachnids, I imagine you'd have to get rid of lots of people. Starting
with just about everyone we know from Winoka."

"So they're living somewhere else." *I've got to find Mom and
Dad. They're probably in Eveningstar. That's how far away,
maybe an hour or two?*

He rubbed his temples. "Doubtful. Jennifer, the sorcery didn't
just change *today.* It changed *history.* Years and years of it. There
were battles that hadn't happened before, victories over dragons
and beaststalkers, reasons *why* Pinegrove is the way it is today.
People died in those battles. Probably your parents, and the
Blacktooths, and—"

"You know an awful lot about this," she hissed. She didn't
know whether he was a liar or a conspirator. Or both.

"Yes, I do know! I just learned most of it. I'm trying to fill you
in, Jennifer. While you were sleeping, I went home and—"

*"Why* was I sleeping, Skip? And why am I still here? If I have
no parents, how am I even possible?"

"Will you shut up and listen!" His impatient anger revealed
a look Jennifer hadn't seen on him before—the same look that
once graced his father's face, in the dungeon where they had once
trapped Jennifer and her father.

She chewed her tongue, willing herself not to strike him. *Find
out what's going on,* she advised herself as calmly as she could.
Then *beat on him.*

"It's like I was trying to tell you," he started again. He was
looking at the frosted grass by his shoes. "I found out last night
that this was going to happen. Mr. Slider told me. I don't know

who told him. But whoever's behind it kept things pretty secret until the last possible moment. I barely had time to make an excuse and get out to you."

"Because you wanted to save me."

"The necklace," he explained, pointing at it. She fingered the emblem of the Moon of the Falling Leaves. "It's a protective talisman, representing change. The wearer can survive all but the most dramatic transformations. It needs a little help to work, and I've learned enough sorcery to enhance it. So even as the universe changed, you survived. With me."

"And what about everyone else?"

He shrugged. "I'm figuring that out now. I spent the morning back at my place. I haven't met anyone yet who's even aware that the universe is any different. My aunt Tavia, Mr. Slider, the newspaper delivery guy, the guy at the twenty-four-hour gas station—they look the same, but they have completely different memories of how they got here. None of them has even heard of Winoka."

"Why didn't you tell me last night." It wasn't a question, but an accusation.

He held his hands out, palms up. "Jennifer, you don't believe me *now*, and it's happened! How on earth were you going to believe me last night?"

"We could have stopped it."

"Jennifer, whoever did this is not the kind of werachnid you just *stop*. Look at what they've done!"

"We could have stopped it!" she insisted. "My mom and dad, they would have found a way! And Eddie's parents, and Mayor Seabright, and the Blaze, they would have helped!"

"Those people don't exist anymore, Jennifer. They never saw it coming. They didn't have a chance. And they certainly don't anymore. According to my aunt here, no one's seen a weredragon or beaststalker near Pinegrove for years. Heck, the guy at the gas station didn't even know what a beaststalker *was*."

"Stop talking!" She put her hands over her ears. "You're lying! There's another explanation! This is a rancid little joke from a really puny mind, and I'll get you for this, Wilson! This is not funny at all!"

"I agree. It's not funny. But it's not a joke, and it's happened. Jennifer, we have to figure out what to do next."

She looked at the houses near her own. The Blacktooth house had also been obliterated by one of these creepy, fat thin houses (this one a pale yellow, like the color of a desert scorpion). Another house—she was pretty sure the family in it had been simply human—was unchanged. Down the way, the Fisk house and the Anderson house also looked intact. She couldn't make out the Elmsmith house.

*Susan!*

She began to walk.

"Susan's not there, Jennifer. I checked. I don't think her family ever moved to this town. Remember, they came here for beast-stalker protection?"

This stopped her in her tracks. "You must think this is pretty damn hilarious, don't you, Wilson?"

"No, I don't. I wish you would believe me."

*I'm beginning to,* she admitted to herself grudgingly. Really, she had no choice.

"All right," she said. *I can handle this. Can't I?* "So we have to figure out how exactly this sorcery worked. Then we have to find a way to reverse it. Maybe we can find friends in this universe who—"

"Jennifer, hold up. I don't think that's what your dad would want."

She clenched her teeth. "How the hell would you know what my dad would want?"

"Because I talked with him."

"How? When?"

"He saw us leave your house last night," Skip explained. "He followed us to make sure you didn't do anything rash. You seemed upset from that argument with your mother, he said. He kept his distance while we had ice cream and walked to the park. After I had you fall asleep, he came up and asked me what I thought I was doing."

"You're lucky he didn't kick your ass."

"No, *you're* lucky. Once I explained to him what was going on, he agreed I was the only one who could save you."

"Why not him, too?"

"The necklace only helps the wearer, and the one who casts the protective sorcery. Your dad and I agreed you were the right one to save."

"*You two* agreed? *You two* made this decision for me?"

"He's your dad, Jennifer. What else was he supposed to do?"

"So you told him off, and he just agreed the universe was screwed, and he left?"

"Of course not. He wanted to strangle me. But we didn't have much time, so he wrote this for you instead." He handed her a folded piece of paper.

She slowly unfolded it. It was a utility bill to the Scales residence at 9691 Pine Street East. ($320.32, she noticed.) On the back, there was a scribbled note. The handwriting was definitely her father's—the same hurried script he used for lists of chores she had to do, or to let her and her mother know he'd be in Crescent Valley for a few days.

*Jennifer,*

*What can I write? There's not enough time.*

*Skip has told me what will happen. When you read this, you will likely be alone. I'm sorry for that. I'm sorry the world separated us before any of us were ready. And our fight—I'm sorry for that, too.*

*But while this may be the end for your mother and me, it cannot be the end for you. Make the best life you can, where you are. Do not try to change anything back. It will get you killed.*

*Grow old. Marry, if you fall in love. Live a rich life. Tell your children and grandchildren about us, if the moment is ever right. It is all a parent can ask.*

*Of course, your mother and I love you. Never forget that.*

*Stay as strong as stone. Stay as beautiful as fire. Stay alive.*

*—Dad*

She read it twice, and then once more. Her eyes took in the words, but her brain refused to recognize them.

Where was the part that told her they would be okay?

Where was the part that told her there was a plan?

Where was the part that told her how to get back?

She crumpled the note in her hands and clenched her teeth.

*Grow old? Marry? Grandchildren? Here? I'm not staying here! This isn't home!*

"I'm not staying here!" she repeated aloud to Skip. "*I'm not staying here!* You can't keep me here! This is insane! I want to go back, right now! Send me back!"

"Jennifer." He frowned as he softly brushed her cheek. "You're not listening. There is no 'back.' This universe isn't parallel. It's a replacement, a patch."

She slapped his hand away. "Then we're *un*patching it! We'll find—"

"Find what? Who?" He shrugged in exasperation. "Who can change it back? Where the hell would we start?"

"Mr. Slider knows," she accused him desperately. "You said yourself he knew this was going to happen. We go to him and we make him tell us—"

He grabbed her by the shoulders. "He won't remember! He's not the same Mr. Slider I left behind! He wasn't in the bubble I cast with the necklace—just you and me. I replaced whatever Skip was already here—not that anyone will know that. As for you, Jennifer, Mr. Slider will have no idea who you are! If you go up to him or my aunt and order them to tell you who changed the world, they'll think you've escaped from a mental institution. And with no family to speak of, that's where you might end up!"

She sank to the ground, dragging him with her. "Skip, you have to help me. I can't stay here like this. My parents are waiting for me. They're worried. We were arguing, and—"

"Jennifer. Your parents are gone."

*"Don't say that!"* From her huddled position on the ground, she pushed him away. *"Don't say they're gone! They're not gone!"*

"Read the note . . ."

She ripped up the utility bill and threw the pieces at him. "*This note is a lie!* You forged it! My mom and dad are waiting for me and you're taking me to them *right now*!"

Instead of arguing anymore, he bent to pick up the pieces of paper.

"What are you doing?" she sniffled.

"You're going to want these," he told her tonelessly. "It's more than either of my parents ever left me."

A moment of curiosity got the better of her. "Are your parents alive here?"

"I haven't looked." He finished gathering the letter fragments and handed the small bundle to her. "If you come to my aunt's home with me, there's time to get you cleaned up. You can wear what you've got, or borrow something of mine, whatever you like. This afternoon, we can go clothes shopping—"

"Shopping!" She grabbed the bits of paper back but did not rescatter them. Instead, she shoved them in a jacket pocket. "I can't go *shopping*! Skip, aren't you going to help me?"

He heaved a long sigh and rubbed his forehead. "Jennifer, what I'd do to help you . . . Can you at least accept we'll need more than an hour here to get the job done? I mean, it's going to take time. And you need a place to stay, and you can't wear the same outfit every day. Right?"

She bit her lip as her face reddened. Of course he wanted to help her. He already had, by saving her from the same obliteration that had taken everything else she knew. And what he said now made sense. Why was she yelling at him?

"I'm sorry," she whispered. "I just can't . . . this is too . . ."

"I know." He slid next to her on the ground and held her. "This is a lot to take in. I can barely believe it myself. We'll work through it together, okay? Come with me."

*The next couple of hours* were a blur. His house was still a two-story Cape Cod with brown shingles and a bright red door and yellow trim, so she guessed not all werachnids lived in grotesque uber-houses with spooky spires. Neither Tavia Saltin nor Edmund Slider were there at the moment. Skip said they were both teachers at the high school now, and the workday there had begun.

The house was decorated much as it had been when Jennifer saw it last, which was a cold comfort to her. Lots of shots of Tavia and Edmund together: formal portraits, vacation photos from camel rides and hiking trips—

She paused over one of them. *Hiking trips.* There was Edmund Slider, formerly bound to a wheelchair, now standing tall astride a forested mountain path, nothing but nature in the background, lifting his girlfriend in his arms and smiling at an unseen cameraman.

*So he can walk now.*

There were pictures of Skip's parents on a wall here and there—

but, of course, that had been true before. Otto Saltin had been Tavia's brother, after all, and Dianna Wilson her sister-in-law. (There were six other Saltin siblings, Jennifer counted from one of the more formal photographs. One such studio photo had all the Saltins in spider form, splayed out on webs, against a traditional blue-gray background.)

Despite the occasional shot of Otto and Dianna, it was clear Skip's parents didn't live here—just Tavia and Edmund. Were they married? She didn't see a wedding photo anywhere.

Moving into the dining room, Jennifer thought of a meal she had eaten in this house, on a date with Skip not long ago, where she had wondered at speckles in the mashed potatoes. She also thought of last night's dream, and the dragons trapped like flies in the thickening web.

Skip invited her upstairs. His wardrobe was about the same in this universe as it had been before—lots of dark, stark colors. Jennifer decided against new pants, opting for her own skirt so she could keep her daggers handy, but she did change her top to a black, buttoned-down, collared shirt. It felt a bit better to put something clean on, and it did smell like him, which was a small comfort. Skip found some agreeable makeup from his aunt's room, so she washed her face and applied some simple base, lipstick, and waterproof mascara: Today felt like a day she was likely to spend crying an awful lot.

They walked to the school, which wasn't too great a distance, and it gave Jennifer a chance to see more of the town. Her first impression of the town was right, as was the population sign—there were more houses than before, packed a bit more tightly, and a few larger condominiums that were doubtless teeming with spider families and old scorpion couples. But there were perfectly normal-looking people coming out to get the mail and check their lawn sprinklers.

*How can some be spiders and some not under this moon,* she wondered idly, thinking of the hunted cows. *Only Skip can change back and forth when he likes.*

*Whoever did this can spin the clock back and change history,* she answered herself. *Changing shape at will is probably child's play to them!*

"Have you been to the hospital?" she asked Skip.

"I haven't had the chance," he replied. Then he answered

her real question: "Jennifer, I really think your parents are both gone."

She held a hand out. "Skip, drop it."

"I'm not trying to upset you—"

"Then don't."

They walked for a while in silence. Jennifer tried hard not to think of her parents, which of course meant she spent the entire time thinking about her parents. The only thing keeping her feet moving forward was the thought that she would find her mother, and then her father. *Then I'll take Dad's note and cram it down his throat for scaring me. Then the three of us will blow this universe apart.*

"Wow," Skip murmured.

They were cresting the hill less than a mile from the high school. The massive, maroon and white brick building appeared no different from the outside. Sure, the sign by the parking lot said PINEGROVE HIGH — GO SCORPIONS! instead of WINOKA HIGH — GO FALCONS!, but Jennifer was learning not to sweat the small stuff.

However, the hulking structure beyond it—what looked like an enormous, metallic golf ball four stories high bound to the earth with a web of massive steel beams—*that* was new.

"What is that?" she asked.

He whistled. "Huh."

"Whatever it is, it's sitting right in the middle of the soccer practice field." This offended Jennifer on a newer, deeper level. She gave it a hard look, and she suddenly felt as if it was giving her a hard look back. A cold light shone on her insides, where her lungs were breathless and her heart was slowing. *Something in there can see me. Right through me.*

"Let's get you registered." He steered her toward the more normal-looking school building.

In the principal's office, Jennifer had her first pleasant surprise since waking up.

"Mr. Sheep!"

The school principal wrinkled his plain nose, and his plain eyes widened a bit in surprise. "My name is Mr. Mouton," he allowed, letting the French word for *sheep* roll off his tongue a bit. "Do I know you, Ms. . . . ?"

"Scales," Skip finished for him. "She's a friend of my family's.

She'll be staying with us for a while, and of course we'll need to get her registered here at Winok— er, here at Pinegrove High."

"Oh." Mr. Mouton shrugged. "Well, that shouldn't be difficult. Welcome to Pinegrove High, Ms. Scales. Do you have a written and signed communication from your parents? We would need that to—"

"Her parents are dead," Skip interrupted. Jennifer felt her chest tighten, but took a deep breath. Whether Skip believed that or not, it was a convenient excuse to get through this meeting.

"Oh! I see." Now Mr. Mouton's simple features were tinged with embarrassment. "My condolences, Ms. Scales. At some point we'll require some formal documentation, but given the fact that Skip's mother and Edmund Slider both work here and can no doubt speak for you—"

"They will," Skip promised. *Just as soon as I talk to them,* his expression told Jennifer.

"—then we can certainly get you started. My assistant will get you going on the paperwork, and then perhaps Mr. Wilson here will be kind enough to escort you through your classes for the day . . . ?"

"I can find my way around," she assured them both. "Skip, go on. If I don't see you around, I'll just meet you out front at the end of the day, okay?"

He took a tentative step back. "Are you sure?"

She nodded. "I'll be fine."

"All right. I'll, you know. Check things out. We'll talk later."

"Sure."

Once Skip was gone and Mr. Mouton had put her at an assistant's desk with a small ream of paperwork, Jennifer carefully considered her options. It was the first moment she had to herself since Skip had told her the horrible truth.

First, she could fight. She had her daggers on under her skirt and a throat full of fire. The plan: Start here in the office, destroy as much of the school and its ghastly occupants as possible, and work her way over to that horrid building in the soccer field.

On the plus side: This would feel really, really good, and that building was important for sure. How could anything that huge and ugly *not* be a headquarters? Which meant she might smash something hard enough to change things back.

What were the cons? She would probably die before getting out of this building, much less *into* the other one.

Her second option was to do as her father asked and give up completely. She would forge a new life here in Pinegrove, come to love spiders and other supercrawly things, and occasionally get out to the countryside just to stretch her wings in peace and quiet. Decades from now, when she was on her deathbed with lots of adoring grandchildren around her, she'd flick over to dragon form and give them all a nifty scare. They'd be shocked but they'd love her anyway, because she made really good Christmas cookies, like all grandmothers do, except these wouldn't be shaped like frosted snowmen and cinnamon angels. Instead, they'd be shaped like little gingerbread ticks and chocolate-sprinkled tarantulas . . .

*Ennnh! No go. Third option?*

Her third option was to finish this paperwork, start classes, and keep her eyes open. She could not possibly be the only dragon left in existence. There would be a few others at least. Maybe they were the dregs of the school social classes, the untouchables of the community—but they would befriend her and introduce her to others. Same with beaststalkers. If the kids wouldn't talk about it, maybe their parents would. She could slowly build up a group who would be willing to—

"Do you need help getting started, dear?" The kind administrative assistant was leaning in closely, and Jennifer suddenly realized her pen had been frozen over the paperwork for a full minute or more. "Are you feeling all right?"

Jennifer smiled at the white-haired woman, imagining her with eight eyes and trying with no small difficulty to refrain from stabbing six or seven of them with her pen. "No, thanks. Just got lost in thought for a sec."

"Happens to me all the time," the assistant said, waving a hand in kind dismissal. "Sometimes, it feels good to pretend you're somewhere else."

"You said it."

*Her schedule of classes* was a bit different from what she was used to. Her first two classes—arithmetic and geometric applications, and history and literature—had already passed by the time she was out of the principal's office. Ahead was music, then lunch, then chemistry, then study hall, and then Spanish. Spanish had an asterisk in front of it. At the bottom of the page was the notation:

*Excused from Introductory Astronomy for one semester.*

*No straight English class,* she noted on her way to the band room. *And why don't they just call math "math"? And what's with the Astronomy class, and the excuse? There were never any Astronomy classes at Winoka.*

She didn't have good answers to any of these questions by the time she got to the band room. Which was good, because she would have forgotten all of them anyway.

The band room was lined with an array of instruments: some typical brass and percussion, and others of completely foreign design. One such device in the center of the room—what at first appeared to be a collision of three or four different harps—had an elaborate wooden frame and reminded Jennifer of multiple legs on strings.

At least twenty other students were in the class, but none carried an instrument. Instead, they were gathered around a grand piano, where Tavia Saltin sat. Tavia looked exactly the way Jennifer would have hoped, with chocolate hair wrapped in a tight bun topping a spindly frame, but the older woman betrayed no sign of recognition.

"So you're our newest student!" She greeted Jennifer with a mixture of warmth and interest. "Tell me, have you had much musical training?"

"Just the normal music program from my regular school. It's, er, a bit like this one."

"That's fine. And do you prefer to morph when you play?"

"Oh! Geez, Ms. Saltin, thanks, but I'm not ready . . . I mean, I'm more comfortable . . ."

"Not a problem at all!" Tavia's beam was wide and understanding. Just as when she first met this woman, Jennifer was unnerved by the overfriendliness. "You just take whatever form makes you most comfortable.

"So let's get started!" she announced to the class as she absent-mindedly poked at the piano keys. A simple but catchy melody emerged, perfect background music for conversation. "I believe we left off yesterday in the middle of our discussion of the more complex stringed instruments. The piano, like the one I'm playing now, is an example of such a stringed instrument—though many would call it a hybrid of string and percussion. But of course you've all seen a piano, so I don't expect that's very exciting for you."

She grinned at the students, some of whom granted a giggle.

"Far more interesting is the web harp," she continued, motioning to the massive instrument Jennifer had noted when she came into the room. "This complex harp was devised in the late eighteenth century when the Welsh settled in Patagonia, now known as Argentina. Nearby native South Americans adopted the simple Welsh harp and . . . improved it. Over the years, the web harp has found favor as a niche instrument, and the past few decades have seen a resurgence in its popularity, especially in South and North American music."

*I'll bet,* Jennifer thought bitterly. She made a note of the time line—"the past few decades." Clearly, the instrument in this room was of werachnid design. If werachnid culture had increased in dominance gradually, then whatever change paved the way must also have happened decades ago.

*How am I going to go back in time and switch everything around again?*

"The resulting music," Tavia continued, "can be astounding. I am not an expert on the device myself, but fortunately, we have a prodigy here at Pinegrove High who can provide a demonstration. I believe many of you know Andeana?"

"Please," came a quiet, tired voice from the front of the crowd around the piano. "Just call me Andi, Ms. Saltin."

Tavia shrugged as a tanned whisper of a girl slid away from the piano, through the tiny crevices between unmoving students, and up to the enormous web harp. Andi's modest nose and cheekbones were of a dark complexion, rooted perhaps from Colombia or Brazil. Her straight dark hair with a soft magenta streak was tucked behind her left ear. Wearing navy slacks, a loose blue sweater, and blue flats, the girl looked fashionable but forgettable, especially next to a work of delicately strung, carved wooden art.

Looking up at the web harp, Andi sighed and began tuning it. Her sleeves kept rolling down, only to be quickly propped up to the wrist again. The instrument dwarfed her; had Jennifer not known any better, she would have mistaken the girl for one of the shorter strings.

"Andeana has agreed—"

"Andi." The girl pouted, rubbing her forearms through the sleeves.

*"Woot, Andi!"* cried out one of the girls—a well-dressed, handsome blonde of unusual size. This got the class chuckling, but Jennifer saw admiration and anticipation, not mockery, in their faces.

"Andi has agreed," Tavia continued amiably, "to play an excerpt from a beautiful composition called 'Sekidera Komachi.' This piece is based on an old Japanese play of the same name about a woman who has lived too long and been forgotten. It is unusual in that it was originally written for two harps, a flute, a koto, and a soprano. I will play the flute part here on the piano; Andi will handle everything else."

If Jennifer expected Andi to turn into a spider and start plucking strings with grotesque tarsi, she was bewildered to find that the girl did not change shape at all. Instead, the girl kicked off her flats (revealing long toes with nails painted ten different shades of blue), sat on a chair placed close to the center of the harp, and began to play. Her feet strummed a sequence of strings that lay along the base of the instrument—something that looked like the sort of koto Jennifer had seen in Japanese art movies.

Even more impressive, Andi's arms were a blur of movement along the arrays of harp strings. There must have been at least four, maybe five or six—and they produced simultaneous flows of music, some soft and gentle, others more staccato or agitated. The musical rivers cascaded alongside each other and splashed over the room, washing the class in a dizzying spectacle of sound. Jennifer squinted at the source of this display: Did she only have two arms? Or was it more?

Before she could figure it out, Andi began to sing. It was a simple sort of tune, with not much in the way of range and some repetition. But it was still gorgeous coming from this girl's plain throat, and her words were perfectly accented Japanese.

Even without knowing what the girl was singing, Jennifer could understand the sorrow and pain of the woman in the song. There was tremendous loss.

Suddenly, Andi switched to English:

> *Where are my loved ones?*
> *I grieve for my family,*
> *And my friends are nowhere near.*

With that, the song ended, and Jennifer nearly leapt over the crowd and into the harp. *They're playing with you!* She steamed, as the class applauded and whistled, forcing Andi to take a tiny bow. *They all know what they've done, and they're rubbing your face in it!*

But she saw as Andi stood up straight that the girl had tears on her cheeks. This was not a performance for an outsider's benefit, she realized. This was a song very personal to this particular musician.

Noticing the girl hugging herself hard and staring at the floor, Jennifer relaxed enough to take in some detail. First, Andi did not look happy even after this fine performance. Second, she did not make eye contact with anyone, even though several students and Tavia were all lavishing praise upon her.

Third, just under the girl's sleeves, Jennifer spotted an angry red railroad of marks traveling up each arm.

*Andi's a cutter,* she realized with grief and alarm. *She feels pain inside, cuts herself to bring it out, and hides the marks.*

Then a few more pieces clicked into place. *She clearly doesn't feel she belongs around here. She sings about suffering and loss. And she doesn't morph when she probably should while playing what is obviously a werachnid's instrument.*

*What is she hiding?*

Straightening when a thrill ran up her spine, Jennifer realized she had her answer.

*She's not like these others.*

*She's like me.*

*After music class,* Jennifer struggled through the hallways to catch up to this strange young woman. The delicious possibilities sped through her mind—*weredragon? Beaststalker? Both?*

She felt a thrill as she spotted the back of the smaller, darker girl's head. *How does she move so fast?* In addition to speed,

Jennifer would have to overcome another obstacle: Andi's companion, the tall blonde who had shouted out to her in music class. The two of them were talking. Well, the blonde was talking, and Andi was just nodding and listening and trying to keep up with the other girl's mammoth gait.

The two of them appeared to be friends, since the blonde was laughing and Andi revealed a small smile when she turned her head from side to side. *Another recruit?* Jennifer wondered. Then she realized she might be getting ahead of herself.

"Jennifer!" It was Skip, racing down the hall to catch up. He had a tentative look on his face. "Hey, you're still okay? How are you getting along?"

She shrugged, trying to contain her excitement about Andi. "Okay. I'm trying to keep up with a couple of girls I just met in music class. Thought I might try having lunch with them."

"I'll come with you." He fell into step next to her. "So how was music class?"

"Interesting. Your aunt was friendly enough. Didn't seem to know me."

"I told you." His voice held a gentle reproach. "Apparently, she's not even an eye specialist in this universe, since the average person's eyesight around here is 20/10. So instead of using her love for music as a therapeutic approach for patients, she teaches the subject here at school. Crazy world, huh?"

"Yeah. Crazy world. So how was *your* class?"

He grinned. "Advanced geometrical applications. Really cool stuff. What Mr. Slider teaches sophomores here is tougher than what I was doing with him in independent study! I also found out something about next year's classes."

This blew all thoughts of Andi and the blonde out of her mind. She stopped dead in the hallway and faced him. "Next year's classes?"

"Yeah, for juniors. Seniors do it, too. They follow this special curriculum called the quadrivium—just four classes, double-length, no study hall, short lunch. Really intense. Arithmetic, geometry, music, and astronomy. That's it."

Jennifer didn't care. She stared at Skip. "*Next* year's classes?"

Finally, he caught on. He swallowed hard. "Oh, hey, Jennifer, I'm not saying we'll be here next year. I'm just giving you the scoop on what I learned—"

"Yes, it's all very fascinating." She started walking again, faster this time so he couldn't see her start to cry. "Thank you for your superduper rundown of how I'll be spending the next few years of my miserable life here at Murderous Freak Show High!"

She raced into the cafeteria with eyes so wet she couldn't really tell who was around her. Holding her books with one hand, she wiped one side of her face well enough to see Andi again as the girl dropped her book bag off at a table next to the blonde's stuff. The two of them got into line. Jennifer dropped her own books on the seat next to Andi's, and got behind them.

Getting a better look at the blonde, Jennifer got the sense she had seen this young woman before. *But not here. Where?*

The girl looked like a Valkyrie with blue eyes and a large, square jaw. Jennifer didn't think her attractive, but she certainly had lots of presence. Heck, her sheer size demanded attention.

She got a messy pulled-pork sandwich plopped onto her tray, and she warily chose a steamed vegetable. The blonde ahead of her laughed again, a dull sound with a cruel edge. *I know that laugh. It's a bully's laugh. It's—*

Her jaw dropped in recognition. *No way. It can't be.*

"Hey, Bobbie!" The voice from behind Jennifer made her turn. It was Abigail Whittier, looking exactly as she had before with beautiful coffee skin and a slightly bored look gracing her elegant features. "Whatcha doin' after school?"

Bobbie Jarkmand—for this *was* Bob Jarkmand, Jennifer saw to her horror—turned and gave a noncommittal shrug. "Dunno."

*Bob is a Bobbie here!* As weird as this was to swallow, the evidence was obvious. The girl was a hulk. And she hadn't seen Bob Jarkmand yet today, so the position was open, so to speak. Somewhere along the line, Jennifer supposed, a Y chromosome didn't get where it was supposed to—a different ancestor or a different chemical reaction because of a strange environment. Who knew?

She paid for her lunch and darted for the table, just in time to hear Andi and Bobbie wonder aloud who had dropped their books next to Andi's chair.

"They're mine," she explained with a slight apology on her lips. She sat down before they could protest. "I hope you guys don't mind. I'm kinda new around here."

Andi plainly had not expected such a direct approach and began to stammer. Bobbie looked Jennifer up and down and decided to ignore her. When the other three girls—Abigail, Anne, and Amy—came in a cluster and sat down around them, they all gave Jennifer suspicious looks.

Finally, as they began to eat, Jennifer introduced herself. She held her hand out to Andi. "I'm Jennifer."

The girl tried to shrink away from the hand, but when it didn't go away she relented and shook it limply. "Andi. This is Bobbie, and Amy, and Abigail, and Anne."

"Hey, guys." The best she got out of any of them was a nod. She wondered where Amanda Sera was. "Listen, I don't want to tick any of you off. If you want me to leave—"

"Naw, stick around," Bobbie said, just as Amy and Abigail both said, "Yeah, buzz off."

It took Jennifer just a moment of noting everyone's reaction around the table to determine who the leader was here. "Thanks, Bobbie."

She didn't do much talking after that, just watched and listened. A glance around the cafeteria confirmed that Amanda Sera was absent . . . *Not in this universe,* she guessed. *Just like Mom and every other beaststalker. Some are gone; some are completely different—like Bobbie here.*

Abigail and Bobbie did the most chatting, with Anne asking the leading questions ("Omigod, so *then* what did you do?") and Amy chiming in with the occasional snide remark. Andi spent most of her time staring at her pulled-pork sandwich, which never had more than three bites taken out of it.

After twenty minutes of observing this group dynamic, Jennifer ventured a comment. "That was a beautiful song you sang in music today," she told Andi.

Andi didn't look up. "Thanks," she muttered.

"How long have you been playing that instrument?"

When Andi didn't answer, Bobbie filled in. "Something I've learned about Andi. It's hard to get information out of her. Wherever she came from, it was a dark place."

*Still is,* Jennifer bet herself. She watched Andi twist her sleeves and poke superficially at her green beans.

"How about you?" Bobbie continued. "You play anything?"

"I'm not good with music," Jennifer admitted. "When it comes to art, I do more drawing than anything else."

"That's cool. What do you draw?"

"Just about anything." The vague response got her blank stares. *Heck, a little white lie couldn't hurt.* "The more legs the better!"

That got Bobbie grinning, and the other girls played along. "Sounds cool. Think you could draw me sometime?"

*So she's a werachnid. Terrific.* Jennifer couldn't think of anything she'd rather do less than have this girl pose with mandibles and thorax on display, but she had chosen this road. "Sure. Anytime. All I need is charcoal and paper."

"Cool. Hey, Anne, you gonna eat that?" And like that, Bobbie had dismissed the topic and pulled the group's attention to her next interest.

That was fine with Jennifer, who turned her attention back to Andi. The girl didn't give another opening for conversation, but she rewarded Jennifer with a faint smile when she got up and left.

*Baby steps,* Jennifer reminded herself as she followed the girl up and out of the cafeteria. *Baby steps.*

# CHAPTER 7

## *Tuesday Afternoon*

*Not so bad,* she congratulated herself as she walked out of the cafeteria. The rush of students around her looked increasingly normal. Even if beaststalkers had never made it to this Pinegrove, there were still plenty of familiar faces. The part of her that wanted to scream and start tearing things down was steadily relaxing—there was no imminent danger here. Andi seemed like an eventual recruit, and there were doubtless more.

*Maybe Skip's right,* she allowed. *Working through the next day or two is the best way to learn how to change things back. We'll think things through better if we take our time. Lessee, chemistry now, right?*

She checked her schedule and saw indeed:

*Chemistry, Sloane, Rm. 265.*

Room 265 was just a few doors away. Even before she entered the room, she could see the familiar periodic table on the far wall. Just like the one at old Winoka High, it was frayed at the edges and bore the mysterious, small, random brown stains of a schoolroom decoration that had simply been up for too long.

She was pleased to see Andi here, and it was even agreeable to see Bobbie come in a few seconds after the bell rang. The others on the A-List weren't around, which Jennifer felt was a good thing. Recruitment was best done one or two at a time.

All she had to do was peel Andi away from Bobbie a bit. The girl was clearly miserable in that group. *Who wouldn't be, in any universe?*

"Class, class!" the teacher, who Jennifer presumed was Ms. Sloane, called out with a mixture of tolerance and impatience. The young, petite redhead in a perky flowered dress and green-painted fingernails cleared her throat and picked up a weathered yardstick as several of the boys in the back of the room began to guffaw at something only they found amusing. Tapping the stick on the blackboard, she cleared her throat. "If we could start, please. Today's lesson is important.

"In fact," she continued while twirling the stick in her hand, "it is the key to everything else you'll learn this year in chemistry—and what many of you will learn about medicine after that. After all, chemistry may not be on the quadrivium curriculum—but it does contain an essential link between life and death."

*There's that quadrivium word again.* Jennifer didn't dwell on this, though, because Ms. Sloan had picked up a piece of chalk with her empty hand and was writing a single word on the blackboard in large script with gentle loops. This word, Jennifer knew just fine:

### POISON

Ms. Sloane put down the chalk and turned back to the class. "Can someone please tell me what *poison* is?"

The chill of insecure apathy settled over the room. *What is poison?* Jennifer asked herself, scanning the empty faces around her. *That's easy. Isn't it?*

"Ms. . . . Scales, right?" Ms. Sloane cocked her head. "What do you think? What is poison?"

She shrugged. "Poison's something your body can't handle. You know, the kind of stuff that kills you."

"Kills *me*?" The yardstick twitched.

"I . . . uh . . . I . . ."

"The truth is," Ms. Sloane continued as she addressed the entire class again, "*anything* can be poisonous, if taken properly. Or improperly. Who can tell me about Paracelsus?"

Andi's slender hand floated up. "Paracelsus was a physician who lived over 500 years ago. He came up with a fundamental rule of toxicology."

"And that rule is?"

"The only difference between a poison and a cure is the dose."

Jennifer raised her eyebrows. Plainly, Andi's shyness did not extend to class participation. *So Bobbie keeps her around for her smarts,* she guessed. *Andi's the thinker. Lots of queen bees keep one around to do their homework for them.* The idea of this wretched girl, chained to this warped universe and bartering her brains and talent for some small measure of acceptance, made Jennifer want to spit nails.

"Correct," Ms. Sloane told Andi. "There are actually people"—and the teacher began writing on the chalkboard again—"who have died from overdosing on essential nutrients."

Jennifer watched three more lines appear underneath "poison":

$$GLUCOSE\ (C_6H_{12}O_6)$$
$$VITAMIN\ A\ (C_{20}H_{30}O)$$
$$WATER\ (H_2O)$$

"Anyone who has ever suffered from diabetes can attest to the consequences of an imbalance of sugars in the blood," Ms. Sloane announced while walking past the first few rows of students. "It is an irony, one of many in nature. Glucose, the most abundant organic molecule on the planet, a building block of life . . . can kill.

"So can vitamin A, or any other vitamin for that matter. Taken normally, in doses of 700 to 900 micrograms per day, vitamin A keeps you healthy and staves off multiple eye disorders. But taken in doses of more than 3,000 micrograms per day for long enough, it can damage the liver or cause birth defects."

"What about water?" Bobbie asked from the back of the classroom, looking as slow and skeptical as she—he?—ever had back at Jennifer's own Winoka High. "There's no way anyone has died from drinking too much water!"

"You could drown in it," a boy near the back of the class suggested.

Andi shook her head. "Suffocation isn't the same as toxicity."

"Correct again," Ms. Sloane agreed with a hint of admiration. Now at the back of the class, she rubbed the end of her yardstick with a long, green fingernail. "When someone drinks too much pure water, the body loses salts like sodium chloride and potassium chloride. Salts, of course, are vital to our existence. People have actually died this way, though very rarely."

"Too much of a good thing," Jennifer muttered.

Ms. Sloane heard her and pointed smartly with the stick. "That's right. Too much of a good thing. Can anyone tell me what homeostasis means?"

One of the larger boys toward the back grinned and started whispering to another. He stopped as Ms. Sloane brought down her yardstick upon his desk, splintering it and snapping the entire class to attention.

"*Mr.* Turnbull," she snarled. "Do you find something amusing in my question?"

The boy slunk down in his chair and shook his head.

Ms. Sloane, not ready to let the issue drop, bent over so her rust-colored lips were next to his reddening ear. "Perhaps you can help me with something, Mr. Turnbull. Despite my youthful looks, I have been teaching chemistry for many years. I notice, every autumn, that when the day comes when I introduce the term *homeostasis*"—her lips massaged the vowels slowly and tenderly, making the boy sink farther into his chair—"there is always at least one boy who needs to remark on the word. Can you imagine why that might be, Mr. Turnbull?"

"Intellectual curiosity?" he croaked.

The splintered end of the yardstick rose until it was just under his nose. "Doubtful. Let me suggest, Mr. Turnbull, that you keep your jocular remarks to yourself."

"Okay."

"Thank you." Ms. Sloane's tone softened as she brought the yardstick up to her own face and picked thoughtfully at the broken end. "So. Who can tell me what this word means?"

Again, Andi's slender hand rose alone.

"Yes?"

"Homeostasis is the state of equilibrium within a living organism. A homeostatic system is stable."

"Correct again. Well done. When someone takes too much of a substance internally—be it a neurotoxin or vitamin A— it throws equilibrium off. A homeostatic system will use negative feedback—a reaction to reverse the imbalance. If you've heard the phrase *for every action, an equal and opposite reaction*, you have a sense of what a homeostatic system tries to do.

"If the dose of toxin is small enough, a homeostatic system will find a way to get back to normal. If the dose is too large, the system will collapse—an organ will fail, for example, and death may result.

"Balance is a concept that runs through chemistry, and the study of poisons. I have two test tubes here"—she held them up—"each with a different substance. The first is the most poisonous naturally occurring substance in the world. The second is the venom of one of the most feared poisonous creatures in the world. Each has a complete opposite effect on the body's neurotransmitters. Would anyone care to guess what they are?"

After several moments of watching the class wait for Andi to raise her hand, Jennifer was relieved when her new friend relented. "The first substance is the botulin toxin. The second substance could be one of several spider or snake venoms."

"Black widow spider toxin, to be precise. And does anyone know how they interact with neurotransmitters?"

Here, despite Ms. Sloane's eager look, not even Andi had an answer.

The teacher finally had to answer herself. "Black widow venom acts by forcing the body's release of acetylcholine, which contracts muscles. On the other hand, botulin shuts down that very neurotransmitter, causing paralysis of the musculature."

Jennifer struggled to recall a news story she had heard once of several dozen people around the country getting food poisoning. A meat-packing company ended up the target of a class-action lawsuit. Hadn't that been a form of botulism? She wasn't sure.

"Class, I have one more question before we get to the heart of the matter today." Ms. Sloane used the splintered yardstick to reach back and scratch her spine, causing her angora sweater to ride up a few inches. Jennifer caught sight of an exotic yin/yang tattoo in the small of the young teacher's back before she turned around. "Can anyone think of what these two very different poisons have *in common*—other than, of course, the fact that they can both kill?"

There were no takers, which didn't seem to disappoint Ms. Sloane. She carried on without missing a beat. "Both substances have led to high-profile advances in medicine."

Now, a hand went up—a boy about two rows behind Jennifer. The teacher accepted the late entry with grace. "Yes, Mr. Taylor? You can fill in a detail?"

"I think my mother once had botulin injected to remove some wrinkles from her face!"

"That may be so, in minute doses. A more medically useful application of botulin is as a muscle relaxant when a patient is suffering from severe muscle spasms or from migraine headaches. Okay, now that we've addressed one of the poisons, would anyone like to take a stab at the medicinal uses of black widow toxin?"

Jennifer raised a tentative hand. "Is it used to create antivenom?"

"Yes, Ms. Scales! In humans and other animals, the introduction of many venoms will inspire the creation of antibodies. For that reason, we can actually use some poisons—like black widow poison—to build medicines that save lives.

"And so we come to the heart of the matter. Class, just like any beneficial substance might be a poison, so any poison *might* have medicinal uses. The demanding dual nature of drugs and other ingested substances leads us to the Central Truth of Poisons."

By this time, Ms. Sloane had laid down the yardstick and was back at the blackboard, scribbling four lines of text.

> POISON IS DEATH.
> POISON TESTS US.
> POISON STRENGTHENS US.
> POISON IS LIFE.

"Class, this Central Truth is essential to your understanding of chemistry—and a great deal else. Because poison threatens death, it challenges us. Because it challenges us, it can make us stronger if we survive the challenge. And by becoming stronger, we increase our chances of survival and prolong our lives. Please repeat after me: Poison is death."

"Poison is death," the class repeated as Jennifer watched with a growing chill in her abdomen.

"Poison tests us."

"Poison tests us."

*This is crazy.* Jennifer kept her mouth shut and her head down.

"Poison strengthens us." The jade fingernails were wrapped around the yardstick again.

"Poison strengthens us."

The broken stick came down hard on Jennifer's desk.

"*Ms. Scales.* You seem to have trouble participating in this exercise. Please repeat after me. Poison is life."

"I— This is just—"

"Poison is life, Ms. Scales."

Jennifer felt the burn of every student's stare on the back of her head. Many of them, she knew, had more than two eyes hidden deep inside. *This is no time to be a rebel.*

"Ma'am. Poison is life."

"Excellent. Again, class, all together now. Poison is death."

"Poison is death." Jennifer said the words with everyone else, feeling very far away from home.

"Poison tests us."

"Poison tests us . . ."

*She was just getting out* of Spanish class at the end of the day— a refreshingly normal experience where they learned words such as *cambiar* and *arquitectura*, and where nobody had a mantra to chant before the bell rang—when a voice down the hallway startled her.

"Hey, Jennifer!"

She tried pretending not to hear as she strode toward the exit, but it was impossible—Bobbie Jarkmand was the only girl in Pinegrove High with longer legs than her.

"Jennifer, wait up!" Bobbie grabbed her by the arm, a strong grip that Jennifer was flustered to find she could not break. Before her attempt to escape led to violence, she decided to relax and turn. The other A-Listers were catching up to the two of them.

"Oh, Bobbie! It's you. Hey, Andi, Anne, Amy, Abigail. What's up?"

"Just thought we could talk. You know, new student and all. So where are you from?" Bobbie's voice did not sound particularly threatening and she had let go of her grip, but the question still made Jennifer nervous.

"I'm—er—from out of state. Just moved here."

"Your parents got a new job, or something? My parents moved me to this shit town five years ago; I could kill them for it." Bobbie took out a compact that looked not unlike the one Amanda Sera used and began to check her lipstick.

"They aren't— I don't have any— I mean, my parents are gone."

The other four girls gasped, but Bobbie barely missed a beat. She smacked her lips, flipped her compact shut, and cocked her head as if she smelled something strange. "That sucks. So where're you living?"

There was no point in lying. "With Skip Wilson."

"Oooh, he's cute. Doesn't he live with Ms. Saltin, the music teacher?"

"He's her nephew, I guess." Jennifer wanted to talk about something else.

Apparently, so did Bobbie. "Huh. So how about that chem class, am I right, Andi? I wonder if Ms. Sloane is ever going to let us take the chug test."

"The chug test?"

Bobbie turned to Amy Collins. "You got any widowmilk?"

Amy's brunette curls hopped up and down mischievously. "Yeah, in my locker!"

"Guys, I'm kinda hoping to meet Skip—"

It was no use. They all scrambled down the hall together, pushing Jennifer along. Jennifer had the presence of mind to seek out Andi, who seemed the most intelligent of the bunch.

"Widowmilk?"

Andi gave her an apologetic wink. "Black widow poison. Bobbie likes to show off for new friends. You should be flattered."

"Why—" Jennifer began, but Anne stepped between the two of them.

"So, you coming to practice tomorrow?"

"Practice? Oh, you mean cheerleader practice. I'm not really—"

Abigail squealed and gave Jennifer a scornful look. "As if! *Cheerleaders!* Hey, Bobbie, you wanna do a *cheerleader* routine after school?"

They all burst out laughing, and Jennifer felt herself redden. "Gee, Abby, I'm sorry I don't know every detail about your lives. I'm afraid I haven't pored over your bios just yet. And I've been here a whole four hours! Maybe you could give me a break and tell me what you're talking about."

Abigail flushed and mumbled something, but Anne and Andi gave Jennifer quick, appreciative winks.

"Soccer," Anne explained. "We play soccer. How about you?"

Jennifer felt herself grow three inches. "Oh, yeah. Varsity starter, back home." Then she stopped short. "It's November. You guys have a late season or something?"

Bobbie shrugged. "A bunch of area schools have a fall-winter season. Yours didn't?"

"No."

"How much milk you got?" Bobbie asked Amy.

"Ssshhh!" The brunette tilted her head at a nearby teacher as they pulled up to her locker. "I've already been busted twice for this. We gotta take it to the girls' room. Here, gimme a sec."

While Amy fumbled with the combination on her locker, Andi filled Jennifer in. "The soccer team has something of a tradition with widowmilk. What we're about to do isn't, well, legal."

"What!?" Jennifer's head swam with visions of expulsion. *That would be bad. Wouldn't it?*

Andi sighed. "It's not a big deal, I guess. Some teachers figure it's harmless and look the other way, but most students don't press their luck like these guys."

"Isn't this the same stuff Ms. Sloane was just showing us two classes ago?"

"Got it!" Amy slipped two small, opaque medicine bottles into her purse, and the six of them were off again.

"She keeps a whole bunch of poisons in the school storage locker," Andi explained. Jennifer was grateful for this strange girl's blend of calm and concern. "Anne's a bit of a teacher's pet, so she has the keys to run supplies up and down. She skims some, and Amy keeps it in her locker."

Both thrilled at the quickly growing rapport she had with this girl and appalled at what was going on, Jennifer scratched her head. "Why the hell do they take it?"

Andi looked down and tugged on the sleeves of her navy shirt. "Some people just do stupid things. But in Bobbie's case, it's not really a danger . . ."

They slipped into the girls' room, giggling and stealing glances into the empty toilet stalls. Once they were sure they were alone, Amy pulled out one of the medicine bottles and a hypodermic needle and handed them to Bobbie.

"You know the stuff about homeostasis that Ms. Sloane just taught us?" Andi asked Jennifer.

"Yeah."

"No one in Pinegrove has a more stable system than Bobbie. Watch this."

A stupid grin gracing her overly broad face, Bobbie held the small bottle high. The other girls began to chant.

"Milk, milk, milk!"

Playing to the audience with a great deal of flair, Bobbie pushed the needle into the vial, extracted all the fluid inside, pulled the needle out, and plunged it into her thick neck.

"Milk, milk, milk!"

It was over in four seconds. Bobbie wound up and threw the empty bottle against the far wall, where it smashed against the tile.

"Woooo!" she gasped and her eyeballs strained, but she never stopped smiling. "My heart is going nuts!" She grabbed Jennifer's hand and put it up against her chest. "Feel that! Isn't that *awesome*?!"

Jennifer was too startled to pull away. The large girl's heart was pounding harder than that of a horse, and faster than that of a mouse. But Bobbie was standing tall and suffering no other effects. In fact, she was using her free hand to poke through Amy's purse. "Where's that second bottle?"

"Take it easy, Bobbie!" Andi warned. "Even you can't do two bottles that fast."

"Not for me, Andi. For Jennifer. Ah, here it is."

Jennifer pulled her hand off of Bobbie's chest. "Uh, no. I've never— I can't— Thanks, Bobbie, but no way. I'm not doing that."

They all stared at her in silence. Bobbie held out the bottle in an open palm. "You can do it, Jenny."

"We all do it," Amy put in with a satisfied smirk. "It's nothing to be afraid of."

"You don't have to do a full bottle," Anne suggested. "Just a half-dose won't hurt you much. We all do okay."

*Yeah, but I'm nothing like you guys!* Jennifer looked around at them, all but Andi undoubtedly werachnid children. Like Skip, they were obviously resistant to toxins. Good for them. But she doubted a dragon's internal systems were as stable. In fact, when she considered skills like fire-breathing and camouflage, she supposed few beings were as volatile. Poison would probably cripple her.

And even if it didn't, this whole scene creeped her out. She took a step back. "I'm really not interested."

Bobbie took a matching step forward. "It's what we do, Jenny. It's a team tradition."

"Yeah, well then, screw your team and its traditions. I'm not doing it. Nice knowing you all."

With that, she turned and made for the exit.

"Wait, Jenny! Okay, you don't have to do it." Bobbie handed the bottle off to Amy and gave chase. She caught Jennifer's wrist and prevented her—once again, the strong bitch!—from going any farther. "You won't tell any of the teachers or Principal Mouton, will you?"

Jennifer sighed and faced them all again. "Bobbie, I'm not going to spend my first day in this school ratting out friends. You want to mess with that crap, go nuts. But don't ever try to push it on me again. That goes for all of you," she added, looking pointedly at Amy, who returned a sneer.

"Don't worry." Bobbie looked back at the others. "We'll all back off. Right, girls?"

They all shrugged. Andi, at least, nodded.

"You've got guts, Scales." Bobbie punched Jennifer lightly in the shoulder. "I'll bet you're a force with a soccer ball."

"I am," Jennifer answered. "But my guts can't handle what you just handled. How are you not vomiting blood?"

Bobbie laughed. With her face this close, Jennifer could make out the scent of onions on the larger girl's breath. "Poison tests us. Poison strengthens us. Poison is life . . ."

That got them all chanting again, and Jennifer slowly backed out of the restroom before another needle contest could begin.

It bothered her that this world was so different. It bothered her that this world was so familiar. It bothered her that she could never tell what was going to be waiting around the corner.

And it bothered her most of all that here at Pinegrove High, she was not even close to being the strongest.

*Tavia Saltin and Edmund Slider,* out of their teacher roles and in the comfort of home, appeared sympathetic to Jennifer's plight as Skip related her "story" to them after school.

"Parents killed by a drunk driver!" Tavia clucked as she rummaged through the foyer closet. "And on top of that, an abusive uncle! No wonder you were so quick to run away with only the clothes on your back. Edmund, it's like I've told you—society today is topsy-turvy. Nothing is right with the world, anymore. Heaven knows who's taken over, but it's certainly not the good guys."

"I suppose," Mr. Slider drawled. He and Jennifer had spent a great deal of time looking each other up and down since their meeting in the house this afternoon. As strange as Jennifer no doubt seemed to him, his appearance was no less stunning—not only because he stood tall, without a wheelchair, and walked as easily as if he had been doing it all his life. (Which, for all Jennifer knew, in this universe, he had been.) But also because his face was partially mutilated. His elegant, tanned European features crumbled into a mess of scar tissue that dominated where his right eye, temple, and ear would have been. From the left, he looked like a Hollywood star; from the right, a Hollywood monster.

"We have got to get you down to the mall and into some new clothes!" Tavia would not hear of any argument. "You can't be wearing Skip's dreary stuff while you're staying with us. Just a few outfits, something that will really cling to that lovely shape of yours. Come on, Skip. Edmund, are you coming with us? It's a nice evening for a walk about the mall."

"I'll stay here, dear. I've work to do." His tone was distant. His hand was working through his slick blond hair as usual, as if he were distracted by other, grander ideas. *Maybe he's trying to figure out how to get his face back to normal,* Jennifer thought with some suspicion. Had he started this sorcery? Was this mutilation the price he paid to get his legs back?

*How did he end up in that wheelchair, anyway?*

It frustrated her that she had no real way to ask him.

*Pinegrove Mall was an* encouragingly familiar sight, with all of the stores Jennifer remembered from Winoka Mall, and in the right order. There was the sports clothing outlet, and the place with overpriced shoes, and the upscale maternity dress shop, and the pet store . . .

Her thoughts trailed off as she looked into the pet store windows. Where once had been two large entryway displays where Daniel's Pets had showcased the "puppy and kitten of the week" was now a series of smaller displays, separated from each other by a series of glass walls.

In each small cubicle was a different eight-legged surprise, each one plumper and uglier than the last. MINI-ARACHNID'S ON SPECIAL, the sign read.

"Ugh, will you look at that! Disgusting!" Tavia spat as she came up behind Jennifer's stricken face. "They've spelled the plural with an apostrophe! Skip, I swear, if you do that on so much as a birthday card, I will drain your blood myself . . . Oh, Jennifer, look at that sun spider! It really seems to like you!"

Jennifer had no preconceived notion what a sun spider looked like, but she guessed that the beige, naked, spindly, grotesque, melon-sized creature humping the glass near her face was it. Reading the sign, s.s.: $240, she found the thing a bit over-priced.

"Let's check out sweaters," she suggested as its legs wriggled for better position.

The clothing stores held no unpleasant surprises. There were no slacks with more than two legs and no eight-lens sunglasses. Like dragons, Jennifer supposed, arachnids kept their fashion needs limited to their human shapes. This was good, because it removed a source of possibly uncomfortable questions. *What's your abdomen size? Pincers or no? Hairy gross body, or smooth gross body?*

Giggling madly to herself in the solitude of the dressing room, she took her time with about a dozen sweater-skirt outfits and let herself think once more. The primary question on her mind: *How long should I stay here in Pinegrove, before striking out for somewhere else?*

The answer, she decided while shrugging into something slinky and electric blue, depended on where "somewhere else" meant. She had at least two options: Eveningstar, which seemed the most likely place her parents would be since they had lived there before moving to Winoka, or her grandfather's farm on her way to Crescent Valley. The two places were in somewhat opposite directions, so she would have to choose which one she investigated first.

*Fabulous,* she praised herself while looking in the dressing room mirror. Then she frowned at the bulges her daggers made in the tight skirt. *Damn. Won't work.*

*Of course,* she realized while exchanging the electric blue for a looser violet wool outfit, *I don't have to visit Eveningstar, do I? I can just research it.* Then she could take her cues from there.

"Hey, Ms. Saltin." She came out of the dressing room and spun around a bit for her new benefactor, who clapped her wiry hands. "Do you have an Internet connection at home? I'd like to check on some news sites for school assignments tonight."

"Oh, Jennifer, that's a lovely set! You have to put that in the 'yes' pile. Of course we have an Internet connection; the computer's right in the living room. We can check the sites together. I'd be happy to help you. Why, I'll bet you've never had a parent or guardian truly take an interest in your schoolwork, have you?"

Jennifer chose not to answer. The Internet connection did her no good if Tavia would be hovering over her the entire time. She would have to research things the old-fashioned way—traveling and poking around.

The remainder of their shopping trip went well enough. Tavia was generous enough to pay for seven outfits—one for each day, she insisted, though Jennifer had no interest in staying around here a full week—and a couple pairs of lovely flats that went with all of them, since Jennifer was a few sizes bigger than her hostess and couldn't borrow.

*It's not real money,* Jennifer told herself as she watched Tavia pay with a credit card. *The real Tavia hasn't paid a cent, and there won't be any imposition once I've gotten everything back in order.*

The logic made her pause. If lying to Tavia and taking advantage of her generosity wasn't wrong because this universe didn't matter, would she rationalize hurting this woman if she ever got in the way? For that matter, why not get her alone and torture her for information? She *had* to know something about that big, ugly domed building behind the high school . . .

Before she could untangle the morality of it all, Skip took her elbow and whispered in her ear. "You want to get ice cream at our favorite place?"

Jennifer tensed. "'Our favorite place' is nowhere near here. Remember?"

"You know what I mean," he said with a sigh. "Can you loosen up just a tiny bit?"

"No. Skip, if you're not going to get to the bottom of things, I will." She shrugged off his hand. "So, Ms. Saltin, whatever happened to Skip's parents?"

Tavia Saltin stopped short in the middle of the mall and turned slowly. For a moment, Jennifer was sure the woman would suddenly burst into evil laughter and reveal herself as behind it all. But instead, there were tears in the slight woman's blue-green eyes, and she directed her first words to Skip.

"Oh, the sacrifices your family has made, my dear boy!" she said to him softly. Then she did look at Jennifer. "A long time ago, they asked Edmund and me to watch over Skip. We've done so gladly. But I know it's hard on him, isn't it, Skip? And you've already given up so much."

Then the werachnid began to cry.

*Back in the privacy* of Tavia and Edmund's guest room, Jennifer chewed her tongue thoughtfully while taping the pieces of her father's note together.

She had not pressed Tavia for any more detail on Skip's parents at the mall. For one, if they weren't raising Skip, then it made sense they weren't around. And if they weren't around, then they weren't useful to her.

Second, Skip had turned white as a sheet when Jennifer had broken open the topic like that. Tavia had recovered well enough, but her nephew remained furious the entire drive home. After dumping her bags full of new clothes in the guest room, he had wordlessly left and slammed the door behind him.

*Stay as strong as stone. Stay as beautiful as fire. Stay alive.*

"Poor Skip," she mumbled at the note's last few words while pressing down a new piece of tape. "What a horrible day this must have been for him, *not* getting ripped apart from his family."

It felt good to say something cruel like that, and she wished he were in the room so he could hear it. While weighing the wisdom of walking down to his bedroom to share the sentiment, she noticed a tiny movement above.

A lone box elder bug was crawling across the ceiling,

moving from some unseen crack in the bedroom window toward the warmer interior of the house.

"You look lonely," she told the insect. "And in a world of spiders, I'll bet you're not too happy."

The beetle continued its near-mindless meandering, working a slow but eventual route toward the wall opposite the window. Once it rattled its black and red wings, considered taking flight, and then settled down into a crawl again.

The tiny buzzing sound it had made reminded her of a much bigger noise, from a much bigger insect—the fire hornet queen of Crescent Valley.

Thinking of that day—it had been just yesterday!—made her think of Ned Brownfoot, and then of Ember and Xavier Longtail. The Longtails had opposed Jennifer's work to bring weredragons and beaststalkers together. Had they been right?

"No," she told the bug that crawled over her head. "They were wrong. If dragons and stalkers had been working together better, they could have stopped this! And if more dragons had been reaching out to more people like Skip, something like this may not ever have happened to begin with!"

The insect did not answer. Instead, it made a slight right turn.

Her thoughts turned to her mother and her father. Her father had told her to stay put and live with this new reality. Would her mother agree?

"She wouldn't," she told the bug. "And not just because she's smarter than Dad. It's because she's not afraid to change the world, and Dad is. She stood up to Mayor Seabright and all of Winoka, when everyone wanted to kill Evangelina. She apologized to the Longtails the moment she met them, even though she knew they'd want to kill her. And she got mad at Dad for lying to the other dragons, just so he and Grandpa could keep the peace. She wouldn't stand for this. She'd know it's sneaky and wrong."

"Jennifer, dear?" Tavia's voice came from beyond the closed door. "Are you all right? Is someone else in there?"

She scrambled to shove the newly reconstructed note under the bedsheets. "I'm okay, Tavia. I'm just—"

The door opened, and Tavia's thin skull pressed through the opening. She scanned the room and Jennifer resting on the bed. "Just coming up to let you know that dinner's ready. Oh, you look tired, dear."

"I guess I am. Sorry about the noise. I'm just talking to the bug." She pointed to the ceiling. "I know, pretty weird."

Tavia glanced up and saw the beetle. Her lips thinned a touch. "It's no problem at all, dear. Dinner will be ready in a few minutes. And don't worry about that bug. It won't last long."

"I guess not. Not this time of year."

But the door was already closed, and Jennifer was no longer sure Tavia meant anything about box elder bug seasonality.

"Man, this place is creepy," she whispered to the beetle after a few moments. "Are you sure you want to stick around?"

With new resolve, she got up, left her room, and strode down the hall to Skip's room. He was at his desk, sketching various spider shapes with headphones on.

"Skip," she called out. *"Skip."*

He finally heard her and removed the headphones. "What."

"Skip, I don't want you to be mad at me. I want your help getting out of here."

He leaned back and flipped his pencil down. "I don't blame you for asking about my parents. But I already knew the answer. I never even had to ask my aunt. I just didn't want to deal—"

"It's okay," she said with a step forward. "I'm sorry, you're sorry, let's just move on. Skip, I need to learn if anything's happened at Eveningstar. I need to know if my parents are there."

"There is an Eveningstar," he answered with a nod. "And we can learn more about them this Saturday afternoon. Their soccer team comes to play Pinegrove then. You up for sticking around that long?"

She shrugged. "My other option is to get to Crescent Valley and see who's left."

"But you think your parents might still be alive and in Eveningstar, right?"

The very thought made her heart buzz with excitement. "Let's be ready for Saturday. If that doesn't work out, then you'll come with me to Crescent Valley?"

He stood up and held her, making her shiver. "Jennifer. I traveled to a whole new universe with you. I'll go wherever you want. Just take the time to think it through."

She hugged him back, the only link she had to the world she used to know.

# CHAPTER 8

## Wednesday

The next morning got off to nearly as bad a start as the previous one. She woke up early and thought to summon a bird of some sort, beaststalker-style. Maybe she would get a golden eagle like her mother could, she reasoned, or at least the snake eagle that seemed to favor her. Something like that could fly high, scout things out. And most important, send a signal to other beaststalkers who might be near.

But what came out of her summoning ritual was a mere kestrel, which had upon the command of its mistress flown out the window and made it about two hundred yards before something gray and hairy leapt out of the trees in the nearby park and brought it down with a deathly shriek.

*Well, maybe I just saved a cow,* she reasoned, and got ready for school. She decided upon the violet wool skirt and sweater set, which really had looked smashing when she tried it on at the mall. Even today, when the post-purchase glow had faded, it still felt like an armor of sorts against the insanity she still faced.

Unfortunately, wool was a poor defense against academic ignorance. She had missed the double-math class yesterday . . . and her first taste of it today was less than savory. Mr. Slider walked briskly up and down the aisles, grinning at his pupils through one good eye and asking questions with a breezy sort of nonchalance. That wasn't so bad, and it did Jennifer's heart good to see the man on two working legs—but the questions!

This universe had seemingly abandoned notions of basic geometry and arithmetic and replaced them with something vicious called differential geometry. Differential geometry, according to the introduction in the wicked, weathered textbook Mr. Slider had handed her, involved "differential equations," "differential topology," and "differential manifolds."

Unfortunately, none of the six authors of the book (all Ph.D.'s in various stultifying and probably imaginary realms of academia) thought to define the word differential. The best Jennifer could come up with was "ridiculously different from anything sensible."

Of course, everyone else in the class had mastered it and answered every question correctly (if Mr. Slider's smiles and encouragement were any indication).

Can manifolds be embedded into Euclidean space? Apparently so.

Can a ruled surface be unwrapped? Apparently not.

Does orienting a Boy's Surface involve anything like what Jennifer would have thought? Not even close.

With her head still spinning from this terminological assault, she stumbled into history class, where she found out three disturbing things about modern Minnesota's history from an earnest teacher named Mr. Cahoon, who had chestnut hair and freckles and looked about twelve:

1. Minneapolis had the tallest building in North America, an architectural marvel finished less than a decade ago. From the glossy pictures in their brand-new history books, the structure had eight shimmering walls and a unique, funneled roof that spun the wind into glorious melodies for the workers within.

2. St. Paul had emerged as the arts capital of the world over the past thirty or forty years, as prodigy after prodigy emerged from nearby towns like Pinegrove and settled in the larger city.

3. Alexandria, a small city in western Minnesota surrounded by lakes, had been the site of considerable civilian unrest sixty years ago. Hundreds of the "instigators" had died. From the grim photographs, Jennifer could make out a few reptilian skulls.

She didn't have much time to explore these events since the

time given to history was considerably shorter than the time allowed for mathematics, music, or even chemistry. The bell rang before she knew it, and just like that she had to close the textbook, promising to study it later that night.

Music was okay. Andi, the guest star for yesterday's class, wasn't there this time. Bobbie was, but something about the blonde Amazon gave Jennifer the creeps. She kept to herself as Tavia turned from the web harp to something a bit more conventional—the piano. She played it with four tarsi, in her spider shape. Like her brother, Otto Saltin, who Jennifer recalled with a shiver, Tavia was predominantly black, with orange and red markings on her abdomen. While four tarsi were not as many as ten fingers, they moved faster and could occupy more ranges on the piano than two hands. The composition, like the player, was striking and disturbing. At the end, Jennifer couldn't get out of music class fast enough.

Rubbing her temples as she walked past rows of lockers on her way to chemistry, Jennifer bumped into a girl racing down the hallway. They both gasped—the other girl in pain, and Jennifer in utter astonishment.

*"Catherine?!"*

The girl's mouth twisted into a skeptical smile as she rubbed her elbows. "Do I know you?"

"Catherine, it's me! Jennifer! How is this . . . How did you get here?"

"Get here? I've lived in this town my whole life. And my name's not Catherine. What's your name again?"

A chill slid into Jennifer's gut. *She's Catherine, but not Catherine. Like Bobbie isn't Bob Jarkmand. Like Minneapolis isn't the real Minneapolis, or my dead parents aren't really dead.*

She composed herself quickly enough to extend a hand. "Um, I'm sorry. You just looked like someone from my old town. I'm Jennifer Scales."

"Oh! The new girl, right? Andi told me about you. I'm Nakia Brandfire."

"Nakia. Um, okay." *At least the last name is the same.* "Do you have . . . um, I'm just wondering, because I knew this girl . . . she had a relative named Winona Brandfire. Do you . . . ?"

Jennifer trailed off, because she saw the expression on Nakia's face. It hovered somewhere between astonishment and terror.

"Forget I asked," Jennifer muttered, and spun away to dash off.

Her thoughts were in turmoil as she slipped behind her desk in chemistry. Catherine was here. The fact that she had a different first name meant little or nothing. What meant a lot more was that she had recognized the name of Winona Brandfire, though not necessarily in a positive way.

*That makes sense,* Jennifer reasoned. *Since Winona was a weredragon, her family would want to hide that fact. Just like Andi wants to hide things.*

Reassuring herself with the thought of two potential allies in just two days, Jennifer waved at Andi as the girl came into class. This actually got Andi to sit next to her, which thrilled Jennifer. She tried hard not to stare at Andi's sleeves—navy blue today— and think about what was underneath them.

Instead, as Ms. Sloane took her position at the front of the class, Jennifer thought about Catherine/Nakia. An unbidden memory pricked the back of her mind. What was it Catherine had told her Sunday evening?

*Don't be surprised if something cool happens later this week.*

Jennifer shook her head. There was no way any of the Brandfires would think of what had happened this week as cool . . .

"This," Ms. Sloane announced as her long, green-tipped finger caressed a small test tube before the chemistry class, "is potassium perchlorate. Also known as potassium salt, perchloric acid, or potassium hyperchlorite."

She turned to the blackboard and wrote in her graceful script:

$$POTASSIUM\ PERCHLORATE\ (KCLO_4)$$

"It has plenty of poisonous properties," she continued. "It's a strong irritant to skin, mucous membranes, respiratory and gastrointestinal tracts, and anywhere else it goes. Causes vomiting, fever, and rashes in light to moderate doses, as in the sample I have here. Heavy exposure—the sort you might get if you play around with this school's locked storage area without knowing what you're doing—leads to a breakdown of red blood cells and can cause extensive kidney damage. And therefore, possibly, death."

A murmur of interest suffused the class. Jennifer felt her insides tighten.

Ms. Sloane put the test tube down on her desk. "We are entering the potassium unit today, class. Potassium is a fine start to any serious study of poison. It is a basic element that, like everything else we discussed yesterday, is essential in small quantities—and deadly under certain circumstances.

"By the end of this unit," she continued as she raised a fresh yardstick (*And how many of those does she have,* Jennifer wondered), "you will make your own potassium perchlorate. Today, however, we are going to do a far simpler experiment, demonstrating some of potassium's basic properties. Please pair up around the experiment stations."

Andi gave Jennifer a nod as the two of them found a station together. While passing out small glass dishes of potassium to each pair, Ms. Sloane related several fun facts about potassium. For example, Jennifer learned that potassium makes up 2.4 percent of the Earth's crust. (*Just this Earth or the real one, too?* she wondered.) Easy to cut with a knife (provided), never found free in nature, and susceptible to rapid oxidation, the samples came doused in mineral oil.

"Goggles and gloves," Ms. Sloane reminded them before they started. "Get a small dish out from under your station and fill it with just a bit of water. Then take a slice of the potassium, and place it in the water . . ."

Distracted by the thought of the potassium chloride and what she might have to do with the poison at the end of this unit—*swallow it? Breathe it in gas form? Smear it all over my face like base?*—Jennifer was only half-listening to the instructions. She grabbed the potassium dish and put it directly under the water faucet, and then cranked the cold water on top of it.

"Oh, no," Andi whispered urgently. "Don't do it that way. You might—"

Jennifer couldn't explain how, but she could *feel* the explosion coming. Whatever sense was operating inside, it gave her just enough warning. A scaled wing shot up as the glass dish flew apart in a cloud of lilac fire. It was a modest explosion but involved blinding light and a sharp, lingering sizzle. A split second later, the wing was gone, leaving only Jennifer's human arms appearing to protect the other girl.

The sound made everyone duck before they turned, and the bright flash from the reaction had sheltered Jennifer's odd shape from everyone—everyone but Andi. The girl now scanned Jennifer up and down, her astonished brown eyes nearly bulging through the safety goggles.

"Andi! Jennifer! Are you all right?" Ms. Sloane hurried toward the back of the room, green fingernails clutching Jennifer by the shoulders. "What happened?"

"I'm sorry, Ms. Sloane." She straightened, trying to ignore Andi. "I used too much potassium, and—"

"Jenny! You're on fire!" Bobbie rushed over from the next table and began pelting Jennifer's backside with a rag.

Bobbie was right. The back of Jennifer's beautiful violet wool skirt was smoldering, from the hem to the waist. It was a miracle that the blades she wore weren't visible. With a small shriek, she dropped to the speckled linoleum floor and rolled back and forth.

Ms. Sloane was quick with a blanket. A few moments later, everyone was standing up and fire-free.

"Scott," the teacher told one of the other students, "get down to the office and tell them we have a mess here that needs cleaning up. Jennifer, are you sure you're okay?"

Jennifer's nerves were still frazzled, but she was grateful that the situation appeared salvageable. If she could just get Andi alone for a moment . . .

"What's that?" Bobbie was pointing a gloved finger at Jennifer's calf, where an inch-long piece of glass was poking out of her flesh. It was more likely it got there as a result of rolling about in the remains of the glass dish than from the explosive force, and it didn't even hurt, but blood was slowly trickling from the wound.

*Aha! Luck at last!* "Oh! Gosh, Ms. Sloane, I should get down to the nurse's office right away, shouldn't I? Andi, could you help me? I might need to hold onto someone."

"Sure," Andi answered carefully, pulling off her safety goggles and gloves. Jennifer still wasn't sure how this girl was going to react to what she had seen. But at least they'd have a chance to talk.

"I'll go, too!"

Jennifer snapped her goggles off. *Crap.* "Thanks, Bobbie. But could you stay until class ends, and take notes—"

"No, it's a good idea for two of you to go," Ms. Sloane cut in. "Class, let this be a lesson to everyone! 'Poison tests us,' indeed! Andi, Bobbie, do come back when you can and let me know how Jennifer's doing."

"Sure, Ms. Sloane," they answered together. Before Jennifer could protest further, they each had a shoulder under one of her arms and were helping her walk out of class.

"Wow, Jenny," Bobbie giggled as they maneuvered down the empty hall together like some limping, six-legged beast. "You were barely in this school twenty-four hours before you blew something up!"

Jennifer tried a short laugh, but it sounded fake even to her own ears. "Listen, you two, don't take me to the nurse's office."

"Why not?" Andi asked.

*You know why not.* A medically trained werachnid might ask inconvenient questions about Jennifer's shape-changing abilities—or worse, might be able to detect differences without even asking. "It's just that it's . . . it's not that bad. I don't want this to be a big deal. It's so embarrassing!"

"Where to, then?" Bobbie asked.

She thought fast. "Locker room. We've got study hall next anyway . . . If this takes a while, no one will miss us. Then I go to Spanish class, while you guys have math and geometry. And then we can meet for soccer practice after that."

"Soccer!" Bobbie couldn't hold back a laugh. "Jenny, you've gotta be made out of steel! Come on, Andi. She's not bleeding to death or anything. If it happened to me, I guess I'd wanna keep it quiet, too."

"That's exactly what I want." She tried to give Andi a meaningful look, but couldn't tell if it had any impact. "Thanks, you two. You're the best."

It was quiet in the girls' locker room. They settled Jennifer down on one of the narrow benches among the lockers, and then Bobbie helped elevate the leg.

"We should get bandages ready before you try to pull that out," Bobbie suggested. "I cut my arm against a shattered window once, and you wouldn't believe how—"

"Where's Andi?" Jennifer's blood chilled.

Bobbie looked around. "Huh. She probably already went to go get some. I'll go help. You okay here?"

Jennifer was in a true fix. If she let Bobbie find Andi, the two of them might talk before Jennifer got a chance to explain anything. If she asked Bobbie to stay, Andi would find someone else—someone possibly less sympathetic.

As it turned out, she didn't even have time to make a decision. "I'll just be a second," Bobbie said, and then she was gone.

Alone, Jennifer figured she had nothing to lose. She reached down and yanked the piece of glass out with a wince. Blood came out a bit more thickly, but a quick morph into dragon shape helped close the wound a bit. Something in the process of changing, she had noticed in the past, seemed to help healing.

It was only a few seconds before she heard both girls' voices echoing through the locker room again. They were using low voices, and she couldn't make the words out. She quickly changed her shape back and was lying down by the time they turned the corner and saw her.

"Oh, you got it out!" If Andi had said anything about Jennifer, Bobbie appeared no less friendly for it. "And it doesn't look like it's bleeding too bad. We found some bandages, and a washcloth. Let me go rinse this out, and then we can start wrapping . . ."

Then she was off again, still babbling about hot water and the state of the school plumbing system. Andi stayed with Jennifer. The two of them stared at each other for a moment, until Bobbie's voice faded.

"You saw," Jennifer finally ventured.

Andi nodded, and her brown eyes fell.

"Andi, please. You can't tell anyone."

The brunette looked around nervously. "I don't know. I . . ."

"*Please*, Andi." She could feel the sweat leaking from her pores. "I'm alone. I shouldn't be here. I don't have anybody I can trust. I need someone, Andi. I need you to help me."

"What are you doing here?"

"It's not my choice, I—"

"Are you going to kill anyone?"

"Oh, Andi, don't be afraid."

"Tell me you won't kill anyone."

"I'm not going to kill anyone. Maybe we can help each other. I—"

"Success!" Bobbie's voice rang out over the lockers a few seconds before she appeared with a steaming hot washcloth. "Let's get started!"

It took some time to clean the wound and dress it. Bobbie tried it first, but she dropped the washcloth and knocked the bandages on the grimy carpet, so she had to get new material. After that, Andi took over, grabbing the supplies from Bobbie and sitting down next to Jennifer.

Even this young, her hands were clearly quite skilled at this sort of work. She briskly rolled up Jennifer's skirt just above the knee, careful to support the wounded calf the entire time. Then she slowly pressed her fingers around the wound, as if looking for something.

"You've done this before?" Jennifer guessed.

"Medicine runs in my family."

"Mine, too." She swallowed at Andi's guarded look. "It did, anyway."

"I don't suppose you can find some hydrogen peroxide?" Andi asked Bobbie.

"Probably locked in the coach's office."

"Hmm." She looked at Jennifer. "You'll probably need to head home once this is bandaged. You're staying with Skip Wilson, right?"

"Yeah."

"He knows?"

"How can he know?" Bobbie interrupted. "We came straight here from chemistry."

Jennifer answered Andi's true question. "He knows." Then she turned to Bobbie. "He knows what to do with an injured leg. He's, um, had one."

"But she can't go home!" Bobbie's face fell. "We were going to have her come to soccer practice!"

Andi pursed her lips. "I don't think that's a good idea." Still cradling Jennifer's leg under one hand, she used the other to gently pat the wound with the washcloth. "Hand me the bandage, Bobbie? Preferably without dropping it."

Bobbie handed her the new roll. "She only has to watch. We've already got a good team, and Jenny says she's played varsity before! I'll bet she's great, Andi."

Chewing her tongue nervously, Jennifer sided with the girl who held her leg—and life—in her hands. "It's okay, Bobbie.

Andi's right. I'll catch practice on Friday. You need me to hold that end?"

"Thanks." Andi began winding the bandage around Jennifer's calf. She slowly lowered it as she did so, cradling Jennifer by the knee instead of the ankle so she could get around and around. "Soccer's important, Bobbie. But it's not everything. The world will still be spinning Friday, just the way it is now. And it will for Saturday's big game, or at the practice next Wednesday for the next game!"

This didn't seem to please Bobbie much, but there was nothing the hulking girl could do. She crossed her arms and let out a deep sigh. "This sucks. Why'dja have to go blow yourself up, Jenny?"

Despite herself, Jennifer began to chuckle. So did the other two girls.

Until Andi's hand accidentally brushed under Jennifer's skirt and hit the dagger strapped to her left thigh.

Jennifer and Andi both froze. Without breaking off her stare with Jennifer, Andi slowly withdrew her hand and finished up the bandage.

"I think we should get you out of those clothes now," she said firmly.

"Oh, no, it's okay, I—"

"Jenny, they're burned!" Bobbie's tone was completely casual, in contrast to Andi's severe expression. "The back of your sweater had holes in it, even before we left chemistry class. I've got some spare stuff in my locker you can use."

"But everyone will—"

"Now." Andi wasn't taking any nonsense.

Jennifer sighed, sat up, and pulled off her sweater. When she examined it, she saw Bobbie was right: The wool had several small burn holes in it.

"Got your shell, too." Bobbie pointed to a yellowish-brown stain on the cream-colored fabric. "You're lucky you had two layers. Get rid of that, too, Jenny. My shirt'll look better." She turned to a locker right next to them and began dialing the combination.

With no reason to argue, Jennifer took the shirt off.

"Your skirt, too." Andi insisted. "It's wrecked all down the back."

She gave Andi a pleading look and received nothing in return but cool air.

"Fine," she said through gritted teeth. "I'm just glad it's my clothes that got hit, and not *yours*, dear. What you're wearing looks so much more . . . *fragile* than what I had on! Thank goodness I could protect you!"

The heavy hint found its mark. Andi swallowed and softened her expression. "I know," she said softly. "Thanks."

Jennifer slid the skirt down, careful not to let it catch on the daggers or the buckles on their sheaths. She had been in locker rooms in front of other girls with less than the underwear she had left, but she had never felt more exposed in her life.

Both girls stared at the daggers. Bobbie whistled.

"Wow, Jenny. You know there's a strict no-weapons policy at the school. Mouton would expel you in a second if he found out!"

"They're j-just for self-defense," Jennifer stammered. "You guys won't tell anyone, will you? I can explain . . ."

"Don't worry. That can wait," said Andi. "For now, you should get dressed. Bobbie, what do you have in there? My stuff's too small for her."

"I always keep an extra gym outfit in here. It's clean. Might be a size too big for you, but it shouldn't matter."

Andi carefully folded up Jennifer's clothes and gave them to Bobbie, who put them away in the locker.

"You'll need to give those up, too," Andi ordered, pointing at the weapons on Jennifer's bare thighs. "The shorts won't hide them."

With a heavy heart, Jennifer unstrapped both daggers and handed them over. Andi passed them on to Bobbie, who put them on top of the folded clothes. The larger girl rearranged the locker contents so that a soccer ball hid most of the contraband from a casual glance, and then pressed the locker shut with a clang.

"Okay, I should get dressed now." Jennifer held her hands out for the clothes.

Andi took the extra outfit from Bobbie, but then held it. "Hang on."

Jennifer felt her whole body turn cold and warm at the same time as she glanced at the secure locker that held her only possessions. She tried to grab for the gym clothes but the other girl took a quick step back. "Andi, please."

"I want you to tell me and Bobbie something."

Realizing Andi could simply run away if she wanted to, Jennifer let her arms rest protectively in front of her chest. "What?"

"I want you to tell us you're going straight home after Spanish, and you won't try to come to soccer practice." Andi flicked her magenta-streaked hair behind her left ear. "Do you promise?"

Jennifer let out a breath. "Yes, I promise. Just, please, let me get dressed!"

Andi grinned and handed her the clothes.

"There's a sports bra in there, too," Bobbie offered helpfully. "It might go a bit better than what you've got on there."

"I suppose," Jennifer answered with a glance at her lacy, lilac bra. "Goodness knows if I burn your shirt off next, I'll want to match underneath!"

That got them giggling again.

"Don't forget sneakers," Bobbie reminded her, tossing her a pair. "Flats don't go at all with what you'll be wearing now!"

*The outfit wasn't exactly* what Jennifer had hoped for—she felt rather conspicuous with shiny yellow Lycra shorts on her butt and an overlarge red T-shirt with FRISKY written in big black letters across the front—but it was, she thought, better than the alternative.

And it did help her learn what the huge, ugly dome was behind the school.

"Hey," came a boy's grainy voice behind her in study hall. "Frisky."

Clapping a hand to her forehead and cursing Bobbie for her casual sense of style, Jennifer turned around. "Yeah, that's me. Frisky. Who are you—Dopey?"

The boy sitting at the next desk was vaguely familiar to her from Winoka High—short and stocky, with lots of stubble on a ruddy face, well-muscled, crew cut, a running back on the football team. Marky? Matty? Whatever. He hung around with Bob Jarkmand, she remembered. When Bob was Bob, and men were men.

"Frisky. That's Bobbie's shirt, ain't it? Sez Frisky."

"I guess."

He chuckled through a leer. "Yeah, Frisky. I remember Bobbie bein' frisky."

*Stop saying frisky!* "What a captivating story. I smell a Pulitzer. You should probably leave me alone and start writing your memoirs right now . . ."

"Yeah," he blundered on, oblivious to her suggestion, "we macked behind the observatory. Got real busy. That Bobbie has real fruit jiggling around her gelatin, if you know what I mean." He sniggered, a slow sort of *heh-heh-heh* as he dully ogled Jennifer's breasts.

"How poetic. I'm sure your way with words is what unlocked the gardens of her passion. Listen, creep, I— What observatory?"

"Huh?" His eyes stayed on her chest, perhaps still working their way through the text.

She snapped a hand out and grabbed the flesh under his jawbone, making him gasp. Ignoring his efforts to remove her hand, she lifted his head until he was looking her in the face. "Awwwb-suuur-vaaaa-torrr-eee. There's one in this town?" *And, ick, a girl actually let you feel her up next to it?*

He nodded as best he could. "Yeah. You know. Behind the school?" His thumb jerked off to the side. "Where all the astronomy classes are?"

Throwing the fool's head back so that he fell off his chair, Jennifer spun around in her own seat and tried to think.

*It's an observatory.*

*Astronomy classes are held there.*

*Astronomy is one of four quadrivium subjects.*

*I'm not in an astronomy class, the only one of the four they excused me from.*

*They put me in Spanish instead.*

*I therefore have no reason to go to the observatory.*

*Clever of them.*

*In Spanish class,* she ignored new vocabulary words like *desatento* and *complot*, and kept strategizing.

Who did she know who went to astronomy class? *Skip, Bobbie, the A-List. How about Andi?* She wasn't sure.

Would any of them help her get in? She imagined she could count on Skip, though she was a bit perturbed at him for not telling her last night that he had a class there. *Maybe it's a morning class and he missed it the first day, like you did with Ungodly Math 909,* she reasoned. She could certainly ask him about that today after school. Maybe they could even agree to sneak into the observatory before Saturday afternoon's soccer game with Eveningstar.

And what about Bobbie? No, she didn't quite trust her yet. Maybe it was who she/he was at Winoka High, or maybe it was the unnerving strength she had shown with that poison in the girls' room. But she didn't seem the type to go along with a plan that didn't have her in a lead role.

That left the rest of the A-List out, since they would probably all blab to Bobbie . . . with the possible exception of Andi. After all, Andi knew her secret now—and she hadn't said anything to anyone. Should she invite Andi to come along with Skip and her?

Just as the bell rang for the end of school, she decided that she would.

*Leaving class,* she was surprised to run right into Bobbie and Andi, along with Abigail, Anne, and Amy.

"Oh! Hey, guys." She let a corner of her mouth turn up. "You checking on me to make sure I go straight home? Don't worry, I'm . . ." She trailed off when she saw their expressions. Bobbie looked angry, and Andi looked miserable again. "What's wrong?"

The larger girl abruptly straightened and put on a shiny smile. "Nothing! Last class was a big bummer. Mr. Frost—our mathematics and geometry teacher—is such a jerk. He spent most of the time yelling at Andi here, just because she doesn't like going up to the blackboard to present stuff. I wish we had Slider; I hear he's way cooler. Anyway, come on. Time for soccer practice."

"But I thought you wanted me to go straight home!"

"Oh." Bobbie tossed her tight bob of blonde hair carelessly. "Yeah, Andi and I talked about that. Your leg's okay to walk, isn't it? You can just come watch. Right, Andi?"

Andi silently examined the corner of the textbook she held in her trembling hands.

Jennifer's head was full of clamoring alarm bells. *She knows. Andi told her.*

But before she could even think to run, the other three girls had surrounded her with forced smiles, and they were hustling her down the hallway, with Bobbie in the lead and Andi trailing behind. Nobody said anything as they walked. Jennifer desperately looked around for Skip, but the hallway was full of strange and unhelpful faces.

"You look great in that T-shirt!" Bobbie loudly called over her shoulder as she skipped into the girls' locker room. "But I think I need it back for soccer practice. You don't mind, do you?" This made Jennifer halt at the doorway, but six firm hands pushed her in.

There was another group of girls passing through the locker room, and Jennifer caught a glimpse of a coach walking out a back entrance, but she knew calling for help would only make things worse. Bobbie took her by the wrist and led her over to the bench where earlier they had wrapped her leg.

"Now." Her strong hand let go of Jennifer's wrist. "How about that shirt."

Jennifer looked from unfriendly face to unfriendly face. They were in a circle around her. Sighing, she yanked the shirt off and tossed it to Bobbie.

"By the way," she shot at Bobbie, "I hear that shirt's been busy behind the observatory."

The remark didn't faze Bobbie. "Sneakers."

She kicked them off. They made sullen thumps against the tile floor. The bottoms of her bare feet itched.

"Shorts."

"Bobbie, she doesn't have—"

"*Shut up*, Andi."

Jennifer took the shorts off and held them out.

"Thanks." Bobbie winked as she took them. "You can keep the sports bra; I never had much use for it behind the observatory. Hold her, girls. I don't want her making a move with the locker open."

Amy and Abigail each took tight hold of an arm. While their grips were not as strong as Bobbie's, Jennifer didn't bother moving. If these girls only wanted to humiliate her, then struggling would only alert others who might want to do worse. And if these girls wanted to do worse themselves . . . Well, she'd worry about that then.

Bobbie undressed and put on the clothes she had lent Jennifer. "Thank goodness I had these for both of us today, huh, Jenny?" She opened up her locker—revealing a glimpse of the soccer ball, but not much else—chucked her dress clothes in, and slammed the locker shut. "You girls get dressed quick. Jenny and I will meet you out there."

Without another word, she grabbed Jennifer's wrist and pulled her through the locker room.

Jennifer panicked. "Bobbie, please, I don't—"

"Shut up." The larger girl tugged harshly, making Jennifer stumble. Then her tone changed back to fake-sweet again. "You know, Jenny, Andi and I had the most interesting conversation with Skip in the hallway. Andi told him we learned about your little secret—the daggers, she meant—but that it was no big deal. I even mentioned we had kinda helped you out. He seemed pretty happy to hear it, and so he got to talking a bit more freely. Imagine my surprise when he didn't talk about daggers at all!"

Jennifer was momentarily distracted when Bobbie didn't go through the outside exit, but rather took her past it to the locker-room exit that led to the gymnasium. *They must practice indoors because of the cold.* Wanting very much to go anywhere but wherever Bobbie was taking her, she strained against Bobbie's grip and managed to kick the door open. That was as far as she got. The larger girl yanked her along the hallway, and all Jennifer had to show for her trouble was a covering of goose bumps from the sudden blast of cold air through the open doorway.

"I got tons of information from him about you, without him suspecting a thing! Oh, by the way, I invited him to practice, but he said he couldn't make it. I told him we'd get you home later."

Bobbie's eyes gleamed with sapphire malice. Jennifer got the message: Skip would not be around to help her.

"Of course, Andi wasn't surprised by what Skip told us." Bobbie's tone turned a bit harsher. "No, *Doctor* Andi apparently knew already. Why she didn't tell me, I'm not sure. I'll handle her later. But you—" She pulled Jennifer to a stop right in front of the gymnasium door. "You I deal with now.

"You're going to go through that door," she continued. "Most of the varsity squad had free time last period, so there are a bunch of players already out there practicing, not counting coaches and parents and everyone else. Big game coming up Saturday, remember?"

"Yeah." Jennifer's throat was getting dry. "I remember."

"Good. Anyway, when you go through that door, you're either going to look like you look *now*"—she reached out with a fast hand and snapped the elastic of Jennifer's underwear with a cruel grin—"or you're going to change into *what you really are.*"

Jennifer swallowed hard. "You don't have to do this."

"Through the door, Jenny."

"I'll leave another way. Please. I'll never come back if you don't want me to, I swear."

Bobbie's eyes traveled up and down her body. "If you wanna lose what little you're wearing, keep talking."

The sounds of girls whispering and laughing increased. Bobbie's friends were coming, having wasted no time in changing so they could see what would happen next. Jennifer couldn't go back that way. But she couldn't go through this door either—not dressed like she was, and certainly not as a dragon.

"Bobbie—"

"Fine." The girl lunged forward. As Jennifer lost her breath against the cement wall behind her, she felt Bobbie's hand reaching under a shoulder strap and pulling hard on the sports bra. A sudden kick to Jennifer's wounded calf made her gasp.

"Bobbie, no! Don't! Please!"

A fast, stiff elbow caught her across the chin. The shock of the blow disoriented Jennifer long enough for Bobbie to flip her around so she faced the wall, with an arm twisted painfully against her bare back. "Don't try to fight, Jenny. You can't win."

Head swimming with pain, fear, and humiliation, Jennifer closed her eyes, clenched her teeth, and began to cry. Where were her friends? Where was her school? Where were her parents? Wasn't *anyone* going to help her?

The catcalls from down the hallway answered her question. "Hey, Bobbie, wait up! We'll get the bottom half!"

Blubbering in short, mucus-filled whistles, Jennifer shoved back against Bobbie, but the larger girl had her pinned. "They're all going to see you," she whispered in Jennifer's ear, breath reeking of onions. She managed to get one strap down over an elbow. "All of you."

Jennifer's muscles strained violently and her spine rippled, but she couldn't go anywhere. Her left arm was pinned by Bobbie's efforts to pull down the bra strap. The right was secured by Bobbie's superior strength. Her brain buzzed with the struggle for freedom.

*Change?* the dragon inside asked desperately.

*Not unless you want to die faster,* she answered herself.

The humming in her brain got louder. Her ears were pounding. Her whistling breaths got shorter and shriller. The other girls were shrieking with laughter. Someone besides Bobbie grabbed her ankles and pulled her feet up off the floor. As she struggled helplessly against the army of hands that held every limb, they took her over to the gym doors. She felt a hand slide down her hip—

—and then the shrieks turned to screams.

The arms and hands on her abruptly let go. Jennifer collapsed to the floor as hundreds of black needles flew through the hallway, wings buzzing furiously as they drove themselves into the other girls' arms, legs, and heads.

*Dragonflies,* she told herself, barely believing the swarm that had come to save her. *Not quite fire hornets, but let's not be choosy.* She crawled a few feet away as Bobbie and the others flailed at the gathering swarm of insects. Looking up, she realized she only had one real way out of this, and it was now or never.

She got to her feet, steeled herself . . . and burst through the gymnasium doors.

If those she saw next were surprised at the nearly naked girl that came running at them, Jennifer was no less stunned at the scene before her.

The gymnasium at Pinegrove High was the exact dimensions as the one she remembered from Winoka High. The floor was familiar hardwood painted cobalt and maize, and the bleachers on either side of her entrance were still uncomfortable plastic. The entire wall opposite was glass, which had always given an excellent view of the athletic fields outside. This November afternoon, there was the slimmest of crescent moons in the darkening afternoon sky.

Everything else was deeply wrong.

There was a soccer net on each end of the gym—or at least Jennifer guessed they were nets. Really, they were two massive webs stretched over the painted cement walls, thirty feet high and thirty feet across. Between these nets, five or six students in spider form were kicking around soccer balls—several at a time—and jumping higher than Jennifer had ever seen a player jump. It looked like eight soccer games happening in midair at once.

*What kind of soccer is this?!*

*Not important!* she answered herself angrily, forcing herself to keep running. *Get moving! You have to do it now!*

She sprinted between the bleachers and out onto the gymnasium floor. Turning, she could take in the dozens of human-shaped parents, little brothers, and others—*Cripes, is that the school's AV class with a video camera?*—in the bleachers she had just run past. The spiders stopped playing and stared. The parents and little boys stopped talking and stared. The AV team stopped talking, stared . . . and apparently kept filming.

*They don't know what you are,* she tried to reassure herself as goose bumps had their way with every inch of her skin. *Not until the others get out here.* Taking a deep breath, she forced more tears down her cheeks and put a hand up to her mouth in her best imitation of a horror-stricken teenaged girl. Given her surroundings, it wasn't difficult.

"*Bobbie Jarkmand's a weredragon!*" she screamed in despair, pointing back with an unsteady finger. "She's in the girls' locker room, attacking Andi and the other girls with a swarm of dragonflies!"

A gasp went through the crowd. "That's impossible!" one of the coaches said, but Jennifer could see his doubt and fear. "I've seen her morph! She's no dragon!"

"*She's half-and-half, I swear!*" Jennifer persisted through renewed sobs, mind racing to stay ahead of her audience. She swatted vainly at thin air. "We didn't *mean* to make her do it, I'm sorry, we didn't *mean* to! We were teasing her about her skinny spider shape after she morphed for practice, and then she got angry, and we got into a fight, and she changed *again*, but this time she . . . *Oh, God, somebody please help me! HEEEEELP MEEEEEEE!!!!*"

With that, she took one last swipe at an absolutely harmless dragonfly that possessed the good grace to wander into the gym at that moment. Then she turned to run for her only possible escape route—the double doors that opened to the outside.

It worked brilliantly. Seeing clear evidence of Jennifer's sinister dragonfly-assault theory, every person in the gymnasium roared in outrage. Parents bloated themselves into eight-legged shapes, and the players already in spider form charged for the door to the girls' locker room. Jennifer had an uncontested path to freedom.

As she charged through the glass doors—which, to her delight, set off the fire alarm and automatic sprinkler system—Jennifer thought with no small satisfaction of how beaten and bruised Bobbie might get in the ruckus, before anyone could figure out what had really happened.

Feeling the chill of November on her skin, she slipped into dragon form and took to the air, saying a silent prayer of thanks to the dragonflies she left behind.

*"Jennifer?!"* The voice from below startled her.

Pulling up and hovering, she turned to see Nakia Brandfire on the sidewalk below, in jogging sweats and sneakers. Her elegant Egyptian features stared up in terror. *She saw me change,* Jennifer realized.

"That's right," she answered defiantly. "My name's Jennifer Scales. I'm a weredragon. And so are you, I'll bet. Your grandmother was Winona Brandfire, who's the eldest dragon. When the universe is right. I can get it back, Catherine. I can make it right for dragons like us. But I need your help. Change now, and come with me!"

"Change?" The question came meekly.

"Yes!" Jennifer turned nervously to the gym's glass walls. Everyone was still stuffed into the hallway to the locker rooms, but this wouldn't last long.

"Um . . . okay."

Nakia flexed her body . . . and to Jennifer's horror sprouted two huge brown claws, eight milky tan legs, and a black stinger that dangled over her segmented midsection.

"Oh, Catherine . . ."

"My name's Nakia," the huge scorpion insisted with a sudden vehemence that made Jennifer pull back in midair. "And I don't know why you keep calling me Catherine, but my grandmother

Winona was the shame of our family. I'm *glad* she's dead now! *Really glad!*"

Jennifer heard a new commotion in the gym. Looking up, she saw three or four spiders coming back out of the hallway. Among their bulbous shapes walked Andi, still in human form, who stared at Jennifer with fresh awe.

*There are no allies here. It's time to go.*

She turned to Nakia. "I won't forget who you really are. Not ever."

And then without letting the scorpion think of a reply, Jennifer was off again, chasing the moon.

# CHAPTER 9

## *Wednesday Night*

Her first stop was a bit less than a mile away, in the middle of a birch forest behind the school. It was dangerous, she supposed, to be this close to where she had played her little trick and escaped with her life. But she was trembling too much to fly straight—and walking around undressed was not an option. Besides, it could only help her to wait until it was a bit darker.

That theory didn't hold up. By the time she felt calm enough to slip over the treetops in the deepening sky and head for Skip's house, she could make out the flashing lights of police cars from more than ten blocks away.

*Of course,* she chastised herself. *Skip's house would be the first place they'd check! You can never go there again.*

She veered away from the threatening strobes and tried to think of where else she could go. Of course, heading out of town was an option—she had been waiting for an excuse to escape for two days—but now she was not so sure. If everyone was looking for her, was this the best time to be flying around?

Not if there was another good hiding place—someplace no one would think to look for a while. Thinking of Skip's family, an idea came quickly.

*Instead of up in the air, maybe I should be down under the ground.*

The sewer culvert where Skip had betrayed her to his father last spring was not far away. She flew low to the treetops the entire way, avoiding streetlights and large clusters of homes. Once again, from above she was struck by the architecture in this town. These houses were so elegantly built, touching the darkening sky with elegant peaks and spiraling chimneys. While disorienting in the sunlight, their strange colors were almost beautiful at dusk.

As she retraced part of the path she had taken away from the school, she caught sight again of the northern grounds. From this angle, she had a clear view of the strange observatory she had hoped to investigate this evening. That would now be impossible, she admitted as she took in the strange dome strapped to the earth within a steel web. By angering Bobbie, alienating Catherine/Nakia, and frightening Andi, she had pulled the equivalent of setting off a fire alarm everyone could hear.

*Scratch that,* she corrected herself. *I* did *set off a fire alarm. With a sprinkler system.*

Before she let the observatory slip away behind the horizon to her left, her eye meandered over the last sliver of its shape. She could not help admiring the striking architecture. It was more than just a building devoted to science—it was a fortress set against ignorance.

*Visitar tutos, imperar tutos.*

The words from the Pinegrove city limits sign came unbidden to her mind. She had asked her Spanish teacher yesterday what they meant. The well-groomed, heavyset man with a clip-on tie, thinning hair, and polyester pants had told her with a booming bounce to his voice: *See all, rule all.*

And just like that, as the memory from class replayed itself, something else swept over her—something from outside herself, from this building. As with the first time she saw it, it was as if it could see her in return. There was something—or someone—inside, ferociously intelligent and strongly expectant.

*Get down,* she urged herself. *Get down and get away.* Immediately, she ducked under the cover of the trees and made her way to the culvert by turf-whomping. It didn't make her feel that much safer, and it wasn't until she was deep in the depths of the sewer, with only the sounds of trickling water to keep her company, that she felt she might relax.

*Jennifer was careful* to make sure there were no artificial extensions to this sewer of the sort Otto had created and stuffed full of spiders before he died. Once her reconnaissance satisfied her that she was truly alone, she curled up in the large junction chamber where she had once done battle alongside her mother, slain a mighty sorcerer, and rescued the boys.

"Long ago," she told the walls that echoed it right back at her.

Otto Saltin had gone to great lengths to trap Jennifer, so that he could make constant use of her blood and pass on her powers to his brethren. It had allowed him to change shape at will, among other things. They had stopped him, Jennifer and her mother, together.

Now it was undone, in a single stroke. Spiders were everywhere, changing shape at will, and doing heaven knew what else. And if they couldn't breathe fire or camouflage themselves, who cared? They didn't have to. Otto's plan had failed, but the outcome he desired had still come to pass.

*You fools,* he had told them right before he died. *You've got no idea what's coming. This is not over.*

So he had been right. They had had no idea.

The chill in the room deepened. She got up, found some moist scraps of wood, gathered them together, and sneezed a small fire for herself.

*A day or so,* she told herself as she began to doze in front of it. *I'll stay here a day or so, and then head to Eveningstar. It's a bit closer to here than the farm, so it's not quite as risky.*

For the next few hours, she took her mind off her worsening situation by taking burnt embers out of the fire and sketching with them on the cobblestones. She drew a dragon—Ned Brownfoot, she decided as she filled in a tortoise under his wing claw. She drew her parents under a moon elm in Crescent Valley. She drew Wendy Blacktooth—the glimpse she had seen of the woman in a hospital bed, with a faint smile on her face. Then she drew her mother and father again, this time lying together with her in her grandfather's farmhouse the first night she had turned into a dragon.

She was just about to search the sewers for more firewood to burn into memories on the floor when she heard footsteps from the tunnel where she had entered. With her wing poised to squelch the fire, she tried to decide if it was better to be a dragon, or a girl, when the eight-legged authorities showed up to drag her away . . .

"Jennifer?" It was Skip.

Breathing a sigh of relief, Jennifer called back. He was a welcome sight, not least because he didn't have an army of spider-people with him.

She shifted shape back into a girl to hug him, but it was brief—she still only had her underwear on, and he coughed in embarrassment until she changed back.

"I can. Erm. Lend you my jacket."

"It's okay." She felt her blue scales turn scarlet. "I'm warm enough like this. No sense in *you* getting cold when you don't have to. Besides, didn't you bring extra clothes for me?"

His look told her immediately he had not. Her embarrassment turned quickly to frustration.

"Geez, Skip . . ."

"How was I supposed to know you would be naked when I found you?" he asked with a shrill, defensive tone.

*"They videotaped me, Skip.* I went out in the middle of the school gym and screamed at a crowd in my panties and bra, and the audio-visual team captured the whole thing on transferable, digital media! After they found out I was a dragon, they probably had the whole thing on the six o'clock news! And the Internet! *Didn't* they?!"

"Yeah," he muttered at the cobblestones by his feet. "You were on the news. And, um, there's a video clip some guys from school are passing around via e-mail."

"And did I have any clothes on?"

He looked up with a defeated expression. "Well, you had your . . . your underthingies on, I guess . . ."

"And now here comes the million-dollar question, Skip: Was I modeling lingerie and sporting a duffel bag capable of storing an extra outfit . . . *or was I running for my life?!*"

When he started to chuckle, she felt the steam pouring out of her nostrils. "Skip, I swear, this is *not* funny. People are trying to kill me. How can I get around town, or go anywhere, if my choices for disguise are (a) dragon or (b) underage porn star?"

"I'm sorry," he said without much regret. "I was really laughing at how dumb I guess I was . . ."

"You were pretty dumb," she snapped.

This yanked him into worse humor. "Shit, Jennifer, I'm sorry I didn't think of every tiny little detail, with police crawling all over my aunt's house looking for you. It took an awful lot to slip out unnoticed. If my aunt or Mr. Slider wakes up and finds

I'm not home, they'll know I'm with you. So I can't stay very long."

"What a shame." She immediately regretted saying it, but there was no way she was going to apologize without a shirt on.

"Yeah. What's your plan now? You blew your secret, so you can't investigate anything at school. And people are probably going to be suspicious of me and my family for a while, since we took you in."

She swallowed the lump in her throat. "So what you're really asking is, when am I going to leave town, so I'm no trouble anymore."

"That's not what I'm asking. And you can't go to Eveningstar anyway."

"Why not?"

"I did some computer research while my aunt and Mr. Slider were occupied with the authorities," he explained as he pulled a short stack of papers out from underneath his jacket. "Eveningstar was destroyed fifty years ago, and then werachnids rebuilt it. Here's a few research articles, and some shots of city hall and stuff."

She flipped through the pages he had hastily printed out. It wasn't ironclad proof that her parents didn't live there, but it sure looked bad. The architecture of the town's main buildings was distressingly similar to the strange houses throughout Pinegrove; they had all been built in the last fifty years, after a "civil unrest" not unlike the one that had taken place at Alexandria.

"Jennifer, it's not safe for you to go anywhere," he told her when she handed back the papers. "You need to keep low. This is a good place; I was kinda figuring you'd end up here, since we both know about it. But you should put the fire out, and keep your dragon shape in case you need to fight your way out . . ."

"I'll go to Crescent Valley."

"What? No, Jennifer, I told you: It's not safe right now. Wait a few days, maybe a couple of weeks. It'll take a while for them to give up and assume you've just flown somewhere far away. And even after that, an awful lot of sharp eyes will be looking to the skies for dragons. You've stirred up an awful lot of fear and anger."

"Fear and anger?" She almost choked on the words. "Gosh, Skip, I hope I haven't hurt anyone's *feelings*! I mean, how rude of me. You all go through the trouble of obliterating an entire universe, and I'm not polite enough to thank you all properly. I guess I—"

"You know I didn't mean it that way. I meant, werachnids are terrified of dragons. We always have been. Jennifer, this whole mess may not have been my idea, but you have to admit we had no choice."

His words slapped her like ice water. "No choice?"

"Jennifer, we were losing the war."

"War?!"

His patient expression crumbled. "Yes, war, Jennifer! You may not have seen it from your cozy vantage point, but werachnids have been fighting for our lives. My father's attack on Eveningstar cost both sides heavily. Dragons regrouped in places like Crescent Valley. We didn't have that option. Do you have any idea how few of us were left, Jennifer?"

She chewed her forked tongue with narrowing eyes. "Apparently not few enough."

"We were on the brink of extinction! Whoever did this was trying to save an entire species!"

"At the cost of two other species."

"I'm not saying I agree with them," he insisted. He was sweating with the effort of explanation. "But, Jennifer, when the order came down to my aunt and me to prepare, I have to admit I was interested to see what it would be like."

"Yes. Well. Now you know. And so do I. It's a freaking nightmare, can we agree on that?"

"It's not what I expected—"

"Then let's change it back. Right? We said we'd do that? Whatever happened to that idea, Skip? You asked me what the plan was. I'm telling you: The plan is to change things back. Are you in or not?"

His body deflated like a balloon. "Jennifer, you don't understand. Even together, we're not even close to a match for this kind of power—"

"Two of us together have a better chance than me on my own. Which I guess is all I've got now. Thanks a lot, Skip. Don't you think you'd better leave now, so you can go back home and *not* bring me my clothes again?"

"You're impossible!" The explosion wasn't exactly shocking to

Jennifer, but it depressed her even more deeply. His mouth curled down into an ugly frown, and his chocolate hair flopped about wildly. "I love you! I saved your life! I came to make sure you're okay, and to warn you from doing something stupid like going to Eveningstar! And I make a simple suggestion—lay low and hide—and you treat me like the enemy! Why can't you lay low? Why can't you hide, and trust me to take care of you?"

She closed her eyes, breathed deeply, and lay down. "Skip, have you ever heard the tale of the Mordiford Wyvern?"

"The Mordiford— No, I haven't. What does that have to do—"

"It's a tale, hundreds of years old. My grandfather used to tell it to me when I was little. A few months after my first morph, he told it to me again and explained what it really meant."

He bit his lip and tapped his foot, so she continued.

"A little girl who lives by the English town of Mordiford finds a baby wyvern—a dragon, cut off from its parents, alone in the wilderness. She thinks it's adorable. She can cup it in her hands and it blows puffs of smoke. So she scoops it up off the moss and brings it home. Her parents, terrified of what they see their daughter holding, order her to put it back where she found it and stay away from that part of the forest forever.

"Ashamed at frightening her parents but unwilling to part with this beautiful creature, she carries it back not to the forest, but to a small cave she uses as a secret hideout. For years, she keeps it there as her pet. She brings it food, and sings to it, and tells it what life is like outside of the cave, and swears to it that she'll always be there for it and protect it from harm. They'll be best friends, you see: the child and her pet dragon."

She paused and took him in. He was standing with arms crossed, still tapping his foot, still angry at her.

"Skip, how do you think this story ends? What do you think happens to the Mordiford Wyvern?"

He didn't answer.

"Do you think it stays in the cave? Do you think it enjoys being this child's pet? Do you think it likes being told how it will live?"

Still, he stared at her with tight lips.

"Do you honestly think the child is able to protect it, when the town inevitably discovers the creature?"

"I'm not a child," he finally hissed.

"Then stop acting like one. I'm not your pet, Skip. I don't want you to keep me in a dark cave and protect me. I want you to help me find my own kind. That's where I belong. If you're not going to help me change things back, at least help me get to Crescent Valley."

He rolled his eyes and gave a snort of disgust. "Crescent Valley. You want to go to Crescent Valley."

"Yes."

"After all I've done for you."

"Good grief, Skip! All you've done? I need—"

He held his hand up. "Yes, I know. It's what you need, Jennifer. It's always about what you need."

He pulled his jacket off and tossed it to her. "You'd better take this. Because you're going to need clothes, and I'm not coming back with any. You want to go to Crescent Valley, go. Good luck."

Somewhere far above, the sound of a police siren wailed, came closer . . . and then passed back into the distance.

Jennifer let out a deep breath. "You know, Skip, it occurs to me: You've already betrayed me once in this sewer. I'd rather not invite a repeat performance."

Leaving his jacket on the sewer stones, she unfolded her wings and rushed past him, up the sewer shaft, through the large culvert pipe, into the midnight sky, and out of Pinegrove.

There was only one place left to go.

# CHAPTER 10

## *Thursday*

*Speed is key,* Jennifer decided as she blazed a nearly invisible path in the dark, just a few feet over the highway ditch. She didn't think she would be able to hit ninety miles an hour like her father could—*can,* she corrected herself—but she was going fast enough to make herself nervous.

Worse than the chance she might hit a stray telephone pole, however, was the chance that the residents of Pinegrove would anticipate her next move and be at the farm to meet her. Since her conversation with Skip, she wasn't sure how much he would help the authorities find places like the farm. On one hand, she had just insulted him. On the other hand, Skip and authorities didn't exactly mix . . .

*I don't need to stay there a long time,* she told herself as she dodged under a steel cable. *Just long enough to see what happened, and to get to Crescent Valley.*

Somewhere in the back of her mind, she told herself it would also be nice to be able to get some rest. Who knew when she would get another chance?

By the time she was at the farm, the slim crescent moon had worked its way lower in the starlit sky. Dragon vision was still excellent in the dark (though not quite good enough to avoid a couple of scrapes on the way up), and she saw all she needed to see within moments of approaching the edge of the Scales's property.

There were no beehives.

There were no wildflowers.

There were no sheep, no horses, and certainly no dragons to be seen.

All there was, in the midst of rugged prairie land and the occasional copse of trees, was a small cabin, maybe one-third the size her grandfather had built, and a familiar-looking barn.

She slowed down, landed softly on the gravel driveway, and assumed a dark camouflage pattern before daring to go any farther. There didn't appear to be anyone about, and there were no vehicles of any kind parked outside.

*Abandoned,* she told herself as she got to the entrance of the barn. The wide doors were flung open, smacking the barn walls at the whim of the November winds. Inside was nothing but a few frayed horse blankets and the distant smell of manure embedded years ago into the woodwork.

She thought she heard a rustling in the woods behind her. Her head snapped around and she squinted her keen dragon eyes. Nothing was there—at least, nothing larger than a raccoon.

Leaving the barn, she went around the east side and surveyed the yard between cabin and lake. The clearing here was overgrown with tall grasses and weeds. Bit by bit, the land was returning to its natural prairie state. But Jennifer didn't know enough about botany or geography to know how long this growth had taken to emerge—ten years? Twenty? Five? A few months?

She glanced briefly at the spot where she and her mother had erected a gravestone for Grandpa Crawford. It wasn't there, of course.

*Is that good news or bad?*

Again, there was a noise—but this was farther off. It was a cry of sorts, perhaps an eagle. Or perhaps something pretending to sound like an eagle.

Whatever it was, it was less likely to find her inside, than outside.

Entering the house, which she knew must have been as much of the cabin as her grandfather finished before things went horribly wrong, gave Jennifer a surreal feeling. Yes, there was the kitchen where it belonged, but the appliances were unfamiliar and rusting. Yes, there was a photo of young Crawford and Caroline Scales over the mantel—but little else, and certainly nothing of anyone else she knew. The wallpaper in the hallway was yellow burlap instead of the elegant flower print she expected, and there was no library or patio facing the lake.

Down at the end of the hall was the master bedroom—the only

bedroom. Jennifer had known it as her grandfather's study. Once upon a time, she had stored some charcoal sketches there. The dresser (which belonged upstairs, which in turn didn't exist) was scarred maple.

She opened the first few drawers, which were empty. In the bottom drawer, she found an old flannel nightgown with a blueberry and daisy print, and a few small holes near the knees. This she quickly put on. The closets were bare, except for hangers, plastic dry cleaning bags, and Styrofoam pellets.

Going back to the kitchen, she scoured the cupboards. There was a can of cheese soup with rust around the edges, and some tea bags. She found a pot and kettle, used a dragon claw to crack open the soup can, and then flinched at what first came out of the faucet. Eventually, the water looked drinkable, and a fire was easy to set in the fireplace. She nestled both the kettle with water and the pot with soup in between the logs. In a few minutes, dinner was ready.

There was no spoon, she then discovered. Or cups, or bowls, or anything else beyond a painted metal serving tray and a broken toaster.

Muttering, she reverted to dragon form and poured the soup down her throat. It was quite hot and reminded her of the day about a year ago she had tried a ritual drink her grandfather had prepared. Oh, well, her innards didn't mind. Then she tore open the tea bags, poured the contents on her forked tongue, and upended the whistling kettle over her open mouth.

That hurt. She swallowed the pain down deep and chucked the kettle into the kitchen behind her, where it rolled back and forth over the moldy linoleum for a while.

*Still better than anything Mom could have made,* she told herself with a stubborn snort.

And then she felt tears fogging her eyes. She kept herself in dragon skin, because the scales made them harder to feel as they streamed down her cheeks.

*Her nap—if she could* even call it that—was short and fitful. Whether it was in her dream or in the forest nearby, she kept hearing ominous sounds. There was the rustling of leaves, and the far-off shrieks of dying things. The carpet in the master bedroom smelled bad, not unlike the sewer in Pinegrove. Were there eyes in the window? Voices on the air? Footsteps in the hallway?

She grumbled at herself, unsure of what to do. Yes, she wanted to be fully rested when she entered Crescent Valley and faced whatever truth was there. But this sleep-deprivation torture was sapping what little strength she had left.

Finally, after unsuccessfully trying different rooms to sleep in (the kitchen linoleum was slippery with mildew, and the hallway carpet was no better than what was in the bedroom), Jennifer decided enough was enough. She braced herself with a deep breath, burst out of the farmhouse, sailed over the lake for as long as she dared, and then plunged into the water.

She emerged a minute later, on the other side.

Some things were still here: the heavy air slowly moving like an ancient breath over her face, the forested shore far away where the moon elms were losing their November leaves, and, of course, the brightly shining crescent moon that kept eternal watch over this world.

But other things were not here, that should have been. There was no sound of insects, she realized. The small water mantises that normally skimmed the lake's surface were gone. So was the gentle, cellolike strum of fire hornets. And the crescent moon seemed more stark for its lack of welcoming fire—the circular signal the spirits of Elders would send to arrivals.

*No venerables?* She sank a bit back into the water. *Where did they go?*

Even worse, there were things here that definitely should *not* have been. Even from this distance, she could make out shimmering lattices that spread from the tops of bare moon elm branches. These delicate shrouds linked the enormous plants into large, unfriendly clusters. Little would pass from above to below, or vice versa.

*Webs.*

She ducked back under the icy water, letting only her eyes and snout stay above the surface. Had anyone seen her?

Her wings and body slowly propelled her, and she slunk across the lake like a miserable crocodile. The initial panic at the prospect of discovery now gave way to a more lasting despair.

*There is no help. Nowhere else to go! Why are you swimming toward the shore? Go back!*

But she didn't. After all, what was there to go back to? She had to stay, at least for a little while, and find out more.

The swim was long and tiring. She saw no movement on the shore as she approached. In fact, it didn't seem as if anything had lived here but the moon elms themselves, for some time. The webs upon the nearest trees, she saw better now, were blowing in the wind, untended and unkempt. *Maybe the dragons drove them back,* she told herself as she caught the crimson glow of lichen from deep within the forest. *Maybe they're still fighting.*

She finally reached the shore and let her skin shift into a rough bark-and-dirt pattern as she skittered over the narrow beach and into the foliage. Dead moon elm leaves crinkled as she curled up into a ball and shivered herself dry under folded wings.

*This is not happening,* she assured herself as she began to sniffle. *This is not happening. This is not . . .*

"Jennifer!"

The sound of Skip's voice startled her. He was running up the lake shore from the south, in nothing but a Windbreaker and some gloves. His bluish-green eyes were slanted in concern, and sweat fixed his chocolate bangs to his forehead.

"Wh-what are you doing here?" she asked in a quaking voice.

"You said you were coming here. I didn't want to leave things the way we left them. It's not right. We should go back, talk things over."

"I need to find them."

"Who?" He waved his arms in exasperation. "Jennifer, who do you think is here? Look around! This place isn't safe for you! The spiders who are here are dangerous. They don't come through the portals often. Some of them have even renounced their human shapes. They could kill both of us!"

She didn't answer. She stared at him.

"Come on." He motioned with a gloved hand. "Let's go back, before someone finds us."

She stared at him some more. And at his gloves.

His *dry* gloves.

"Skip, how did you get here?"

He sighed impatiently and stepped toward her. "There's a cave about a mile south of here," he explained. "The lake isn't the only way into this world, Jennifer. There are several doorways, at least. They're pretty easy to find, once you know where to look."

*Once you know where to look,* she repeated to herself.

"Jennifer, come on!" He was still several feet away, but held out his hand for her to take. "The Quadrivium used sorcery to create awful things out here. Stuff even we wouldn't recognize. You don't want to run into any of it!"

*The Quadrivium.* She thought about it for some time, slowly unwinding herself out of dragon shape and flexing her arms. The wind billowed her nightgown and the air was cold on her November skin, but she knew she had to hold this form for a bit. He stomped his foot when she did not move any farther.

"Jennifer, we've got to go!" He took another step or two.

Close enough for her to reach him.

She slapped him, hard.

The smack reverberated across the beach and the lake. Neither of them said anything for a few seconds. Then Skip rubbed his chin and nodded solemnly.

"I don't—"

She slapped him again, harder. This time his head snapped around all the way and he staggered back.

He turned to face her as she closed the distance herself this time. His hands were up and blood trickled out of his nose.

"Jennifer, I get that you—"

She did not hear him. The fire burned in her ears louder than a dragon's howl. She felt the bones within shift, wanting to change shape, but she willed them quiet. It would be better to do this as she was.

With her bare hands.

She knocked him down effortlessly and then fell upon him, hammering his pretty face with furious fists. He tried to shelter himself with his arms, but they did no good. Her blows were too fast and too powerful. She slowed down as she finally began to speak, one word with every strike.

"You. LYING. Piece. Of. Shit. You. Sold. Us. OUT. And. Now. They're. GONE!"

The reality of what she said hit her, and she yelled in anguish. She couldn't help it—the dragon was coming. Her nose horn was breaking through the skin and her spine was churning. Dimly, she wondered why Skip didn't change, too.

His restraint made her swallow hard and try to end the turmoil inside her. Holding herself like that, half-human, half-beast, took great effort. What if she got too tired? She couldn't rest here.

"What's the Quadrivium, Skip? *Who are they?*" She could see immediately from his expression that he would never tell her. There was only one thing to do. She slammed her crested forehead into his temple.

Disoriented, he was unable to defend himself as she resumed pounding him. He coughed and sputtered; she slammed and snarled. It felt better and worse at once, the more she did it. Piece by piece, she felt her humanity disintegrate, until it was her wings battering him and her double-pronged tail wrapped firmly around his gullet.

What finally made her stop? It might have been the way his eyeballs bulged with the escape of air. It might have been how her blows began to glance off his slippery face. Or it might have been the last shred of her compassion, tapping her scaled shoulder in a gentle reminder before it slipped away.

When she did stumble off of him, she gave him a last kick with a powerful hind leg. Skip groaned and rolled over.

"Never again, Skip." She wiped her bloody wings against her tearstained face. *"Never."*

He raised his head and tried to say something, but instead a battery of coughs convulsed him. One hand came up to his swollen throat; the other began to drag his body down the beach, back toward whatever cave lay to the south.

She breathed in the air of desolation around them, and resisted the impulse to kick him again. "Crawl back under your rock, you spider! You monster! *I hope you die! I hope you ALL die for what you've done!*"

The roar came from within. She could not have stopped it if she had wanted. It cracked the twilit sky open and made the stars shudder. Skip screamed and held his hands against his misshapen ears.

When she was done, she heard an answering sound from far away. It was not a hot roar of passion; it was a cold shriek of alarm. A chill wind blew down from the crescent moon and pressed upon her back.

Another cry went up, and then another, and another. Soon the screams came in distant waves—communicating, alerting each other to the intruder.

She looked over at Skip's creeping form and remembered what he said: *They've used sorcery to create awful things.*

The ground trembled. Whipping her head around in the direction of the sound, Jennifer barely had time to spread her wings before the trees to the east gave way to a shape—a single brown cylinder, longer than five moon elms laid end to end.

It was a leg.

It slammed into the ground under her as she rose on startled wings. She traced it back—across two highly placed joints with dark bands—until she finally found the body. A cobalt blue egg the size of a mansion hung suspended by this leg and seven others just like it. While there may have been eyes on top, Jennifer couldn't be sure—the entire northern hemisphere of the body loomed out of sight. Best she could tell, this thing could stand above five or six soccer matches going at once, and never know the scores.

Without another thought for the boy, she darted away from the enormous creature. A biology lecture from Ms. Graf last year echoed in her mind:

*"Harvestmen are sometimes called 'daddy longlegs.' But in truth, class, most of them don't have disproportionately long legs—nor could all of them possibly be male, of course! Some people think they're venomous, but that's just a myth. They don't even have fangs to deliver any sort of poison."*

*Poison seems beside the point,* Jennifer reflected grimly as she ducked under another leg that had groped blindly for her before smashing into the lake below. Realizing the only safety was far above, she twisted her body and pushed herself higher and higher into the indigo sky. The air cooled rapidly around her, and the thumping of the thing below became more distant.

She looked down and saw the entire harvestman. *More like ten soccer matches,* she guessed now. Triple-jointed legs plied the earth fruitlessly in search of prey. There were lumps on top of its body that suggested a place for eyes. *Is it smart enough to look up here?* she wondered.

A small, black, screaming missile abruptly shoved those thoughts aside. It came from the north, maybe the northeast, and it might have hit Jennifer had its shadow not briefly come between her and the moon above.

"Jyeh!" She flipped herself out of the way just in time. The leaping thing—whatever it was—sailed by her and fell back to the earth, landing with a distant *sploosh* in the lake.

Farther upward she went. *How far can they jump?* She couldn't possibly know, and she didn't want to find out the hard way. By the time she looked back down again, the harvestman was down to a respectable size from her perspective—and only a jet would be able to reach her.

Far off to the west, Jennifer could make out the mountainous shapes where her people—the creepers, the dashers, the tramplers—had once made refuge. Where they had hunted alongside the mysterious newolves, and held Blaze in their giant amphitheater.

*Not anymore,* she told herself. She noticed the patchworks of webs topping clusters of trees as far as she could see, and she knew no newolf or fire hornet would have survived this place. The werachnids here might have kept some herds of oreams alive for food, she supposed. But there would be nothing recognizable left in this world. Nothing except the most basic of topographical features, like mountains and . . .

*Stay as strong as stone. Stay as beautiful as fire.*

The words from her father's note suddenly made sense. Her father had left her a message!

She made for the north immediately. *Stone would survive the change. And we used dragon fire to write messages in the stone.*

*What will the stone plateau tell me,* she wondered as the moon followed her north to find out. *Will it tell me where to find anyone else? Will it tell me what to do next?* The excitement of piecing together her father's hidden message consumed her. *Dad hadn't trusted Skip either! He knew. That's why he spoke in code like that! He might even be there, at the stone!*

What a fool she was for not thinking of this earlier! How much time and pain she could have saved had she understood her father and come here right away!

She flattened her features and increased her speed. The moon-lit air gave way around her, as if clearing a path free of wind resistance. *They could be fighting these things right now,* she realized. *They need my help! I'm the Ancient Furnace, and I can help! Every last one of us counts!*

After about an hour's flight, she saw it: the great rock plateau that sprang from the forest like an enormous stone tree stump. Dragons used it for funeral ceremonies, including her grandfather's, just last month.

Images of strange swirls carved into molten rock pricked her memory. If she remembered right, those whorls marked up a bit less than half the plateau's surface. Would she be able to read what was there? Who might still be left to help her? How would she learn anything if she couldn't read the Elder language? And how long would she have to make sense of any of it?

While the treetop webs lessened in frequency closer to the rock formation, Jennifer could tell the forest was still tainted by their presence on all sides. No dragon was immediately apparent—though of course, they would probably be in hiding. She thought briefly of calling out, but then decided against it. Even if the werachnids and pets who met her at the lake could not travel as fast as she could fly, they doubtless had cousins nearby.

She dared a landing—at least she had to see what was written!—and found herself stricken with disbelief the moment her claws touched down.

There was no spot on the entire surface that was free of carvings. Where she stood—about where her grandfather had been buried, near the center of the plateau—was only the halfway point in a relentless story of death, carved in a language she didn't need to read to understand.

She walked in every direction, skittered along the perimeter of the formation. It was all the same. Swirl after swirl, whorl after whorl, name after name. Some parts of the plateau were raised with bony ridges—the carbonized remains, she supposed, of a carcass too quickly disposed of. One or more funerals had doubtless suffered interruption.

*How many in all?*

Jennifer remembered the rough size of her grandfather's grave markings. They had taken up space roughly equal to a large desktop. By that reckoning, she estimated the small, ten-yard radius around her contained several hundred markers. She drifted queasily on her wings, slowly expanding the radius.

*Hundreds . . . thousands . . . tens of thousands . . . hundreds of thousands . . .*

Gasping increasingly shorter breaths, Jennifer suddenly realized she had always counted on finding someone: maybe another beaststalker trapped at Pinegrove or Catherine (*not* Nakia!) Brandfire or some weredragon at the farm or in this world. She had assumed there would be help somewhere.

She had thought she couldn't possibly be alone.

Finally, on the last patch of flat rock she could find, she landed in front of carvings of a different kind. These were not deep swirls embedded in once molten rock. They were scratches, hastily made in English, by a last author.

*There is no one else left,* they began. Jennifer couldn't hold back a whimper, but she read on.

*There is no one else left. I am the last. All of the others have died.*

*Those who just died, at our final stand not far from here, count in the dozens. I will name them. No one will be left to name me. It is enough to have been their loyal friend.*

*Matthew and Melinda Hotwing.*

*Grace Ann Coals.*

*Ned Brownfoot.*

*Stephen and Atheen Whisperwind.*

*Crawford and Caroline Scales, and their brave young son, Jonathan.*

The list went on, but she couldn't bear to read anymore. Falling to her knees, she collapsed upon her father's name and began to cry.

*She had no idea* how long she lay there—a few seconds, several minutes, even hours. What did it matter? Lying on her belly and sobbing, she only wanted to die.

The noises she had heard before—the shrieks from the lakeside—gently entered her consciousness. They had found her. They were closing in, she had no doubt. Maybe a minute left before the end.

There was no place else to go.

Her tear-filled gaze went up to the crescent moon. She cursed it under her breath. So much pain had come into her life since she had discovered its power.

She released herself from dragon form, for what she knew would be the last time. Back in the shape of a fifteen-year-old girl, she felt around with her hands for a sharp fragment of stone. Lifting a small, jagged rock in her hand, she thought wistfully of her beautiful daggers. She had lost them, in that other world. She had lost everything.

Holding the stone firmly in her right hand, she held out her left wrist. She flexed her fingers and watched the blue veins shudder under her starlit skin.

*I miss you so much, Mom. You, too, Dad.*

The noises in the forest were closer. She could make out movement in a few of the taller trees. They would be upon her in seconds.

She pressed the edge against the skin, saw some blood seep out . . . and then abruptly stopped. Gritting her teeth, she removed the rock from her wrist and stood up. *Not like that,* she promised herself. *I won't do it for them.*

"Come on!" she screamed out to her predators in the dark. The stone felt fierce in her hand. *"Come on!"*

She did not see the attack come from behind.

There were three of them that took the first leap together—the bravest of the creatures that faced this intruder.

They were the first to die.

Jennifer felt the shadow ripple over her—she could tell it had wings—and then heard three simultaneous crackles of electricity. She whipped around in time to see the follow-through of an enormous, triple-pronged tail as it sent a trio of burning corpses sailing back into the shadowy forest.

The newcomer descended to the plateau next to Jennifer and looked at her with a mixture of alarm and wonder. She looked back with nothing but an open mouth. *Can anything possibly be this shape anymore?* she wondered.

"Let's go!" the dragon shouted at her, offering its back. "Get on!"

Suddenly, the voice registered in her memory. She took in the dark scales, the golden pattern on the underside of the wings . . . and the triple-pronged tail that had once viciously knocked her unconscious, back in a happier, friendlier Crescent Valley.

*It can't be!*

"Girl!" The large dasher's voice betrayed some familiar impatience as it rose above the gathering buzz of predators. "You need help! It's available for about another two seconds. Get on or die!"

She got on.

They were up in the air in time to see hundreds of hog-sized spiders land upon the edges of the plateau, each shrieking a bitter siren. The surrounding moon elms shook with the force of larger legs pushing aside trunks, and eight-legged shapes of all sizes were leaping from treetop to closer treetop.

"Hang on hard!" he told her, just before going completely vertical.

She closed her eyes and dug her hands into the joints where wings met spine, as he rocketed straight up and left an angry fountain of darkness leaping and dancing beneath them. In no time, the plateau was a small stone far below, and they were safe in the embrace of the crescent moon.

Or at least one of them was.

"Level out! Level out!" Jennifer gasped, kicking the open air as her fingertips cramped with pain. "I can't hold on!"

"Right," he agreed, and in an instant the dragon was horizontal again, soaring among the few wisps of clouds that laced the autumn landscape.

Jennifer blinked a few times, trying to move her mind from the despair and fatalism she had just felt to the shock of what—who, actually—had just rescued her.

"Xavier Longtail!" she managed, which was still nearly enough to surprise him out of the sky.

"How did you know my name, girl?"

"You're—I—we've met." It was all Jennifer could think to say.

"Hmph. I can't imagine how. You're not a spider, are you?"

"No!"

"No, I didn't think so." There was a long pause as Xavier plainly thought of how he wanted to ask his next question. "I don't suppose you would know anything about that roar I heard a while ago, would you? It sounded like it came from about where the old lake portal was. That's what got me out of hiding and looking around."

Jennifer bit her lip. She didn't know why she hesitated. Maybe she wasn't ready yet to trust again.

"You know about the lake portal, of course. Don't you?"

She chewed her tongue.

"I could just tip over and let you go, girl, couldn't I? You wouldn't mind one bit."

And just like that, he did.

She slid off his suddenly pitching body, shifted right into dragon shape, and spread her light blue and silver wings. From a few feet above her, she heard the strangest and most wonderful sound.

Xavier Longtail was laughing—not a cruel or cynical laugh, but a genuine laugh of surprise and joy. "I thought so!" He chuckled, and descended just enough to fly alongside her. "It seems I haven't forgotten what one of us looks like, after all. Though I suppose it's possible I'm dreaming. Or insane. My noodle"— he pointed to his skull with a crooked wing claw—"is not quite as sharp as it used to be."

"How can you be here?" she asked.

"I might ask you the same question! But let's start with your name."

"I'm Jennifer Sc— Um . . ." She realized he probably wouldn't believe her if she told him her family name right away. *How could he possibly accept that? He buried my father at the plateau.*

"Jennifer Scum? I suppose I've heard worse. Still, you might consider taking your husband's surname if you ever get married, modern times or no . . ."

"Just Jennifer will be fine. My family told me a lot about you."

He shook his head sadly. "I just don't see how that's possible. I haven't seen a dragon since . . . since . . ."

"Since you wrote that message down on the plateau."

His golden eyes wavered. "Yes. Since I wrote that message on the plateau. More than twenty years ago."

"But how—"

"Give us a moment," he interrupted her. "We should find a place to land. Then we can talk."

"Okay. Um, how do we find a place that's safe?"

"He'll take care of it." Xavier's head motioned to his left shoulder. From under his wing, the most unlikely creature emerged, clinging to his host's skin with a silly reptilian grin.

The red and green markings on its back were unmistakable.

*"Geddy?"*

The gecko stared at her from his winged perch, and licked his eyeball with a spoon-shaped tongue.

"I'm afraid I don't know any Geddy," Xavier told her without looking at her. "But Goodwin here's the only friend I've had for years. He'll help us find a good landing spot."

Geddy—or Goodwin—turned away from Jennifer and skittered up Xavier's shoulders and skull, until he was right between the dasher's eyes. From there, he twitched his tail in what looked like random fashion, until Jennifer realized the Elder dragon was using the small lizard's motion to steer.

"You're letting the gecko drive?"

Again, the genuineness of Xavier's laugh surprised her. "It may sound a bit strange," he admitted. "But Goodwin's not an ordinary lizard."

"I'll bet he's not."

"He knows where *they* aren't. Has a sixth sense or something about spiders. I wouldn't have survived all these years without him. Yep, Goodwin, you're right. That looks like a good patch down there."

They began a sharp descent, angling for a thin stretch of ground between two lakes Jennifer had never seen before. This part of Crescent Valley was beyond her experience, even before last Sunday. She checked her bearings—which way had they been going? Northeast? It appeared so.

"They're pretty sparse out here," he called out as they leveled off a few feet from the spongy ground. There were few moon elms nearby, and the reddish-orange glow of the lichen lit up their claws as they landed. "They don't care much for large bodies of water. The best hiding places are even closer to the ocean than we are now."

"The ocean?" Jennifer had heard the lake that held the portal eventually emptied out into the ocean, but she had never seen it. She sniffed, but there was no salt in the air, just the familiar scents of gently churning lake water and moss-covered earth.

"Out over the water is the safest place of all. I tried to get us out there back when . . ." He trailed off and sighed, absentmind-edly scraping the lichen with a hindclaw. "More of us could have survived, I'm sure of it. But tradition held strong for too many of us. Ned and the others weren't willing to let go of that plateau. It meant too much. It was their end. Our end."

She didn't know what to say. Finally, he looked up at her. "Anyway, it *was*. Until you showed up today. So it's Jennifer, eh? Great guns. How are you even possible?"

"I . . . I'm the Ancient Furnace." It sounded lame to her ears, but it was all she could offer.

His reaction stunned her. "Of course you are," he said as if she had told him the sky here was sort of dark.

"How did you know?"

"Any *regular* dragon wouldn't be able to hold human shape here, would they? And as a dragon, you're an obvious blend of the types. The prophecies spoke about you."

His unwavering faith filled Jennifer with unexpected warmth. "You know who I really am."

"I know what you represent. A second chance. Hope." His golden eyes glittered. "You are going to set things right again!"

The warmth dissipated, leaving anxiety behind. What did this Elder expect of her? "Uh, yeah. See, I'm not sure how I can—"

"I don't know either. But you being here is no accident. You and I are going to figure it out together. Oh, Goodwin!" He jumped up, held his gecko out high on a wing claw, and let out a whoop. "We're not alone after all!"

*And neither am I,* thought Jennifer.

# CHAPTER 11

## Thursday Night

Stretching out on the spongy ground, tracing swirls in the yellow, then green, then blue lichen for Goodwin to follow as he scrambled about the ground, Xavier told Jennifer all he knew about the advance of the werachnids over the past few decades. He didn't ask about her own origins; he just accepted that she was here to help. This made her glad, not just because of his confidence, but because she wasn't sure how to explain it all anyway.

It had begun around the time he was a child. "I was eight years old," he told her. "And I'm seventy—no, scratch that, seventy-one—now. It was a good time for dragons. Beaststalkers were in fewer and fewer towns, and they had always been our primary enemy over the centuries. But as a child, I remember not being afraid of them, since no one had seen one in years. They became excellent fodder for campfire ghost stories, and our Elders began to relax their guard, hoping against hope that we had seen the last of such killers. We weren't great in number, but we were growing.

"That all changed when the werachnids attacked Alexandria, which was where most of our Elders lived when they weren't in Crescent Valley. The aggressors used a weapon we had never seen before—poison in the air. After smothering the town in it, they attacked. They were led by a champion some of the arachnids called The Crown."

"The Crown?" Jennifer frowned. "What was he like?"

"None of our number who saw him survived. The few dozen who made it out of Alexandria, including my own family, had lived on the fringes of the city. We didn't stay long after the poison cloud descended. Of course, there were rumors. Some said he was a mere teenager, but had extraordinary intelligence. On top of that, he clearly had powers unlike any spider or scorpion—the poison gas was evidence enough of that. But his future attacks drove the point home."

"Eveningstar was next," Jennifer guessed.

He nodded. "It was twelve years later. A few of us had dared to hope that the werachnids wished no more violence, being content with overrunning Alexandria. But they were merely pausing. They did nothing hastily. Every plan took time. Every trap was sprung after careful consideration.

"With Eveningstar, their method was to begin with the river, which curled alongside the town. They dumped something in it that caused the entire body of water to boil, sending up a curtain of poisonous steam. With the north and east cut off, even for flying creatures, the werachnid army came from the south and west. This time, The Crown showed the first evidence of necromancy. With a word, he crippled six Elders at once, dropping them from the sky like wounded flies. With another word, he struck them blind and pulled their wings off. Those he let survive, to carry his message. Just about everyone else in the town perished."

"How did your family escape?"

"They didn't. My father, Jacques Longuequeue, was one of the six Elders The Crown mutilated that day. My mother, Martha, he outright killed. As for me and my brother, Charles, and some other young dragons, he thought it amusing to leave us alive, pinned under the piled-up corpses of our fellow townspeople. We weren't rescued for two days."

"That's horrible." Jennifer didn't know what else to say.

"It was. And fifteen years later, they came after Pinegrove. This time, the mere specter of their advance caused the town to empty. There was no battle at all. We scattered like dandelion seeds, some of us going to Crescent Valley, others of us finding refuge in twos and threes in the countryside.

"But even that was not enough for The Crown. Efforts to disperse and settle in small groups around and outside of Minnesota were unsuccessful. The Crown had assembled a small team of prodigy werachnids like himself—there were three or four of them, perhaps. This team had a particular talent for seeking us out and exterminating us. Eventually, we realized dividing ourselves was even worse than sticking together. We gathered again in Crescent Valley, with a small outpost at the farm by the lake portal—the one you came through. Crawford and Caroline Scales, and a few others of us, volunteered to stay out there, and feign a last stand. Our hope was that The Crown would assume we were the very last of our race, wipe us out, and never know the rest of our number were hidden in another place."

"And that didn't work." Jennifer sighed.

"The Crown didn't even come to do battle. He sent his elite team—three of them, anyway, to the farm to talk. Under a crescent moon, they came under human shape. A girl and two boys—teenagers, mere children like you! And with supreme arrogance, they told us exactly what to do if we wanted to survive. They revealed that they knew where Crescent Valley was. If we surrendered it and the lake portal, they would let us flee to the most remote corners of the world, and die off in peace. Or we could stay, fight, and die more quickly and violently.

"Our choice was obvious: We weren't going anywhere. Charles got off a good tail shot to the head of one of them, and that was our answer. That cost him his daughter. Ember wasn't even five years old, and the young woman put her to sleep with a word before she left. The little girl never woke up."

"What did these three look like? Did they have names?"

He scratched his horns. "My memory's not good with faces," he admitted. "And they never used names. But the woman was kind of skinny, with dark hair. Smiled a lot, but you got the feeling she might not mean it."

*Tavia,* Jennifer guessed. *And young Edmund Slider, then?* "Did one of the boys have blond hair, with sharp features and black eyes?"

"I'd suppose so," he said, squinting. "But I'm sure I can't remember the third one at all, other than he was a tall drink of water. It was cold out, and they had hats and other gear on.

"The next year was hard," he continued depressingly, as if what he had been relating to that point was all sweetness and light. "More and more arachnids seemed to show up without ties to the crescent moon. That meant they could show up when we were mere humans, and arrive as humans if it suited them to do so while we were trapped in dragon form. We adopted some tactics that— Well, the year was hard." He shook his head and avoided detail.

"There was a short but fine moment of victory less than a year after Ember died," he recalled. "The Crown himself came to the portal to do battle. He killed a few of us effortlessly, before a young creeper with a real knack for camouflage—Crawford's kid, name of Jonathan—leapt out from under The Crown's feet and sank his teeth right into the bastard's throat. With no way to speak sorcery, and losing blood rapidly, The Crown fell. Then Jonathan and his father incinerated the corpse."

Jennifer sat up straight at this and couldn't hold back a small grin. "Jonathan Scales killed The Crown."

Unaware of what this meant to her, Xavier rambled on. "He sure did. That kid was a reckless son of a bitch—all due respect to his mother, Caroline—but he was a vicious fighter. Seeing their mighty Crown die put the scare in his followers. They didn't come back for another year after that.

"When they did, there were simply too many of them. And the Quadrivium—that's what The Crown's inner circle started calling themselves—really came of age. They overran the cabin, and we had to get back to Crescent Valley. And then the real nightmare began. Our last refuge, precious and pure to us, came under attack. First, the wereachnids only knew about the lake portal."

This made Jennifer squirm in her seat.

"But then invaders showed up in places far away from the lake, using entry points we had rarely used or forgotten. Worse, what showed up wasn't just arachnids anymore. It was new things, horribly mutated. The sort of things you saw today. The Quadrivium experimented with their own kind, and then sent them into the fray. It was a terrible thing to do, and it worked extremely well."

He stroked Goodwin's back a few times before he spoke again. "You know the story from there—it's all written on the stone plateau. Three years after we gave up the outside world, we lost this one, too. After our last stand, when Ned died in my own wings, I scratched the last grave on that plateau and fled. It was cowardly not to go out fighting, I suppose. To run and hide, year after year, and slowly fade away."

"You're not a coward," Jennifer protested. "If you had gone out fighting twenty years ago, you wouldn't have been around to save me today, when I thought I wanted to die—but I really didn't."

"Hmmm," he allowed, his yellowed teeth showing. "Well, that's my story. A long and sad one, I'm afraid. And now I'm left to wander here by myself. The Quadrivium stopped looking for me in earnest once they were sure I was the only dragon left. Crescent Valley has been left to rot. What possible harm can I do, before I die?"

Jennifer raised her head and licked her teeth. "You wanna find out?"

*Xavier volunteered to keep watch* and scout the area with Goodwin while Jennifer stretched out and tried to get some sleep. There was a lot of excitement in his voice, but Jennifer wasn't sure he had much notion of what to do next.

*Great, the Ancient Furnace has shown up. So what? What can he and I possibly do together? Repopulate the species?*

She snorted and twitched her tail as she dismissed the idea. The old guy was something like five times her age; and while this version of Xavier Longtail seemed okay, she hadn't quite forgiven the old version for being such an ass. And even if she had a kid, by any father, so what? The kid got to die alone a few years after his or her parents. Not exactly a rousing tale of recovery.

No, the answer wasn't repopulating this universe. It was restoring the old one. But could they? And should they even try?

She recalled the note her father had written her. It was probably still in Tavia's guest room with all of her clothes, assuming Skip hadn't moved it. She felt a pang of guilt. He had told her to sit tight. He had told her to accept this world and make a life. The first time she had read those words, she had resisted the idea. But with a couple of days under her belt here, she wondered if he might have been right. Given how powerful these werachnids were, fighting would probably get her killed. Her father wouldn't want that.

*But he reminded you about the stone plateau,* a new voice in her head argued. *He wanted you to fight. He just didn't want to tip off Skip.*

This was certainly possible. Of course, it was hard to be sure either way. Jonathan Scales had probably had less than five minutes to write words that would pass Skip's inspection and still mean something to Jennifer. His mention of stone and fire certainly seemed like a code now—but it may have been a code to check out Crescent Valley, and give up if this refuge was lost. And lost it was.

*And why is it lost?* the voice persisted, making Jennifer roll over restlessly. *Who lost it, Jennifer? Who brought the enemy through the portal, revealed our deepest and most ancient secret, and then got angry at the dragons who thought it was reckless to do so? How many names are on that plateau, Jennifer? How many people did Skip kill when he gave the Quadrivium the location of Crescent Valley? How many people did you kill?*

The guilt was more than she could bear. She covered her head with her wings but she knew the voice would not let her sleep. Not with that knowledge. Not until she had set things right.

*It may kill me, Dad. But I can't let that plateau stand like that.*

The voice in her head accepted that resolve as down payment on her debt, and it quieted down long enough for her to slip into an uneasy slumber.

# CHAPTER 12

## *Friday*

The lichen in the nearby copse of trees was graduating from orange to yellow again when Jennifer woke up. Even without the visual cue, she would have known it was morning: The enigmatic warmth that radiated from the ground at the start of each day was, at least, a familiar comfort. She remembered asking her father about it on one of her first trips to Crescent Valley. He had told her it was the breath of Brigida, the first dragon, who no one had ever seen die thousands of years ago.

The thought of an ancient dragon breathing somewhere in the deep earth to provide warmth for an entire world comforted Jennifer, even though she knew intellectually that such a thing was impossible.

Xavier was not around, but Goodwin was back, staring at her. Jennifer stared back, stretching her wings.

"So what's your story?" she finally asked. "You the same little guy I left back home in his terrarium, or what?"

Goodwin's tail twitched.

"Hmm. Not exactly a decisive statement." She craned her neck and caught sight of a cluster of cobwebs, far above in the branches of a nearby moon elm. The dew on them had frozen, and the gentle wind blew the crystallized strands like ghost's hair. "Okay, how about this? Lick your left eye three times if you're part of the secret plot to screw up my life."

Neither his tongue nor his eyes moved. Jennifer realized he wasn't looking at her. He was looking over her right wing.

*Tail twitching . . . looking behind me . . . uh-oh.*

In half a second, Jennifer shrank back into the shape of a girl, which caused the black spider the size of a soccer ball to miss as it jumped at her. The hairs on its legs brushed her ear, and it landed with a piercing scream on the ground in front of her.

It was more than a spider, she saw now: twelve legs, four with clicking claws. It had quills on its bloated abdomen, and its mandibles opened wide to reveal a blue forked tongue.

Picking up one of the flat, heavy stones spread throughout their camp, Jennifer raised it over her head with both hands and brought it down hard. Though the results were spectacular, she immediately regretted the move.

*Ick. Mutant spider guts all over my nightie!*

"Jennifer!" She looked up to see Xavier sailing above, coming from the direction the spider had. "I'm afraid we have to move on. I've been scouting. They've definitely gathered in numbers to find us. You have awakened something violent in them, I think. Can you fly, or do you need to ride?"

"I can fly. Just needed a quick change to pick up a rock. Come on, Goodwin!"

The gecko scrambled up her leg as she shifted shape again and set to the air. From above, she could see a black mass of creatures approaching from the southwest. "Wow, it didn't take long for them to find us. Where do we go now? Can Goodwin find us another place that's safe?"

"Of course," Xavier answered. "But he's been doing that for decades. I think it's time for something different. Follow me!" He appeared quite pleased with himself, and even began to hum as the infested landscape below disappeared under sunlit clouds.

While she found this charming, Jennifer was not content to let the matter rest. "Um, Longtail? If you've got a plan, I'd like to hear it."

"All in good time—"

"Uh, no." She pulled up short and hovered impatiently, forcing him to pull up himself. "Dude, I know yesterday and today probably rate as a high point in the last several years for you, but for *me*, this week sucks dead horse eyeballs. I've lost my friends, my family, and everyone else I've ever known. Every place I go is like a nightmare reflection of itself. And those freaking *things*"—she pointed as another screaming black missile tried, and failed, to reach them in the sky—"are driving me nuts. *What the fuck are they, anyway?* Never mind—I want them gone. I want the whole thing gone. No offense, I want *you* gone. I want the cranky Xavier Longtail back, with the niece who hates me and my parents because they did horrible things in the past, but it's *my* parents and *our* past, and I want that all back, too. I want Winoka instead of Pinegrove, Catherine instead of Nakia, and Susan . . . instead of nothing at all! I want it all back, do you hear me? And I want to know how you're going to help me do it. *Right now!*"

He watched her for a while as they both dangled up and down in the sky, like self-propelled reptilian marionettes. His yellowed teeth were presented as something between a smile and a sneer. It was very old-world Xavier, Jennifer thought. A bit of perception, and a bit more of contempt.

"Well, my little princess," he finally said. "It sounds like you have quite a performance to put on, and very few volunteers around who can satisfy your high standards. If you don't think I'm dancing fast enough, I'll just collect Goodwin, say good-bye, turn tail, and take my chances with our arachnid neighbors. I've led a long life—not necessarily a happy one, but certainly unique. I can last a little longer on my own. And I certainly don't want to be a burden to the Ancient Furnace!"

She didn't reply, so he went on.

"Or you can trust me and give the signal for us to get moving. Your choice, kid."

Chewing her tongue in frustration and wretchedness, she finally relented. "I want to change things back. But I don't know how. If you have a way to get me help, I could really use some. P-pl-please." She felt her eyes get wet. *Again! Cripes! I can't believe I have any tears left!*

He cocked his head and groaned. "Aw, hell, girl, don't cry on my account. I haven't had much company for the past twenty years, and I'm afraid I've forgotten most of my social skills. Look, we're kinda going out on a limb, and I just didn't want you to worry. About the only lead I can think to follow is a scrap of a story my mother taught me before Eveningstar."

"Wh-what's that?" She sniffled.

"There's a creature named Sonakshi," he told her. "According to dragon legend, he's a prophet. He might have clues to steer us right."

Jennifer waited for more, but when Xavier began flying again, she had no choice but to follow. "He might have clues? What kind of clues? Does he have any powers? Can he help us fight?"

"He's not a fighter; he's a prophet. If he exists at all."

"What good will a prophet do?" Jennifer tried to sound inquisitive, rather than upset. She was sure Xavier was doing his best; but this hardly seemed helpful. "I mean, a prophet just tells the future. We're not trying to change the future; we're trying to change the past back the way it was."

"My mother once told me," came the answer as the lands began to thin and the water became more plentiful below, "that a prophet is not someone who can tell the future. A prophet is someone who can see the change in the present."

"Okay, that might be useful. We'll have to see exactly what's changed, I suppose, if we're going to change it back. But will this Sonnyshack—"

"Sonakshi."

"Will this Sonakshi be able to tell us *how* we can make things right again?"

"No idea," he called back as he increased speed. The air was decidedly cooler now, and the growing shimmer beneath them suggested to Jennifer that they were totally above water, with at most a few lingering strips of land flung out into the mysterious expanse.

"One more question. Where is this Sonakshi?"

His long, black head craned back. Jennifer could just make out the tiny form of Goodwin perched upon his elderly skull. His tone was very old-school Xavier as he nodded down at the glistening surface. "Where do you think?"

*They were riding chilled air* currents over the ocean for over two hours before Jennifer thought up another question she thought Xavier would tolerate. "So, is this Sonakshi supposed to be a dragon?"

"Nobody really knows what he is," the dasher admitted. "The most frequent explanation is that he's the most ancient of the lurkers."

"Lurkers?"

"Yes, lurkers."

She pulled up next to him. "You're losing me. Like, sea monsters?"

His expression suggested he didn't believe her ignorance. "No, lurker as in the dragon type."

Since she was too embarrassed to say anything, he continued. "You're the Ancient Furnace, Jennifer. You have all dragon types in you—dasher, creeper, trampler, and lurker. How can you not know about lurkers?"

"Um, I know . . . that they, um. Lurk."

"Great oceans, Goodwin," she caught him mumbling. "We get saved by the Ancient Furnace, and it turns out she's an ignorant twit—

"—Ow!" he exclaimed with a grin after she rattled his skull with a flip of her tail. "And a pretty good shot, too. At least that's something: You know dasher skills."

"Skills?" The plural confused her.

He let slip a wary hum. "Yes, skills. You know more than tailwork, don't you?"

"Well, I know lizard-calling, and camouflage." Suddenly, she felt inadequate. His reaction didn't make her feel any better.

"But what of the Elder skills?"

The phrase did trigger the memory of her confrontation with Ember Longtail. "Oh, like calling up a swarm of insects! Yeah, I guess I can do that."

"And how about meteor diving?"

"No. It sounds painful."

"It's the dasher Elder skill," he explained. "Great fun, especially over the ocean."

"Why would someone want to meteor dive?"

"It's a good way to make a little room," he answered with a wink. "You just hold your breath, curl your tail so the prongs are up by your head, start dropping . . . and then sneeze through your ears. You really have to see it to . . . Here, I'll just show you!"

Before she could ask him what sneezing through ears entailed, he had curled into a ball and dropped like a stone. As his velocity increased, a faint burn enveloped him, and then right before he hit the surface of the ocean . . .

*KAPOW!*

At first, Jennifer thought he had exploded in a massive fireball, and she screamed. But then she saw the splash right below the expanding fire cloud. He had ignited right above the surface, it seemed, and then dropped into the ocean.

*Poor Goodwin,* she thought. But then again, Goodwin seemed the sturdy type.

"Try it!" His voice came up faintly from the dark, sparkling water. "Don't forget to sneeze through your ears!"

"Yeah, sure, I'll sneeze through my ears, you crazy old fart," she muttered, and then held her breath and pulled her tail up so the prongs scratched her chin. Like that, she stopped flying and started falling.

*How am I going to sneeze through my ears how am I going to sneeze through my ears omigod the ocean is coming up really fast and am I catching fire how am I going to—*

Just before she hit the water, she stopped thinking and just did it, forcing as much air as she could through her aural canals.

The results were spectacular. She had never been *inside* an explosion before. An orange and purple starburst coursed over the ocean as she dropped into the water with a glorious splash.

"Wow!" she heard Xavier say nearby as she regained the surface. "That was pretty damn good for a first try!"

"Thanks." She really was grateful for the diversion. It was the first time she had actually done something *fun* in days. After lifting themselves out of the water, shaking themselves off, and making sure Goodwin was still firmly attached to Xavier's wing, they continued.

"What other skills have I missed?" she wondered aloud as they climbed back into the sky.

"Not too many," he admitted. "Of course, the legend of the Ancient Furnace suggests that in addition to Elder skills of the four types, there are unique powers that no other dragon has."

"Huh." She decided she didn't like this turn in the conversation. She didn't want to disappoint her new friend any further. "So if there are such things as lurkers, have you ever seen any? Did they help you fight? Are they all gone?"

"I've never had the chance to find out before today. The legend of Sonakshi is such that the lurkers never show themselves without their chieftain. And I've never been able to summon him on my own. We couldn't do it twenty years ago, either."

He answered her question before she even asked, with a short verse:

> *Far from the shores where other dragons be,*
> *Where moonlight shines upon the blackened sea,*
> *Spill stalker's blood with ancient tooth,*
> *To summon forth the court of Sonakshi.*

"Ancient tooth," Jennifer repeated. "You mean, my tooth. The tooth of the Ancient Furnace."

"That's right."

"And stalker's blood?"

A quick cough escaped Xavier. "That's where I think we might run out of luck. Beaststalkers aren't exactly plentiful anymore. I was thinking you could just, you know, take a bite out of me. Maybe my blood will do."

She stared at him, and he misinterpreted her look.

"Dammit, Jennifer, we don't have a lot of choices! If you know where we can go to find a nice, juicy beaststalker, now would be a good time to—"

"It's okay, Xavier." She began to laugh. "*I'm* a beaststalker."

"*You're* a—" He almost fell out of the air. "Is that a joke?"

"What, you have a problem with that?" A memory reemerged of Xavier Longtail in Blaze, smashing rock with his tail and proclaiming her an abomination to all who could hear.

"Hell, no!" he shouted. "Jennifer, if I could find twenty beaststalkers to join us, I would! We could have used them as friends, before the end came."

"You get one," she told him. "That's going to have to be enough."

"Let's get out a little farther and try our luck!"

As it always seemed to be for adult men who were in charge of driving during a trip, "a little farther" meant about three hours. Jennifer could see no difference in the black, sparkling surface that stretched out beneath them now, and the one in which they had practiced meteor diving.

"We should try it here," he called out to her as they gently descended into hovering position about twenty feet above the calm, rippling expanse. "So if you'll just, um. Bite yourself."

She rolled her eyes as she scanned herself for a good spot to take a chomp. *Tail? Too narrow. Wing? Need it to fly. Flank? Too painful . . .*

Finally, after Xavier began clicking his tongue impatiently, she decided upon the fleshy part of her hind leg, above the knee. She arched her neck down, opened her jaws, and—

*"YEOUCH!"* she bellowed into her thigh.

With a mix of satisfaction and irritation, she noticed right away that she had really nailed an artery. Blood streamed down her leg and dribbled into the water.

"Nice job!" Xavier encouraged her. "Now I can initiate the ritual call!"

"Terrific. Everyone has a role to play."

But he wasn't listening to her. He was flapping his wings hard and calling out to the ocean. "Sonakshi! Sonakshi!"

*"That's* the ritual call?" she asked, trying to staunch the flow of her blood. "'Sonakshi, Sonakshi?' Cripes, I could have done that, while *you* gnawed on your own leg, old man . . .'"

"Sonakshi! Sonakshi!"

Somewhere in the distance, a silent flash of lightning burst from underneath an indigo thunderhead. And before the noise of the bolt could reach them, the endless water rumbled with its own answer.

The ocean, which to this point had resembled nothing more than an endless swarm of sparks bouncing off each other, took on a more definite shape below them. The infinite reflections of moonlight organized into an enormous swirl, and steam began to lace the water's churn. Like fleets of racing sails, long rows of triangular shapes emerged on the edges of this circle.

"I'll be damned," she heard Xavier whisper next to her.

The triangles grew taller, and then seawater washed off of them and onto vast, reptilian coils. Jennifer could not tell at first if it was one large serpent, or several smaller ones. "Smaller" being a relative term here, since even the shortest coil was longer than Pine Street back home.

*Home,* she mused as the thunderhead raced toward them, darkening the twilight and sprinkling rain upon nearby waves. *How quiet it must be for them, in their home far below. Did anything change for them at all?*

The ocean suddenly swelled, washing the writhing coils below with a surge. The thunderhead settled above their position . . .

and opened up with a single, massive firework that lit the sky brighter than a beaststalker's cry, and pounded them with a force that knocked them several feet down out of the sky.

"Are you sure about this?" she shouted at him as the storm unleashed. The wind whipped up the waves to meet the sheets of water cascading from above, making it not only difficult to fly, but to tell where the rain ended and the ocean began.

"Sure we've found the right place? Yes," he answered, before a gust of wind took him. Then, from some distance: "Sure we'll live through this? No."

The coils with the triangular plates rose higher in the maelstrom, swirling around their position like a birthing tornado. Enormous strings of kelp trailed off their snakelike bodies. Jennifer guessed from counting heads through the watery chaos that there were four of them, their features grim—dark hues laced with silvery streaks. Two of the heads were dragonlike, with distinctly human shaping around the eyes and ears. The other two heads were best described as a cross between a seal and an elephant— long, whiskered snouts leading large, floppy ears.

"Which one is Sonakshi?" she asked.

"None of them," he replied, peering into the sea's waves. He struggled to point a wing claw downward, against the burst of air that rushed up from the surface.

What emerged from the depths of the watery vortex made Jennifer scream. The tentacles were first. Eight were the thickness and height of moon elms, and they splayed around the two dragons as though seeking to capture them. Two more tentacles were even longer—the height of redwoods, perhaps, though they did not stand still long enough to measure. They were thinner than the other eight, but still substantial enough to slap either of them from the sky without a second thought. Covered with severe spikes, they extended far above, and then descended along with the other eight appendages.

But before Jennifer could even flinch, the tentacles had receded and splashed back in the stormy water. Then the eye shone.

It was large enough that Jennifer was pretty sure she could have parked Catherine's Mustang convertible on it. An unfathomable disk of obsidian was surrounded by a golden iris that shone with a glow powerful enough to pierce the unsettled sky like a searchlight.

"Sonakshi," she heard Xavier exclaim in reverence. It was difficult to tell if the droplets covering his black, reptilian face were tears or the spray from below. *"Sonakshi!"*

The serpentine beasts riding the surging vortex around them continued to circle, but with open mouths they began to swallow seawater, and sound, and even darkness. It became quieter, and the starlight shone more brightly. The massive eye of the squid below them glided from one visitor to the other. Then the pupil settled upon Jennifer, and a voice with the low, mysterious pitch of whale song crooned in answer.

> *You come far, ancient girl, to return to the sea;*
> *Destiny's tides pull at you, you yearn for the sea.*
>
> *Ancient girl, have you forgotten your ocean kin?*
> *Your kin that died on land used to burn for the sea.*
>
> *What you left behind does not drown or drift away,*
> *Ocean depths stay faithful, though you may spurn the sea.*
>
> *Daughter of fire, daughter of water, fly true*
> *And when air and earth betray, return to the sea.*

*Great,* Jennifer thought as she chewed her tongue. *The gargantuan squid likes poems.*

Hoping she didn't have to respond in kind, she called out over the swirling waters, "We're lost. The universe has changed. We need to put things back where they belong. Can you help?"

For a few moments, she thought Sonakshi had not heard her, or didn't want to answer. But before she could repeat herself, perhaps in some sort of metered rhyme, he continued:

> *Sorcery spins on the surface, never deeper;*
> *Swim beneath it, unravel it, ever deeper;*
>
> *Where the crescent moon lights the ocean on fire;*
> *Lies Seraphina's Isle, however deeper;*
>
> *Strength she will give you, to stand grimly by your side;*
> *Then you must find strength within, endeavor deeper;*

*Heal the world, ancient girl, and poison the poison;*
*Set the moon elm's roots in stone, forever deeper.*

*Aw, shit, it's a poem* and *a riddle,* she almost screamed. *He can't just give me a map and a gun?*

"Thanks," she said instead, and looked up to Xavier. "Anything else you want a really long, undecipherable answer to?"

Xavier stared at the giant squid for a long while, his lips tight and face full of grief. He didn't seem to know how to say anything, but then the words poured out.

"Where were you?" he finally screamed. "We came out here, years ago, and called for you! We needed your help, and you ignored us! We were dying, and you ignored us! We buried the last of our dead, and flew alone for years, and you ignored us! *Why didn't you come?! What have you been doing out here all this time?!*"

The golden searchlight slid dispassionately to consider the dasher, and a last answer came, more slowly than the first two:

*The fight you fought years ago, outside of water,*
*Carries on, beneath these waves, in hidden slaughter.*

*Do not waste any more time here, friends.*
*Hurry, before it is too late.*

And with that, the giant squid and the host of sea serpents submerged, leaving a chaotic residue of foam behind on the surface.

"Hey, that last line had too many syllables," Jennifer protested. "He had to—"

"We're going," Xavier spat bitterly into the ocean. He ascended into the skies, leaving Jennifer to rush after him.

She tried to recall the pieces of the poem. "Where are we going to find where the crescent moon lights the ocean on fire?"

He did not turn to look at her. "I've been out this way many times, and I've never seen anything like that. So I'd guess farther out."

"My wings are a little tired."

"Yeah, well, my friends and family are dead."

"Hey." She flew up close to him and nudged him, not in an entirely friendly way. "So are mine. I'm just saying."

"We don't have time to float around like ducks." His voice held barely restrained anger.

"We could at least swim for a while, and exercise a different set of muscles."

"You want to swim, swim. I'm flying."

"Okay, smiley. You win. We'll keep flying."

If she thought the concession would earn her an apology for his rotten attitude, she was wrong.

*It was six more hours* before either of them said a word to each other again. By that time, Jennifer's wings felt like they were going to fall off. The only thing that might have changed was the crescent moon: It seemed larger than it usually did, but that could have been her eyes playing tricks on her after virtually an entire day of staring at a twilit horizon.

"Xavier!"

He did not turn. He was quite a distance ahead by now, with his profile quite small and Goodwin just a barely visible crown on the dasher's silhouette against the moonlight.

"Xavier! Aw, screw you. I'm going for a swim."

"We're almost there," he called out.

"Sure we are. What does that mean—another three, four hours? No thanks. I need to rest." She was already turning over and dumping the air out of her tired wings; her limbs embraced the change of position.

"Jennifer, if you just—"

"You lost your nagging privileges when you turned back into a bitter old turd," she called up to him. Her altitude continued to decrease. "For almost a whole day, I thought you might be different from the guy I left in the other universe. *That* Xavier Longtail was a snarky slice of toe cheese, too. Why I thought you'd be different, I have no idea." She was almost touching the water now; the velvety surface offered liquid comfort.

"You're going to want to—"

"Save it, Toe Cheese. Yes, that is my new name for you: Toe Cheese. As in, 'Toe Cheese is something I don't enjoy spending time with.' Or 'Excuse me, sir, but could you please remove this Toe Cheese? It displeases me.'"

She gently lit into the water and relaxed all of her limbs,

spreading out her wings on her back and forming a sort of shallow boat. "You spend twenty years alone with no one but a crappy little lizard for company—no offense, Goodwin—and then the Ancient Furnace shows up. The Ancient Furnace! I'm a big deal, pal. You could at least— Hey, this water's kinda warm."

"I should think so," Xavier replied. He was hovering now, staring off into the distance.

She ignored him. "Kinda like a Jacuzzi, but with saltwater. Wow, that feels nice. You should really come down here and feel this, Toe Cheese. Not that I care if you do."

"And *you* should really come *up* here and see *this*."

"Okay, I'll turn my head. But that's it."

That was enough. The glow from the far east was unmistakable.

"Is that fire?"

"It sure is."

"On the ocean?"

"Yes."

"Wow. No wonder the water's warm. So, this is where Seraphina's Isle is, huh?"

"I don't see it. We'll have to look around."

"Hmmph." She wiggled her wing claws. "I suppose that means I'm going to have to get up out of the water."

"No, please, don't let me interrupt your bath. I'll do it myself. After all, it's not like I was up all night doing reconnaissance while you snored up a storm."

"I do not— *Hey!* Flying away while I'm talking is not proof of snoring!"

He was out of sight for ten minutes or so. When he came back, he lowered himself into the water next to her with a sigh.

She kept staring up at the sky as they drifted in circles around each other. "So. How'd it go?"

"The fire looks pretty spectacular," he replied with an exhausted voice. "But there's no island anywhere near here."

"That doesn't make any sense. Where else would an ocean be on fire? Look at those flames!" She pointed lamely with a wing claw at the distant, floating inferno. "They must be, like, thirty-feet high."

"More than a hundred, actually. You want to go up and take a look, feel free." He lapsed into silence. Then, "We're not looking at this the right way. *Why* is the ocean on fire?"

"Hell if I know. Oil slick?" The air around them was getting stuffier, and Jennifer noticed the current was carrying them closer to the flames. They were still a distance away, but the seawater was shifting from warm to hot. "Xavier, I think we might need to—"

"The only other thing that catches fire around here is the crescent moon," he said. "Or it did, back when the venerables served as host to Crescent Valley. But I haven't seen that signal since . . ."

"How did the werachnids manage that?" Jennifer asked. "I mean, venerables are already dead, right? Why wouldn't they stick around?"

Xavier's voice was soft in thought. "They left right before the last stand. We saw the streak of fire leave the crescent moon and disappear over the eastern horizon, and we despaired. We thought they had abandoned us for the heavens. But we were wrong. They came out to the sea . . ."

He lifted himself out of the water and pointed at the inferno, which raged only a few hundred yards away now.

". . . and dove through this spot . . ."

Now Jennifer got up and hovered next to Xavier, suddenly understanding.

". . . and went deeper," they finished together.

And without any hesitation at all, they plunged into the depths.

# CHAPTER 13

## *Friday Night*

The portal through the ocean was much deeper and took much longer than the lake portal had. The column of fire extended into the depths, providing them with light, warmth, and a path to follow. Holding her breath wasn't much of an issue, and Jennifer passed the time deep in excited thought.

Were they crossing back into the correct universe? Skip had told her that wasn't possible—but again, that had been Skip. If he was wrong (or lying), how would they reconcile the two worlds? Would they even have to? If she got back into a Crescent Valley and outside world where her parents were alive and all was right, who cared if she ever went back to this crappy, spider-infested one? Let it rot where it was.

Their emergence into the new world was sudden. The column of fire washed out all of the visual signals they would normally have seen upon a surface approach. For a moment, Jennifer thought they must have gotten turned around, for the ocean here looked pretty much like the ocean they had left, and the fire raged on next to them. Then she saw two spectacular differences.

First, the crescent moon was twice the size of the moon they had left behind. It almost appeared as though they could reach out, grab its hooked end, and pull themselves out of the water.

Second, behind them was a break in the water—a volcanic isle that loomed tall above them. Its sides near the water were barren rock, though there might have been something growing higher up. At the top of the island, where the volcanic crater crested, there was a single, shimmering point. While it was impossible to tell exactly what it was, it was clear to Jennifer that it was shifting, and that it was their destination.

"Jennifer, look!" Xavier pulled himself out of the water and pointed with a wing claw. "Around the moon!"

She squinted, looked hard, and gasped. Against the surface of the massive crescent, she could make out thin trails of flying shapes. Like tiny ants working a trail across a shiny plate, they all moved loosely—but surely—in the same direction.

"The venerables," she whispered. *Grandpa's up there!*

Xavier's voice sounded thin and stretched. "I can't believe it. Seraphina's Isle really does exist."

They approached the volcanic crater cautiously. The dark isle was a mile in diameter and half a mile high, which meant they had to fly up the rocky side rather than climb. Closer and closer they came to the crest, with Jennifer more and more certain that what she saw at the top . . .

. . . was a tree.

*Impossible,* part of her mind told her. *It's too big.*

It was a moon elm of spectacular size, several stories tall. There were thousands of branches, and every branch had hundreds of gleaming leaves. The ground around the tree was lush with strange grasses and wildflowers. Jennifer thought immediately of the wild gardens back at the Scales farm. The vegetation clung to the tip of the volcanic isle the way snow might grip the upper heights of a mountain.

Once they were only a few hundred yards away, Jennifer spotted the source of the movement she had seen from the ocean. An endless fountain of green snakes was cascading down the tree, from branch to branch, leaping at the small white butterflies that rose like confused snow from the flowers below. As the snakes reached the very lowest branches, they launched themselves into the air, flattening their thin bellies and gently coasting into the wildflower fields. From there, they replenished the fountain by climbing up the tree's enormous trunk again.

*This is it,* she guessed. *The moon elm Dad told me about that appeared before him and Mom.* It seemed impossible that this plant could have been anywhere but right here, ever.

"Since we've found Seraphina's Isle," she asked Xavier, "perhaps you could tell me who Seraphina is? Because I'll bet we're likely to meet her now."

"We are indeed."

Before Xavier even spoke the words, the entire tree shivered. Something deep within the branches was uncoiling, disturbing the creatures around it with a long, soulful hiss.

"Behold Seraphina," Xavier continued, "daughter of Brigida, the first perfect dragon."

"How can that be?" Jennifer asked as the coils within the tree continued to unravel. She still couldn't see either end of the creature. "Grandpa told me Brigida lived more than two thousand years ago."

"More like two thousand five hundred. Seraphina was born over two thousand years ago, about the time Brigida disappeared. The daughter lived an incredibly long time, hundreds of years, during which time she is said to have created Crescent Valley. After giving birth to the first Ancient Furnace, Seraphina left the valley she created and promised she would tend to the venerables. Most dragons took that to mean she died and joined them."

"But instead, she created this place." At last, Jennifer thought she could see a head rustling the upper leaves, working its way down.

"That's right. A Crescent Valley beneath Crescent Valley. A place that no one could reach, except for us. A place to keep things secure, if Crescent Valley should ever fall. It was a pleasant legend in my mother's mind, one I always hoped was true—but no one could ever prove it."

"You needed the Ancient Furnace."

"We needed the Ancient Furnace."

"I'm sorry. I showed up twenty years too late to help you."

His eyes did not leave the serpentine shape that now emerged from the moon elm. "Time is not over yet, Jennifer Scum."

"It's Jennifer Sca— Oh, never mind."

Seraphina was a cobra as black as the sea that surrounded them, as long as the trunk of the tree she nested in, and as quick as the wind that whistled through her branches. Two wings, feathered midnight, were folded up against her body. An ancient, powerful scent swirled around her like burial spices. Jennifer was absolutely unsure if what she saw before her was living, dead . . . or something else.

"Welcome, Ancient Furnace," the creature said in a low, guarded alto, and raised its head high enough to affect a slight bow. "You have come to set things right and restore balance to the universe."

Jennifer breathed a sigh of relief. *No poetry, and we don't have to explain a damn thing. Thank heavens.* "Sonakshi sent us here. Can you help us?"

The feathers whispered to each other as Seraphina's coils drew closer. "If you move quickly, there may be time. This is the sole place left untouched by the sorcery of the Quadrivium. Like a distant limb on the far side of the body from where a poison enters, the muscle spasms have not reached here yet. But they will. Only by finding Sonakshi and following the trail left by the venerables have you kept alive our hope that you can keep this place pure and restore the silver moon elm."

*Restore? It looks fine.* Then: *Okay, don't argue!* "I'll do all of that and more. But you have to help us figure a few things out."

"Sonakshi spoke in rhyme."

"It was a little cryptic," Jennifer admitted. "He said you'd give us strength, and that I'd have to find my own strength, and that I'd have to heal the world by poisoning poison and setting the moon elm's roots in stone." She looked up at the tree behind Seraphina. "No offense, ma'am, but I have no idea how to move that thing. Couldn't we just leave it where it is?"

"If you do everything else, the tree will take care of itself. First, you will need strength. I can give you that."

Jennifer looked up and down the massive coils of Seraphina. "You'll do great! I'll bet you can whip the Quadrivium with one wing tied behind your back."

The hissing sound might have been laughter or impatience. "Not me. My place is here. Your help will come from above." Her hooded head gently lilted toward the crescent moon, where the eternal parade of venerables flew on.

"Grandpa?" Jennifer felt a surge of excitement. "You can bring Grandpa Crawford back to help me?"

"*Grandpa* Crawford?" Xavier's voice seemed far away to Jennifer. "Your grandfather is Crawford Scales? But how can—"

Seraphina ignored him. "Reach out, Jennifer Scales. You will find what you need."

"Reach out how?" As she had when Xavier grilled her about her nearly nonexistent Elder skills, Jennifer felt inadequate. "I have no idea how to do this."

The tip of Seraphina's tail slid over her wing, wrapped itself around the claw, and squeezed gently. "You are the Ancient Furnace, child. Have faith in yourself. Look to the crescent moon, and seek what you need. You will find it."

Jennifer stared at the bright sliver. *He's up there! He's really up there!* She let her vision relax and take in the moon's surface. The crescent rushed down to greet her, and in an instant she could see them—see them so closely, it felt as if she were among them.

Her gaze floated over dozens, hundreds, thousands of them. They were an endless legion, pale and silent shadows of cerulean, violet, and jade. On translucent wings, they soared over stark stone craters. Every one of them charged at the horizon, with not even a glance to either side.

Grandpa? Are you out here?

The dragon host continued, more and more rushing past her in silence, even though many had jaws open in what could have been terrible roars. It was unbearably cold, Jennifer realized. She wouldn't be able to stay here much longer.

Grandpa! I need your help! Please!

Niffer.

His term of endearment made her shiver. She spoke aloud now, frantically searching for his image among the multitude. "Yes, it's me! Grandpa, I'm alone! I need to get back! I need your help."

You need family.

"Yes."

You need strength.

"Yes!"
He did not hesitate.

You'll have it.

A gentle chill ran up her spine to the top of her skull. Before she realized it was him, his unseen wing had pressed her gently but firmly down, away from the host and the moon. She gathered speed as she rushed back to herself, until she suddenly found herself rolling backward upon the rocks below the giant moon elm.

As if chasing her, a ball of flame came tumbling down from the moon. It hit the elm with the force of a meteor, sending up a terrific explosion of sparks, splinters, and startled snakes. The fire consumed the massive plant in a matter of seconds, turning each branch into a withered, burning arm. Moments later, the trunk cracked and sent a shudder across the rocky island before it collapsed upon itself in a torrent of cinders.

It was a while before any of the three of them dared approach the burning remains of what had once been the silver moon elm. Instead of rising, the heat seemed to cascade down the sides of the island and push them back. Not even their dragon skin could bear the radiation.

Finally, the flames died down enough for Seraphina to slither up the stones and examine the wreckage. Her horn probed the ashes and coals.

"It worked," the ancient dragon confirmed. "A new presence is here. But—"

"Grandpa!" Jennifer charged up the hill, desperate to see him again. She hadn't realized how much she had missed his face, his stories, even his somewhat short temper. But now that he was back—

No, Jennifer. Not Grandpa.

The familiar voice wrapped around Jennifer's mind and spine, stopping her dead in her tracks. The tone was full of spite and dark amusement.

Murk seeped up through the smoldering ashes, pulling up an unseen head and torso. Out of this shadow, six black legs and two tattered wings rediscovered their balance, shoving aside the revered figure of Seraphina as the new arrival turned and faced them.

"You have *got* to be kidding," Jennifer snarled.

Sister!

*So let me get this straight, dear sister.*

Evangelina's voice hummed inside their minds with gleeful irony.

*You're abandoned and alone in this strange, dangerous world. No family, no friends, no apparent way out . . .*

"Correct." Jennifer was back in human shape, gritting her teeth, hugging her knees, and rocking back and forth. *How could Grandpa send her? This isn't help! We nearly killed each other last week!*

*. . . and you need me—me!—to get out. Why, that's . . . delicious, sister. Absolutely delectable.*

"Forget it." Jennifer abruptly stood up and walked away, back toward the shore. She had no idea what she would do when she got down there, but there was no way she was staying up here. "I'll do it alone."

"Wait, Jennifer!" Xavier scrambled down the rocks after her. "I'm not sure what's happening here, but—"

"She's my sister!" Jennifer spat. "My horrible, awful Half-Sister From Hell! Half-dragon, half-spider, completely insane. If Grandpa ever comes back from the dead, I'll *kill* him . . ." She clenched her fists and screamed up at the moon. "This is *not funny*!"

*Grandfather sends his regrets.*

Jennifer tried to push the voice out of her skull, but Evangelina was too powerful to deny. Communication was on her sister's terms.

*He felt I was the better choice.*

"How. How? *How!?*" She turned and stormed back up the hill, spittle flying in outrage. "How could you possibly be the better choice? A rabid orangutan would be a better choice than you!"

Evangelina's reaction surprised Jennifer. There was anger, of course, but also genuine hurt there, before her sister thought to cloak her emotions.

You asked for strength. I have strength. More than Grandfather has. He knows it. So do you.

"This is so unfair!"
Evangelina's thoughts simmered with discontent.

I couldn't agree more. But Grandfather asked, so I am here. He thought this would be appropriate penance for me.

Jennifer kicked a rock. *Penance? Hmmph.* She couldn't argue with that: Evangelina had done some fairly awful things not long ago, murdering her grandfather among them. If he saw fit to send her back, who was Jennifer to argue?
"You'll really help me?"
Deep within the shadow, Evangelina allowed a thoughtful pause.

Yes.

"You'll do what I say?"
A sound like escaping steam filled her mind.

Don't push me. I'll *help* you.

Jennifer jutted her chin out at the smoking, monstrous shape. "Change back."

Change back?

"To the way you were the last time I saw you."
Evangelina was clearly confused at the request, but within seconds the shape softened, the darkness dissipated, and there stood the young woman from a parking ramp a world away. If she dyed her own hair black ten years from now, Jennifer knew this is what she would look like. The gray eyes and the pale skin

were definitely Scales trademarks. *Come to think of it,* she realized, *the dark hair is, too.* It was only because of her mother that Jennifer was a blonde.

Thinking of her parents made her tremble. Would she ever see her family again? She was beginning to dare to hope. After all, wasn't family standing in front of her?

"Talk to me." Jennifer stepped closer.

Evangelina's head cocked to one side.

I don't know what you want me to—

"No. Open your mouth and *talk* to me." They were face-to-face now, sister to sister.

Evangelina flipped back her dark bangs in irritation. Her vocal chords, bitter from disuse, scraped the words out. "You're a lousy fighter."

Jennifer couldn't help it. She reached out, grabbed the bitch by the shoulders, and hugged her.

# CHAPTER 14

## *Saturday*

While Seraphina slithered over the rocky surface of her isle, surveying the remains of the moon elm and tallying the few surviving creatures, Jennifer and Xavier tried to get some sleep under the dubious watch of Evangelina. It had been days since Jennifer had slept without jitters or horrific dreams, but she finally did so here, where she felt nothing bad could reach her.

Well, there was the half-sister who had tried to kill her. But other than that.

The sleep was deep but short. She woke up before Xavier did, to see Evangelina and Seraphina huddled over something. Their two black, scaly shapes seemed to fit together, as if one were the descendant of the other.

*And she is, isn't she? She's Dad's daughter, just like me. And if I'm an Ancient Furnace, and Seraphina gave birth to the first Ancient Furnace, then she's our great-great-great-hundreds-of-times-over-grandmother.*

They were talking, the two of them. Jennifer sharpened her ears and began to track the topic, which appeared to be on the ground in front of them.

"And you call it *what* again?" Evangelina's voice was still gravelly and impatient.

"Paradise tree snake," came the smooth reply. "My favorite, really, from my old travels through Southeast Asia. They're friendly, observant, and wonderful conversationalists. Handy if you've secluded yourself on a magically remote island for thousands of years. And it gives me peace, to watch them glide from tree to air to land."

"And they land on top of . . ." Evangelina trailed off. "What? People?" Clearly, she was not as charmed by the species.

Again, Seraphina's mysterious hiss preceded her answer. "They are only dangerous to the butterflies, and perhaps to the gentleman's gecko."

Jennifer quickly checked over the sleeping form of Xavier. Fortunately, Goodwin was alive, asleep, and tightly tucked inside his master's wing.

"I don't trust them," Evangelina's voice grated. "Snakes don't fly."

"She didn't say they flew," Jennifer corrected her sister as she walked up to them. "She said they glided. And is your voice ever going to get better?"

"I'm only using it because I have to," Evangelina spat. She motioned to Seraphina without taking her gaze off of the wounded paradise tree snake that struggled to return to the splintered trunk of the silver elm. "I can't enter her mind."

Seraphina's hood rippled, and Jennifer thought she caught a small rise at the corner of the giant cobra's mouth. "My mind is not a playground for your amusement, child. You will need to save your talents for the other world, where they will help your sister."

"Fine." Evangelina turned, and while Jennifer couldn't see the face inside that dark cloud, she was sure the expression was a bit nasty. She, of course, heard her sister's telepathic jab loudly and clearly.

### FINE.

She ignored the provocation. "So where are your brothers? You look like you have their qualities in this shape, but they didn't show up when you took human form last night."

The shroud around Evangelina's head and shoulders fell a bit, revealing an outline of sadness. "None of them were strong enough on their own to endure as venerables. To persist at all, they had to join with me one last time on our way to the crescent moon."

*That's a shame,* Jennifer thought. One of the brothers had been rather cute and had seemed to have a thing for Susan Elmsmith. But Jennifer supposed that match was never going to work, anyway. "So what's it like up there?"

Evangelina snorted. "You were just there."

"It felt cold."

"It is next to the moon."

"Is every conversation with you going to be like this?"

"No. Most will be shorter, and quieter." Evangelina's shadow extended again, and her body turned toward Seraphina. "I'm hungry. What do you have down here to eat?"

Seraphina motioned to the wounded tree snake. "It will die soon, anyway. Better to serve as nourishment."

"It's young." Evangelina's comment gave Jennifer goose bumps. It had been the unearthly hunger for young prey that had tested her half-sister's sanity in the inhospitable dimension where she grew up. "Are there more?"

"Help yourself." Seraphina's detached voice surprised Jennifer. Weren't these snakes her companions? She couldn't imagine summoning a bunch of black mambas just for food. If they weren't going to show up to help her fight in Pinegrove, they certainly weren't going to show up to serve as hors d'oeuvres on her crazy sister's buffet.

Of course, she noticed as she surveyed the destruction at the top of the crater, with no habitat or food, these snakes would probably die soon anyway.

Xavier twitched in his sleep and gave out a long sigh. This had Goodwin up and flitting about, and after a moment Xavier opened his golden eyes.

"So, do we have what we came for?" he asked. "Should we get moving?"

"We could, if we actually had a plan," Jennifer answered. "What is it, exactly, that the three of us are going to do? There's an observatory behind Pinegrove High School. It looks like a headquarters, and we know that Tavia Saltin and Edmund Slider work at the school. Do we just storm the observatory and force whoever's in there to change things back?"

"It can't be that simple," Evangelina said through a mouthful of chewy snake.

"It isn't," Seraphina confirmed. "Remember the rest of Sonakshi's rhyme: You will need to 'poison the poison,' in order to heal the world."

Jennifer kicked idly at a rock. "That doesn't make much sense."

Evangelina rooted around the stones for another snake. "Is there a place in your town where they store poisons? We could investigate." It didn't sound much like she cared if they did or didn't.

Suddenly, it all snapped into place for Jennifer. "Seraphina, you said the change in the universe happened as a sudden seizure, like the way some poisons affect the muscles of a body."

The cobra looked at her evenly, waiting for the logic to unfold.

"Well," Jennifer continued, "if a sorcery *contracted* those muscles, and that sorcery works like a poison, then if we wanted to 'poison the poison,' we'd need to find something that would relax those muscles. Something that would restore the natural position of the universe."

"It's very likely the original sorcery required poison as part of the ritual," Xavier said. "So if we knew what poison the Quadrivium used . . ."

". . . then we could figure out the right ingredient in a sorcery to reverse it," Jennifer finished.

Evangelina radiated waves of impatience. "This information will not help us unless we can figure out what poison they used, where to find it, and who can perform a reverse ritual. Then, of course, we have to convince them to reverse that ritual. All of these occurrences are unlikely."

"Not really. Black widow venom violently contracts muscles. Either that venom, or something like it, was probably used. And if that's the case, we can use botulin toxin to gain a reverse effect. It's a muscle relaxant."

"Where did you learn this?" Xavier asked.

Jennifer straightened her spine and shoulders. "My high school chemistry class."

Evangelina began to chuckle, a completely patronizing sound. Jennifer ignored it. "And I'll tell you something else," she continued. "We can find both of those things at the high school, in the secured storage area. And we know at least two members of the Quadrivium—Edmund Slider and Tavia Saltin. Skip Wilson is also a likely member," she threw on top of it all. She wasn't sure about that last part, but the idea of putting the jerk on everyone's hit list appealed to her.

Evangelina kept chuckling, but Xavier and Seraphina seemed to take Jennifer's ideas seriously. "Botulin would make sense," Seraphina said. "I have heard of sorceries woven with this toxin before. But the obstacles before you are still large, Ancient Furnace. If your plan is to work—"

"Plan? This is no plan!" Evangelina's amusement bordered on outrage.

"If this plan is to work, then you will have to make use of the element of surprise. You must acquire this toxin from the werachnid stores, find the Quadrivium, and force one or more of its members to cooperate, without giving them time to regroup and resist you. The strength of werachnids lies in their ability to plan. The strength of dragons lies in their ability to act."

"Clearly, my sister is not a werachnid."

"How droll. Did you know you have a black hole for a face?"

Seraphina's gaze left the two quarreling sisters and hovered somewhere in the distance. Her forked tongue extended far, over and over.

Jennifer knew enough about reptiles to turn and look. "What do you smell?"

The ancient cobra did not answer. Instead, she unfolded her feathered wings, pushed off with her coils, and sailed down the steep slope toward the rocky coast of her island.

When the other three (four, counting Goodwin) joined her at the bottom, where the waves were beating the rocks into smaller stones and salty gravel slid through the open spaces, they saw a single creature washed ashore.

It looked at first like a large blue crab, perhaps the size of a tricycle tire. On eight segmented legs, it scuttled from side to side, navigating the treacherous pull of the waves and finding purchase higher and higher on the beach. Its large pincers—Jennifer saw that it had three, instead of just two—clicked in anticipation.

They barely had time to look the creature over and wonder at its purpose when Seraphina gave a short spitting sound. An instant later, the crab was on its back, legs shriveling, with a smoldering nine-inch fang sticking through the center of its body. Pieces of its carapace were already washing away.

"Sonakshi's strength is failing," Seraphina observed. "How-

ever many lurkers still live in his waters, it will not be enough
to stop this new onslaught. Ancient Furnace, they are coming for
you. You must go."

"Go?" Evangelina shook her head. "But we have no real plan! I
refuse to help a wretched girl who can't even— *Owww . . .*"

Seraphina reached into the darkness around Evangelina's head
and plucked out the fang she had just spat. It made a juicy *pop*
as it exited. "You'll do as your ancestors instruct, child. Or you
will find this island a mere way station on a continuing journey
downward."

"All right then," said Xavier. "If we have to go, let's go!"

"One last gift for the Ancient Furnace," the winged snake said.
With a swift motion of her wing, she caught a flat, glimmering
shape that had been riding the coastal winds. She approached
Jennifer and offered it: a single leaf from the silver moon elm, a
five-pointed firework caught in time.

"For whatever else you may need on your journey, I lend you
this."

The leaf draped over Jennifer's wing claw like a silk scarf.

"Hurry, Ancient Furnace. If we lose this island, we lose it for
all time, no matter what you may recover elsewhere."

"How much time do we have?" Xavier took to the air and hovered anxiously. "I mean, how long can you hold them off?"

Somewhere out to sea, a shrill cry penetrated the air. They
looked out and saw a silhouette against the ocean's flames, something that might have been a whale or a very large lobster, with
countless legs and eye stalks.

"If that's the largest thing they have," Seraphina answered
thoughtfully, "a day or two."

Jennifer was impressed. "You have enough teeth in your
machine-gun mouth to hold *that* off for forty-eight hours?"

The winged cobra graced her with a faint smile. "Teeth," she
replied, "will be the least of their problems. Off you go. No, not
the way you came! Through the crater now. It is a one-way portal
that will take you back more quickly, and more safely."

Jennifer led the way, looking sadly upon the ashen remains
of the silver moon elm as she crested the top of the volcanic
crater, and then plummeted down the shaft into utter darkness.
She just had to trust that there was something there, at the other
end.

\* \* \*

*To her surprise,* they emerged from the lake near her grandfather's cabin.

"Neat trick," she muttered as she headed for shore. Xavier was right behind her, with Evangelina lagging.

The first two had just landed in the yard behind the aging cabin when Xavier started to groan. He fell on top of his wings and clutched his belly. Goodwin abandoned his rolling host and sought the safety of the cabin's cinder-block foundation.

"Xavier! Are you all right?"

He could not answer. His yellowed teeth began to crack and his wings were shriveling. Jennifer pieced it together just as Evangelina came up behind them and motioned to the sky.

No crescent moon. He's changing.

Panic overwhelmed Jennifer. *How could I be stupid enough to forget this?*

Once again, sister. Stellar plan. Really, I'm in awe.

"Shut up, Hole." She had an unkind thought about Xavier. *What good is he to us, as an old man?* It dissolved into horror as the elderly dasher writhed on the overgrown lawn. He might have been getting a bit smaller, she supposed, and his face was bulging. But he wasn't actually changing shape. "Why isn't anything happening?"

His body does not remember how to change. It will take time. If he doesn't die first from the shock.

"But I don't want him to change at all! He's better off staying back in Crescent Valley. Let's take him back, before he's really hurt—"

A shiny object at the tip of her wing—what she was holding—distracted her, and she immediately breathed a sigh of relief.

"Xavier, take this!" She handed the silver moon elf leaf to the dasher. With a wild motion, he grabbed it.

It took a few moments, but he began to relax. His dark, robust scales regained their gleam, and the gold under his wings began to glitter again. "Thank you, Jennifer. If it's not too much trouble, I'd like to hold onto this for a while."

"I think you'll need to hold onto it for as long as we're out here," Jennifer replied. "The next crescent moon isn't for a few days."

"Fair enough." He sat up. "I'm feeling much better now. Goodwin, come back, boy! I promise not to crush you . . ."

**There's something close.**

Hearing the echoing voice in her head, Jennifer turned to Evangelina. "Just because Seraphina isn't around anymore doesn't mean you can intrude on our minds."

**Tough. My help, my terms.**

"Fine. We don't want your help anymore. Go back to Seraphina and explain to her why you were such a stubborn ass. I'm sure she won't be too busy fighting off the last outpost of our civilization to forgive you."

From the depths of shadow came a growl of frustration, and then her sister's grating voice. "We can't stay here long. There are minds and memories in this forest. They are too mixed and too far away to read well, and I can't guarantee all are friendly."

"Fair enough." Xavier regained his hind legs. "If we can do better than dead snakes, we could look for a bite to eat in this house, and then get moving."

Jennifer shrugged. "Go ahead and look around. I've already eaten at this joint. It sucks."

# CHAPTER 15

## *Saturday Afternoon*

They stayed a short time at the cabin, but the constant mumblings from Evangelina that there was "something out there" provoked Jennifer to the point where she finally snapped.

"Maybe you're sensing that moment in time when you slipped into a cabin just like this one and killed our grandfather," she suggested.

Her sister began sulking and to get her moving again Xavier suggested that they didn't have infinite amounts of time to get everything done. By noon, they were up and flying. Jennifer was painfully aware that of the three, she was the only one capable of disguising herself in any kind of camouflage. But as they went farther south, the cloud cover increased and gave them a higher altitude where they could stay hidden.

The cold wind whipping against Jennifer's closed eyelids reminded her of the previous Saturday, and a ride with four friends she had taken in a Mustang convertible. She opened her eyes and took in the clouds below, and the tiny yellow sun that tried to warm them from a November distance.

*Up here, they can't reach us. Nothing has changed.*

It was Evangelina who first gave the signal that Pinegrove was near. She sensed Jennifer's lingering memory on the edge of town Tuesday morning, of Skip Wilson and a place gone horribly wrong.

"Just how far does that little mind radar of yours work, anyway?" Jennifer asked as they began their descent.

"Depends," came the grudging reply. "If the person is close to me, I can trace them from far away. There are exceptions . . . like you."

Once again, the specter rose of that night at Grandpa Crawford's cabin where each of them had surprised the other.

"I wonder why that is."

Evangelina shrugged, then turned over to dump the air from her wings. "Some minds are harder for me to read. Beaststalkers like your mother. Others are simply stronger and harder to read. Yours, for example, is stronger than most."

"Really?" It was the first compliment Jennifer had received from her sister. "You really think so?"

A burst of resigned exasperation leaked through Evangelina's telepathy before she answered. "Bear in mind, I still kicked your ass that night."

"You so completely did *not*."

They broke through the cloud cover and were surprised to find billions of heavy snowflakes dropping alongside them. Through the curtain of weather, they could make out the landscape of Pinegrove. From the thin sheen of white on the ground, it looked as though the storm had just beaten them here.

"A little bit of good luck, then!" Xavier called out over the brisk winds. "I don't think they'll be able to see our approach in this weather."

The high school was easy to spot. They made for it, getting low as quickly as they could and keeping the strange observatory as far away as possible. Jennifer didn't sense anything creepy about it. Perhaps the eyes within were sleeping or focused elsewhere.

"Which entrance to get to the storage rooms?" Xavier asked.

"Any should be fine," Jennifer replied. She rebuked herself silently for not thinking ahead enough to plan a specific route, but then again, she wasn't exactly sure where the storage area was, anyway . . .

Basement level. Thirty yards from the west entrance and stairs. Your chemistry teacher is on the grounds, and she is easy to read.

Her sister was surprisingly tender with her telepathy, and Jennifer sent back a grateful thought as she repeated the instruction aloud to Xavier.

The school doors were locked, but Evangelina tore them down. Their sleek, monstrous shapes slipped down the stairwell and into the dark basement hallway.

"Is Ms. Sloane in this part of the school?" Jennifer whispered to Evangelina.

"No. Somewhere on the east side, with others."

"Near the gymnasium." The big soccer game against Eveningstar was tonight. Jennifer briefly wondered whether they should have waited a day, or at least until evening—but then the thought of Seraphina holding off whatever hellish arachnid navy was emerging reminded her that the wait was not worth the risk. "Okay, so that looks like the storage area over there."

They could easily see the locked door in the dark, and pushing through it was not a problem. However, a quick glance into the room told them that dragon shapes would be more hindrance than help.

"Xavier, keep watch. Evangelina and I will shift and go in."

The storage room had all sorts of supplies for all sorts of classes: paints and brushes, small animals in formaldehyde jars, old maps and Latin textbooks, and finally in the far corner, a huge fenced-in storage locker with jars upon labeled jars of chemicals and other poisonous substances, as well as a large steel refrigerator.

"Jackpot," Jennifer muttered as she kicked this door open herself. "All right, we're looking for the botulin toxin. I don't know if—"

"In here." Evangelina flipped back her dark hair and strode confidently to the refrigerator. "I can smell it."

They looked up and down and found a shelf of plastic containers marked *Clostridium botulinum: Keep 2–4°C*, and small glass vials marked *Botulinum A: Keep 2–8°C*.

"Which do we take? How much do we need? How're we going to keep it cool enough?"

Evangelina shrugged. "No idea."

Jennifer chewed her tongue and scanned the locker. "All right. Over there." She pointed and then picked up a small plastic cooler, which had a bit of dust in it but nothing else. "Let's take one of the plastic containers and a few of the vials. If it's not enough, one of us will have to come back and get more, that's all."

"That's all?" Evangelina's smirk was not totally unkind as she located ice from the freezer compartment and filled the cooler. "You have an awful lot of faith in yourself, sister."

"I have faith in *you*. You'd be the one coming back. You're the strongest. Okay, let's get the poison in there. Make sure there's ice all around it."

The older girl's mouth twisted. "Hmmm. You were right about where the poison was. If you're right about the observatory—"

"Can you feel anything from over there? They're pretty close."

Evangelina shook her head. "That building felt closed. Nothing in, nothing out."

"Can you feel Skip?" As soon as the question was out, Jennifer thought better of it. "Never mind. I don't care. He can go—"

"He's been in the school recently. But that could mean anything."

"Ladies!" Xavier's voice came from the doorway. He was trying to squeeze in. "We have company."

*At least three of them,* Jennifer guessed from the footsteps and voices echoing down the stairwell on the opposite end of the hallway from where they had entered. She closed the cooler, wondering if they should engage the newcomers or just run for it. *Do they even know we're here?*

They did not, it was immediately clear. The voices were giggling and whispering and shrieking, like teenagers trying to scurry away from some authority figure and do something ill-advised out of sight.

"Did Coach see us leave the locker room?" one of them asked, and Jennifer's teeth clenched hard. It was Amy. And if Amy was one of them . . .

Bobbie's voice was breathless but still firm. "No way. Stop freaking out, Amy, we're on the other end of the school! So how much you got?"

"A vial for each of us. But we gotta hurry. Game starts in twenty minutes!"

Feeling a cloud over her head darker than anything Evangelina could muster, Jennifer turned to the other two and forced her voice down to a whisper. "I'm not running from these people again."

Evangelina only had to connect for a brief moment before Jennifer felt her sister's caution turn to fury. "These are the bullies who threatened your life. They are predators."

*Like she used to be,* Jennifer thought. *And still is.* She felt a simultaneous desire for penance and vengeance—the chance to do right by doing wrong—rise in her sister's mind.

"We don't have time for this!" Xavier urged them both. "They're still far down the hall. If Evangelina and I move now, Jennifer can use her camouflage to cover our—"

"I am *not*," Jennifer repeated, "running from these people again. Xavier, take the cooler. Evangelina—"

But her sister was already out the door, morphed, and racing down the hall toward the other girls.

"Jennifer!" Xavier pleaded as she pushed the cooler into his wings. "You could raise an alarm!"

"There won't be an alarm." Jennifer followed her sister.

Bobbie and the others were so consumed with their quest to get high that they did not see the attack coming. Evangelina rolled down the hallway like a blackout, snuffing the exit signs and nighttime lights one by one. By the time any of them realized anything was wrong, it was too late.

Jennifer shifted into dragon shape so she could see a bit better. Even then, there was little detail available. Someone screamed—Abigail or Anne—and then she heard a shout of anger from Bobbie. Amy's brunette locks emerged from Evangelina's darker shadow briefly, but then a tattered wing with a stark claw yanked her back in.

After a few moments, Bobbie broke free of Evangelina's trap and found the time to morph into a spectacular black widow specimen, dominating the hallway at seven feet tall and ten feet long. Anne's unconscious shape stumbled into view and careened to the floor, and Abigail screamed again from somewhere unseen, but Amy managed finally to scramble into the open and under the protective new shape of her friend.

"Who the hell are you?" Bobbie demanded.

"We're the visiting soccer team!" Jennifer answered, and before anyone could figure out where she was, she took wing just behind Evangelina, plunged through her sister's dark aura, and burst out again right in front of Bobbie, turning to swing her tail. "Penalty kick!"

The black widow took both prongs right on the side of the head, stumbling under an explosion of sparks. Evangelina advanced and grabbed Amy by the neck. The girl sputtered as her body was lifted off the floor and slammed up against the wall.

You thought it was funny to attack my sister. You saw the blonde bitch make her bleed, and you joined right in.

"I'm . . . sorry . . ." Amy gasped.

You are young. Stupid. Tasty.

Another creature emerged just under Evangelina's body. It was Abigail, gathering herself to try to help. The girl's scorpion shape was strong but elegant, with an olive segmented body, lean crimson head, and swift orange appendages with brown markings. Her black tail struck blindly at where Evangelina's head likely was, and apparently scored a hit.

Ow.

Evangelina threw Amy back down the hallway, where the girl's limp form came to a halt near a horrified Xavier. Then she sized up Abigail's scorpion form, swung her tail around like a scythe, and broke off one of the girl's snapping pincer claws.

While Abigail screamed, Evangelina raised a foreleg and brought the pincer end down, stabbing the scorpion in the back and pinning her to the hallway floor.

"Evangelina!" Xavier dropped the cooler and raced toward the fray. "Stop! You'll kill her! Jennifer!"

The monster turned to Jennifer, who had Bobbie's dizzy head pinned to the wall with a strong hind leg.

Don't pretend that would bother you, sister.

Jennifer didn't know how to answer; she could only watch Abigail's crippled shape stagger back and forth across the locker-room entryway. Did scorpions regenerate limbs? Would others around here know a sorcery that could help her? Would—

A sudden blow across her jaw interrupted her thoughts and

broke her grip on Bobbie. The spider brought another limb up and struck Jennifer in the midsection, knocking Jennifer back and giving her opponent the chance to scramble up the nearby stairs. She was fast, Jennifer calculated through her pain, faster than any of the three of them.

*But not faster than fire.*

It only took one ball of flame to knock the spider down. The projectile from Jennifer's jaws hit its target squarely in the bulbous thorax, and the carapace began to combust immediately. Bobbie screamed as she lost her balance and tumbled back down the stairs.

Jennifer kicked the burning monster in the abdomen, then pushed her up against the wall and pinned her there. *Just like she pinned me.*

"You wanted me to turn into a dragon," she spat at Bobbie. "Here. I. Am."

The spider tried to regain its balance, but Jennifer kept her foot planted firmly on her back. She gave a short whistle—just enough to reignite the fire that had been consuming the girl's body.

"Jennifer!" Xavier's shock echoed down the hall. "No!"

Bobbie tried to shift back into the form of a girl, but she kept burning, her chest heaving in pain.

Jennifer gave Xavier a hard stare, but then smothered the fire with her wings. "Stop screaming, you insufferable baby. Get up." She turned to Xavier. "We're going to have to put them all in the storage locker, so they can't get out and alert anyone else."

Bobbie's clothes were still smoking. "Make it stop!" she shrieked. "Please! It burns! Please! I'll do anything. Just make it stop, make it stop!"

Let her burn.

"What?"

They might escape the storage room. Besides, we ruined the door. Easier to kill them.

"Jennifer!" Xavier's reptilian features were full of pain and worry—not for Bobbie or Abigail, she realized, but for *her*.

"Don't do this! Don't lose yourself! That's not our way."

Evangelina picked up Abigail with a single claw, threw her against the wall, and then reverted back to human form. Her grating voice was full of disdain. "Your way, old man? What exactly is your way?"

"Whatever it is," Jennifer guessed, "it hasn't done much good these past fifty or sixty years." She took a deep breath. *Can I do this?* "Evangelina's right, Xavier. We have to kill them."

"Please don't," came a new voice. "You said you wouldn't."

Andi was standing on the stairs, wearing shorts and a sweatshirt and holding a small gym bag. The small girl was biting her lip and examining Jennifer's dragon form.

"Are you going to kill anyone?" she had asked.

Jennifer had certainly toyed with murder since she became a dragon. She had finished off an already dying Otto Saltin, and beaten down Evangelina to the point where the spirit of Crawford Scales could carry her away. But had she ever done anything like this before? Ever knocked a wounded girl down as she was running away and let her burn to death?

"I can help them," Andi offered. She took a step down. "I can heal them. It's what I do, remember?"

Jennifer surveyed the scene. Bobbie burnt, Anne and Amy unconscious, Abigail in scorpion shape with a claw missing and a hole through her abdomen.

Andi took another step down. "I can keep them alive, for a while. Until help comes. That's all I want to do. Whatever you came to do, I'm not going to stop you."

"I don't trust her," Evangelina snapped. She grew back into her shadowy form. "I say we kill her, too, and finish the others off."

But seeing Andi again had awakened something in Jennifer: the memory of another girl in pain, who was almost a friend. *Maybe still is.*

She gently held her sister back. "Evangelina, please. Let's stop here, and go."

"You want me to show mercy."

"Like you showed my mother. Remember?"

"I remember." Evangelina looked at Andi. The quiet girl was already pulling bandages and other supplies out of her gym bag to tend to Abigail, who had shifted back into the form of an armless human. When the black beast spoke again, it was with deep anxiety. "I can't help it, sister. I'm hungry."

"Pardon?"

"Hungry. Being where I was, where our grandfather still is, I never wanted for anything. I was never hungry like I had been before. I didn't need to feed on anything, or anyone. But now that I'm back here . . ."

"I just need you for a little longer, Evangelina. Then you can go back to the crescent moon, and never be hungry again."

Evangelina slipped away from Jennifer's grip and took a step toward Anne's unconscious body. "Why not enjoy ourselves while we're here?! It's not like any of these people will know or care what happened, once our job is done. Half of them won't even exist anymore."

"You know that's not the point. Andi deserves the chance to try to save them."

"How do we know she won't raise the alarm?"

"Hey." Andi interrupted them with a look full of pride and anger. "If I had wanted to raise the alarm, I would have done it while you were fighting. Jennifer said she was my friend, and that maybe we could help each other."

"That's right, Andi. I said that. And I meant it."

Sizing Jennifer up much as she had while bandaging her in a locker room days ago, Andi finally reached into her gym bag again and pulled out two shining objects. Jennifer gasped as they came skidding harmlessly across the floor at her.

"Bobbie gave me those, after you left. She said she didn't want to get caught with them." She gave Bobbie's scarred body a bitter glance.

Jennifer shifted back into a girl and picked up the two blades—*her* two blades, the metal hilts sticking out of their strapped sheaths. How they shone in the faint light from beyond the stairs! She squeezed the handles and felt herself grow a foot taller. *We're going to win.*

"Do you need any help here?" she asked Andi.

Andi gave her an incredulous look that said it all: *Haven't you done enough?*

"Right. I'm sorry, Andi. I know they're your friends. I hope you can help them. We'll— I'll—" *Never see you again? Not if all goes well.* "Take care of yourself."

* * *

*They left the school* the same way they had entered, Xavier and Evangelina in their larger shapes and Jennifer still feeling the thrill of holding her daggers in human hands. Even in the cold November snow with nothing but a flowered berry nightgown on, she felt invincible.

Staying low, they worked their way around the northwest corner of the school. The observatory was off the northeast corner, which meant they would have to cross at least two hundred yards of open ground, with no cover and the tall school wall to their back, to get to their target.

*And just where is the entrance to this thing?* Jennifer wondered as they moved. She tried to remember if it had doors anywhere. Yes, she thought she remembered a set of double doors on the west side. *Wherever they are, as long as we don't need to teleport in, we'll be fine.*

As it turned out, there was a lovely pair of doors right where she expected them: in the center of the west side, where anyone could walk in. Of course, they would first have to make it past the six dozen giant, stark spiders ranging from desert tarantulas to silver argiopes who stood guard on the field north of the high school. The silent snowflakes gently fell upon their bloated bodies and stuck to their wiry leg hairs.

One of them—maybe all of them—spotted Xavier's golden wings the moment they came around the corner, and the alarm went up.

"Too many!" Xavier shouted.

"We can take them," Evangelina insisted. The cloud around her body extended, and Jennifer felt her sister's psyche brace for combat.

"Evangelina, are you sure we—"

DOWN.

The air buckled around them, and a shock wave burst over the field. It melted the snow and scattered a tangle of spindly legs. Spiders tumbled over each other and into the latticework of steel beams surrounding the observatory. Jennifer leapt forward, seeking advantage in this opportunity her sister had given them.

Before she could engage, another shriek went up, and another two dozen spiders came marching around the edges of the observatory.

"We can't take them all!" Xavier called out.

As the first group of spiders recovered, the trees far off to the northeast began to rustle with movement. *More of them,* Jennifer guessed.

Jennifer shifted into dragon form, clinging to the precious cooler with a hindclaw. She let a jet of flame escape her mouth to keep the advancing swarm back. But it was half-hearted—the memory of what she almost did to Bobbie haunted her—and before long she saw even more dark legs scrambling to bolster the ranks that faced them.

"We need to get out of here!" Xavier took to the air. Evangelina cursed and followed him.

Jennifer took off after Xavier and Evangelina. *Andi can't have told them. They were already in position. They knew before we even got here!*

The spiders pursued them for a short while, with some of the jumpers taking a shot at them before the dragons were at too high an altitude to track. The arachnids' screams followed them even as they punched through the clouds far above the borders of Pinegrove.

Before it had even begun, the assault on the Quadrivium was over.


"*I've seen horrible things* in my lifetime," Xavier spat as they soared out of Pinegrove and back toward the cabin. "Awful, terrible things. But I'm not sure that didn't top them all, Jennifer Scales."

"That's not fair! We had to retreat. You saw how many—"

"I don't mean our retreat," he snapped. "I mean you and your sister's actions in the school hallway, before that doctor friend of yours put some sense in your brain."

"What do you— How can that— That was nothing!" Jennifer protested. "You should see what my sister used to do to people."

He didn't answer. Jennifer gently chewed her forked tongue

between sharp teeth, and her tail twitched as she swerved a bit. "I told Andi I was sorry. I couldn't help myself, for a while. I was angry."

"Of course you were. And I'm angry, too—at what they did to all of us, including your father and grandfather. But you won't ever see me stab one of them in the back, or torture them for fun. It's beneath me. It's beneath you, too."

*It's not beneath me.*

This Evangelina offered from a comfortable distance behind them both.

"No, that appears to be right at your altitude, hot stuff," Xavier spat. "But maybe you'll learn better before the end."

They spent the next hour or so in relative quiet, letting the stars above hold a twinkling conversation. It wasn't until they were a few miles from the cabin that Xavier spoke up again. He veered in close to her so he didn't have to shout.

"Jennifer, I regret snapping at you."

"It's okay. I accept your apology." Smiling warmly at him, she wondered if the Xavier Longtail in the other universe ever apologized to anyone.

"I'm offering regrets, Jennifer. Not an apology."

Her warm feelings vanished. "I can't wait to hear you split hairs over the difference."

"Jennifer, I can remember what we were like before the trouble started. Before the rout at Alexandria, before they crushed us at Eveningstar, before they entered Crescent Valley and pushed us to the brink of extinction. We weren't perfect, but we had pride in who we were. We thought ourselves better than our enemies.

"But as our numbers dwindled, we became more desperate. More and more of us began to lash out, to do things no dragon had ever done before. Some even reveled in embracing the beast within. My brother, Charles, and I argued against them, but the years wore us down. Then he died, of course."

"How did he die?" Jennifer asked, holding her breath.

"It was when we barely had a foothold in this world anymore. Charles tried to stop a group of young dragons from firebombing a nuclear power plant near a werachnid town. He tried to explain what could happen, not just to werachnids but to everyone. Instead of listening, they turned on him, accused him of conspiring with the enemy, and killed him. Their plot failed, eventually. But neither their failure, nor his murder, taught them anything.

"After we were pushed off this side altogether, we slid into oblivion. The longer we stayed in Crescent Valley, the worse it got. After decades of getting pushed around this world, and another five years confined on the other side, our worst characters came out. We became as primal and thoughtless as those experiments you saw. Yes, the ones werachnids eventually abandoned, because they were uncontrollable."

Here he nudged himself closer.

"The worst part, Jennifer, is that *we still lost*. We gave up everything about ourselves that meant anything at all. And in the end, it did nothing to protect us."

"You mean you would have won if you had acted differently?"

"I don't know, Jennifer. I suspect we would have inspired ourselves to last longer, since we would have had more pride in who we were. And maybe we would have even inspired unseen allies to join our cause earlier—like Sonakshi and the lurkers. More to the point, we would have forced the werachnids to fight us, rather than the mindless, bloodthirsty shadows we left behind."

Jennifer sailed along quietly. She was pretty sure how this related to what had just happened at Pinegrove High, but she didn't want to admit it to herself.

Xavier closed the loop for her. "Jennifer, when I met you just a few days ago, you weren't just the first dragon I'd seen in more than twenty years. You were a dragon . . . who was still a dragon. Don't let *her*"—he jerked his head back—"change that. Don't let her change *you*. Once you set the world straight, it will need you the way you are."

The air left her wings. *Once I set the world straight?* "As if we can possibly succeed now."

"I know it looks bad," he told her, "but I've seen worse. The three of us will just need to regroup, is all. Come up with a new plan."

"We're running out of time. Seraphina can't keep holding off whatever's attacking her. Crescent Valley probably emptied everything it had on her."

"We'll make it," he promised her. "Together, we'll finish what we started." And with that, he split off from her and began his descent toward the cabin.

Had it not been for the tiny whistling sound, Jennifer wouldn't have already been looking down at Xavier when he grunted. She would have missed his wing spasm, the way his body suddenly jerked, and his quick and uncontrolled spiral toward the ground.

# CHAPTER 16

## Sunday

Evangelina and Jennifer dropped immediately to follow Xavier's body. They lost him for a moment through the treetops, but within a minute they found him again.

He was on his back in the brush, splayed out like a giant black and gold butterfly on top of a cluster of raspberry bushes. The cold, snowless wind pushed the vegetation and the body on top of it back and forth. Had there not been a thin, black, carbon-aluminum arrow sticking out of his heart, Jennifer would have thought he was relaxing. As they got closer, Jennifer heard him muttering.

"Stupid, stupid, stupid . . ." He spoke between shallow breaths, and his glazed eyes tried to focus on her. "I flew too low, too early, even for this side of the lake. I should never have relaxed my guard."

"Maybe we can do something," she offered frantically. She looked over at Evangelina. "What if we pull the arrow out?"

"Jennifer Scales." Xavier smiled. "I'm glad we found each other. Even if you were a bit difficult, and foolish . . ."

"What if we pull the arrow out!" She shouted the question at Evangelina.

Her sister shrugged.

**Then he'll die faster. It might show mercy.**

"That's not helping!" She tried to lift Xavier's body off the brush, but he was too large, and she didn't know what good it would do anyway, so she stopped. "Xavier, tell me what to do!"

"Watch over him," he answered in a whisper. His wing claw opened, and two things poured onto Jennifer's trembling wing claw: the moon elm leaf, and the red and green curl of Goodwin, still alive. "Until you and I meet again . . ."

"You can't die!" Jennifer felt the panic rising in her throat. "I need you here!"

The Elder's yellow smile remained, but he said nothing.

"Xavier!"

He's gone. I can't sense him anymore.

Jennifer fell to her knees. "No! Not him!" Her mind raced back to that moment on the stone plateau, when this ornery dasher had rushed in from nowhere to save her. All of the thrill she had felt at that moment, and all of the hope she had accumulated since then, crumbled away. "He can't be gone! I need him! He was the last!"

Not the last.

Evangelina reminded her gently.

"But now there are only two of us! We can't take on the entire town of Pinegrove!"

Have faith, sister. We are not finished yet.

"Faith," she snorted through her tears. "That's almost funny, coming from you."

She felt Evangelina's attention turn elsewhere.

They are coming, the ones who did this.

"Who, werachnids? They've followed us from Pinegrove?" *Or from Crescent Valley?* Or perhaps it was not even from that far. Jennifer remembered the sounds she had heard during the night she spent at the cabin.

Not werachnids. Something else.

Her sister turned to look at her.

Something familiar.

Even though Evangelina told Jennifer there were several of them hiding nearby, only one was brave enough to emerge out of the brush and confront them. It was a young man dressed in grim brown clothing and archer's gear. His quiver held dozens of thick, black arrows that looked exactly like the one sticking out of Xavier's corpse. He stepped up and inspected the fallen dragon. He might have let out a small gasp at what he saw, but Jennifer couldn't hear too well past the throbbing blood in her temples.

"He's mine," she growled, pushing her sister aside. She spread her wings and cleared her throat, ready to incinerate the soldier . . . until she saw him raise both hands and his face to her. Sorrow and reverence clouded his sparrowlike nose and soulful eyes.

"Spirit! Forgive me!"

She squelched the fire building within, choking in shock. *"Eddie?!"*

He stiffened in fear. "You know me, Spirit?"

"Eddie Blacktooth!" Had it not been for the dead dragon not ten feet away from them, Jennifer would have hugged him. As it was, she was shocked at his appearance.

While lean from hunger, this Eddie Blacktooth was clearly a warrior. He held his composite bow in muscular hands, and multiple scars curved over the ripples on his arms, neck, shoulders, and chest. He wore mostly camouflage gear, with patches of animal skin sewn in places where the fabric had worn thin. Three hunters' knives of varying sizes hung off his utility belt.

But above all, he held his sparrowlike face high, not dug into his chest like it always seemed to be back home. Jennifer could not reconcile this young man with the pathetic boy who had cowered before Winona Brandfire last week.

"But how did . . . Skip told me . . ." She trailed off, realizing she had answered her own question. *Why would Skip tell me the truth about anything? And who's to say Skip had any idea?*

He looked at her, confused. "I didn't know what flew overhead. In my fear and haste, I assumed it was one of . . ." He cleared his throat and spat. "One of *them*. Jumping high."

She looked over at Xavier. "Oh, Eddie . . ."

"Take my life in payment," he declared abruptly, standing up and offering her a small knife with both calloused hands.

*"What?!"* Jennifer panicked as she watched several other young men and women come out of the woods, similarly dressed, each with head bowed and hands holding out some convenient implement of death.

"I've wronged you," Eddie told her again. "You and your spirit brethren came to help me, as omens of good fortune. I repaid your divine gift through murder. My life is forfeit."

Jennifer gasped, and then steamed silently as she heard her sister's mocking laughter inside her head.

They think we're gods. Splendid.

"Eddie, haven't you *ever* seen a dragon before?" Of course, she knew the answer before he gave it with reverent brown eyes.

"Dragons have been dead for longer than we've been alive," he explained. "Only Mother remembers seeing one alive, as a child. All that are left are spirits like you . . ." His features turned desperate. "I cannot curse my family. I owe them everything. Please, divine Spirit—"

"Stop calling me that!" Jennifer shifted out of dragon shape and motioned to her sister to do the same. Evangelina reluctantly followed suit. "I'm not a spirit, and you don't owe me your life. But Eddie, you killed a friend . . ."

His jaw dropped open. "Spirit in human shape!" he cried. Then he shielded his face. "I cannot look. Only the most blessed of mortals may— *Aaarrr!*"

Twisting the ear she held, she pulled him closer. "Eddie, shut up and listen! My name's Jennifer. I can't explain why I'm here. Not now, anyway." Her mind was working again now, and she took in the dozen or so warriors that gathered. They looked at her with alarm, but also enough respect for her to continue.

"We need a ceremony. For my friend. I can't take him back where he belongs—" She had a brief but grim memory of the great stone plateau in Crescent Valley, and the creatures that guarded it. "But I think he'd be okay if we laid him to rest near here. Someplace safe. Maybe near the cabin. You know the one just northeast of here?"

"Yes," he answered, keeping his head still.

"Great. Can you help us move him?"

He put his hand to his ear as she let go, and then he nodded. "Yes, we can move him. It will be an honor to bury him. What was his name?"

Jennifer sighed at Xavier's fallen body and thought back to his last words carved in stone. "He just wanted to be known as a loyal friend," she told them. Then she turned to Eddie. "And it's *him* you owe a debt to, not me. You want to repay your debt?"

"More than anything," he told her, bowing once more.

"Then take his place and help me."

He didn't hesitate. "Absolutely. I will stand at your side."

*It was well after midnight* on Sunday morning by the time they had buried Xavier. Jennifer had him put where Grandpa Crawford's grave would have been, and then decided she should doze while she could. Evangelina offered to stand guard, needing little in the way of sleep. Meanwhile, Eddie and a few others stayed at the cabin, while the rest of his patrol made for their headquarters, which they told her was a campground a few hours' march away.

By the time dawn broke, Jennifer had a fresh set of tears ready. She lay in the downstairs bedroom for a while, listening to the heartbeat of her vigilant sister outside the door, wondering which of the two of them would be the next to die.

Or would it be Eddie? Of course, it had occurred to her the moment she had seen him that he and his fellow beaststalkers could be the new source of strength she needed. But would they come along? And did she want them?

She got up, and she and Evangelina joined the small troop of beaststalkers who had been camping outside. (They had refused her offer to sleep indoors, out of courtesy to the dragon-spirit in mourning, and she had been too tired and exasperated to force the issue.) From their tents and packs they supplied her with proper clothes, and it was a relief to take off the nightgown that she had first found at the cabin several days ago. Then Eddie and the other young warriors—none of them knew what a beaststalker was—shared a few key facts.

First, the entire "family"—the entire loose group of warriors who lived on the run and in a variety of makeshift homes throughout this part of Minnesota—numbered about thirty individuals. For years, there had been intermittent contact with other, similar groups. However, it had been months since they had last heard from anyone else.

Second, while some parts of their clothing were primitive, these people had technological savvy. The bow Eddie had was top-of-the-line, obtained through a series of trades with trusted contacts and supply chains. A few of them had legitimate jobs and simply wove themselves into the fabric of society, just as weredragons and werachnids so often did in the real world.

Third, they lived a bloody existence.

"How are you not dead?" she asked them plainly, after hearing a few of their recent adventures.

Eddie bowed his head. "Many of us have died, Jennifer-spirit." *Jennifer-spirit* was the compromise they had reached on her possibly divine identity. "And most of us die before our time. But those who remain are strong. I myself have slain over thirty spider-beasts with this bow. No one else in our family, not even Mother, has done this before turning sixteen." His face changed from pride to sorrow as he remembered his last kill. "The spirits have blessed me . . . until now."

"So you believe in dragon spirits, do you?" Evangelina's throaty voice was a bit playful with Eddie. "And you worship them."

Eddie nodded. "Native American tales of the spirit world are strong. While Mother says it is mythology, many of us grew up with relatives or friends who insisted some spirits do exist—such as dragon-spirits. Dragon-spirits were a strong, divine force that once kept the spider-beasts at bay. We have heard of the times when dragons were plentiful and lived peacefully alongside all others."

Jennifer narrowed her eyes at Evangelina's snort. "Legends can exaggerate. But I remember a little of the times you're talking about."

"Then you must be older than you look!" He looked at her with new respect.

"Hey," she protested, "I'm not *that* old . . ."

"Will we see your mother?" Evangelina asked Eddie with some anxiety. Jennifer figured the memory of her sister's fight with Wendy Blacktooth had awakened some small measure of guilt.

"She's dead," Eddie explained with no visible regret. "She and my father fell in battle when I was four years old. The last I saw of them, they were back to back, fighting off hordes of enemies. Piles of dead, eight-legged monsters lay at their feet. The others in the family raised me from that point. Now I am an elder, and I help raise others."

"So wait. You've been talking about a mother, but you just said she died. Who's Mother, then?"

They were interrupted by a clamor in the nearby forest—the howl of something that sounded like a cross between wolf and wildcat. Jennifer leapt to her feet with the others, but there was something recognizable about the sound. She recalled the hunts of Crescent Valley . . .

A huge, furry shape crashed through the underbrush and came at Eddie. Rather than pull out a weapon, he laughed and held his arms out. The newolf—that is, after all, what it was—crashed into him and began licking his face.

Jennifer nearly fainted in shock at the sight of the animal. She could not tell for sure if this was the exact creature she had once met on the side of the road last spring, but it shared an auburn coat and a thoughtful set of animal eyes. "How many of these are still around?"

"Just Phoebe, as far as we know." He chuckled while giving the deadly animal a noogie. "Down, girl, down! She has a terrific sixth sense. Mother keeps her at her side, at all times."

*Phoebe. Mother.* Jennifer barely had time to put it all together before what looked like the rest of Eddie's clan stepped into the clearing. At the front of this grim band, none of whom were smiling, stood the most forbidding figure of all: six feet tall, honey blonde hair, and sharp emerald eyes.

Jennifer rushed forward for a hug, but her target was too fast. With a quick dodge to the right, the woman brought down the butt of a sword on the back of Jennifer's head.

*Jennifer woke up to darkness* and the anxious outrage of Evangelina clouding her mind. Through her sister's thoughts, she gathered the beaststalkers had surrounded them both, and Evangelina was about ready to kill them all. Only an argument between Eddie and the woman who was certainly Elizabeth Georges-Scales—*She's alive!*—was delaying the slaughter.

You're awake. Are you all right?

*I'm fine. What's happening?*

The idiot boy is challenging the bitch who resembles your mother.

*Resembles?* Jennifer's spirit, which had risen upon the memory of seeing her mother alive again, sank a bit. She stretched a hand out into the darkness. "Help me up, please."

Evangelina's claw grabbed her wrist and pulled her up into the morning light. The move startled the crowd of beaststalkers around them, but Jennifer could plainly see they were all too terrified to attack. The only one who urged them on was the woman, whose face was contorted in rage and disgust.

"I can't believe how stupid you are!" she was screaming at Eddie. "You shoot one down, and then rather than finish the other two off, you lead them to a comfy lakeside cabin and stand guard! Did you also cook them breakfast?"

Eddie took a step forward. "Mother, will you *listen* to me?!"

"I will not. You disappoint me, Eddie. If any of us die here today—"

"Nobody's going to die!" Jennifer interrupted. "Mom—Mother. Eddie. My sister and I are not going to hurt any of you. In fact, we need your help. If you could—"

"Quiet, beast. Your pretty façade doesn't fool me. My scouts told me the true shape you took as you came down from the heavens to mourn your friend. You've got a forked tongue, and I'll cut it out if you say another word."

Jennifer took a step back. "But I'm your daughter . . ."

"Enough." The blonde woman raised her sword and came at them.

A quick left from a spindly front claw sent her staggering back.

"You're cute," Evangelina croaked. "Let's play again."

"Take it easy on her. That's my mom!"

"Stop," the woman said while regaining her feet, "calling me 'Mom.'"

"Mom mom mom mom mom this universe sucks and I'll call you what I want mom mom mom mom mom!"

"Phoebe, attack!"

The newolf, crouched between the woman and Eddie, snarled at Jennifer and Evangelina . . . but stayed put.

"Mother, she's not going to attack them. Don't you remember the legends of wolves who once hunted alongside dragons?"

Phoebe got a swat across the snout for her insubordination. "Those are tall tales, campfire stories! Dammit, dog, if you're not going to behave—"

"Look." Jennifer raised her palms and took a cautious step forward. "You've given me plenty of reason to fight you. You've coldcocked me, tried to get your friends to kill me and my sister, and sicced your wolf on me. But I'm still not going to do it. I'm not going to fight my own mother. Can we just—"

"Stop calling me that."

"*Dammit*, look at my face! Can't you see it? Are you that damn stubborn?! I'm your daughter!"

The woman lowered her sword. "Am I to take it that none of you are going to help me fight this creature and her grotesque friend?"

Nobody moved.

"Fine." She sheathed the weapon and walked away. "Disobey me, if you want to play with the funny-looking woodland creatures. But keep them away from me, Edward, or I'll kill *you*."


*The next couple of hours* were harder for Jennifer than just about any she had suffered this past week. After trying multiple times to approach Elise Georges—that was, she learned from Eddie, the woman's name—Jennifer tired of the increasingly violent reactions and accepted Evangelina's advice. Instead, she stuck closer to those beaststalkers who still appeared eager to befriend them.

*At least,* Jennifer told herself while huddled near the campfire with Eddie, Evangelina, Phoebe, and about fifteen others, *she hasn't left completely. Though that's probably because the dog likes me.* In fact, she was scratching the newolf behind the ears right now, just like she used to scratch the smaller black dog with the same name. While she didn't actually think this was a new incarnation of her favorite border collie–German shepherd mix, she was enjoying the naming coincidence.

"Do you think we should try to talk to her again?" she asked Eddie for the eighth time in three hours.

His shoulders shuddered in a silent laugh. "No."

"The way she talks to you. It's awful. I can't imagine her talking to me like that."

He shrugged. "It's the way she is. I know she loves me."

"People who love you don't talk to you like that. Do you really believe you're a disappointment to her? That she'd actually kill you?"

These questions plainly bothered him. "It doesn't matter, Jennifer-spirit. Mother has made a decision. She will stick to it. If you ask me to follow you, I will follow you. I cannot guarantee you how many others will come. I know Mother will not."

"That's not good enough. No offense, but we tried with three. It just doesn't cut it." This conflict grated on Jennifer. *Thirty beaststalkers!* It would be enough, she was sure. And she couldn't believe that fate would dangle this opportunity so close to her face, and yet deny her. If she was any kind of ambassador between dragons and beaststalkers, she was meant to make this work. But how?

"What did Elise teach you about dragons?" she asked Eddie.

"Not much. What I learned, I learned from my true mother, and others who have since died. Elise's experience with dragons— she was, as I told you, the last of us to see one alive—was not as friendly as others I heard from. While some dragons seemed to ally with us years ago, others kept fighting. One killed her brother, she told us."

Jennifer recalled her uncle Michael, the butcher from Virginia she had barely known, but who had made her the weapons she wore today. "So she's bitter toward all dragons."

"She killed the last one she saw. Some say that brought bad luck. A few weeks later, werachnids destroyed the town we lived in, and ever since our family has had no real home."

"So you've never had one at all," Jennifer observed. "And yet, Eddie, you're . . . you're so different."

"Different? You mean from Mother? I suppose I am."

That wasn't what Jennifer had meant, but she let his interpretation stand. "Does Elise lead you all because she's a doctor, or because she's the oldest?"

"Doctor?" Eddie snorted. "You say strange things. You call

this woman your mother, even though she rejects you. And now you say she can heal."

"She can't? I mean, she doesn't?"

"She's a warrior, Jennifer-spirit. Aside from putting a quick bandage on a bleeding wound, she has never healed a person in her life."

Once again, Jennifer's heart sank. Seeing this rough, incomplete shadow of a woman was worse than seeing her father's name etched in stone.

Evangelina and Phoebe, both of whom had begun to relax around the campfire, raised their heads at the same time. Jennifer almost laughed at the way they sniffed the air simultaneously.

"Who's coming?" she asked. But then she heard the sound herself—an engine with an impressive amount of horsepower, being driven at an unsafe speed down the gravel driveway.

Unable to believe anything she was hearing, she leapt into dragon form and sailed over the house. Sure enough, down the driveway came a single car. The top was up, but Jennifer recognized it without any trouble at all.

It was a Ford Mustang. It parked just south of the house, and two figures climbed out to face the gathering beaststalkers.

"Catherine! Andi!"

*"I've told you," the young* Brandfire said with a bemused stare while sitting at the campfire between Jennifer and Eddie, "my name is Nakia. And why exactly are we camping outside in November, when we have a perfectly viable house right behind us?"

Jennifer shrugged, just happy to see these two girls here today.

Evangelina was less welcoming. "It has occurred to you, I'm sure," she told Jennifer with a bored sort of tone, "that the appearance of these two the day after we attack the Quadrivium stronghold is suspicious. Right?"

Jennifer rolled her eyes. "I'm not a moron, sis. But I think we can certainly hear them out. So why are you two here, anyway? And how did you find us?"

"Finding you wasn't hard," Nakia answered. "Just about every werachnid knows this is the last place on Earth anyone ever saw a dragon. It's where The Crown died, and where the Quadrivium drove dragons out of sight forever."

"Not quite forever," Evangelina purred.

"As for why we're here . . . I'll let Andi speak for herself, but I'm here because I'm running out of choices. I'm not really welcome in Pinegrove anymore."

"Not welcome?! Why not?"

"I was seen with you. The night you caused that commotion in the gym. Several werachnids saw me outside, talking with you."

"So what? They saw you change into your scorpion shape and tell me off. That's suspicious?"

"It is," came the reply, "when your grandmother was a dragon, who only had children and grandchildren because she was . . . forced."

Jennifer's jaw dropped. "Raped?"

Nakia nodded without looking anywhere but in the fire. "A few years after she fled Alexandria, she was raped. My grandfather's name was Motega. He left her a few years later, because he didn't want to raise a kid who might end up being dragon. She had a hard life, and most people avoided her and my father. He was a werachnid, but it didn't matter. He finally met my mother—a trampler—and married her despite my grandmother's objections. She was already ashamed of him and wanted her bloodline to end with him. But they were married, and I was born. This time, it was she who left a while later, for pretty much the same reason my grandfather left my grandmother. And so I got to grow up the same way my father did—ignored and bullied. The fact that I'm arachnid means nothing. Especially now, with you around."

When Nakia finally looked at Jennifer, it wasn't necessarily with kindness. "My father's disowned me. He told me he doesn't believe that I'm not your friend, that I'm too much like my mother, and that I should get out. I've got no place else to live. So I thought I'd come to the only possible place where I might be wanted."

Jennifer had no clue what to say. The fire crackled on, until Eddie spoke up.

"And you, Andi? Why are you here?"

The small, brown-skinned girl pushed back her magenta streak and then stuffed her hands into her own loose jacket sleeves. "After you left me and my friends in the hallway, I did what I could to save them. Amy and Anne turned out okay once they woke up, and Bobbie's recovering in the hospital burn ward. But Abigail's dead."

·

"Oh, Andi. I'm sorry." Jennifer tried hard not to look at Evangelina, who didn't seem to have a reaction. "I know you did your best."

"I'm still learning," Andi explained. "My own upbringing . . . I never really knew my parents. I was raised in a strange, cold home. Once people saw my talent, they used it. They used *me*. I became a caretaker. What I wanted, what I needed, made no difference."

She was rocking back and forth, Jennifer noticed, and her arms were shaking.

"And it was werachnids you grew up with?"

Andi nodded. "I didn't quite belong, of course. I was different, and I knew I always would be. I will never have a shape like them, never really be accepted by them."

"And so you started cutting yourself."

Evangelina's bold comment startled Andi out of a sort of reverie. The smaller girl appeared fearful for an instant, and then firmly closed her eyes. "I don't know what you're talking about."

"You cut yourself," Jennifer added. "Multiple times. I've seen the scars myself."

"I don't want to talk about it."

Jennifer recalled the video her middle school teacher had once shown their health class, about girls who hurt themselves. One of the girls interviewed, a cutter who had since stopped, had said something that had stuck in Jennifer's head.

"You're trying to get people to know you're hurting," she recalled aloud, "and at the same time, it pushes those same people away."

For the second time that day, Andi gave them a startled look.

Looking at this girl, who seemed so different from the strange world around her, Jennifer thought of Susan Elmsmith. *She's just a regular girl,* she told herself. *Different from the world around her because she's not so different. And it hurts. I wonder if Susan would ever cut herself? No, because her hands are so important to her, for sculpture. But then, Andi's hands are important for music, too, aren't they?*

She suddenly focused on Andi's sleeves, and the hands working themselves within. "Andi! You're doing it right now, aren't you?"

The girl froze, her look utterly unconvincing. "Doing what?"

"You're cutting yourself!" Jennifer got up, at first quickly and then more slowly, so as not to scare Andi into doing worse. "Please, Andi, you've got to stop."

The girl pointed her face down, concentrating once more on her unseen forearms. "There are times I can't help myself. I know I don't belong, Jennifer. I know there's something wrong. But I don't know . . ."

She trailed off. No one said a word. Jennifer looked at her; at Eddie and the other beaststalkers, who were similarly spellbound; at Evangelina, who watched with what appeared to be detached interest; at Nakia, who seemed surprised by this turn of events; and at Phoebe the newolf, who was licking Goodwin's red and green scales.

*So much about this world is different from the last,* Jennifer thought as she watched Andi's suede sleeves undulate as she mutilated her own arms. *New music, new buildings, new people. And so much about this world that hasn't changed at all. People who kill other people. Friends who betray each other. Girls who hurt themselves.*

"Andi, please stop."

The girl's beautiful brown eyes held Jennifer's. "You said maybe we could help each other. You said—"

"We can, Andi. We can help each other. Just, please, stop. Please?"

Andi took a deep breath, and another, and then her sleeves separated, releasing a bloodstained steak knife into her lap. "Okay. Yeah. I can stop. If you can make it better, I think I can . . ."

Jennifer reached over, very slowly and carefully, and pulled the knife out of Andi's lap. "Thank you, Andi."

*"So what do you think?"* she asked Evangelina later inside the house, once they had bandaged Andi's arms and everyone had settled down to sleep. The two of them were in human form again, relaxing over some hot tea from the beaststalkers' stores. "Are they telling the truth?"

"Andi definitely cuts herself. You saw that. And her fear has taught her much. Beyond the fear, there is incredible strength in her. She shuts her mind very well."

"Agreed. And Nakia?"

"Nakia . . ." Evangelina took a longer sip of the tea, which soothed her voice temporarily. "Almost the opposite of Andi. Her mind was completely open to me, but still nearly unreadable. Too much churning, too many emotions. It reminded me a little of myself, when I first escaped the dimension I was born into. She wants to strike out, wants to punish."

"Punish us or them?"

Evangelina offered a small, nasty smirk. "Great question."

"Keep an eye on her for me, sis."

The other girl began to cough. "Keep an eye on her? Yes, and on this girl Andi, and on Elise Georges, and on Eddie and this whole troop of beaststalkers. And on whoever else manages to show up before we try to take on nearly a hundred full-grown werachnids and the Quadrivium. You keep an eye out, too, sis. For *me*."

*As the sun lowered* in the sky, Jennifer and Eddie were busy compiling a short list of those willing to join them in the return to Pinegrove—less than ten even counting the two of them along with Evangelina, Nakia, and Andi—and devising an uphill plan of attack. Suddenly Jennifer discovered an unexpected weakness in their skills.

"None of you have heard of it?"

Eddie cocked his head. "No. Show me."

She looked around nervously. "It will probably draw attention."

"If it's half as powerful as you suggest, Jennifer-spirit, isn't it worth the risk?"

His earnest voice and complete trust in her convinced her to show him. As he and a few others looked on, she unsheathed her daggers and stood up. A brief kiss on the blades, a deep breath, and . . .

"Jennifer-spirit!" Eddie staggered back on his feet, as did everyone else behind him except Evangelina, who stretched by the fire and idly flicked her brunette hair. Phoebe, the newolf, lay down flat on the ground and put her paws over her eyes. "You brought the sun screaming back! How did you do that?!"

"You can do it, too," she told them. "All of you. It's called a beaststalker shout. It's pretty harmless to human forms, but will damage the ears and eyes of any magical creature. Do you want me to show you?"

Twenty-nine of the thirty warriors who had gathered nodded wildly. But Jennifer only had eyes for the thirtieth, who spat and walked away.

About an hour later, she had trained every willing warrior, though none could do it as well as Jennifer herself. Eddie could make quite a bit of noise using the mere tip of one of his arrows. Her stock went up considerably within the camp, and Eddie was soon finding new recruits.

"How many now?" she asked him.

"More than twenty. And with their new skill . . ."

". . . we may have enough," she finished for him. *At least enough to get inside. Who knows what else the Quadrivium can throw at us?* It was time to find out.

*Nakia was inside,* sipping instant coffee with Andi and a couple of the friendlier warriors, and teaching them . . .

". . . trigonometry?" Jennifer repeated. "Really? They want to know that?"

Nakia shrugged at the warriors as they nodded and left. "They don't get much formal schooling, that's for sure. They seem pretty hungry to learn something besides hunting, camping, and killing."

"So you figured sine, cosine, and tangents were the way to go."

"It's what I know." Nakia winked. "You know screaming at high volume, so that's what you were just teaching outside. Anyway, are they all trained? You ready to head back to Pinegrove?"

"That's what I wanted to talk to you about. I'd like to be better prepared this time. Can you tell me anything—anything at all—about the Quadrivium?"

Nakia's face fell. "I'm sorry. Nobody knows much about them. Just a few basic facts: They live in Pinegrove, and there are four—"

"I know two of them. Edmund Slider and Tavia Saltin."

Andi nearly spat out her coffee, she began giggling so hard.

"Tavia Saltin? But that's so . . . so . . ." She couldn't come up with the right word. "I mean, she's not even a particularly good piano player."

"What does that have to do with anything?"

"There is a verse that describes the Quadrivium—"

"Of course there is."

"—and it suggests one has musical talent:

> *Four formed the Quadrivium:*
> *One to build a new dimension,*
> *One to create new numbers,*
> *One to relight the stars,*
> *And one to sing the song of change.*

"If you pay attention," Andi continued, "you'll notice that there are four in the verse, corresponding loosely to the four major subjects at Pinegrove High."

"Edmund and Tavia are faculty," Jennifer pointed out. "Edmund would know all about new dimensions, and Tavia does teach music."

"So are you saying the Quadrivium are faculty at Pinegrove High?"

It didn't jibe with her theory that Skip was involved, but Jennifer felt there was something to this line of reasoning. "Why not? What two lines are left? Creating new numbers . . . that would be math . . ."

". . . and Slider again," Nakia pointed out.

"There are other mathematics faculty. Andi, don't you and Bobbie have someone different from Slider?"

"Yeah, Mr. Frost. But I doubt he's the type . . ."

"No one ever seems the type." Jennifer sighed. "We have to assume he is. Okay, who's the astronomy teacher?"

Andi shrugged. "Only those on eight legs go into astronomy class."

"Nakia?"

Nakia's brows furrowed. "I've never been cleared for astronomy class. Remember? Trust issues. I take advanced Spanish instead."

Jennifer slumped into a chair, head in her hands, and rubbed her eyes. "We can't fight what we don't know. We could take out three of the four members of the Quadrivium, and still be left with whoever's in there. And he or she could be unbeatable."

"So you are still trying to kill them?" Andi asked. Her face was inscrutable.

"I may have to," Jennifer said. "I'm sorry, Andi. But it's not like your friends in the hallway. This Quadrivium—"

"What will killing them accomplish?"

"I don't want to kill them," Jennifer persisted. "I meant it when I told you that, Andi! But I need them to do something for me. They've messed things up, and they have to make things right."

"So you'll hurt them, like you hurt Bobbie."

"Andi, that's not fair. I don't have a lot of choices anymore."

"Have you tried asking them?"

Nakia's royal Egyptian eyes rolled at that. "Don't even answer that, Jennifer. Nobody who knew what they were talking about would ask that question."

"I'm sorry if I'm being naïve," Andi said. "But I don't like seeing the people around me get hurt."

"It doesn't strike you as a bit strange," Nakia countered, "that someone who hates seeing pain slices open her own arms on a regular basis?"

Jennifer had to put a stop to this. "That's not getting us anywhere. Andi, I'm going to try to get this done with as few people hurt as possible. That's all I can promise. You don't have to come with us. But don't try to get in our way."

"I won't get in your way. I came here to help! But I won't . . ."

"You won't fight. I get it. That's fine. You could maybe help out those of us who get wounded?"

Andi seemed relieved at the out Jennifer had offered. "Yes. Okay, I'll do that."

"What will you need?"

"Antivenom," Andi answered. "Lots of it."

"Eddie must have some in his supplies. I'll talk to him." Jennifer turned to Nakia. "How about you? Can you fight with us?"

"I can try."

"That's all I'm asking. With you two on board, that's just about everyone. We only have a few standouts among the warriors here, and I don't think anything I do or say now—"

"Jennifer Scales." The voice made them all turn around. Elise Georges was in the entryway to the cabin, the newolf Phoebe at her side. Uncertainty softened her hostile emerald gaze. "Do you have time for a walk?"

*The first minute or so* of the walk was silent, mutual torture. Jennifer could sense that something had shifted in Elise's demeanor, but the woman wasn't ready to express it. Meanwhile, Jennifer wasn't sure if she wanted to burst into tears, confession, protest, or all three—but she *was* sure Elise was not interested in finding out which would happen.

As it turned out, the newolf helped break the ice by rubbing up against Jennifer and licking her hand.

"Phoebe likes you," Elise allowed. "That's unusual for a stranger."

"I'm not a stranger. I'm your daughter."

The woman stopped in the middle of the prairie, where horses and sheep and wildflowers would normally be. "So you keep saying. Would you care to explain how that's possible? And if you call that *thing*"—she pointed vaguely back toward the cabin, but Jennifer knew to whom she was referring—"your sister, does that mean I'm *her* mother, too?"

"No! No, it's more complicated than that. You have to understand, things aren't the way they're supposed to be—"

"Don't I know it. I'm supposed to have parents, and a brother, and friends. Not a horde of unruly teenagers who barely follow my commands. You're taking them into a battle in Pinegrove itself, without my permission."

"You could join us."

Instead of the immediate rebuke Jennifer expected, Elise licked her lips and raised the collar of her jacket. "Battle's coming, no matter what I do. If two children tracked you here, the Quadrivium certainly will. And I'm fine taking them on. Relieved, actually. But you know nothing about tactics, kid. You're about to return to the same battlefield where you got your ass kicked not twenty-four hours ago. You'll have even less surprise on your side than you did before."

"Not necessarily. They won't be expecting all of you. And if you guys didn't know what a beaststalker shout is, I'll bet a bunch of them have forgotten, too."

"Maybe." Elise began to walk again. "You have obvious

skills. You're not like any dragon I've ever seen before. Maybe you could help us . . . make a dent. Before the end comes."

"The end?"

"There's no avoiding it, kid. We're going to die soon. Me, Eddie, Phoebe, every last one of us. How we've stayed alive these last few years, I couldn't begin to guess."

"You may have had something to do with it."

The woman shook her head. "I've taught these children how to kill. And they're good at it. And we know how to survive, how to hide. But lead them? They don't turn to me when they're hurt. They don't turn to me when they're afraid."

"The mother I know is exactly the kind of person folks go to when they're hurt."

"The mother you know isn't here," Elise snapped. "What the hell do you want from me?"

Jennifer silently cursed the tears running down her cheeks. She had sworn to herself she wouldn't cry. "I want you to come with me. If I'm going to die, I want my mother there."

"That's the attitude that will get you killed."

"So come along and teach me different."

"It won't make a difference. Whether you succeed or fail, no one will ever know. The world will keep spinning. People will keep dying."

"I know better than that. And if you had grown up differently, maybe you would know better, too—"

"I grew up differently enough from these kids to learn something valuable," Elise growled. "Everything is born for no reason, limps through life for no reason, and dies for no reason. You can't control the gears of death. But you can, if you're willing, throw your body into them before your time. If that's what you want to do, then do it already!"

Hearing these words come out of her mother's mouth broke Jennifer's heart. She sank to the ground and pulled Phoebe close to her. "Why did you ask me out here?"

As if snapped out of a nightmare, Elise threw her head back and sighed. "Yes. I asked you out here. I thought about doing so earlier today, so that I could kill you and end this nonsense."

"So have you changed your mind?" Jennifer found she didn't care anymore. The Quadrivium was too strong. Her father was dead. Her mother was twisted beyond recognition. Why drag what few friends she had left into a suicide mission?

"That depends," Elise replied, "on what you can tell me about this." The woman reached into her coat pocket.

"What you were teaching the others caused a lot of light and noise," Elise explained as she pulled out the object. "Phoebe was restless, so I took her for a walk near here. We were at the edge of the woods just over there when she suddenly broke away, running off despite my commands. You can imagine, it's hard to stop a newolf who gets a notion. She rousted a couple of wild hornets' nests—yes, they're alive and well in November around here, and I have a couple of nasty stings to prove it!—and I finally found her snuffling at this on the ground."

Jennifer was barely listening; instead, she was clambering to her feet and checking the pocket of the jacket Eddie had lent her that morning. *There can't be two!*

Elise continued in a whisper. "I went over and picked it up. Almost immediately, I felt . . ."

Jennifer retrieved a mirror image of what Elise held out—a frail, silvery starburst from a moon elm that no longer existed.

"I felt," Elise managed through quivering lips as she rubbed the edges of her own leaf, "like I was missing something. I've lost so much in my lifetime, but this was like losing something worse." She looked up at Jennifer. "Do you think you can help me find it?"

Jennifer's jaw tightened as she struggled to keep her face composed. "Oh, yeah. We're going to find it. Tell you what: Let's start with you showing me those hornets' nests."

# CHAPTER 17

## *Monday*

Getting everyone in vehicles to Pinegrove wasn't difficult, though it did involve some grand theft and automotive know-how. By the time morning twilight came, they had embedded themselves in the snow-frosted forest on the southwest fringe of the town, with the high school grounds just a few miles away. Nakia's teeth were chattering and Andi seemed depressed, but everyone else looked grim and prepared under the moonless sky.

"I just want you to know," Evangelina murmured in Jennifer's ear as they took position, "that I still don't think this is going to work."

"Hey! You helped with The Plan this time. And so did Elise and Eddie."

"The Plan is still flawed."

"The Plan is strong, like bull. You love The Plan and you know it. Now get to work." She turned to Elise. "Our new friends're still with us?"

"Y-yes. They seem to have kept up with the convoy."

"Great. I'll, um. See you out there."

The woman stared back for a few seconds. "If you die," she finally said, "how would you like to be buried?"

"Thanks for the rousing speech, General Patton. You know what? Just leave me to rot. I don't want to be any trouble."

This actually provoked a small grin. "See you out there, then."

\* \* \*

*The hundred or so arachnids* guarding the observatory were not stupid, Jennifer supposed. They knew about Jennifer and Evangelina, so they were scattered more evenly over a wider area. They also would suspect the two of them would not be alone, so they had increased their overall numbers.

What they did not expect, however, was a missile from above, directed right in their midst.

She chose a spot just fifty yards from the observatory as her target. As she plummeted, she held her breath and prayed like mad that the cocoon of fire building around her would do something—anything—to absorb the impact of her landing.

The results were spectacular. She didn't see them because she was deep in a crater of her own making, but she figured from the screams and fireworks that she had caused a bit of commotion. Before she even got up (with sore hindquarters, but no other injury), she whistled through her teeth for her bodyguard.

The horde had already been waiting for her signal, and it rushed in from the northern skies with the roar of a thousand buzz saws. Elise and Jennifer had found not just one nest of hornets in the woods near her cabin, but ten. Perhaps they were a strange mixed breed or descendants from the beehives Crawford Thomas Scales had once faithfully maintained. Or perhaps they were a rival species that flourished once the competition had gone. Either way, they obeyed Jennifer fervently. A swarm the length of a pterodactyl's wingspan came crashing down next to Jennifer's crater.

Before the werachnids could regroup, their third and greatest surprise came: The early dawn bore down as if the sun were riding a locomotive into town. With a quick shift to human form, Jennifer watched the warriors advance upon the observatory from the forest's edge. Elise led them, riding her newolf Phoebe, screaming louder through her sword than any of them. Her daughter felt no small pride, and a twinge of remorse at the thought that in a different Pinegrove, years ago, a similar group of beaststalkers must have adopted the same tactic against her own ancestors. She wondered if Glorianna Seabright had found her own motives so blameless.

*No time for philosophy!* She readied her daggers and took up a position near the hornets. The swarm had not suffered at all during the barrage of beaststalker shouting. Every arachnid around them, however, was in incredible pain. Scorpions and spiders curled up and shrieked under the glare of pure light. Many of the smarter ones thought to shift back to human form.

And that was when Evangelina descended upon them.

### RUN!

She shouted to the terrified guards around her, sending a new shock wave rolling over them. And run they did.

Jennifer had given her sister strict orders. No killing, unless there was no other way. While she knew she couldn't change Elise and the warriors who followed her, Evangelina was special to her: The two of them were the last dragons. They would follow Xavier's values and the values of their ancestors and show the world what dragons could truly be.

Despite the growing hunger she had sensed, her sibling appeared to enter the fray with a smidgeon of restraint. The lingering light and noise from the beaststalkers did nothing to faze her. She could be, as Jennifer had learned before their own fight, blind or deaf at will.

The hornet dragon stung and chased away those few that withstood Evangelina's thought weapon, driving them south toward the school.

"Look to the air!" Elise called out from Phoebe's back. She had ended the newolf's charge some distance from the observatory and now swung back to ensure a secure flank to the north. A dozen of her warriors kept up with her, pushing back their bewildered enemies and hacking at those hairy limbs that dared get in the way.

Jennifer followed Elise's voice and saw a sight that made her swallow hard: A dozen bulbous shapes flew through the air toward them, aiming for the center of Jennifer's small force.

Only ten landed alive. Eddie's quiver was now low two arrows, but he quickly pulled another from behind his back and readied a third shot.

Nakia got to his target before he could fire, plunging her claw into the head of a deep blue jumper with white markings. Jennifer felt a bitter pang as she watched the friend she knew as a gentle lover of newolves and fun cars disembowel a fourth spider that tried to leap on top of her.

"Bitch," she heard the troubled scorpion spit. Then, "Die. Die, already!"

She hadn't wanted it this bloody or this personal. Wasn't there another way to get past these spiders?

She changed into dragon form and blew fire in a circle around her, which caused several of the new jumpers to back off. Evangelina held off another surge, a few dozen regathering from the south, by coating one of their number in acid. *Not exactly following the spirit of our agreement,* Jennifer told herself, but it did scatter the rest of them without hurting more.

With most of the field won, they pushed hard at the observatory.

Here they met the stiffest resistance. A ten-foot-tall horned baboon spider with a clipped front leg and three fat-tailed scorpions of only slightly smaller size pulled back to a small door near the base of the spherical observatory. Inspired by their courage, another dozen or so humans shifted back into their spider forms and tried to make a last stand.

Jennifer kissed her blades and gave them a burst of light and sound. They shuddered but held their ground.

Evangelina pounded on them with her mind. They flinched, but held their ground.

Then Elise flew off her steed straight into the middle of them all, swinging her sword, and they began to falter.

Elizabeth Georges-Scales, as Jennifer anxiously tried to recall while watching the scene before her, was a caring soul full of optimism and grace who healed the sick and wounded. Elise Georges had a grace of a different kind—the grace of inevitable death as it clears a battlefield, and the grace of a killing blow as it slides past even the tightest defenses.

There was a moment when that grace was nearly not enough. A brown funnel spider lunged forward upon Elise's blade, impaling itself deeply enough to land a bite on her shoulder before dying. Pulling back in pain, she did not see the horned baboon spider rush forward and lift up its orange and black maw for a killing blow.

"Mother!"

Eddie Blacktooth's arrow was true, flying straight between the giant spider's mandibles and emerging from the back of its many-eyed head. The arachnid crashed to the ground in a cloud of snow and dust.

*Success!* Jennifer congratulated herself on the fact that only Elise appeared to be hurt, with a minimum of werachnid casualties. And Jennifer herself had killed no one. Xavier would have been proud. They had made it to the entrance of the observatory, Eddie's warriors were scattering the last of the guards, and Jennifer had just located Nakia and Andi on the field about halfway between the observatory and the high school. Suddenly she heard Evangelina's voice. For the first time, her sister radiated worry.

Sister! Something is here! It is strong!

*This is it, then. The Quadrivium. Edmund? Tavia? One of the other two?*

The observatory door opened, and out came a father and his son.

Jennifer had hoped it would not be true after all this time, but she had to believe what she saw. "Oh, Skip . . ."

But it was not Skip who stepped forward first. Otto Saltin, werachnid and sorcerer, was alive. His chocolate hair was slicked back with sweat, and his eyes bore none of the friendliness he had faked with Jennifer the time they had first met.

*This is not over,* he had told Jennifer a few months later, with a blade through his belly. She had had no idea how much he meant it.

He saw Elise, peeled his lips back into a sneer, and said a single word.

"Numb."

Unlike her first experience with Otto's sorcery, Jennifer actually saw the magic this time. A icy bluish streak leapt from Otto's lips and slammed into its target. Elise gave a wail and fell to the ground, sword clattering to her side. Otto stepped forward onto her back, pressed her down with his winter boot, and opened his mouth to say another word.

Before it came out of his throat, it was cut by a long dagger—one with a beautifully ornamented hilt carved in the shape of a tiny dragon—that had flown through the air with deadly accuracy.

Andi and Nakia rushed forward to help guard Elise's paralyzed body. Jennifer stepped up to the dead man who lay next to her and bent down.

"If I had to kill someone," she told him, yanking her blade out of his ruined throat, "I'm glad it was you."

She straightened and looked into the eyes of the man's son, who looked like he wanted a dagger of his own. She knew there was nothing she could say or do that would salvage Skip. And she didn't want him back anyway.

Expecting him to shift into any one of a number of spider shapes, she raised her knives.

He hesitated, started to say something, and then took a step forward.

Something whistled by Jennifer's elbow, and then there was a black shaft sticking out of Skip's right shoulder. He bellowed in pain.

Eddie had another arrow nocked and his bow aimed before Jennifer could even turn around to identify him as the source of the shot. With tense limbs, Evangelina drew up next to the archer.

Andi pulled Elise back away from the entrance, and Nakia covered the retreat in scorpion shape. The beaststalkers beyond Eddie and Elise took up positions in a tight circle near the entrance, facing outward and preparing for a counterattack.

Skip staggered back several steps, until his back was to the observatory entrance. His beautiful blue-green eyes glanced at Eddie and the next black arrow pointed at his heart, and then turned to Jennifer. He let a cocky grin crawl over his bleeding mouth.

"Can you believe it, Jenny? Eddie fucking Blacktooth."

He pulled a black object out of his jacket and pointed it at Eddie. Jennifer looked at it for a few seconds before she realized it was a gun. He fired it three times.

Evangelina had already thrown her dark aura out to cover Eddie. The boy cried out, but Jennifer couldn't tell how many of the bullets hit him, or where. Not satisfied with this knowledge, Skip aimed blindly into the shadow and fired five more times.

There were a few tense moments when Jennifer and the others were not sure what had happened. But then a quiet laugh from the darkness settled the matter.

*Brother. Are you through?*

He emptied the clip.

A low purr of annoyance spread like the darkness itself. Evangelina advanced, and Skip gave a small whimper. The gun went sailing into the gloom, useless.

*Why isn't he changing?* Jennifer wondered.

Before she could determine why, Evangelina's tail plunged through Skip's abdomen, lifted him up, and threw him. He crashed through the doors and skidded into the darkness beyond.

"Evangelina!" Jennifer rushed forward to check on the boy, but stopped short of entering the observatory. "You didn't have to do that!"

Selfish. Arrogant. Hurtful. Unrepentant.

Evangelina withdrew her aura with an air of indifference.

You thought these things of him, even before he betrayed
you.

"But that doesn't mean—" Jennifer stopped short when she turned and saw Eddie. He was sitting on the ground holding his left elbow. Blood trickled down his forearm and over his hand. A grim nod told her he was hurt, but okay.

A cold shriek distracted them all. The bulbous form of Tavia Saltin filled the entryway. She took in the sight of her dead brother and nephew, then Jennifer, and foam formed on the tips of her mandibles.

"You little bitch! I knew we should never have let Skip save you! He should have left you behind with the rest of your pathetic kind! I'll rip you apart! I'll—"

Tavia.

Jennifer turned to Evangelina, but knew even before she saw her sister's stunned expression that she was not the source.

Let them in, Tavia.

*Edmund Slider?* Jennifer wondered. But the voice in their

heads didn't sound like him. Tavia certainly didn't respond the way one would expect her to treat her boyfriend.

"Let them in?!" the spider screamed at the unseen source. "They deserve to die and we could kill them all, right now, if you had the guts!"

**Tavia. Please. Let them in.**

Evangelina's expression evolved from shock to utter bewilderment. Before Jennifer could stop her, her sister was a helpless young brunette pushing past the giant spider-Tavia and walking into the observatory.

A few quiet seconds passed. Jennifer felt a wave of recognition come from within the observatory, then fear, then . . .

**Mother?**

# CHAPTER 18

## *Quadrivium*

Jennifer wasn't sure she wanted to step into the observatory. But curiosity and her own desire to have this battle end, one way or another, won out.

The inside of the observatory was not what she would have expected from photographs in science textbooks and magazine articles. There were no computers tallying astronomical distances or painting interstellar photographs, no swivel chairs with old astronomers sitting in them while peering through a telescope. Indeed, not even a telescope in sight.

Instead, the inside of the observatory was smooth obsidian, and the ceiling and walls took the same spherical shape as the exterior. There were small pinpricks of light all over the interior surface, and Jennifer realized right away that she was looking at the nighttime sky. Enough illumination pooled at the bottom of the room to see the occupants.

The floor ahead was smooth and sloped slightly upward. About halfway up the slope was a striking blond spider with red and white facial markings. Seven of the eight eyes were scarred shut—*Edmund Slider, I presume!*—and he stood still as Tavia rushed to his side. Evangelina was already past them, barely caring who they were.

It was the third figure in the room, a brunette woman of striking height, who caught Jennifer's full attention. Jet-black hair cascaded down her pale, freckled shoulders and back. Jade accents matched her simple gown. Tiny freckles peppered her gentle nose, broad cheeks, and the pale forehead above her carefully shaped eyebrows. And beneath those eyebrows were the most mesmerizing points of color Jennifer had ever seen.

They were black, Jennifer was sure at first. But then the woman shifted a tiny bit, and the gaze turned indigo. Then a step forward, and the eyes were clearly as green as her dress. Each movement brought a new hue into play.

Right now, those eyes were focused on Evangelina.

Daughter.

It was the same voice Jennifer had heard in her head when it called to Tavia just a few moments ago, as clear as a horn's call in winter, but tender as a fern's touch in spring.

It's really you. You're here.

Evangelina stood, transfixed. It wasn't clear if she was overcome by emotion or trapped like an innocent opossum in a truck's headlights.

Dianna Wilson's gaze flickered briefly to Jennifer—*I'll bet she heard that*—but then rested again on her daughter.

Are you afraid, Evangelina?

I can't shut you out

That was all Evangelina could say. Jennifer saw immediately that her sister was simply trying to find a secure place to take in this new development. She wanted a place where she could think for herself. But the weapon she had used for weeks upon escaping her awful dimension was not powerful enough here. Just as Evangelina had forced herself into her victims' thoughts—Jack Alder, Grandpa Crawford, and Elizabeth Georges-Scales—so now this woman was doing to her.

*Predator to prey,* Jennifer realized.

That thought definitely got Dianna Wilson's attention. Startled, she severed the link. "I'm sorry," she offered in a dry but melodious voice. "I don't mean to— Daughter, you have nothing to fear. I'm so happy you're here."

Evangelina seemed lost in her mother's graceful features. Neither of them moved as more people entered the observatory. Eddie first, then Nakia, then a few of the beaststalkers, and then Elise stumbling upright with Andi's help. Phoebe the newolf hovered by the doorway, whining through her nose at the lifeless body of Skip Wilson.

"Dianna!" the blond spider called out, taking a few steps back with a sobbing Tavia. "If we are going to end this, we ought to do it now, don't you think?"

"A moment please, Edmund." Dianna reached for Evangelina's face and caressed the younger woman's chin. "I've been waiting for this for some time."

"But your son is dead!" Tavia spat. "They killed Skip!"

I'm sorry, Mother . . .

Dianna hushed Evangelina with a single black fingernail, and she glanced past Jennifer out the doorway. "First things first. I want to hold you, daughter."

Of all the sights Jennifer thought she would see when they started this battle, much less when she woke up in this town a week ago, the sight of her newly dead sister hugging her father's long-dead ex-wife while her ex-boyfriend lay in a pool of blood was nowhere near the top of the list. But they did hug, and Jennifer was sure she saw a rust-colored tear slip down the older woman's face.

"Dianna!" Tavia was plainly losing patience. "They will kill us!"

This finally broke the embrace. "Oh, Tavia. They're not here to—"

"They've already killed Otto!"

"Well, Otto was a bit of a twit, wasn't he?" Dianna sighed.

"He was your husband!"

"Yes, he was." Dianna stepped around Evangelina, letting her jade dress flow behind her. "Not a very good one. Skilled at sorcery, horrible at interpersonal relations. And so he died. Twice, I believe? Which brings us to our first guest."

By now she was almost nose-to-nose with Jennifer. Dianna Wilson had not cast any sort of spell—if she could even do such a thing—but Jennifer had never felt less able to move in her life.

"Jonathan's daughter. Jennifer, correct?"

With great effort, Jennifer was able to raise her hand and shake the one Dianna had offered. "I have no idea what to say to you."

"You could start by telling me why you're here today."

"Why not just read my mind?"

Dianna walked past Jennifer and gauged the force that had assembled inside. "If I have occasion to doubt you, I will. But your father taught me long ago how dangerous it can be to pry continually into a teenager's mind. Can we just talk?"

"Fine, let's talk. You and your friends ruined my universe. I want it back."

"Marvelous." Dianna had completed her circle around Jennifer and beamed at her. "Isn't she marvelous, Edmund? Tavia?"

"The exact adjective fails me," Edmund said in a strained voice, "but that is probably not the one I would choose."

"Then you choose poorly. Jennifer Scales has done exactly what I wished she would do. What no other person could possibly have done."

"And what's that?" Jennifer snapped, angry at being talked about as if she wasn't there. "Put up with the stench of your husband twice without retching?"

Tavia Saltin cried in outrage and tightened her body into bipedal form. "Have some respect for the dead!" She straightened and spat a single word: "Low."

It was sorcery; Jennifer could see that much right away. *Strange,* she thought, *it moves more slowly than Otto's.* In fact, it was a simple matter for her to step to one side and deflect the orange blur with her blades, sending it to the floor to dissolve harmlessly.

"Numb." Advancing on Tavia now, Jennifer knocked this blue spell aside, too.

"Poisoned." And this sickly green one.

"Marred!" Jennifer parried the breath as if it were a slow thrust of a crimson mace, and then shoved it back into Tavia's mouth. Then she crossed her blades under the woman's spindly throat and pushed until Tavia was pinned against the wall, breathless.

"That's enough out of you," Jennifer snarled. "And if your boyfriend doesn't take a step back, I'm going to send you where I sent your brother."

Reluctantly, Edmund Slider receded from her peripheral vision. At the same time, Dianna entered it on the other side.

"You've made your point, Jennifer. Let her go, and we can continue our conversation. I was enjoying it."

"You were saying," Jennifer said as she lowered her blades but didn't look away from Tavia, "that I did what you wished. And that was . . . ?"

"You brought my daughter to me."

That got Jennifer's attention. "Pardon?"

Dianna's vermilion eyes sparkled. "Only you could do it, Jennifer. My search for Evangelina kept coming up empty. It cost me my ability to remain in the normal universe, and it nearly cost me my life. By the time I located Evangelina again, she was where I could not get her—in the world I had left behind, rampaging after your father. Worse, she was beyond control, and no one could get close enough to her to bring her to me in this universe."

"You were still looking for me," Evangelina said.

"I never stopped, darling." She turned back to Jennifer. "At the same time, the Quadrivium was ready with its own plans for conquest. Despite our best plans, I could not see a way to both change the universe and retrieve her. In fact, had I any choice at all, I would have gladly chosen her and left the universe as is.

"But it seemed hopeless. And then last week, right before the four of us were ready to take action, the most marvelous thing happened."

It came to Jennifer like thunder. "Evangelina died."

"Not only did she die, but your grandfather generously arranged for her passage to the perpetual crescent moon among the venerables."

"You know about the venerables?"

"Of course I do," Dianna said. "During our secret relationship, your father was able to close many parts of his mind to me, but not all of it. Through him, I learned enough: what the venerables were, and what might happen if Crescent Valley were to fall. I even heard of the legends his parents had taught him: of Seraphina, her island, and the silver moon elm. While I never could determine where these places were, I saw the path of events that could lead to Crescent Valley, and Seraphina's Isle, and ultimately Evangelina."

"And only one person could travel that road," Evangelina guessed.

"Correct, daughter. The Ancient Furnace. Only she could retrieve you, because the portals were guarded by powerful forces who would listen to no other.

"She would have to have a reason to want you here. She had, after all, a difficult relationship with you. And so the pieces fell into place: What the Quadrivium already had planned served as the perfect motivation. I knew, Jennifer Scales, that you had to be part of the new universe, and that your efforts to change things back would eventually lead you to Evangelina . . . and then to me."

"You manipulated me." Jennifer felt warm under her collar. "This whole thing was just a setup."

"It was a plan," Dianna corrected. "And a long shot, at that. Last-second opportunities are both gifts and challenges. So many things could have gone wrong. You could have not survived the trip to this universe, you could have given up, you could have failed at any one of a number of points. But to me, you were my only hope. As a bonus, I got to keep alive the daughter of Jonathan Scales: a girl as remarkable as her father had been."

"Stop talking about him like he's dead!" Jennifer shouted. This was humiliating, to have been shuffled and yanked around like a puppet. "And stop talking about him like you ever cared about him. All you cared about was your own daughter. And you destroyed my world to get her."

"You have no idea," Dianna answered gently, "what a parent would do for a child. I planned the sorcery with a heavy heart, because I was not sure it was the best path. But when the moment of truth came, I served my role on the Quadrivium."

"And all four of you agreed to do this, just to free my sister?" Jennifer couldn't understand why Otto, or Edmund, or Tavia would have cared.

"The Quadrivium had four members," Dianna admitted, "and four different motivations. Mine was exploration; Otto's as always was domination. As for the other two . . . " She trailed off with a sigh in Edmund's direction. "They can speak for themselves, if they like."

"I would hope," the blond spider cut in, "my student here could figure that sort of thing out for herself."

"Yours was revenge," Jennifer replied. "I remember how bitter you were about Glorianna Seabright when I saw you in the hospital last week. So you joined the Quadrivium to get rid of her."

"Fine logic, Ms. Scales." As usual, the geometry teacher's voice managed both admiration and condescension. "In fact, Glorianna Seabright was ground zero for the explosion the Quadrivium set off in history. She was more important to beaststalkers than you may realize. Before she came of age, her kind was scattered, and not very skilled anymore. Many of the beaststalker arts had been lost over the centuries, and even the best among them were decent swordsmen and little more. We needed to crush them before she changed all of that.

"So we went back in time and found The Crown when he was a young werachnid. Once we told him what Ms. Seabright would become, and where she lived as a girl, we could step aside. It was an easy matter for him to find her and kill her—thus completing our sorcery. Glorianna Seabright never had a chance to grow up and unify beaststalkers in the way that became so threatening to our kind, and to dragons, truth be told.

"With her dead, picking off beaststalkers became easier. The Crown's legend grew, and he became more powerful than any werachnid before him. He knew that the Quadrivium had yet to be born in this time line, and so he made a point of finding and nurturing us. Three of us came to power quickly and helped push the dragons back into Crescent Valley—"

"I already know this," Jennifer interrupted. "Xavier Longtail, the dragon you could never kill, told me. I'm glad my father killed your precious Crown!"

"His death, as it turned out, was incidental by then. The three of us were powerful enough to finish the job. Some years later, all four of us were ready, and the circle was complete. Four members of the Quadrivium, each with some sort of imprint in the two universes—past, present, or future. Otto, for example, was dead on your side, but he still existed here, and that was enough to forge a link. We other three could do the same, and so together we wove a sorcery capable of pulling two time lines together. As we exchanged universes, those in the Quadrivium who already existed in both, became the sum of both lives."

"So you killed all those dragons and beaststalkers just so you could walk again." Jennifer shuddered. "I can't believe I actually admired you once."

"My walking had little to do with it, Ms. Scales. Though it was a nice byproduct. In this universe, you see, I was never hobbled."

The word *hobble* evoked Jonathan Scales's description of the beaststalker practice and her mother's loathing of it. "Glory hobbled you?"

"Goodness, no." Edmund's chuckle was mirthless. "That would have been beneath her. One of her minions hobbled me, upon her command. But, of course, in a universe without Glory, beaststalkers didn't enjoy the revival from their heyday of centuries ago. They never rediscovered so many nasty skills: never learned to hobble, never learned to shout. They were soft, like the warriors you brought with you today."

"Hey," Eddie growled, cocking an arrow through blood-tinged fingers.

"And once beaststalkers were out of the way, we could focus on dragons. A tougher battle, to be sure, but one we could win."

"Especially once you knew where Crescent Valley was," Jennifer finished for him. *Because of Skip.*

"You're upset with my son," Dianna said. "Because he gave us the last piece we needed. The only thing I couldn't learn."

"He betrayed me. He betrayed my friends. Because of him, my father is dead. Because of him, Susan's gone. Because of him, Catherine's . . ." Jennifer motioned vaguely behind her to where the scorpion-Nakia stood.

"He only did what his family asked of him. If your family asked the same of you, wouldn't you listen to them?"

"I don't know," Jennifer answered honestly. "I don't think my family would ever ask me to do anything like that."

Dianna stepped in closer. "I know you have no reason to believe me, Jennifer. But there are things we've done here that I'm not proud of."

"I'll make sure they etch that on your gravestone."

"When you do something like this, two lives become one. The dream you had becomes your life, and the life you had becomes more and more like a dream. For seventeen years, I did not hurt a soul. I had faith in peace. I married your father in secret, with the hope of showing the world someday how love could prevail. Past the disaster of losing my daughter, through more than twenty years of putting up with Otto Saltin's dreams of conquest, I did not kill.

"Then, in the space of a single evening last week, I slaughtered tens of thousands, maybe hundreds of thousands of souls." Her voice trembled. "I have not left this observatory since the new world was born. I can already see too much from here, as it is, especially in the new life I've created for myself. Things are twisted beyond my recognition, even myself and my loved ones. I am a killer. My son became a liar to the girl he loved most. My husband, Otto, dead in the first world, spent his new life here conducting horrific experiments in Crescent Valley. While these things won us our victory against dragonkind, it turned a place we coveted into a place we avoided. And I let it all happen. I couldn't help myself. I have become what I feared most: an adult addicted to death and desecration."

Jennifer spared a thought for Seraphina, who was probably still fighting Otto's creations on the last island left to them all. *Or is she even still alive?*

"You created new life!" Tavia protested to Dianna. "The werachnids are strong now, because of what the Quadrivium did! You have your daughter! Edmund can change, and walk!"

The bosom inside the jade dress heaved with a sigh. "Otto made arguments like that to me, all the time. One life, traded for another. Werachnid in, dragon out. We're creators, and yet we're also murderers. It doesn't feel like an improvement."

She reached out tentatively to Jennifer, who let her replace a strand of platinum hair behind her right ear. "On top of that, I made an orphan of the daughter of the man I truly loved. And, of course, my own son is dead." Now, finally, Dianna walked over to where Skip lay. Those in her way parted quickly to let her pass. She knelt down by his body, letting her dress soak in his blood. Her breath came heavily, and for a moment Jennifer believed she was trying to cast a spell that might bring the boy back to life.

Whether or not that was the case, it did not work. The breathing turned to sobbing, and Dianna turned to Edmund and Tavia with pale eyes. "I want to put things back the way they were."

"That's easy for you to say," Tavia snapped. "You've gotten what you want."

Edmund crouched slightly. The threat behind his posture was

hard to miss. "Dianna, don't make us regret including you. Otto told me he had his doubts—"

"I know what Otto told you," Dianna snapped. "His mind was always simple, always open to me. He took things too far. And now he's dead."

"Is that a threat?"

"It's an instructive reflection." Dianna stood up, letting the thick blood trickle off the hem of her dress. "Please tell me you have more sense than him!"

Feeling the shift in the room, Evangelina morphed into her stronger, darker form and stepped close to her mother. Jennifer joined her, and Elise and Eddie closed ranks. The other warriors and Nakia followed suit. Andi, dark eyes wide, edged toward the doorway. Jennifer saw the small girl's fingers flex around her forearms, and she spared a hope that Andi had no knives hidden on her person.

"I can't believe this," Edmund snarled, his good eye rolling. "We finally get things the way we want to, after years of planning. Decades of planning. And you want to throw it all away!"

"Throw *what* away?!" Dianna asked with a stomp of her foot. The small demonstration of impatience rocked the observatory and startled Jennifer. "One of the Quadrivium is now dead. Three are left, surrounded by the allies of a fifteen-year-old girl who crushed our guard and entered our inner sanctum. Edmund, we changed the universe . . . and we still lost! It's over! How long do you think we'll be able to hold this universe together as the paradise you believe it to be? How many more people will have to—"

"We have to stop her, Edmund." Why Tavia bothered to whisper, Jennifer had no idea. Not only were Dianna and Evangelina telepaths, but even the smallest voice became a magnified echo in this cavernous room. "We have to kill her!"

Evangelina showed no interest in waiting for them to strike first. With a snarl, she forced the tendrils of her dark aura forward.

Edmund was directly in her path and had his back to the wall. As the darkness overtook him, he blinked an eye, and vanished, leaving Evangelina to crash into the wall. A moment later, the blond spider reappeared, clinging to a point about halfway up the observatory wall.

"Settle down, daughter." Dianna sighed. "Edmund Slider's jumping skills are, shall we say, better than average. You can't catch him. And we don't need to."

Evangelina did not listen. She began to chase Edmund around the room. Jennifer heard her try to sound out where he would go next before he teleported, but he was too good at clouding his mind.

"Evangelina, please! You're embarrassing yourself."

"Don't tell me what to do, Mother."

Jennifer almost laughed. *That didn't take long.* With a wry smile at Elise, she admitted, "You and I have a special mother-daughter relationship, too."

In the commotion, she barely noticed Eddie, who still had an arrow nocked in his bow. He began to track the movements of the pair with the point of the dart.

Tavia ignored it all and made her last plea to Dianna. "You can't make us give this up! Look at him! He's so beautiful as a spider. In that other world, he's never going to change. He's never going to stand."

"And in this world," Jennifer heard Eddie mutter, "he's never going to see."

He released his arrow just as Edmund arrived at a point on the opposite wall, just a few feet up. The missile plunged right into Edmund's last eye, knocking the spider off the wall with a blood-curdling scream.

"Edmund!" Tavia rushed to his side and tried to staunch the blood running down his face.

Jennifer located Andi, who was still in the doorway. "What are you waiting for? *Help* him!"

Andi nodded and jogged over, gym bag in hand. Her delicate features widened in concern as she tried to keep Edmund's head still. "If you hold him steady, I can . . ."

But Tavia released him as soon as Andi had him, and she charged across the room without a thought of changing or casting sorcery or anything else other than getting to Eddie. "You little piece of shit! You won't leave this place alive!"

Eddie nocked another arrow instantly and leveled his bow. Jennifer did the only thing she could, and stood in front of him with her back to Tavia. "Eddie, no!"

In a flash, Dianna was back to back with Jennifer, palms out at her sister-in-law. "Tavia, wait!"

"Dead!"

The severity of the word and the tone Tavia used in her sorcery made Jennifer turn, keeping one hand on the point of Eddie's arrow and raising a dagger to defend . . .

But the sorcery never made it that far. It was suddenly not a woman behind Jennifer, but a pulsating mesh of bright and dim green lights, with hints of reds and yellows, suggestive of a spider rather than actually detailing one. Set against the twilight of the observatory interior, her shape reminded Jennifer of a strange aurora borealis.

A being of pure energy, Dianna swallowed Tavia's black sorcery whole, adding it to her own kaleidoscope. She reached out with a leg (or what Jennifer guessed was a leg) and tried to stroke her sister-in-law's face.

"Tavia. See to Edmund."

The other woman pulled back from the touch with hate deepening the wrinkles in her brow. "You've ruined everything!" she cried out in a hoarse voice. "Otto was a strong man, and Edmund was magnificent, and then you ruined everything! I'll never forgive you for this!"

"Tavia—" The aurora dimmed and wrapped itself back around Dianna's human form, swishing again like a dress.

"I hope you die!" The word *die* echoed through the hollow sphere. Tavia looked at each and every one of them—Dianna, then Eddie, then Evangelina and Jennifer, and then everyone else. "I hope you all die for what you've done!"

"Are you going to help me save him or not?" called out a thin, clear voice. It was Andi, looking angry. One of the girl's hands was on Edmund's bloody chin, trying to keep the man's head straight. The other one alternated between trying to pull the arrow out, and trying to keep her patient's flailing arms from tearing at her.

"Not," Tavia sneered at Andi, "because it doesn't matter. Not if Dianna has made up her mind. We'll all go back to last week, and everything will be back the way it was. Nobody will remember anything of this world. Skip will be alive. Edmund will be in a wheelchair. Otto will be dead. And you, my pretty little nurse, will have never even existed." The thought seemed to amuse Tavia in her hysterical state. "Meanwhile, my dead brother's wife here gets to float about, wherever it is she floats about, all warm and joyful! Because I'll bet she'll find a way to keep her precious daughter around. Won't you, Dianna?"

Dianna sucked in her cheeks and narrowed her eyes. It looked as if she was going to say something to Tavia, or perhaps level her, but then she let out a breath and turned to Jennifer. "You want your life back."

The open offer stunned Jennifer, in spite of all she'd heard. She managed to open her mouth. "Yes. Please."

"You may have it, on one condition."

Jennifer braced herself. *I have to complete another quest? Or grovel? Or worst of all . . . not kill Skip the moment I see him again?*

"I want you to forgive my son."

*Dammit!* "Why?!"

"Because of his sacrifice."

They both turned to look at Skip's lifeless body. His face was paler now. Strands of chocolate hair clung in cold sweat, making small weblike patterns along the fringes of his face.

"What he did out there wasn't sacrifice," Jennifer protested. "He shot at your daughter! He could have ruined everything for you."

"And yet he missed." Dianna shook her head with a sad smile. "He didn't know what he was doing, dear. He never did. All he knew was that he wanted to save you."

"So you let him."

"As I said before, I wanted you along, too, by the time he knew what would happen. But us *wanting* you here was one thing. *Having* you here required sacrifice. Skip stepped forward. He gave something precious, for something precious."

Jennifer walked over to Skip's body. Hearing his mother's words, she knew right away what he had given up. *That's why he never changed, all week long. No matter what I did to him. Oh, Skip . . .*

"You hobbled him."

"Gently, yes. Hobbling doesn't require the brutality of the beaststalker ritual. The right poison, applied correctly, will do the job without pain. He could walk, but he would never change again. And he asked me to do it, for you." Dianna extended a hand of velvet and lifted Jennifer's chin to face her. She measured this girl, judging her worthiness of the sacrifice. "The boy who was to become my people's most powerful leader, hobbled himself so you could live. I took his gift, and spread it across all our kind to break our bonds from the phases of the moon."

Jennifer wanted to believe this woman. *Why would she lie about it? He's dead now.* "He wasn't a member of the Quadrivium."

"No."

"He really only came along to save me."

"Yes. He could have left you behind, using his sorcery for himself alone, bringing nothing but his betrayal into this world. Or he could have let the change happen without protecting himself, which would have left him in this universe without any knowledge or memory of you. He couldn't bear the thought of either path. Only saving you made any sense to him."

"And he only betrayed Crescent Valley because you told him to."

"We all told him to, and yes."

Jennifer looked straight into Dianna's colorful eyes. They were pale yellow now. She raised a dagger and pointed it right between them. "Then fine, I'll forgive him. And you'll set things right. And then the next time you and I meet, we're going to settle this with a good, healthy dose of violence."

The woman's lip curled up. "I suppose I'm going to have to hope it never comes to that."

"Don't patronize me."

The curl didn't go away. "I'm not. But I'm flattered you think I'm in a position to do so."

Jennifer looked her up and down. Was Dianna as strong as she seemed? Or was her strength limited to certain situations? In a knife fight, would a simple beaststalker tear right through her?

*Find out afterward.* "Whatever. If you're going to change things back, how about less talk, more back-changing. I'd like to see my parents and friends again."

"Yes, of course you would. You'll tell your father what has happened, I imagine?"

"Yes."

Dianna turned and walked toward Evangelina. "Could you

please tell him I'm sorry? For leaving him, I mean. I didn't mean to hurt him. It just . . ."

". . . came naturally?" Jennifer offered.

"It just got too hard," Dianna finished with a sigh. She walked into Evangelina's aura, and the darkness faded around her. She stroked her daughter's reptilian skull. "But let him know I'm happier now. Perhaps he is, too. And let him know our daughter is safe."

*What will happen to me, Mother?*

The sorceress graced her daughter with an enormous, warm smile. "Oh, Evangelina, dear. Don't fret. Just stay at my side."

"What do you need to do?" Jennifer asked. "To reverse everything. Is it difficult?"

"It's always easier to undo, than to do. My role in the Quadrivium was to bend the stars." Dianna looked up at the starlit sky within the dome, and it flexed as she breathed. "All we need to unbend them is a bit of poison to relax what I've constricted."

"Will this do?" Jennifer went over to the gym bag, where Andi was storing the cooler with the botulin toxin. "We've had it under ice, and it's been pretty cold out to begin with . . ."

The sorceress took the cooler from her and peered inside. "You are prepared for anything, aren't you? Just like your father was. I mean, is," she added hastily.

"I don't know about that. A good swift kick seems to catch him off guard."

"You will also need something from outside this manufactured world."

Jennifer patted herself down with the growing sense that she was going to have to give up one of her beautiful daggers. *It's worth it,* she told herself as she examined them both. *But which one? Can Uncle Mike replace either one as easily? Would I even want him to?*

Then she thought of Goodwin, who she had placed in Andi's gym bag before the battle, for his safety. *Maybe he's Geddy and he'll work. Or maybe he's just Goodwin, which will blow up the whole— Oh, hey!*

She placed her hand in her jacket pocket, where the silver

moon elm leaf still rested intact. Victorious, she held it out for Dianna to take.

"Finally," the woman told her, "we will need a beaststalker's blood."

Jennifer bit her lip. "How much?"

"All of it."

"Nothing else will work?"

"Glorianna Seabright's young blood," Dianna answered patiently, "cemented this sorcery. Only a beaststalker's blood can unglue it."

Swallowing hard, Jennifer looked around the room. She hadn't told any of these people what this was all about. Sure, some had heard about a new universe, but did any of them know if they would still be alive in it? And what if Dianna really was tricking them? Neither Sonakshi nor Seraphina had said anything about a blood sacrifice. Could she ask any of these people to die for what could be a dumb, horrible mistake?

"Take mine," she finally offered, rolling up her right jacket and shirt sleeve.

Dianna shook her head. "You wouldn't—"

"Hey!" Elise snapped through clenched teeth as she grabbed Jennifer's shoulder and spun her around. "I'm still not your mother, but if I was, I'm pretty certain I would be pissed off at you right now!"

"You don't—"

"Eh, why'm I even talking to you." Elise shoved Jennifer to the floor and turned to Dianna. "You spill her blood, I spill yours. It's not an option."

"Are you offering yourself in her place?"

"No!" Jennifer shouted it from the floor at the same time Eddie did while lowering his bow. Eddie was faster, and he pushed Elise first, who tumbled back into Jennifer and sent them both sprawling.

The arachnid sorceress could not help but sigh as she watched the three of them. "You all make quite an impressive force."

Eddie didn't answer. Instead, he stripped off his jacket and tore at the shirtsleeve where Skip's bullet had already made a hole in the fabric. Then, keeping his brown eyes fixed on Dianna, he presented his arm.

"Very well," she said.

Before either Elise or Jennifer could stop it, Dianna had dissolved herself and sunk two barely visible shafts of green light into Eddie's wound. He sucked air through his teeth but did not complain as she began to drink. All around the room—Jennifer and Elise staring from the floor, Tavia glaring next to a barely alive Edmund, the warriors around them looking on in awe, and Andi and Nakia gazing anxiously from where they stood—people watched Eddie Blacktooth die.

The spider drank from him, steadily and deeply, until he fell to his knees.

"That's enough!" Jennifer reached for her daggers as she raced forward. "You've taken enough! Let him go! Eddie!"

There was no need to strike. Dianna abruptly released Eddie and shifted back into human form. The woman's throat was still engorged with blood as she staggered to the center of the chamber floor. From one hand, she fed herself the moon leaf, and from the other, she washed it all down with a vial of the poison Jennifer had offered.

A nova's light filled the observatory, and then dimmed enough for Jennifer to see the stars unbending on the walls around them. From somewhere unseen came a profound series of bass tones and the faint scent of sulfur filled the air.

From where the nova had begun, a frail light now shone in front of Dianna—white and spindly, like a thin spider curling and uncurling its legs. On top of the bass tones, a soft melody arose. It sounded strangely familiar, so much like the tune Jennifer had heard when she fell asleep in Skip's arms on the Winoka park bench. She did not pay attention to it for long; Eddie was slumping to the floor not far from Skip's torn body. The boy's sparrowlike eyes glazed over. *There's no going back now,* she knew. *The only Eddie that's alive is back home. Oh, please, let this work.*

Dianna stood near Jennifer and pointed to the frail light. "Take your place there! When you are ready, reach out and hold the light."

"And that's it? Everything will change back?"

The sorceress nodded as she stepped closer to Jennifer. "As I said before, unraveling is simpler than weaving. Given who you are, the fabric of this universe will quickly disintegrate in your hands. All will return to last Monday evening, before the sorcery started . . . and it will simply never happen. Nobody except you will even know what truly happened—not even Skip, or Edmund, or Tavia. Who you tell and how much, of course, is up to you." Now she leaned in, gave an indigo wink, and whispered, "I'm glad you and I didn't have to fight today, Jennifer Scales. And not just because you are my dear Jonathan's daughter."

"*Your* dear—?"

"One last favor? Please give this to Skip." She handed Jennifer a sealed envelope, the color of her own dress.

Jennifer was confused, but nodded as she put the envelope in her pocket. "Sure. Uh, what about Evangelina? Shouldn't she come with me?"

The right side of the woman's mouth curled up. "We'll be spending some mother-daughter time together. I hope your grandfather doesn't mind."

"Time together?! Where? Neither of you will be alive anymore!"

Dianna's brows lifted. "You're a lovely young woman, Jennifer Scales, and a hell of a fighter. But if you think I'm going to spill all of my secrets to you right here, Jonathan hasn't raised you to be as bright as I'd expect. Now, off you go!"

Despite the woman's firm (and somewhat rude, she thought) pat on her buttocks, Jennifer stayed where she was. She looked around the room one last time. She saw its stark architecture in the obsidian arcs above, which caught the music of the spiders so softly just before bouncing it back down upon them. She saw Nakia, her bright olive skin shining, eyes aglow as she witnessed the play of light in the center of the observatory. She saw Andi next to Nakia, head bowed low and reverent before the display of sorcerous power and resonant music. She saw Eddie sprawled upon the floor with his bow lashed to his back, blood still spilling from his muscled arm, and Skip behind him, leading the other boy on the cold path of death. And last of all, she saw Elise in front of the remaining warriors, looking back at her and everything around them in wonder. They stepped toward each other.

"You did it," Elise said.

"*We* did it," Jennifer corrected her. She took a last glance at Eddie's empty brown features. "We all did it."

The woman reached into her jacket and drew out her moon

elm leaf. *The last one left in this world,* Jennifer reminded herself. "Take this," Elise told her. "I won't need it here anymore."

"You won't miss anything. Not ever again," Jennifer promised her, sliding the leaf into the pocket of her jeans. She turned, walked into the brilliant magic of the sorceress, and seized the light in her hand. As she collapsed into a deep sleep, she heard the same words she had heard nearly a week ago.

*She'll be home soon.*

# CHAPTER 19

## *Monday Night*

Jennifer woke up with her face on a plush, carpeted floor. Opening her eyes, she saw forest green, with piles of dirty laundry in the distance. Her head jerked up.

*My clothes. My bedroom.*

*My house! My world!*

She stood up and took everything in. Geddy was in his terrarium, lapping up the last of his water from the molded plastic bowl. Not far from him, a cricket hid behind a cactus. Out the window, a crescent moon shone brightly through the window.

*It's last Monday! It worked! I'm back!*

She couldn't wait to see everything again the way it was supposed to be: her home, Winoka High, city hall, the farm, Crescent Valley! It would all be right again. She had to see it all!

But first things first.

"Eddie!" She flung open her door and ran down the hallway to the guest bedroom. He was there, beautifully alive, wearing gym shorts and a T-shirt, with no signs of grimness or pain. And best of all, there was no blood seeping from his elbow.

Red-faced, he stuffed whatever he was reading under the pillows and jumped off the bed. "Jennifer! I was just—"

Her mouth was already on top of his. He had brushed his teeth, thank heavens, but he still wasn't that good at it. Jennifer didn't care. She stayed with the kiss until they both had their eyes open again.

"What's going on?" he asked, bewildered. "Y-you said—"

"I was wrong," she told him. "About you. I'm sorry."

"No, you were right. When you needed me, I—"

"When I really need you, Eddie, you'll be there. I know that now."

"How—"

"I'll explain another time. Right now, I gotta go."

"Huh. Okay, but this was really weird."

"Don't I know it."

Jonathan no doubt heard her as she ran down the stairs into the living room, but he nevertheless was surprised when she grabbed his wing claw and pulled him toward the front door.

"I'm sorry, I was a jerk, come on, let's go."

"Honey, I know your mother's upset, but now is not the time. She'll calm down and be back in a little—"

"She's— Wait! Hey, Phoebe!" Jennifer bent down and gave her modest black dog a hug. "You were so brave. Thank you." The dog accepted the affection with her typical, unconditional enthusiasm.

She looked back up at her father, who had a bemused look on his face. "As I was saying, she's waiting. And the time *is* now."

He wrinkled his scaled forehead as she let go of Phoebe and shook her wings and tail out. "She's what?"

"We're going, we're going!" she yelled at him, pushing his squirming body out the door. "I'll tell you everything on the way!"

"On the way *where*?"


*Jennifer had guessed* from the moment of her return that there was really no other place her mother could be. Nevertheless, she was relieved when she saw the minivan parked outside the lake-side cabin.

"Huh," Jonathan said. "She backtracked on us. How'd you guess?"

She didn't answer him as she landed on two human feet, but instead reached inside her coat pocket and handed him the only object she had left from her lost week: the leaf Elise had given her.

Its image sparkled in his silver eyes. "Jennifer, is this—"

Before he could finish his question, his winged body trembled. His scales shrank and paled, while the horns at the back of his head disappeared. His tail withered away, and his teeth grew blunt. In a matter of a few seconds, he was standing in the twilit backyard on two bare feet.

The leaf crinkled in his tightening palm. He wiped his bangs out of his face and looked up at the crescent moon. "It looks larger," he noticed.

Jennifer averted her eyes with a snort. "Not from where I'm standing, it doesn't. Here. You should, er, take my jacket." She dangled it on the end of a finger behind her, refusing to look at him.

He chuckled, taking the jacket. "You know, I've got clothes inside. Though I hardly expected to need them for another few days."

"Then, please, pretty please, let's go inside."

They went up on the porch, Jennifer first. Everything was the way it was supposed to be, from the well-kept porch to the new library wallpaper visible from beyond the glass doors. Once they were inside, Jennifer could see her mother, blonde hair disheveled, hunched over the kitchen table facing away from them. She could also hear the clink of a spoon against a ceramic ice-cream bowl.

"Mom?"

The woman turned, and for a moment Jennifer thought she was looking at the cold, hard stare of Elise Georges. Then the face softened a touch, before Elizabeth Georges-Scales turned back to her ice cream. "What are you doing here?"

*Keeping my promise.* "I'm . . . I've been . . . I missed you."

Jennifer heard her mother sigh and the spoon clatter into the bowl. "I missed you, too, honey. I'm sorry I drove off earlier. It's just that your father sometimes—"

"—drives you into the seductive arms of double chocolate ice cream?" Jonathan guessed, stepping out from behind his daughter.

His voice made Elizabeth turn again, and she gave her husband a skeptical look up and down before dismissing him. "Your idea of an apology needs work. Put some pants on to go with that jacket." She pushed her chair back and brought the empty bowl over to the sink.

"Elizabeth. Look."

"Dammit, Jonathan, I've seen your—"

*"Mom!"* Jennifer lost all patience. *"Look!"*

Elizabeth bit the inside of her lip and squinted at them, still not understanding what they meant. Finally, though, she saw the silver moon elm leaf in Jonathan's hand. A brief expression of wonder escaped before she slammed her features shut again.

"Liz, I'm sorry." Jonathan stepped forward and held the leaf out to her. "I never told the Blaze about what really happened that night, because I was too scared of what they'd do. Not to me, but to you."

"I can handle myself." Elizabeth put her hands on her hips, but did not move away as he got closer.

"I should have told them the truth that day. I should have told them the truth when we got married. I should have told them the truth when Jennifer was born, when she had her first change, when Evangelina showed up. I had so many chances, and I blew them all. If you forgive me, I'll do it right tomorrow. Actually, I'll do it right even if you don't forgive me. You deserve that."

Elizabeth didn't move for some time. She pinned him there, standing half-naked in the kitchen, with her emerald gaze.

Finally, Jennifer couldn't stand it anymore. "I found him for you, Mom. You told me you were missing him, and I helped you find him again. I promised I would. You have to forgive him."

Her mother shook her head. "Jennifer . . ."

"You have to forgive him!"

"For heaven's sake, Jennifer, calm down! It's not what you think. It's like I told you on the highway. I don't need your relationship advice."

With that, the woman reached into her jeans pocket and pulled out . . . her own silver moon elm leaf.

"I figured I'd spend the night here and clear my head," she explained. "As I drove up, this flew into the windshield. At that point, all I figured I had to do was—"

"—eat a bowl of double chocolate ice cream?" Jonathan guessed.

Her eyes narrowed again. "I was going to say, 'wait for the love of my life to show up.' But at this point, Mr. I-Can't-Let-My-Wife-Finish-a-Single-Sentence, a second bowl of ice cream is looking better and better."

Seeing a possible opportunity slip away into sarcasm, Jennifer panicked. "So are you forgiving him or what, Mom?"

"Of course I'm going to forgive him, honey. I'm just mulling over the price." A sly grin spread over her face, and she reached out to grab her husband's earlobe.

Jonathan returned the smile. "How about we go negotiate upstairs?"

"Deal."

"Oh, that's—" *Ugh. Gross? Twisted? Sweet? Romantic?* "Gross! Yes, please, you two, take it upstairs." She continued calling after them as her mother's clothes came tumbling down the stairs. "By all means, celebrate our family reunion by ditching your daughter for a blundering roll in the hay! It's not like you owe her anything, not even a simple 'thank you!' Because you know what? *You're not welcome!* Yeah, that's right, you're not . . ."

"Jennifer, honey." Her mother's voice came drifting down along with her father's giggles. "You're really killing the mood here. How about you fly around the lake for a while, pick up some firewood, rake some leaves, build a shed . . . ?"

# CHAPTER 20

## *New Tuesday*

Jennifer was still fuming by the time she staggered into school Tuesday morning. She had spent hours circling the cold farm last night before she had finally lost patience with her parents, reentered the house, and screamed up the stairs that she was going back home to commiserate with any teenaged boy who happened to be staying there as a guest. That had gotten them moving, but they hadn't made it home until after midnight. Unfortunately, school started just as early here as it had in the other, more wicked universe.

She ambled blearily through the front door, letting Eddie race ahead with an energetic wink good-bye. Trying to wink back, she ended up closing both eyes and drifting off until a group of kids bumped and shoved past her. *Beaststalkers.* She sighed to herself. *So rude. They don't even appreciate what you did for them. Where are the balloons and cake? Where's the welcoming committee?*

Working her way to her locker, she was just reaching for the handle when the most beautiful voice in the world sounded behind her.

"You're still a bitch for blowing me off."

"Oh, Susan." With a slow sigh, Jennifer stumbled around and draped her tired arms around her best friend. "I missed you. I'm sorry. I'll cancel on Amanda and Bob as soon as I see them."

"Hmmph." Susan kept her back rigid and her books held tightly against her chest as Jennifer tried to make herself comfortable, maybe get a quick nap in. "I guess you sound sincere. Hey, what the hell happened to you last night. You've got circles under your—"

"My parents did it. Like, for two hours."

"Oh, you poor thing!" The brunette let her books drop to the hallway floor and accepted Jennifer in a warm hug. "You poor, wretched thing! Did you go to your happy place? Whenever my dad brings a date home, I use a memory of snorkeling off a Caribbean beach with no one there but me and some completely asexual fish . . ."

*I have a happy place, too,* Jennifer thought. *And I'm back in it.* Her nose nuzzled Susan's neck, taking in her friend's cheap, apple-scented perfume.

"Woot! Go, girls!" The dull roar of Bob Jarkmand's voice startled them both out of the forgiving embrace. He and another football friend were mere inches from them. "Matty, check it out, my date's goin' at it with another babe! Yeah, Jennifer, you can bring Sandy along here with you to Amanda's Friday night! The three of us can—"

Susan was actually faster than Jennifer. She reached up, grabbed Bob Jarkmand by the lapels of his letter jacket, and shook him violently. "My name is Susan very simple name Susan S-U-S-A-N and I wouldn't go to a party with you or kiss you or do anything else with you even if you flayed the skin off my fingers and IT'S A VERY SIMPLE NAME!"

"Bob," Jennifer added with as soft a smirk as she could manage, "I've had a change of plans. I can't go to Amanda's Friday night."

"Aw, man." His dreams of sexual adventure in tatters, Bob hung his head. "So, um, when do you think we can go out?"

She reached up and locked fingers with Susan's hands, forcing her friend to relax and let go of the giant boy. "When you can remember my girlfriend's name. You, me, her, Eddie, Amanda, a few others. It would be nice to go out to the movies, maybe talk a bit. No macking. No feeling. No girl-on-girl action."

"Huh. Whatever." With all interesting options removed from consideration, Bob put a desolate arm around his buddy Matty and walked away, grumbling about fickle girls and a certain time of the month.

"He's a real winner, Jennifer. I can see why you fell for him."

"Yes, a rude comment about female anatomy really is the way to my heart."

Susan took Jennifer's arm and walked her down the hall. "Hey, by the way, did you do your geometry homework last night? Most of that stuff, I couldn't get. I don't think Mr. Slider even cared if we got it all done!"

*Mr. Slider.* The name made Jennifer draw a sharp breath. *Is he here? Did he survive? Does he remember anything?*

The sight that greeted Jennifer in geometry class nearly broke her heart. Edmund Slider was there, in his usual position at the head of the class. His useless legs spilled off of the wheelchair, and his blond head was in his hands, unkempt strands of hair escaping through his fingers, with elbows jammed against awkward knees. The clothes he wore were wrinkled and scented with stale sweat. The only parts of him that looked presentable at all were his feet, enshrined in two polished black shoes that had certainly never been used.

He raised his head off his palms as she passed, and she found her legs fixed to the floor as if he had cast a sorcery upon her. She could not look away from him. There was no anger there, just overwhelming frustration and despair. They stared at each other, she clearly wanting to say something but not knowing what, and he clearly not ready to hear anything at all.

The bell rang. Everybody else took their seats.

"If you would turn to page 252 in your texts, class." His voice was a hoarse whisper, and he did not look away from her.

She tried. "M-Mr. Slider, I—"

"Page 252, class." He did not move. "Ms. Elmsmith, if you would be so kind as to read aloud from the beginning of the chapter."

Jennifer didn't turn, and she knew Susan was also unsure of what to do. After a long pause, her friend began to read:

"'Chapter Seven. Geometric Transformations. A *transformation* is a change in the *form* of a mathematical *object*. By the end of this chapter, you will be able to: First, *explain* the basic types of transformations; second, *make use* of transformation terminology to describe elements of the changing world around you; and third, *change shapes* using interactive computer software modules that illustrate rotations, reflections, translations, and enlargements. You will also . . .'"

*It didn't work,* she mouthed silently to him as Susan kept reading. *It's over.*

There was no humor in his voiceless reply:
*Wait.*


*"Wasn't he weird?"* Susan wrinkled her nose at the memory of Mr. Slider's class. He had not said another word the entire time, other than to change chapter readers at intervals. "I mean, he never even asked us for our homework!"

"He will," Jennifer said thoughtfully. "He doesn't know what went wrong, but he'll try again."

"Well, duh, he is the teacher. You sure you're okay? You've been acting weird today."

"I'll explain later. Maybe over lunch, if there's . . . Hang on, there's the A-List. Hey, Anne!"

The freckled blonde broke chatter with Amy and Abigail long enough to look up. "Hey, yourself."

"Where's Amanda?"

Anne shrugged.

"If you see her, tell her I'm out for Friday."

Amy examined Jennifer's figure and smirked. "What, Bob decided he could say 'no' to you after all?"

Susan stepped in front of Jennifer as they walked by. "No, she's just spending the evening with friends. Thanks for passing on the word to Amelia."

"Amanda."

"Whatever." And with that, Susan pushed past the A-List, letting Jennifer grin as she stumbled behind.

A few steps later, Susan stopped short. "Jennifer!"

Jennifer followed the direction her finger pointed down the hall. When she spotted the target, half her heart leapt while the other half sank.

"He looks terrible."

Jennifer had to agree with Susan. Skip Wilson was at his locker, staring down the hall, without really seeming to see her or anyone else. His chocolate hair was more unkempt than usual, and there were bloody spots on the whites of his tired eyes.

"Give me a sec, will you?"

Jennifer walked up to him and handed him Dianna Wilson's jade envelope. "This is for you," she told him. "Your mother asked me to deliver it."

Suddenly recognizing her, Skip reached out and opened the note. He read it for a few moments, and Jennifer backed up a step or two when she saw tears escape down his cheeks.

"You've read this," he said when he was done.

"No," she answered truthfully. "But I don't have to. I can imagine what's in there pretty easily."

"It was you. You stopped it all. This morning, when nothing changed, Mr. Slider and I tried to figure out what happened. *You* seemed like the most likely explanation."

She sighed. "Your mother stopped it. She saw the consequences, and she didn't like them."

"But you had something to do with it, I'll bet," he barked, crumpling the paper up and jamming it in his jacket pocket. "The Great Jennifer Scales, Wonder of All Wonders. Couldn't stay out of it. You ruined everything. You always—"

"HEY." She stepped toward him and grabbed him by the front of his shirt. "You can gnash your teeth some other time, buddy. You're lucky you're still alive, after what you tried to do."

He shook her hand off and wiped his face. "You would have been fine! I was going to save you."

"I know," she said. "But as it turns out, I ended up saving you."

One side of his mouth rose in an uncertain sneer. "You're not making any sense."

"It doesn't matter. You don't have to save me, Skip. What you thought would happen today—it will never happen. Your own mother won't allow it, and your family can't do it without her. You're stuck with the world you're in, for better or worse." She briefly remembered Mr. Slider's threat—*Wait*—but pushed it firmly out of her mind.

He rested his head against the locker behind him and slumped his shoulders. "So that's how it is. Jennifer Scales gets her way, yet again."

She resisted the impulse to knee him in his intransigent groin. "I know it's hard when you're not in control, Skip. When it feels like the whole world's against you. I found friends, when I needed them. You just have friends, too. You just have to reach out."

"Friends." He spat. The familiar defiance was returning to his features. "Friends like disowned Eddie, or babbling Catherine, or useless Susan. No thanks."

"I'm sorry you feel that way. I guess I have something else to tell you, then." Leaning in close, she gently smoothed out the fabric of his flannel shirt. "I promised your mother I'd forgive you this time. And I have. But right now, my parents are putting out word to every dragon and beaststalker about what you and your family have tried. I would expect an awful lot of eyes will be on the Saltins, Wilsons, and Sliders of this world, for a very long time." She looked up meaningfully at him without smiling. "Be careful, sweetie. I would feel horrible if you got hurt."

Looking back down at her, he bit his lower lip. "So I'm supposed to be afraid? I don't care. Witch-hunters like your mom and the mayor don't scare me. Nobody does."

"I know." She sighed and touched his ear. "That's why I still kind of like you."

He backed up a step. "You only like me as long as I behave. As long as I stay on your leash."

"Skip . . ."

"It's all about control with you, isn't it? As long as you can stop me from doing things you don't like, you'll tolerate me. I can be your pet, as long as I'm house-trained."

"No, I'm . . ."

"You stop me from reuniting with my mother by turning her against me. You stop me from connecting with my half-sister by murdering her. You even stop me from getting close to you by lying through your teeth. You're just an expert at stopping things, aren't you?"

"Skip, that's not fair—"

"That's the difference between us, I guess," he finished with a vicious arrogance. "Guys like me try to *create* and *make* things happen, and uncaring bitches like you just get off on *stopping* things from happening. Do you get that from your mom, or—"

She slugged him across the jaw.

"Gosh, Skip, I'm sorry," she said as he reeled back and fell against his locker. "I just couldn't *stop that from happening*! I must not be as good at this sort of thing as you say I am."

She turned quickly so he wouldn't see the gathering tears and marched away.

*   *   *

*Jennifer was standing* alone for a moment, reflecting on the laughing and jostling teenagers filing out of the cafeteria, when she saw someone who nearly made her drop her textbooks.

*How is this possible?*

"Hi, Jennifer."

"Huh?"

"I kinda tagged along when you left."

"I don't . . . I . . . how did you do it? Are there other—"

"Relax, Jennifer. I'm the only stowaway. When we shifted the universe the first time, we realized it might not work out. This was our Plan B. Unlike our bloody Plan A, the only thing Plan B has cost is a single life—someone to keep the balance. I chose Amanda Sera. Nothing personal against her. I'm just not a big fan of queen bees."

Jennifer didn't really hear the last couple of sentences. "*We* shifted? *Our* Plan B? *You* were one of the . . . ?"

"Oh, come on, Jennifer. It can't surprise you that much, can it? I mean, you suspected Skip from the start; so it's not like you *always* thought it was four adults behind all of it."

"But you're not . . . you don't . . ."

"I'm special. Let's leave it at that."

Jennifer bit her lip. "So if you, and Dianna, and Otto were . . . then either Edmund or Tavia wasn't . . ."

"Tavia Saltin's a talented gal. But not Quadrivium talented. Edmund Slider had to bring her along, just like Skip brought you. It cost him half of his sight and hearing, a price he gladly gave. I was the one who 'sang the song of change,' as the verse says."

Jennifer didn't know what to say. Sweat tickled her cheekbones, and her breath came up short. *Edmund Slider was right. There's still a plan. They're going to try again. They're going to take away—*

"Jennifer. Please, don't panic. We're not going to try to take away your universe again. Whatever you may think of Dianna Wilson, she keeps her word. She really did love your father. She told me so many times, when Otto wasn't around. She said leaving Jonathan Scales behind for your mother was the one mistake she'd correct, if she could."

"That." Jennifer put a hand up against a locker and tried deep breaths. "Doesn't necessarily. Make me feel. Better."

The girl pulled her long sweater sleeves up, rubbed her palms, and smoothed her green-streaked hair behind one ear. Jennifer noticed how much straighter she stood. "You have a great universe here. Worth fighting for, I can see already. Thanks again for opening the door so I could come home."

And with that the small, dark girl Jennifer only knew as Andi stepped up, kissed her on a clammy cheek, and pranced off to history class.

*Jonathan and Elizabeth didn't want* to hear much about Andi when Jennifer got home. They were preparing for their next trip to Crescent Valley.

"This girl sounds like she's rather fond of Winoka," her father pointed out as he put on Jennifer's silver moon elm leaf. The strange cellulose was tough enough for them to puncture a hole through the leaf and put on a simple necklace chain. "If she's up to mischief, I doubt she'll be able to plan much in a day or two. And if she has no troubling designs, so much the better."

That made enough sense to get Jennifer in the minivan with Eddie and her parents. They started the drive talking about their plan for the visit.

"Two things have to happen this trip," Jonathan said as Elizabeth peeled out of the driveway. "First, I have to tell Winona Brandfire the truth. Second, we have to show a true effort to bring more beaststalkers to the table."

"I'll help this time," Eddie said. He held Jennifer's hand tightly. "Dr. Georges-Scales, thanks for taking me to see my mom earlier today. I think you're right: We can start with her."

"She'll be able to check out of the hospital in about a week," Elizabeth advised. "Once she's out, we might want to wait a few more weeks before trying to take her through the lake. Meeting the others at the cabin will be best, for a while."

Jennifer squeezed Eddie's hand back. "Will she stay at your house with your dad?"

He shrugged. "I don't know. The two of them haven't talked since I moved in with you. He hasn't even tried to visit her."

"Oh, Eddie. I'm sorry."

"My dad did most of my training. Until my mom gets better, I guess I'm going to be pretty pathetic with a sword."

"Huh." Jennifer chewed her tongue and held his hands up to

her face to smell them. He had used her soap that morning, she could tell. "Have you ever considered archery?"

He gave her a quizzical look. "What, like, you mean a bow and arrow?"

"I'll bet anything you'd be really good at it."

"Geez. I guess I could try it, but I don't think my mom knows much about—"

"Actually," Elizabeth interrupted from the front, "your mother was on the archery team in college. She won quite a few trophies."

"Wow! I had no idea," Eddie said. "Maybe I should ask her once she's doing better in a few weeks."

"You don't have to wait. I can get you started before then."

"*You* did archery, Mom?"

"Sure did. It's been a while, but I was in those competitions, too."

"Thanks, Dr. Georges-Scales. But I can wait. If my mom won all those trophies, I should probably learn from the best."

Elizabeth's eyebrows lifted in the rearview mirror. "You would be. I didn't say she got *first* place trophies."

Jennifer gave a snort and turned to her father in the passenger seat. "Dad, who else are we meeting besides Winona?"

"Catherine will be there, I think. And Xavier."

Eddie almost cried out as Jennifer crushed his hand. "Xavier Longtail? Why did you invite *him*?"

"He deserves to hear the full truth, too."

"Is he bringing his niece?"

"I don't believe Ember comes out of Crescent Valley much, anymore. It should just be the three of them."

As it turned out, there were four dragons waiting for them around the barbeque pit in the farmhouse's backyard. Xavier sat next to another dasher—not Ember, but a young male with soft cobalt scales and lavender wings. Jennifer couldn't tell his exact age, but from his wide golden eyes and the way he deferred to Xavier, she guessed right away that he was a relative.

Indeed he was. "Jonathan. Jennifer." Xavier looked at Elizabeth and Eddie, but did not acknowledge either of them. He motioned to the second dasher. "This is my great-nephew, Gautierre Longtail."

"Ember's son?" Jennifer asked, reaching out to shake Gautierre's wing claw with one of her own.

"Yes, Ambassador." Xavier nodded appreciatively at Jennifer's morph. She couldn't help it—the last time she had seen this man, they had both held dragon form, and he was dying with an arrow in his heart. The gesture of respect seemed natural. "He turned fourteen some weeks ago. Like you, Ms. Scales, he had his first morph earlier than the average dragon. This is not so unusual among those of us who raise our families in Crescent Valley."

"Raise your families?" Jennifer turned in amazement to her father. "In Crescent Valley? Before first morph?"

Jonathan sighed. "It's not supposed to happen. But Crescent Valley is a big place, and not every rule is easy to enforce."

"Not every rule is a good idea, Elder Scales."

"Rules like letting beaststalkers into Crescent Valley?" Jennifer shot back.

Xavier's reaction surprised her—he actually snickered. "The Blaze has forgiven my niece her indiscretion, as I believe it has forgiven yours, young lady."

"I hope forgiveness is the order of the day." Jonathan sighed. "Because I have a great deal to tell you, Xavier. Winona. Catherine." He nodded at each of the dragons.

Suddenly realizing what she was looking at, Winona Brandfire gasped at Jonathan. "The crescent moon is still in the sky! What has happened here?"

"My daughter can explain that later," Jonathan said. He turned to Xavier. "I hope you and your great-nephew will not begrudge me keeping human form tonight. I am enjoying a rather exceptional opportunity."

"Don't mind us," Xavier said with a bit of gruffness. "Tell us why you've called us here. You mentioned it was urgent you speak to us, and only us."

"I will speak before the full Blaze later. But you deserve to hear this first, in private."

Jennifer held her breath while her father told the Brandfires and Longtails everything about that night twenty years ago: the secret relationship with the beaststalker, the appearance of the silver moon elm, and the attack by the tramplers. Winona stiffened the moment these two entered the story, and she still had not moved by the time Jonathan finished his confession of murder in the defense of Elizabeth. Meanwhile, Catherine gave her grandmother a confused look. *Did anyone even tell her what her parents were doing when they disappeared?* Jennifer wondered.

"The Blaze should know," Jonathan finished, "that I am solely responsible for your daughter's death, Winona. And her husband's. I am also solely responsible for deceiving the Blaze afterward. Elizabeth had nothing to do with these transgressions. She thought I had owned up to it all long ago and received forgiveness. Forgiveness I hope to receive from you, if you're willing, in your time."

The fire in the pit crackled for a long time after Jonathan stopped talking. Waiting for the others to react, Jennifer recalled her own reaction on the side of the highway, when she found out about all this. She looked at Catherine, who was still looking back and forth between her grandmother and the man who had killed her parents. *Dragon faces are so hard to read. Is she confused? Outraged? Sad?*

Finally, Winona stood up on her hind legs. It appeared to Jennifer the elderly trampler was going to step forward to embrace Jonathan, but instead she veered and began to walk toward the lake.

"Eldest?" Jonathan called out. "You have nothing to say?"

Winona paused but did not turn her head. Steam rose from the water's edge in front of her. "Elder Scales. You have broken faith with me, for the last time. Catherine, let's go."

"Jennifer." Catherine's voice quivered with despair. "Please tell me this isn't true!"

"Catherine, I didn't know until last night . . ."

"We-we're moving into Winoka," the young trampler stammered. "That was the surprise I hinted at Sunday afternoon. We close on our new house this week. Jennifer, Grammie wanted to move because she believed in—"

*"Granddaughter!"* The earth shook, and the water bubbled near Winona's wings. Large coils moved through the water, but Jennifer could not make out if it was one creature or ten slithering over each other.

Without another word, Catherine followed her grandmother as they heaved their large bodies into the air and made their way over the lake. Whatever Winona had summoned disappeared under the surface.

"Catherine?" Jennifer knew her friend couldn't hear her, but she could not believe she was gone. Again.

Her mother's hand on her wing comforted her, and she even

accepted an apologetic look from her father. He didn't know, she told herself. *He had no idea the tramplers attacking his girlfriend were parents. No idea their daughter would grow up to be my friend. No idea Winona would walk away from this family, after all these years.*

Gautierre got up to leave.

"Sit down."

Gautierre sat down with an exclamation of protest. Jennifer stared at Xavier Longtail. The Elder dasher had not moved from his position by the fire.

"Uncle X, they murdered Catherine's parents! Shouldn't we go?"

"We're not leaving just yet."

Jonathan gave him a weary glance as he sat down across the fire from the dragons. "You want to fight instead, like your niece? Go ahead, Xavier. Take your shot. I'm not going to stop you."

"I will," Jennifer warned them.

Xavier's black-scaled features broadened into an ironic grin. "Frankly, my friends, I find myself unable to go. The violence and drama surrounding your family is fascinating. I simply must stay and see what horrific revelation comes next." He turned to his great-nephew, who was impatiently twitching a triple-pronged tail. "Who knows, Gautierre? With a little luck, we may be the next victims!"

"Longtail, I'm not in the mood for—"

Xavier raised an apologetic wing claw. "My gallows humor. Yes, very well. But I would like to stay, Jonathan. If you and your wife don't mind. You see, I also have something to share."

"You're going to tell them?" Gautierre huffed as he stood again. "But shouldn't we tell Mother first—"

"Your mother," the Elder dasher said through sharp, gritted teeth, "does not always have the most rational perspective. Sit down, kid."

"Where is your niece, anyway?" Elizabeth's tone was understandably anxious, Jennifer observed.

"Back in Crescent Valley. She is—how can I put this?—unaware we are here. I felt her presence would only be disruptive."

*That's kind of funny coming from you.* Jennifer congratulated herself for not saying it aloud, but Xavier seemed to read it in her face anyway. His next comments were to her. "Since you and your parents left Crescent Valley, Ms. Scales, my niece has become obsessed with you. Worse, she seems intent on taking some sort of vengeance upon you."

Jennifer felt her mother move to her side and look up in the air. Eddie took up position on her other side, and Jonathan scrambled to his feet. In response, Gautierre sat up on his haunches and curled his wings.

Alone among them all, Xavier sat still and breathed in the smoky fumes from the barbeque pit. "This is not an attack. Had I agreed with my niece, I would hardly have put you on your guard. Not exactly my style."

"No, your style is to fly up behind people and smack them on the back of their head," Jennifer recalled.

"Xavier, you said you came to tell us something." Jonathan dared to sit back down again, which made the others relax. "Perhaps you could get to it."

"We received your summons early this morning," Xavier began. "Gautierre and I were patrolling the ocean far to the north. At first, I intended to leave my grand-nephew in Crescent Valley and come here alone. But on our way back to our lair, we passed a sight I have never seen before. The very sight convinced me to bring him here."

"What was it?" Jennifer asked.

The dasher licked his teeth. "If you trust me, Ms. Scales, I would like to show you."

She didn't need to think about it for long—just long enough to remember the dragon who had saved her from a suicidal last stand, who had shown her the deeper power of the Ancient Furnace, and who ultimately had given his life to help her.

She stepped forward. "Okay, let's go."

"Jennifer!" Elizabeth tried to hold onto her daughter's shoulder. "Are you sure?"

"I'm sure. Ready when you are, Longtail."

Elizabeth and Eddie went through with them all, and clung to their rides—Jonathan and Jennifer—with shivering cold hands as they emerged into Crescent Valley. Jennifer almost cheered when she saw the venerables' fire signal around the crescent moon, but then she thought of Evangelina, which made her think of Dianna Wilson again.

She pulled in close formation with her father as they sped north, the Longtails leading the way. "Dad, do you think of Dianna Wilson much?"

"Jennifer, you may not have noticed, but my wife is hanging onto my back right now, and she's got long fingernails."

"I don't mean that! I mean, now that we know she's alive . . . do you think we'll see her again?"

Jonathan exhaled mist into the frosty air. "Given what you've told us about what she's done, I would expect so. The only question is when."

"What she started . . . Dad, I don't know if we can stop someone like her if she tries again. Even Seraphina knew her island wouldn't last long."

"Do you know if she lasted long enough?" Elizabeth asked. "Seraphina, I mean. You said she was already under attack when you left."

"I don't know what happened," Jennifer admitted. "I had no way to find out. And with the venerables still here in Crescent Valley, there won't be any fire on the ocean. I don't think we can ever stumble on the portal there again."

"So the island may have been overrun by the time you were able to face the Quadrivium," said Elizabeth.

"Yeah." Jennifer hadn't thought too much about Seraphina since she had succeeded in setting everything straight. But now with an everlasting crescent moon over her head again, she wondered what sort of creature was left standing on that island, once all else had changed back.

Nearly an hour later, she felt closer to an answer.

They came in low above the treetops, taking in the scent of pine. Jennifer guessed by now they were headed for the stone plateau. *But why go there? What could possibly be . . . Oh!*

She saw it first as a faint light over the horizon, and then a shining peak, and then a growing mass of greenish-gray movement. *The paradise tree snakes,* she told herself. *And the butterflies.*

The silver moon elm grew larger as they approached, as alive and strong as it ever had been on Seraphina's Isle. Jennifer felt a fresh tear at the corner of her eye. They went over the edge of the stone formation. The top was beautifully smooth and empty of any funeral carvings. The trunk of the moon elm pierced an unmarked portion of the surface as if it had been thrown down like a javelin by the venerables themselves, and its roots gripped the stone depths.

"This was here when you passed over this morning?" Jonathan asked Xavier. They pulled up to land on the rock just a few steps from its outmost branches. Snakes and butterflies rained down around them and chased each other back toward the tree's trunk.

"Yes. I don't know when it showed up. We Longtails are among the very few dragon families who come out here when there isn't a funeral."

"If it hasn't moved by now, I wonder if it is here to stay."

"It is," Jennifer said. She walked under the canopy of branches until she was next to the massive trunk. Her fingertips traced swirls on the bark. "It's been here since last night, and it won't move from here."

"Who put it here?" Gautierre asked.

She reached up and plucked two leaves from a nearby branch, remembering the last line from Sonakshi's verse. *Set the moon elm's roots in stone, forever deeper.* "Seraphina did it. I don't think she could come stay here with it, but she's still alive."

"So why put it here?" Xavier wondered. "Why not keep it on her island, where it's safer?"

Handing each of the Longtails a leaf, she replied, "Because she wants us to use it."

The moment each of them took the leaf in their wing claw, the transformation began. Xavier's face betrayed some fear at what was happening to him, but Gautierre seemed more calm. Jennifer thought back to Xavier's struggle behind the farmhouse after twenty years of holding a dragon shape, but this was nothing like that.

In a few seconds, all seven of them were on human feet under the moon elm. Xavier Longtail was an older man with tanned Gallic features. His wrinkled eyes and stern nose were framed by dyed-black hair, pulled back into a triple-braided ponytail. He rubbed his stern chin with a couple of well-manicured fingers, each of which held a thick gold ring with dozens of tiny diamond chips.

His grand-nephew was even more striking, with charcoal hair pulled back into three braids like his grand-uncle. But unlike

Xavier, he had neither a tan nor jewelry. His well-defined muscles were his only decoration.

"Wow," Jennifer said after she spent some time staring into the boy's pretty face. Then her eyes strayed downward. "Wow."

With an edgy sigh, Xavier reached forward to pull the moon elm leaf out of his great-nephew's hand. Then he dropped them both, and their bodies reverted to dragon shape. "An interesting trick, Ms. Scales. But I would prefer my grand-nephew and I maintain our dignity while we talk about this phenomenon. You say Seraphina wants us to use this tree. How? Other than letting us lose our powerful dragon shapes, what possible benefit can it have?"

"It's not just for changing from dragon to human," Jennifer explained. "If you're under a different moon, it gets you from human to dragon."

Xavier licked his teeth. "So why put it here?"

"It would be too obvious in a place like Winoka," Eddie supposed. "Or even by the lake. But here in your refuge, it's safe."

"Out here," Jonathan added, "we can grow enough leaves to unchain every dragon from the moon's phases. We can decide when we will change, and for how long."

Xavier looked up at the elm, and then at them. "And who will decide who gets these special leaves, and who does not? Is the spirit of Seraphina here in this tree, to guard the prize and separate the worthy from the unworthy?"

"No separating!" Jennifer was adamant. "Xavier, this should be something any dragon can enjoy. It belongs to all of us."

"Another noble sentiment from the ambassador." He sniffed. "You might change your mind once Winona Brandfire decides to use these leaves to hide the next wave of assassins who'll come after your mother. Or your father, this time."

"And would you happen to be one of those assassins?" Elizabeth asked, with her typical stoic expression.

The Elder dasher flared his nostrils and faced the beaststalker. "I wondered, *Doctor*, when you would finally have the courage to address me again. No, I am not an assassin. I am a warrior, like you."

"Not like me," she replied with a stiff lip. "It's not who I am. I haven't fought since the day I met your brother. He changed me."

"And it only cost him his life." Xavier flexed his wings and stretched his neck, but it was not a threatening gesture. Instead, he sighed at Elizabeth. "What did my brother change you into, exactly?"

"Something better."

"Just like you," Jennifer added. "When I was . . . when the Quadrivium . . ." She stalled, trying to explain it properly. "When we were in another place together. You were different. You were a hero."

She reached into her pocket and pulled out Geddy. The gecko had made the trip quietly and with his usual silent grace. "He belongs to you. You asked me to watch over him, until we met again."

"I never . . ." He let the green and red lizard crawl from Jennifer's hand to his wing. Geddy worked his way up Xavier's shoulder and settled upon the dragon's head—right where Jennifer had seen Goodwin settle in for a long flight.

"Mr. Longtail." Elizabeth stepped forward again and reached out for his wing claw. "I've spent my life since I was fifteen years old trying to do penance for your brother's death. I'll spend every day I have left doing the same. If you require anything else of me—"

"Doctor." He winced as he took her hand. "Come with me."

The two walked together, the others following, past the tree and onto an area on the plateau where the swirls of strange dragon-writing were thick. Jennifer wished she could read what they all said. There were so many lives recorded here, each carving a path to the venerables' ceaseless flight around the crescent moon. Who were they? What had they done in life? How had each died?

"This one here," Xavier finally said. He tugged Elizabeth's arm until she stumbled to her knees in front of a patch of worn stone. "Read it."

She looked at the arcane whorls and markings. "I can't read this writing."

"You can." He grabbed her hand again, put his other wing claw on the text, and then breathed fire over the stone pattern. "Read it aloud, so the others can understand."

Touching the dragon that breathed fire over his brother's grave, Elizabeth began to translate the strange inscription:

CHARLES LOUIS LONGTAIL. FIRST SON OF JACQUES AND MARTHA
LONGUEQUEUE. IMMIGRANT CHILD, ORPHANED SHORTLY AFTER HIS
FIRST MORPH. ADVOCATE FOR PEACE. DOCTOR AT WHITE LAKE AND
EVENINGSTAR. BELOVED BROTHER. HEALER. DIPLOMAT.

"A healer and a diplomat," Jonathan murmured.

"I wonder," Xavier said with his raspy voice close to Elizabeth's ear, "if you see anything familiar in this obituary. Anything you can relate to."

"You know I can."

"Good. Because my forgiveness and tolerance, to the extent you want it, will only last as long as you can do so."

Elizabeth nodded. Then she saw something else in the swirls still hot with dragon's breath. "Wait! There's more written here."

> *Fire is death.*
> *Fire tests us.*
> *Fire strengthens us.*
> *Fire is life.*

Jennifer's jaw dropped, but Xavier's reaction was cooler. "Yes, those are words my brother taught me when we were young. Character-building nonsense, I considered them for many years. But he always was the wiser one of the two of us."

He turned to Jennifer. "So you bring your repentant mother to me, and this new boyfriend of yours"—he motioned to Eddie—"and you give me a pet lizard, and you believe we will be best buddies, Ambassador Scales?"

"No," she answered immediately and honestly. "But we both know we're better people with the other one around. And we both value the same thing."

Through a crooked smile, he sniffed. "And that is?"

"Honesty."

His bark was almost a laugh. "True enough! Since you revealed your dual nature to us a few months ago, you have not lied once to me . . ."

"Though I *have* let you know what a jerk you are."

". . . and perhaps you could have been less blunt, at times." He said this with a glance askew at Gautierre, who could not stifle a juvenile snort.

"What about Ember?" asked Jonathan. "Will honesty be enough for her?"

"I doubt it. I will have to tell her what has happened, because I will not lie to her. But I expect she will try to prevent Gautierre from seeing much of me, for as long as I do not seek the same revenge she does."

"And do I have to obey her?" Gautierre asked with an offended air. "If you trust this girl, then why shouldn't I? And why shouldn't Mother?"

"Good questions, Gautierre. Each dragon will have to come up with his own answer. I will support you in finding your own. All I ask is that you remain honest with your mother. We will not keep secrets from her."

"A good policy," Jennifer agreed, with a meaningful look at her own parents.

Gautierre gave Jennifer a piercing stare. "I want to learn from the Ancient Furnace. I want to see a new and different world."

*Be careful what you wish for,* Jennifer thought with wry humor. She returned Xavier's skeptical look, while Eddie cleared his throat and stepped up close enough to her to take her hand.

Standing up from the grave markings of Charles Longtail, Elizabeth nodded at Xavier. "If your Eldest will not receive our family anymore, Eddie Blacktooth and I will bring those beaststalkers we can find to seek audience with you. You and my husband will need to convince the Blaze to follow through with Winona Brandfire's original plan. Maybe if we can pull together enough from both people, we can regain her trust."

The black dragon stretched his neck to the heavens. "Brother Charles. I hope I am doing the right thing. I would like to join you someday, on the endless flight."

"You will," said Jonathan with a grin. "Just like I'll join my father."

"Enough of that!" Jennifer cut in. "Let's all stay down here for a while!"

They agreed, and then sat on the rock together for some time, watching the crescent slowly roll over the silver moon elm, listening to the snakes rustle after the butterflies, and talking in hopeful tones about the days to come.

# THE ULTIMATE IN FANTASY!

From magical tales of distant worlds to stories of those with abilities beyond the ordinary, Ace and Roc have everything you need to stretch your imagination to its limits.

**Marion Zimmer Bradley/Diana L. Paxson**

**Guy Gavriel Kay**

**Dennis L. McKiernan**

**Patricia A. McKillip**

**Robin McKinley**

**Sharon Shinn**

**Katherine Kurtz**

**Barb and J. C. Hendee**

**Elizabeth Bear**

**T. A. Barron**

**Brian Jacques**

**Robert Asprin**